PRAISE FOR

A River of Royal Blood

AND

A Queen of Gilded Horns

★ "Joy's writing is exemplary; a strong plot, even pacing, and character growth (not only Eva's) all lead up to an ending that should satisfy even the pickiest readers . . . A strong and satisfying conclusion."

—*Kirkus Reviews*, starred review of *A Queen of Gilded Horns*

"The world of this book is fascinating, the characters and their relationships are compelling, and that plot twist—wow! Readers of fantasy will enjoy it immensely."

—*VOYA* on *A River of Royal Blood*

"A dark and bloody delight of a debut, Amanda Joy's *A River of Royal Blood* is a seductive tapestry of extraordinary magick delving into the terrifying lengths we will go to claim our destiny."

—Dhonielle Clayton, *New York Times* bestselling author of *The Belles*, on *A River of Royal Blood*

"[This] engrossing, North African–inspired series opener draws effectively on real-world prejudices to inform [a] richly created universe."

—*Publishers Weekly* on *A River of Royal Blood*

★ "At its core, this story dives deep into the themes of family, belonging, identity, and sibling rivalry. These themes are adeptly blended with a fast-paced plot and incredible world building . . . The stakes are incredibly high in this stunning conclusion to the duology. Highly recommended for all collections."   —*School Library Journal*, starred review of *A Queen of Gilded Horns*

"A surprising twist and multiple unsolved mysteries will leave readers looking forward to the next book . . . A compelling debut."   —*Kirkus Reviews* on *A River of Royal Blood*

"[A] fast-paced magical adventure . . . Filled with mythical creatures, ancient traditions, sibling rivalries, political intrigue, and epic world-building, this book stands out as a masterful adventure." —*School Library Journal* on *A River of Royal Blood*

"A sibling rivalry like nothing you've ever read before. Joy weaves a dark yet delicate treatise on race, heritage, and power whilst never losing that addictive 'just one more chapter' allure. I devoured it in one sitting!"

—Natasha Ngan, *New York Times* bestselling author of *Girls of Paper and Fire*, on *A River of Royal Blood*

★ "Joy's debut has all the trappings of a riveting fantasy novel: enviable world building, elements of magic, and scintillating glimpses of a powerful backstory . . . not to mention a slow-burning romance sure to get readers swooning . . . Gripping political intrigue and cinematic action."

—*Booklist*, starred review of *A River of Royal Blood*

"Joy creates a complex, intriguing fantasy world . . . [Readers] will enjoy exciting fight scenes and a variety of abilities reminiscent of Kristin Cashore's Graceling trilogy."

—*The Bulletin of the Center for Children's Books* on *A River of Royal Blood*

"Tensions are high in this sequel and Joy's language is just as melodious, her world-building just as spell-binding . . . There's no denying Joy's talent, and readers will bask in the sisters' character arcs and the book's gratifying ending."

—*Booklist* on *A Queen of Gilded Horns*

"A dark and complex fantasy of bloodlust and rich imagination . . . Fascinating characters, both regal and warrior-like, fill the narrative, and the pageantry is richly detailed in a swirling cacophony of colors, dance, and swordplay . . . This first book in a series is riveting . . . [and] will leave readers wanting more."

—*School Library Connection* on *A River of Royal Blood*

ALSO BY AMANDA JOY

A River of Royal Blood

A QUEEN OF GILDED HORNS

AMANDA JOY

putnam

G. P. PUTNAM'S SONS

G. P. Putnam's Sons

An imprint of Penguin Random House LLC, New York

First published in the United States of America by G. P. Putnam's Sons,
an imprint of Penguin Random House LLC, 2021
First paperback edition published 2022

Visit us online at penguinrandomhouse.com

THE LIBRARY OF CONGRESS HAS CATALOGED THE HARDCOVER EDITION AS FOLLOWS:
Names: Joy, Amanda (Amanda Saulsberry), author. | Joy, Amanda (Amanda Saulsberry). River of royal blood.
Title: A queen of gilded horns / Amanda Joy.
Description: New York: G. P. Putnam's Sons, 2021. |
Summary: After learning the truth of her heritage, Eva is on the run with her sister, Isa, as her captive,
but with the Queendom of Myre on the brink of revolution, Eva and Isa must
make peace with each other to save their kingdom.
Identifiers: LCCN 2020047805 (print) | LCCN 2020047806 (ebook) | ISBN 9780525518617 (hardcover) |
ISBN 9780525518624 (ebook)
Subjects: CYAC: Magic—Fiction. | Sisters—Fiction. | Fantasy.
Classification: LCC PZ7.1.J8 Qu 2021 (print) | LCC PZ7.1.J8 (ebook) | DDC [Fic]—dc23
LC record available at https://lccn.loc.gov/2020047805
LC ebook record available at https://lccn.loc.gov/2020047806

Manufactured in Canada

ISBN 9780525518631

1 3 5 7 9 10 8 6 4 2

FRI

Design by Suki Boynton
Text set in Fournier MT Pro

For all the Black girls busy dreaming up worlds.
I see you.

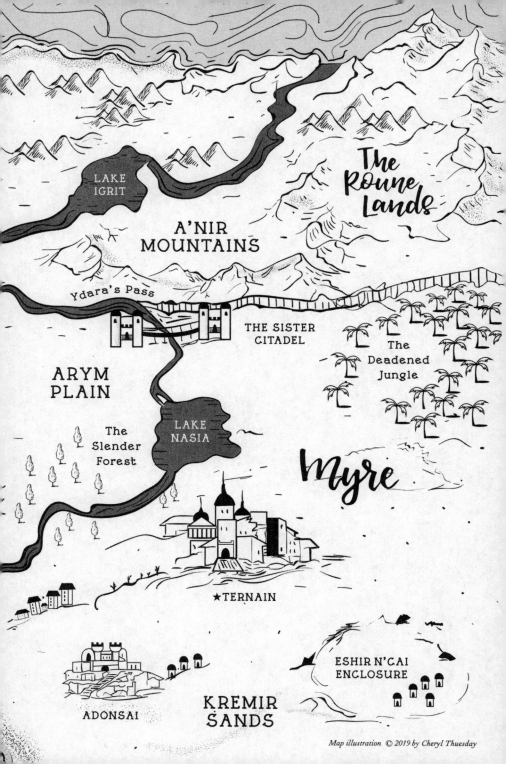

✸

ROMEO

Is love a tender thing? it is too rough,
Too rude, too boisterous, and it pricks like thorn.

MERCUTIO

If love be rough with you, be rough with love.

—WILLIAM SHAKESPEARE,
Romeo and Juliet

⪘ PROLOGUE ⪘
Ysai of Ariban

THE SKY ABOVE the sprawling camp at the foot of Mount Ariban was a bruised purple—a sign of the storms to come and the snows that would follow. This far north in the Roune Lands—the lawless territory east of Dracol and north of Myre—a handful of weeks was all it took for High Summer to turn into Far Winter.

The smaller peaks rising around the valley were limned in gold from the sun's recent descent. The silver light of a hundred thousand stars and a sickle moon would have been enough for most in the camp to see by, despite the copper lamps hung in concentric rings around their tents. For most in this camp were khimaer—horns adorned their brows and their bodies were an elegant amalgam of animal and human—and they could see even in darkness. The few who were not khimaer were fey or bloodkin, their vision as sharp.

The lamps were magicked to keep time and would only be doused when all the day's work was done.

Seated upon a tree stump carved with snaking vines and

budding wildflowers, Ysai eased a narrow blade around a length of buttery *noshai* wood in a slow spiral.

So used to the feel of a carving knife in her hand, Ysai focused her attention solely on her students' upturned faces and the significantly duller blades in their laps. Until her gaze slid past them to the nearest copper lamp, throwing warm light in a spray of pinpricks, waiting for it to flare and signal the end of her day.

The children of the camp took lessons well into the night after history and weaponry and magick during the day. Blessedly this group of eight-year-olds was Ysai's last lesson in charm-making for the day.

Instead of the sacred noshai, each clutched a bit of spare wood left over from the older children's lessons in their sticky palms. The noshai trees, the tallest and most ancient of all the beings who dwelled in the North, only grew in the A'Nir Mountains north of Myre's borders. It was a curious thing, how many.

In millennia past, the wild fey who dwelled in these mountains offered noshai saplings to the first Queens who ruled most of Akhimar, both north of the river and south of it. Back when the realm was known by just one name, instead of the three nations it was split into now. Yet the noshai trees rarely thrived in the South, so the tradition became the offering of a charm of protection carved from the trees. In the centuries since it had been forgotten, until the Tribe fled Myre after the Great War and adapted the tradition, making carvings of their own.

Most created charms in the likeness of the animals they were akin to and hung them from the trees around their tents; the charms were a small magick, prayers and wishes to their Goddess Khimaerani bolstered by a simple offering of power. The hundreds upon hundreds around the camp created a strong ward that set off a wave of foreboding for anyone who might venture here.

"Sister Ysai," Kisin, one of the smallest and thus most outspoken of the group, called. Lamplight caught the gold rings adorning the tips of his pronged horns, and huge sand-fox ears dominated either side of his face. His coppery skin and fur were the exact same hue, and though the spray of white freckles across his face reminded Ysai of a fawn, the boy's expression was distinctly tricksome. All wide-eyed innocence at odds with his toothy grin. "What will you carve for us today?"

Ysai had been planning on a cunning leopard. The children, having never ventured far enough south to see the great cats of the Arym Plain and the Deadened Jungle, were fascinated with the large predators.

Yet Kisin, she knew, would request a fox, like he had the last few lessons.

"I haven't yet decided. Perhaps Tosin can help us," Ysai murmured, offering a smile to the fox boy's twin sister.

Unlike her brother, Tosin never spoke unless prompted. Her big, glossy black eyes were always slightly out of focus, lost in a dreamland. Ysai hoped that meant her imagination would be a bit more well developed than her brother's.

The girl blinked a few times, fox ears twitching, before she explained, "Mother Moriya told us about the *krakai* in the desert."

Ysai's heart sank. She had learned the stories of the krakai that crawled up from the sea into the desert, but she had no sense of what the creatures truly looked like, having never been more than fifteen miles beyond the Myrean border, let alone thousands of leagues south to the Kremir Sands. "I think I would require a larger canvas to carve a krakai, Tosin.

Maybe another time." Then she pitched her voice low. "But I do know another story, and it's Mother Moriya's favorite. Has she ever told you about the leopard who was so clever it trapped a snake and tied its tail into a knot?"

The children giggled and inched forward until they were practically atop Ysai's boots, tugging on her skirt. Mother Moriya was the leader of the Tribe, but Ysai rarely used the honorific, as Moriya was actually her mother.

She'd been in the South for two months on what was meant to be a quick raid across the Myrean border, and yet Ysai tried not to worry. Moriya would be safe; the other Tribesfolk with her on the incursion would die to keep her safe.

Ysai began to tell the story as she carved the body of the pouncing cat. She used magick to shift her throat and mouth until she had the growling voice of the leopard. She snarled and hissed at her students when she could tell she was losing their attention. Until she felt the deep vibration of hoofbeats beneath her feet and relief coursed through her, golden as good Myrean wine. She quickly finished the story and sent her students running for the cook fire at the center of camp.

Though darkness had long ago fallen, the camp was in a flurry of motion. Horned, fanged, and pointy-eared folk spilled from their tents, anticipating the return of the raiding party. Only humans were truly unwelcome here. When Moriya became the Mother of the Tribe near sixty years ago, she began seeking out any Myrean exiles who ventured north into the Roune Lands and welcomed them into the Tribe. That had swelled their numbers from less than a hundred to the near two hundred and fifty members now.

Ysai considered going to the tent she and her mother shared and sleeping until her mother had finished being welcomed home. But she wanted to hear firsthand what excuse Moriya would offer to her people about the length of the trip.

Would she admit that this journey had been more of a fact-finding mission than a pure raid? Or would she continue to hide her true plan to venture south and take back the throne?

Ysai was betting on more deception. The Tribesfolk and Elderi Council were notoriously fearful about any plans to return to Myre; they were exiles for a reason, and without a clear plan, they would be facing annihilation from the human Queen's armies.

But now that Moriya had a vast network of spies in place, she believed the time was more right than ever. Ripe for revolution.

Or so her mother believed. Ysai herself was not so certain.

The human queens were merciless and powerful. Their entire nobility heartless enough to require fratricide as a stepping-stone to the throne.

She did not dare long for the throne, not when seeking it endangered everything she had ever known. The Tribe has remained safely hidden for centuries, and yet any attempt to complete their original purpose—to lie in wait until the time was right to take back the throne—might very well mean their destruction.

It was a risk their ancestors expected them to take. When all hope of victory in the Great War was lost, the original thirteen Elderi who had served the last khimaer Queen crossed the A'Nir Mountains to preserve their race. All in the hope that they could one day take back their ancestral home. Eight generations had passed—while eight unlawful human queens sat on the Ivory Throne—and they had made no real progress on that goal. The humans had armies numbering in the tens of thousands and they were a few people, hiding in the mountains, longing to return to a country that had forgotten they existed.

Ysai fell into step with the rest of the Tribesfolk making their way to the front of camp. The large, circular clearing in the shadow of Ariban had been reinforced with a wall of trees bound with twine and packed with mud on the slim chance any of the other raiding bands in the Roune Lands made it past their wards and sentries.

By the time the tide of the crowd carried Ysai to the front of the wall, the front gates were swinging open. The sound of thundering hoofbeats rang in the air and Ysai's stomach clenched as she caught sight of the first rider.

Anosh, her mother's second, a man of eagle wings and storm-cleaving magick in his veins, rode not a horse like most of the folks behind him. He sat astride one of the *shahana*, a rare antelope found only in the far north. Like all shahana, the massive beast was a few hands taller than a horse, with long nimble legs and splayed hooves perfect for navigating the snow and ice of upper reaches of the mountains. White spiraled horns sprang from the sides of her triangular head and her pitch-black fur was flecked with snow-white spots. A crest of equally snowy fur covered her chest.

Ysai knew the beast well, for it was her mother's mount. She pushed through the crowd gathering at the gate as an uneasy silence spread.

It was shattered a few moments later as two men carrying a stretcher came into view.

Ysai broke into a sprint as the crowd opened before her. Roaring filled her ears, and between one blink and the next, she was on her knees in the dirt as the stretcher was laid on the ground.

Only to be greeted by her mother's smile. The silver hair and antlers Ysai had inherited were bright in the dark night. Ysai scanned her mother's face—the only sign of pain was faint tightness around her eyes—before turning her attention to the arrow protruding from Moriya's waist. A deep crimson stain bloomed around the wound.

Before she could say a word, the Mother of the Tribe crooned, "It is not so fearsome as it seems. I was shot as we crossed the border." Moriya reached up to catch a single fallen tear on Ysai's cheek. "Do not worry."

Moriya's smile slackened to a painful grimace as she reached within the heavy folds of her woolen cloak to pull out a journal. She pressed it into Ysai's hands.

"Do you understand?" Moriya asked. "I need you to be strong now."

Fear clanged through Ysai. She knelt there frozen in the dirt until someone, she did not notice who, hauled her to her feet.

She followed the path Moriya's stretcher cut through the gathering khimaer, barely hearing the explanations from the dismounting warriors.

We were ambushed at the border . . .

Be assured . . . the Mother will be well.

Human scum . . . cowards waited until we . . .

Ysai tuned it all out, numbly trudging after her mother as she held tight to the book.

She knew Moriya wouldn't have given her this book unless things were truly dire. It was deceptively plain, hand-bound in twine with a Godling symbol inscribed on the cover. One of the dozens of journals Moriya kept, but never once before let Ysai look within.

Finally Ysai skidded to a stop before one of the white canvas tents where the Tribe's healers worked. Sentries waited out front, blocking the entrance. Only patients were allowed within, and it wouldn't do to disturb their work. Still fear writhed in her gut like an eel.

She settled on the ground, close enough to the lanterns hanging outside each tent to read. She flipped through the pages until she reached the last entry.

At the top of the page were notes written in a cypher; not written for Ysai's eyes, though she would attempt to translate them in time. She ran her fingers over a splotch of blood staining the corner. It had seeped into several pages.

In the center of the page, her mother's sloping handwriting switched to plain Khimaeran.

Ysai,

My mother once told me I would know my death when it came to me. She said all women gifted with Khimaerani's power do. I didn't take her warning seriously. But as soon as the bolt struck, I knew I'd been wrong. I could feel my death rushing toward me; I knew I wouldn't survive the healing required to save my life. Already I feel weakness seeping through me like poison, and every one of my hundred years weighing upon me like stones. There is chaos in the South, chaos that will serve our plans. Learn the cypher, you will see. And call the Hunter home; he will be essential. There is one last thing. Someone else has inherited the gift we share. You must lead our Tribe south, free the khimaer in the Enclosures, and you will find her there. She will be Queen.

The words were rushed and sloppy. Ysai could barely make sense of it. Her eyes were still scanning the page as she climbed to her feet.

She wiped the tears gathering beneath her eyes and approached the guards. "Please, I need to speak with the Mother. It's urgent."

One of the guards opened his mouth, likely to deny her entrance, but his voice was cut off by a scream from within. Ysai shouldered past them, the whole of her trembling, as she ducked beneath the tent flaps. She could only assume it was by virtue of being the Tribe Mother's daughter that the guards didn't hold her back.

Inside, two healers knelt on either side of Moriya, who lay on a pallet of soft furs. Her stomach was exposed, the arrow having already been removed from her side. Yet the dressing on the wound was soaked in bright red blood.

"What is wrong? Why haven't you healed her?"

"We are trying," the closest healer, a jackal khimaer with liquid-black eyes, explained. "It resists healing. There is no poison in her blood, but the internal damage, it resists our healing."

At Ysai's approach, Moriya's eyes flew wide, almost seeming to glow as they latched on to her daughter, pinning her in place. Her usually rich bronze skin had gone ashen.

"Oh, Ysai, yes, good . . . ," she rasped. The hairs around her brow were soaked in sweat. She rose up on her elbows, managing to a firm look at the two healers. "Thank you for all you've done. Know you are not to blame for what is to come, children. Leave us."

A gust of wind yanked at the scarf around Ysai's neck as the tent flaps opened and closed upon the healers' exit. Once they were alone, Ysai sat beside Moriya and began mopping the elder woman's brow. Her softly curling silver hair was tangled around her horns. "I don't believe you," Ysai said. "Great-mother was *wrong*. We'll call for more healers."

Moriya frowned, pushing Ysai's fumbling hands away. "Do not worry, child. We have little time now. The King is dead. The human Queen and her daughters may yet destroy each other and that will be our chance. You will be named Mother in the days after I am buried. You must promise me, Ysai. Promise me you will take us south and see a khimaer take the throne."

When Ysai hesitated, Moriya caught her hand, squeezing painfully. Ysai was surprised her mother still had the strength with that pained, dying light in her eyes. She could tell her mother was using all her immense will to hold on to life a bit longer. Perhaps if she gave the healers a chance, they could extend the time she had left.

Ysai tried to pull away, but Moriya's grip was tight. "Mother, how do you expect me to convince them? The Elderi still think I'm a child. It will take decades to gain the Tribe's trust."

"I know you will find a way, Ysai. Promise me," Moriya repeated, eyes fervent.

And so Ysai of Ariban, who had hardly left this snow-blasted valley in the twenty years of her life, said yes.

Her mother fought the fever burning through her until finally she went peacefully at dawn. Not one of the many Tribesfolk blessed with healing gifts could root out the fever. They said it was as if her body had simply given up.

In the numb days that followed, Moriya was burned on a pyre. The morning after, when all the Tribe watched as two Elderi placed a headdress of crescent-shaped plates of gold over Ysai's shoulders and swore their allegiance to her, the new Mother of the Tribe, Ysai thought only of that promise and a stain of blood.

Take the Tribe south. Lead them to slaughter or steal the throne right under the humans' noses.

She added another task: Seek revenge on the soldiers that killed Moriya and obliterate all who stood between her people and the throne.

- I -
PRINCESS NO MORE

And so the Enchantress said to the maiden, *I have stolen your magick. I will take your throne and you will wear my crown of horns. You can be Princess no more.*

—Child's tale, of human origin

∗ CHAPTER 1 ∗

Eva

I DREAM OF fire. A river of blood and a column of smoke rising so dark and thick as to blot out the sun.

I dream of gnashing blades and crunching teeth and the foul reek of viscera spilled upon marble floors. I dream of a knife buried in my chest and a crimson crown balanced atop Isadore's golden brow. I dream of the Hunter in chains, eyes red-rimmed with sorrow, shackles wearing down his flesh to the bone. I dream of Court and coronations and fine silk and gossamer gowns drenched in gore.

I dream of the Patch and *chatara* and my bare feet dancing upon the broken paving stones until they run with blood.

I dream and dream and dream, conjuring every darkness seeded deep within me. It feels like magick, this dreaming. In my waking hours when everyone seems to watch me from the corner of their eyes, worried I will finally show signs of breaking, I know my dreams have protected me. I can smile and pretend for them, waiting for night when I will wake screaming and only Aketo will be there to see.

At least I had the dreaming; much as the terror ate me up inside at night, by day it bolstered me. Look, see how I could seethe and weep and be so afraid and, yet, come morning I could hold it all in with a will of steel and a biting smile.

Because I couldn't afford to be broken.

Not when I'd stolen my sister halfway across the Queendom to keep my mother from crowning her when the truth of my heritage spread. Not when I had dragged half my guard along with me, making them betray their oaths to the throne. Not while I sought a way to keep all of us safe, Isadore included. Not while I needed to soon decide what my future would hold.

There could be no breaking under such circumstances.

I had to find a way to survive first.

I inched forward on my elbows, eyes slit against the cloud of golden soil that rose at our every move. The sky above was an unbroken stretch of cerulean and the midday sun hammered against my back, but anything that dulled the bite of the wind that swept through these lowlands had my gratitude. The bare skin on my arms pebbled as another gust rolled past, tugging apart the loose braid at the nape of my neck.

High Summer was well and truly gone, but by virtue of my greatly diminished wardrobe, I hadn't yet given up the sleeveless tunics and thin leggings of the warm months.

It had been six weeks since my nameday on the last day of High Summer, and what little warmth left in the year still lingered on the Plain. A chill had begun to flow south. Autumns were long in Myre, the land slow to cool for a short and bitter Far Winter.

Far Winter being the season when cold came down from the A'Nir Mountains all the way to the Red River. Soon the silks and cottons of High Summer and autumn would be exchanged in favor of wool and furs. And most of the clothing I'd brought from Ternain would be of little use.

If we stayed in the North on the path I had set.

That remained to be seen, considering we'd been stuck for the last week, waiting.

As the dirt settled, I peered through the battered eyeglass I'd acquired three weeks ago before venturing onto the Plain. I blinked, gaze focusing on the small village that lay just a few miles north. From our vantage point atop a rock outcrop that jutted up from the Plain like a tooth—more a misshapen molar than the smaller, fang-shaped stones that dotted the vast golden plain—I could cup the village in my palm. Anali and I pressed flat to the ground, hiding in a fold in the rock that kept the few villagers going about their day from spying us.

Arym meant "gold" in Khimaeran, and the Plain had been named for the bright ocher dirt that glittered faintly in the sun. It was a hard region, with hundreds of miles of flat grasslands, shallow lakes fed from an offshoot of the Red River that ran deep beneath the earth, and low, lifeless hills peppered with undersize, knotty trees. Few traversed the Arym Plain for fear of the lions and magickal predators that roamed it. Not to mention the roving herds of wildebeest and antelope and Gods knew what else. Any land left to grow wild and free in Myre kept secrets even the oldest storybooks didn't speak of.

But even shining dirt couldn't pretty up the small village curled up in the shadow of a considerable estate. Orai wasn't so much a village as a handful of sturdy clay homes with latticed windows painted in jewel tones scattered around the walled estate. There wasn't much more to the small, dust-covered place: two inns that looked like they'd seen better days; a run-down Temple; and a market that was stirring to life just now. A sizable flock roamed on the outskirts, tended by two shepherd girls no older than twelve. The girls' hair hung down to their waists in thick plaits weighed down with beads and charms. Older women of the village wore their hair wrapped in elaborate whorls of dyed cotton, one of the few signs of finery here.

On every map we'd consulted before crossing the Plain, Orai was the only village noted besides Sellei Lake and Meteen, an outpost for bloodkin nomads who regularly traveled the region. But while Sellei, now a dried-out basin, and the outpost were marked correctly, Orai was not fifty miles west, as every map indicated. It took an extra week of searching, but two days ago, we finally found it. Miles south and hidden behind a rise of stone outcrops still resonant with the scent of earth magick.

I'd briefly fantasized about the wondrous place someone had gone to such lengths to keep hidden. I conjured great marble walls rising around a vast khimaer enclave. But this speck of a village deep in the Plain?

It made *sense*.

Sense that crawled over my skin, along with the realization that had I looked to find it, had I focused and listened and questioned my father more, I would have known he was keeping a secret. The King of Myre and Lord Commander of the Queen's Army had come from this forgotten place, and his family never followed him to the capital to bask in the wealth his marriage brought? Of course they were hiding something.

Whoever *had* looked closer at my father's life must have ferreted out the truth and killed him.

Sunlight graced the limestone wall of the estate, which

rose tall enough to kiss the relentless lapis sky. It dwarfed every other structure in Orai several times over. A simple teakwood door sat in the center of the wall, and the limestone bricks were etched with ancient beasts. A detail I could not make out from so far away, but our first night here, Anali and Falun had ventured close enough to take note of them.

Twin spires, lit like bars of golden sunlight, peeked out behind the wall, the only detail of the estate that was visible.

Even with an eyeglass, this was all I could see from miles away. All I had seen of my father's family and home, after two days of surveilling the estate and Orai. In those two days, no one had gone in or out. No one from the village approached the estate or so much as glanced its way. I watched the windows high up on the wall for signs of movement, even knowing there was no use.

No figures would come to fill them. My guards had been keeping watch all day and all night. They saw no more than I did. And everyone they questioned in the village either shook their heads and ignored them, or said the house had been silent for a year.

What was the family living inside that wall to this village? How could the Lady of the House lead it without interacting with it? I came here seeking answers about my father and how he'd managed to hide as a khimaer for so long, but I couldn't deny my hope for a plan. A list of allies and nobles sympathetic to our cause would help. Or even better, a way to persuade the Court and my mother to accept a khimaer Queen, when a lengthy set of laws designed to keep khimaer from amassing any power stood in my way. I'd searched through all my father's things before leaving Ternain and found nothing.

I hoped Papa's family would be able to give me those answers. If not, well, I wasn't sure what I'd do.

"How much longer must we wait?" I asked, slapping the eyeglass shut. Sweat coated my skin, and I shivered as it cooled in the wind.

Anali ignored my question. "You saw exactly what I did. There's been no movement."

"How long must we wait?" I said quietly, not bothering to hide my impatience.

Anali's sooty eyes flitted to mine and held. Her ice-white hair, a sharp contrast to her darkly luminous skin, was braided tight to her scalp. In the weeks since we left Ternain, she'd woven colorful bits of fabric through the braided ends and fine gold chains hung from the ram's horns that framed her face, dangling violet beads that matched her feathers. Neither was a decoration she would've been allowed in the Queen's Army, though the masculine cut of her clothes was the same. "A week, then we can be sure—"

"In a week, soldiers could arrive. Do you want to remain here long enough to get caught? It was dangerous enough coming here."

We'd searched for any sign that soldiers from the Queen's Army had been to Orai. So far, blessedly, there had been none. But that didn't mean they wouldn't soon arrive. This village and the family that supposedly dwelled in it were my last tethers to my father. But coming here was a risk I was willing to take.

"And yet, we are here," Anali said, voice hard. "No need to rush and endanger us further."

I sat up, tucked the eyeglass within the heavy belt around my waist, and began the climb down the stone. Pain stabbed at

19

my abdomen, and the copper tang of blood filled my mouth as I bit my tongue.

The pain receded and my thoughts became unfocused. I centered my attention on the craggy rocks beneath my palms. An easy calm slipped over my skin as I worked my way down, moving mostly by instinct. I half slid, half bounded down the near-vertical wall of rock.

Soon, too soon, I reached the ground. I flexed my fingers. Thick black claws curled over my fingertips, caked with bits of clay from the climb. I prodded the bandage low on my stomach, hissing through my teeth until I was satisfied the wound hadn't split and begun bleeding again.

Another luxury I had come to miss: healers at hand.

At the crunch of my Captain's boots on the rocky dirt, I crossed my arms to hide their trembling. I didn't want to remind anyone of the injury, least of all Anali. "Maybe I will walk down in the night by myself. I bet I could scale that wall quicker than the rest of you."

I bet I could slip down there at night without any of you noticing and acquaint myself with whatever lies behind that wall before sunrise.

None could kill me but my sister. On the evening of my nameday, at the start of the celebration, the Sorceryn had placed a complex spell on Isadore and me so that only we would be able to kill each other. Its power would even bar accidents from taking our lives. The only way for either of us to die was by the other's hand. Now that Isa was my prisoner, I was safe. Safe at the least from death. Better to use me than risk anyone else.

Anali arched a salt-white eyebrow. "So you will force me or the Prince to carry you back to camp."

I offered her a dry smile, curling a hand in invitation. "Maybe I won't let you."

I was stronger now and faster than I'd been. One of the benefits of breaking the block on my magick, I assumed. Not to mention whatever strange power I now had that made climbing the Plain's craggy hills and buttes as easy as walking or swimming. Well. Perhaps not as simple as walking. But the power coiled in my limbs had grown, and with it, so had my sense of the earth.

Anali's face softened with mirth. "While the idea that you would easily best Aketo and me together is hilarious and might make for quite a show, it does not sound as though it will get you any closer to your goal. I understand you tire of this delay, Eva."

"It's been too long, Anali. We've been gone too long and have nothing to show for it." All we had done since my nameday was run from one village where I couldn't show my face to another village where the same rule held. Six weeks had passed without news from the capital, but we all knew it could come to an end at any time. My mother would have to reveal what happened, if she hadn't already, and once she caught my scent, who knew what she'd send after me.

Two more months and Far Winter would be upon us.

Every day the air grew colder and the nights stretched longer until soon even the sun wouldn't be enough to keep us warm. Cold would roll down from the mountains like a specter, freezing earth that had been baked dry by the High Summer sun. Snow would follow and chase most of the animals who lived on the Arym Plain south across the river until spring.

"I know you're tired of waiting, but we can't afford

mistakes," Anali repeated. "If you go into that village and someone recognizes you, word will travel."

I brushed a hand over the base of my horns, claws clacking against their ridges. The horns grew an inch into my hairline and every nearby curl wound around them in dense tangles. I missed Mirabel's steady, patient hands braiding my hair. The haphazard twist at the back of my neck was the best I could do.

"Few will recognize me like this." My voice was soft, so much so that I was surprised when Anali heard it over the wind.

Her eyes hardened. "Even if they don't know who you are, tales of a horned girl on the Arym Plain will travel. The Arym Plain, where your father's family has lived for centuries. Whoever *else* knows about the King will know exactly what that means."

I couldn't argue with that, but my mind was not going to be changed. Six weeks and I was no closer to understanding my khimaer magick. No closer to learning who I really am.

Six weeks with Baccha gone. And now two days here, wasted as we waited and watched. "We've been lucky all this time. The Queen won't wait forever to strike. And we're too exposed. We need shelter. We need baths." And we needed to consider what would come next.

I needed to consider my future, and Myre's as well.

Anali frowned but, after a long moment, nodded. "What are my orders, Your Highness?"

I cringed at the honorific and cut Anali a sharp look. She blinked in apparent innocence, knowing well enough that references to my nobility irritated me now more than ever. I expected to hear news that I'd been stripped of my land and my titles soon enough. I imagined it would give my mother great pleasure to do so. "When we return to camp, call everyone back. Tonight we plan, and when the sun goes down tomorrow, we are getting inside the wall."

"As you say," Anali said with an incline of her head. "You are so like your father."

"What?" I blurted, every thought in my head going still at the mention of Papa.

"I always knew the sight of a terrible plan forming behind his eyes, and I know the sight of a fool one forming in yours."

"Better a daring plan than a safe bet—those always go awry," I said with a smirk. I remembered those bright eyes. Papa could stare into space for hours, working out a plan, moving around all the pieces in his head till they fit.

That was one change that had come in these six weeks. I could think of my father without seeing his dead body. I felt a stab of guilt at just that small measure of comfort. How dare I be comfortable with, or even accepting of, my father's murder? I had left Ternain with my promise to find his killer unfulfilled.

Despite Katro's insistence that his mother, Lady Shirea, had been behind the plot to kill my father, I was certain she'd only done so at someone else's direction. Someone at Court, someone I knew.

And I could get no closer to the truth out here.

Anali and I trotted through the scrub grass in silence until we reached the edge of camp a few miles away. At dawn, Falun had led a group of four scouts—all we could spare—far out into the Plain. They must have already made it back, because we passed one—Arame, a human with earth and water magick, ice-chip eyes, and rich, golden-brown skin—as he sighted down his arrow.

There was a meaty *thunk* as he shot two guinea fowl racing

through the underbrush. Anali walked over to speak with him as he set off to retrieve the birds.

I didn't wait for the Captain to catch up. As soon as I stepped foot into our small camp, Falun walked into my path and slung an arm over my shoulder.

I loosed a sigh and managed to smile up at him. "Back from hunting already?"

He nodded, muttering something about a herd of wilde-beest and needing to chop wood to make new bows, before an unsubtle pivot to the real reason he'd approached. "How did you sleep?"

"Fine," I lied. I had woken screaming, unable to shut out the last image of my nightmare—my body swinging from the Queen's Palace gates—and the smell of rotting flesh, so vivid in the dream, seemed to still fill my nostrils. I hoped Aketo hadn't told him about the nightmares. I didn't need more of them worrying over me.

Even though I knew what was coming, I couldn't help but flinch when Falun spoke again. "And the other thing?"

My jaw clenched as I struggled to think of a way out of this conversation. I never should have told Falun I'd been considering looking in on Baccha. The more he appeared in my dreams, the more I couldn't help but want to know exactly where he'd gone.

And yet, I refused to give Baccha the satisfaction of worry-ing over him.

Falun, who'd seen Baccha's sudden, unexplained departure for the betrayal it was, hadn't been able to hide his disappoint-ment when I mentioned Baccha. *We have enough on our hands without worrying about him.* He *should be worried about you.*

And if his silence was any indication, Baccha wasn't

worried about me. The bond we'd created, using our blood to make our magicks coalesce, allowed us to communicate mentally. I could still feel Baccha like an anchor on the other side of the bond, tugging at me whenever I let my thoughts drift toward him. Baccha had gone off, likely to fulfill his duties to the Tribe, and declined to include me in his plans.

So why did I want to check in on him? Maybe I was still searching for a reason to put my faith in him again despite every indication he could not be trusted. In my weakest moments, I allowed myself to fantasize that Baccha had gone off to the Tribe to beg them to help me gain the throne. But it was foolish to believe Baccha had anyone's interests besides his own in mind.

"I changed my mind."

Some tension around Falun's ultramarine eyes eased as he arched one cinnamon brow. "You're sure? Of course I'm glad to hear it, but last time we talked about him, you seemed worried."

I shrugged, chewing on my bottom lip. "You were right. It's not like our bond is broken. If he wants me to know where he is, he can inform me anytime."

"Just," Fal adds, gaze darkening, "like he could've told us the truth the entire time."

Before my nameday I told Falun about Baccha's lies and the Tribe being the real reason the Hunter returned to Myre. Fal hadn't held it against Baccha at first, but when Baccha left, making it clear he really had been using me the entire time, all Falun's affection for him had melted away.

Baccha fled when we needed him most. He would have to come crawling back.

When I said nothing, Falun slung an arm around me again,

the long tendrils of his hair tickling my cheeks. He smelled of freshly turned soil and honeyed fey wine. "You don't need him. We don't need him."

I wasn't so certain.

I wouldn't have made it out of the last few months alive without Baccha. But there was no use pointing that out, so I nodded and wrapped an arm around Falun's waist, drawing him farther into camp. "Come on, I've left Aketo alone with my sister long enough."

By now I could admit one of my more spectacular mistakes of the last year was kidnapping my sister with only a vague plan to control her. All I'd been sure of at the time was that I couldn't leave her in Ternain. My mother would've crowned her in my absence. But the difficulty in keeping a prisoner, especially one I hoped to persuade not to kill me, hadn't dawned on me until we fled.

Chains were one thing—and had their uses. Before we left Ternain, Anali and Falun had stolen a set of shackles from the Palace dungeons. They were an invention of the Sorceryn, with spells woven through the iron to keep whoever wore them from summoning magick. Their weight was light enough to keep my sister mobile, and crusted with glowing runes, she was impossible to miss while wearing them. My stomach had curdled when Anali explained that these were used to transport khimaer to and from the Enclosures.

When Isadore first woke as my captive, bound to a horse tethered to mine as we left Ternain's outskirts, she had barely seemed to notice the shackles.

Her eyes grew wide as she took in the scene. Fury wicked through her like flame and she began to shake with it, eyes rolling as she searched for a weapon. Before she could say a word, I gripped the bone handle of the dagger at my hip and held up the stoppered silver bottle hanging beside it. "I brought enough to drug you for a month straight. If you cause a stir or use your magick, I will be glad to dose you again. If you endanger my friends, if any of your actions get any of them killed"—I glanced at the guards riding low on their mounts around us—"I will return the favor in kind."

I wasn't sure what I expected, but when Isadore grinned at me, hatred filling her stare, I went still. So still that I didn't react when she rose up in her saddle and leaped from her horse.

Or attempted to leap, but Aketo was there, catching her around the collar before she could shatter her legs or break her spine trying to escape the beast. The fog of the drug should have weakened her, but she bucked in the saddle like a wild animal, trying to throw him off. I caught her mount's bridle, thanking the Gods the horse had remained calm enough for me to do so, and had to dodge Isa's teeth snapping at my hands.

Aketo guided his mount forward. His eyes flitted to me and I nodded at the question in them. He wanted permission to use his magick to subdue her. Aketo could command the emotions of anyone he touched. I'd seen how effective it was as a means of control when we interrogated Katro.

"I'm sorry," he told Isadore, and wrapped her bound hands in his.

Isadore bared her teeth in a grin. A grin that seemed to hold back a scream. "Don't bother with that. We both know what this is."

Her words landed like a knife in my stomach. She knew because she had spent years doing the same—controlling people with her magick.

I knew without scenting the air that his magick flowed through her. Isadore's limbs went slack and she swayed in his grip. Her eyes now dull, but no less etched with hate, Isadore growled, "I will get free. And then I will kill you. Both."

"I think we're beyond all that now, Isadore," I said softly, but the moment I spoke, she turned away.

We didn't stop then, barreling down a road that would take us west to the coast, in the small hours of the morning. So Aketo rode on the other side of Isadore's horse, and whenever she thrashed in her chains, he touched her wrist and a druglike tranquility swept through my sister once more.

He did not stop apologizing. And the knife in my gut did not stop twisting.

That night we reasoned that the shackles had weakened her magick enough that Aketo's overwhelmed her. Unlike the night she had taken him, she was vulnerable now and I knew she hated it. Might hate the both of us for it forever.

Finding Aketo beside her horse once again the next day, she had made no declarations of revenge or mad escapes. She rode quietly between us, rage wafting off her like acrid smoke. No violence beyond a few curses under her breath promising me a frightful death, and no words exchanged between the three of us. Aketo and I traded meaningful glances whenever Isa seemed to forget our presence.

That was how it began at least.

How we had gone from that to the scene before me now in just six weeks was still a mystery.

Isadore and Aketo sat in front of my tent, a woven

teal-and-goldenrod blanket from the Isles spread out beneath them. They bickered over the cherik board before them, even though the chipped enamel game pieces—what players called the "sacred animals" in sky blue and slate gray—hadn't even been set up.

And yet there they sat fussing like children. Almost like . . . brother and sister.

It might've been comforting if it weren't so infuriating. Though she'd promised to kill the both of us, somehow she and Aketo had made up. But that promise was the last time Isa had spoken directly to me in weeks.

Her hair, without the straightening irons of the capital, now fell in silken curls around her face. The color a richer gold than I could remember ever seeing it. A spray of cinnamon freckles danced across her cheeks and pert nose. In a sleeveless bronze tunic that showed off tattooed arms corded with lean muscle, and soft calfskin tights, she looked as lovely as ever. If not for the conspicuous lack of weapons stashed about her person, she might have passed for a member of the guard.

Laughter danced in her eyes even as she rolled them at something Aketo said. Isa leaned close, murmuring words I was still too far away to catch.

Aketo looked up, sensing my approach. He smiled, broad and bright as the sun, and stretched out his hand toward me. The weeks on the road had been good to him. His dark curls were streaked with hints of gold. The cotton shirt he wore stretched taut across his back and shoulders. There was a long-handled knife thrust through his belt, and his longbow and quiver rested just out of Isa's reach.

As I anticipated, my sister fell silent the moment she caught sight of me. Sitting with her feet tucked beneath her, Isa shifted until I could make out the shackle that bound her ankle. It was attached to a stake in the ground a few feet away. I nodded, but said nothing as I passed by them and ducked into my tent.

After a beat, I heard Aketo murmur something to my sister before he followed me inside. He sat beside me as I dug through my remaining saddlebags, searching for one of the sweaters I'd bought in Dahn, the nomadic bloodkin city between the Silvern Coast and the Plain. After we left Ternain, we'd ridden west to the sea and then took a ship north past the great port cities at the mouth of the Red River to a rocky coastline dotted with small but well-fortified towns that thrived off trade from the Isles.

Dahn, meaning "roaming city" in Khimaeran, made its home in a fertile valley a few hundred leagues from the sea. The city was home to old bloodkin families who lived and traveled in intricately carved, fancifully painted wagons. Over the years, Dahn had also become a meeting place for peddlers with their vast merchant caravans, who requested permission to travel with the city. There we divested ourselves of most of the supplies brought from Ternain and traded for supplies for our journey on the Plain.

Much smaller than the tent I'd slept in on the ride to Asrodei, my current lodging could hardly fit two people comfortably. I was used to sharing the cramped space with Aketo, though.

His knees pressed against mine, his skin warmed by the sun. Desire flickered through me.

My face heated. This was becoming embarrassing. No matter how many nights I spent in this tent curled up beside him, my attraction to Aketo had not waned. Remembering that he was as aware of this as I was did not help.

"Well?" Aketo asked, his breath warm against my cheek.

I leaned away and kept my attention on the search. It was so easy, I'd learned these last weeks, to let Aketo's presence suck up all my attention.

Most days, most nights especially, I needed the distraction. But not now.

"We'll make our plans tonight and go inside tomorrow by nightfall."

"Did you see someone? At the estate?" Aketo pressed.

I shook my head. "No, but we can't continue waiting here indefinitely. Staying in one place for too long is dangerous."

"Yes, and so is rushing into an unknown situation, Eva."

I faced him, our noses bare inches apart, and sighed through my teeth. I should have known he'd preach caution. "I know that. Better than most, but sometimes these things are necessary. Need I remind you what might have happened if I'd left you with Isadore?"

A muscle in his jaw jumped. "I don't require reminders of that night or how dangerous your sister is."

"Are you sure?" By my estimation, he needed a daily reminder. I remembered my sister's knife at his throat. She was softening him, not using her magick, but persuading him that he could relax around her nonetheless.

Aketo's brow furrowed, gaze falling to my neck and the pendant that hung from it. The courtship gift he'd given me before everything went to shit. "Perhaps I have not been expressing my . . . gratitude toward your fearless nature adequately if you have need to remind me."

Spying laughter in his eyes, I protested, "No need! Your appreciation"—Aketo smirked outright as I went on—"is well documented at this point, my Prince."

"Good to know." He pressed a soft kiss to the corner of my mouth. Tempting, but we both drew back. "I'm just worried.

31

The more time passes, the more crucial our every move. It feels like if we even look in the wrong direction, everything will fall apart. I want to keep you safe." He closed the space between us, and added in a near-silent whisper, "I'm afraid."

I shivered, recalling my dreams of the last few nights. Bodies swinging from the Gate of Skies—the main entrance to the Queen's Palace that opened to a vast public courtyard. In the nightmare, sackcloth bags covered their heads, but I knew who swung beside me: my guards. One body had the scaled feet of a lizard.

The dream was a warning. Any mistakes I made now would have deadly consequences. And this time I wasn't gambling with just my life.

I kissed Aketo's cheek, daring a nip at his chin. "I am too. But if this search for my family is to yield nothing, then let us be done with it and move on."

"And do you have a plan if there is no one inside?"

I did. One I should have shared with him and Anali when we first set off from Ternain. But the final truth left unspoken between us stilled my tongue. Beyond our first conversation about why he'd come to Ternain, I had not questioned Aketo about how he came to know my father so well.

Aketo's and my father's conspicuous lack of explanation made me certain I would not like the answer.

I had a feeling that if no one here could tell me about my father's intentions, Aketo's mother might be the next best chance at understanding what Papa wanted.

I eased away from Aketo. "Tonight after we make our plans, can we talk?"

His fingers laced through mine, nimbly avoiding the sharp points of my nails. "We can talk now."

I did not miss the hesitation in his voice. "We shouldn't leave Isa alone any longer."

He offered a relieved smile. "Shall I unchain her? You know Isadore *loves* your walks."

I snorted and Aketo's broad laughter sent a pulse of warmth through me. Yesterday she'd told him, just loud enough for me to overhear, that our forced time together was tantamount to torture.

"No, finish your game." I turned my attention back to my bags and fished out the sword gifted to me by my father. The bone hilt was now wrapped in leather, but I could still feel the hum of energy beneath. "I need to think."

Aketo gave my hand a final squeeze and left the tent.

And though I sensed his attention when I followed a few moments later, sword strapped across my back, I kept my eyes to the ground as I walked toward the edge of camp.

Soon, though, I caught one of the guards following me at a respectable distance. It was Kelis, my tail and personal guard since we left Ternain. She was tall and bronze-skinned with an unruly mane of copper waves and wide-set umber eyes. She was like a wolf, equally quick to offer a fanged grin as to growl in reproach.

When we first set off, Mirabel had asked Kelis if she would serve as my body servant while we were away, should circumstance demand it. Kelis agreed, despite my objections, that weeks on the run from my mother would offer few opportunities to pretty me. It seemed that she had been given an additional task by her Captain—to protect me.

All a waste of her time. The only threat to me was chained to a stake in the middle of camp. I often dreamed of the night Isa and I had stood before the Court while two Sorceryn wrapped us in shining ribbons of magick, binding our souls in a terrible alliance. It was not quite the cruelty I once believed it was. It had saved Isa's life and cut down my list of potentially murderous enemies to one. For once, I felt safe.

Though I had been wrong about that before and didn't doubt I would be again. I mourned my old surety, born of growing up largely insulated from my own poor judgment and the harsh realities of a common life. Even at Asrodei I'd been waited on hand and foot since I was an infant.

And yet here I was asking my guards to trust me now.

Every soldier who remained loyal to me after they'd seen my true form—fifteen guards, plus Aketo, Falun, and Anali—had likely already been named traitors to the crown. The punishment for which was public hanging, like the ones in my dreams.

I very much doubted my khimaer magick had come with a gift of clairvoyance. The only khimaer known to wield that power were long-dead Godlings.

No, I was not concerned with omens, but the fact that if we were caught, my friends would die alongside me. I'd let them place their trust in me, while I was still reckoning with the impossibility of what I wanted. How would I gain the throne when I refused to kill my sister, as the law required? And how could I even hope to be crowned when I was khimaer?

But as long as I had even the slimmest chance, I had to fight for the throne. The freedom of thousands of khimaer depended on it.

When we had finally found Orai a few days ago, we made our camp in the shadow of a outcrop of striated red-and-white stone. The Plain's dense grass was sparse here and we were downwind of the village's only well. And still close enough that we risked trips to it at night.

When I reached the high grass at the perimeter of the camp, I undid my sword belt and laid the weapon on the ground. I waved at Kelis, who stopped about twenty feet away, and she saluted in reply.

I began the way Anali first taught me when I moved to Asrodei. I bent at the waist and planted my palms in the dirt. In our first lesson, she had bade me to listen to the pulse of the earth. I didn't truly understand what she meant until Aketo's lessons in *kathbaria*.

Now I dug my claws into the rocky soil and let my mind fall silent. Wind knifing through the grass reached my ears. Finally energy crackled in my hands and I surged up, as if to cup the sun itself.

I cycled through the stretches until I forgot everything but the strength and rhythm of my body, which was its own song.

I included a few new movements focused on my neck and shoulders. It was easy to forget that I had horns until I lay down on my bedroll at night, my back aching. I was still getting used to the weight of them. Next I practiced a series of hand-to-hand attacks Aketo taught me until my limbs were warm and loose.

Finally I retrieved my sword. I lifted the blade, sighting down it to an imagined foe, and lost myself in the savage dance.

I dashed to the right, blade singing as it slashed the air. Breath blossomed in my chest, a near-jubilant feeling taking over me as I spun. The sword was light as a dagger and seemed an extension of my hands. I flowed through the sequence of sword forms easily, with enough strength behind each strike to kill.

I pushed my body harder, bade my limbs to move faster.

When I slowed, I fell to my knees as fear threatened to upend my stomach.

Not just fear, but joy at the power that sang in my veins.

I was not winded. The burn of muscle fatigue did not weigh down my legs. I could have gone an hour more. Two.

No, *ten*.

I'd suffered long hours after leaving Ternain, worried I would never get used to my new body. That perhaps everyone but me would adjust to it, so that I'd always seem a stranger to myself. But I hadn't anticipated how much my body truly had changed. Freeing my magick had done more than shift my physical features.

All the newfound strength, speed, and stamina stole my breath, but I was determined to control my new well of strength. And understand it.

I knew no better way to learn my body, and make it mine again, than to work like this.

So I stood and began again, sweat stinging my eyes, old wound aching.

I did not allow my thoughts to linger on whatever other changes—and magick—would come. Baccha would call me a coward for it, but I found I didn't care.

✎ CHAPTER 2 ✎

Eva

BY THE TIME I finished, the sky over the Plain was ablaze. Burnt orange and gold-flecked crimson streaked through the sky from the setting sun as it tipped into the horizon. The sparse leaves of a massive baobab tree danced like tiny flames in the distance. But that was nothing compared to how this golden hour before nightfall transformed my sister.

Her golden-brown skin had deepened and the sun had seen fit to turn her light brown skin to a deeper bronze. Her hair looked spun of the finest yellow gold, her cheeks dotted with flecks of copper. Even in an ill-fitting tunic and pants, and a streak of ocher dirt across one cheek, she was still very much a creature of the Court.

I found myself wondering about her father's identity. He must have been the source of her staggering beauty. Had whoever told her about Papa revealed that to her? I would never get her to tell me, but I wondered at whatever man had stolen our mother's heart, then spurned her. Who would reject a Queen? And if there had been love between them, might my childhood memories be wrong? Maybe there never was any love between her and my father and that was why Mother was so determined to use his death to cloak her own ambition.

I made no effort to hide my survey of Isadore, just as she made no attempt to acknowledge it. She never did. Even on our walks she remained quiet. Isa had requested the exercise through Aketo—"Unless my sister *intends* to let my muscles atrophy so that I will be weak when she works up the courage to kill me"—assuming I would let him take her rather than endure her silence. Right now I half wished I had.

Typical of Isadore to find the only way to exert control over a situation in which she had none.

The last time we had spoken at any length was the first night we made camp after leaving Ternain. We'd ridden nearly seven hours straight, heading west to the Silvern Coast. Simply because I knew my mother would not anticipate such a move and, if we did have a tail, I did not want to lead them directly to Papa's family.

That night as the guards set up camp, I pulled Isa aside. I'd brandished the stoppered bottle—milk of the poppy—Mirabel had procured for me.

"You decide how this will go. If you can refrain from using your magick, I will allow you to walk freely among us."

Before we left the capital, I told Aketo and Mirabel of my plan: offer Isa the choice we'd never been given. If she could set aside what the Rival Heir laws intended, I would grant her freedom, bit by bit. Though they'd both cautioned against it, I wanted—*needed*—to try. I had to give us a chance at something other than death. If we could learn to trust each other, maybe we could be sisters again. Or at least something other than enemies.

If Isa couldn't set our rivalry aside, then at least I could keep my mother from crowning her for as long as we stayed on the run.

At my words, Isa had snorted and rolled her eyes. "How kind of you, sister." She held up her wrists, grimace darkening her gaze. "And what of these?"

I swallowed, throat dry as the southern sands. "If I have your word that you won't make an attempt at escape, I will remove the irons from your arms."

"And my legs?" she asked, voice deceptively light.

"No," I said, jaw set. Isadore would take advantage of any weakness I offered and she hadn't rescinded her threat of revenge. However naïve Mirabel thought I was being, I would not let her roam free. "Well?"

"You have my word. I promise."

I waited, eyes narrowed.

A long moment passed, during which I worried the glares passing between us would set one of us aflame. Finally Isa loosed a sigh. "I swear by my title not to use magick or attempt escape should the opportunity present itself."

I hoped then, as the old stories said, the Gods would frown upon her if she broke that promise.

But if any God heard my request, they must have laughed. Two weeks later, when Isadore broke her oath, she did so in spectacular fashion.

We were a short ride from Soli Port, where we would catch a boat sailing north. For days I'd smelled the salt of the sea, reminding me, unhappily, of my mother's perfume. At dawn we broke camp. I'd been about to climb into Bird's saddle as Isadore slipped a knife from my belt, as deft as a cutpurse in Ternain. Before I noticed its absence, she'd buried the blade in my stomach to the hilt. She tore the pouch where I kept the key to her chains from around my neck.

I had no time to release even a grunt as Isa's magick attacked on the heels of pain. She had my mind in her grip. I could do nothing as blood soaked my tunic and pants. None of the guards even noticed Isadore until she mounted Bird and galloped from our camp.

She didn't make it very far. As shouts of warning went off, Falun was nocking an arrow. He loosed two before she'd gotten a hundred paces.

The first punched through her shoulder.

The second struck the back of her neck, but the arrow that would have killed her didn't even pierce her skin. And only seemed to stun her. Her magick broke as she slumped in the saddle.

I found myself crying out, "Help her." A moment later, I fell to the ground, the hilt slick with blood still protruding from my side.

Without Baccha, there was no one with a gift for skilled healing. Sylban, one of the fey members of the guard, sewed up the wound and stopped the bleeding with rough combat healing. The wound was still tender, and likely would be for weeks more. Some part of me was glad it had happened. Falun's arrow had proven the Entwining's effectiveness: no hand but mine could kill Isa.

And Isa had proven she was not as driven to kill me as she once seemed.

During the week we spent on the *Silversong*, the river cutter Anali hired to sail up the coast, I'd healed enough to ride. And had asked Isadore half a dozen times why she broke her promise and why she hadn't killed me when she had the chance, but she refused to speak to anyone but Aketo.

When he reported that Isa hadn't *intended* to break her oath, only to see how far she could get if she really wanted to escape, I'd nearly given up on my plan. She was still lying and playing games with me, even as my prisoner. I might as well forget a truce between us. I had no way to convince her, and nothing she really wanted. Even if she did agree, I could never trust her.

And still I wanted to trust her and be trusted by her again.

My gaze drifted to the bandage peeking out from her collar, covering the puncture wound from Falun's first arrow. I hoped it pained her as much as mine pained me. I prayed it reminded her. Our destruction was mutually assured now. If she killed me, the spell that kept that arrow from piercing her neck would unravel the moment my heart stopped beating.

And then my guard would be free to kill her.

Beside me now, Isa stared at the sea of yellow grass, eyes narrowed.

"Planning your next attempt?" I asked.

Her eyes flitted to mine and just as quickly darted away.

"You'd only need to run a hundred fifty miles west to reach the coast," I continued.

I stumbled as laughter sprang from her lips. "Yes, you have me well and truly trapped here. You must be so pleased with yourself."

Before I could reply, she went on. "Though that does not make you any less a fool."

Gritting my teeth with the effort of maintaining a civil expression, I inclined my head. We might as well have been at Court, performing for each other. "Go on, then. Tell me."

Isa arched a blond brow. Pretty as a painting and silent as one.

"Oh no, don't stop now. You've resisted criticizing me for weeks. I know you must long to inform me of my inadequacies." How else could she bask in her superiority? "You always do."

"Why," Isa snapped, "should I bother to open my mouth when you already know that I'm right? To come to Papa's home." She chuckled. "Why bother escaping? The army will catch up with us soon enough. Mother has likely already dispatched them to this place."

"If they have as hard a time finding this place as we did, I think we're safe for a while. And I thought you said Lei wasn't your father," I whispered. I could barely breathe around the knot of anger in my chest.

She waved a hand, brow furrowing with annoyance. "Did I? Well, if Lei is not my father, then I have none. So I think I shall keep him, liar that he was."

"And what of Mother, who has lied to the Queendom since you were born?"

Isa frowned and the scent of caramel began to waft from her skin. The air around her shimmered, the color of her hair flickering back and forth between Mother's pale blond and her own dark gold.

I sucked in a breath, grasping the long-handled dagger hanging from my belt. Isa often lost control of her magick because of her temper, but the fact that she could still summon any of the persuasive magick she used to change her appearance while wearing those shackles was chilling. The runes etched into the shackles flared with silvery lavender light.

"Isa," I warned, "control your magick."

She glared at me, shivering violently, before her appearance finally stabilized. "Mother did what she had to do."

"And so did Papa." By the set of her jaw, Isa did not agree, but she didn't argue. A few minutes passed in silence before I spoke again. "What would you do in my stead?"

"Flee north—to the Roune Lands. You won't survive in Myre long as a rebel Princess. They will call you a traitor, an imposter attempting to steal the throne. Papa is dead. There are no allies for you to gather.

"This country is not good to rebels. You face death here," she finished softly.

I shrugged. "Well then, my fate hasn't changed. I've run toward death for as long as I've lived. With every day that I avoid death, I fear it less and less. And you have grown more afraid."

I understood now that she'd always been afraid of me, as I feared her. Mother or the Rival Heirdom, I wasn't sure who to blame for that.

"Of course I'm scared. You have me stuck here. You can kill me anytime."

"But I won't. I didn't bring you with us to hurt you, Isa. I swear it."

"Well, I don't trust you."

"I could have killed you a hundred different times by now. I could drag your body back to Ternain and make Mother choose between crowning me, a khimaer, or starting a war of succession. But I haven't."

"Why?"

Her eyes were veiled with distrust, but behind that, there was genuine curiosity. I tried not to let my relief that I'd finally baited Isa into a conversation show. "You remember my nameday?" Isa nodded, lips flat with displeasure. As if it was rude of me to bring up the night she'd tried to kill *me*. "I meant the Entwining . . . before everything else happened."

"That night," I continued, "I thought this was just more power they were taking from us. Robbing us of our ability to choose anything but fratricide. But I was wrong. I can't believe no other Rival Heirs ever figured it out. The Entwining is a gift. If we choose peace, they can't make us kill each other, Isa. We don't have to die. The spell ensures our safety."

"There are worse things than dying." Isa's bright green eyes scanned the horizon until they settled on the rise of rock outcrops hiding our camp. "How many of their throats would Mother have to slit before you decided it was worth killing me, if just to keep them safe? Maybe I'm wrong and you would let them all die. They are soldiers, after all, and death comes with the job. But what happens when she brings in children off the street, poor bloodkin boys and girls, too young to have even had their first taste of blood? Will you let them die for me? I doubt it, Eva."

"Gods, Isa, must your every decision be driven by fear of Mother?" I snapped.

Isadore seemed to look down her nose at me as she answered, "I make my decisions by not being completely naïve. You're of age now, Eva; you should try it."

"You should try to have a little faith that not everything in our lives must be terrible."

"And why would I do that when all evidence indicates our lives *should* be miserable?"

Isa fell silent and refused to add anything further. We resumed our slow procession around the camp. That hour parrying imagined blades beneath the sun earlier had done its job of quieting my mind. Our conversation hadn't been painless, it soothed me somehow.

Though it hadn't made my planned truce seem any less futile.

∹⋆∹

We ate supper by the light of torches hanging from stakes pounded into the earth. The camp was arrayed in a half circle, the lights marking this central meeting place. Behind each stake was a row of tents. Our tents were made from the same nondescript, muddied-brown canvas, but lined with shearling for warmth. Nights were brutally cold on the Plain, even in High Summer.

We'd sold our old tents in Dahn. The last place I'd been able to walk about freely, home to bloodkin and many part khimaer.

In Dahn, I'd divested myself of nearly all my jewels to equip us for the three-week trek across the Plain. Where we would not ride, but walk and run several miles a day to reach Orai. Our only pack animals were two camels who kept pace with us just fine. All I'd kept were the adornments of my title—the Rival Heir diadem, my signet ring, and the ceremonial necklace and headdress worn alongside the diadem—and a few gifts I could not replace. My father's ring and Baccha's horn bracelet, now worn stacked atop mine on my left wrist.

I had debated dropping it in the sea once, but when I tried, I could not bear to remove it. Even though all it did was remind me that this tether to Baccha was severed, another, deeper connection—the coalescence—kept our minds enmeshed.

Dinner was the fowl roasted beneath a pile of hot coals and a stew of sweet peppers, onions, and yams.

Anali had chosen fifteen guards when we left Ternain, and I was surprised all remained with us still. I'd been sure we would lose a few to Dahn. What I once offered them—my protection and a steady wage—was long gone. Part of me wanted to ask them to leave, to flee to the Isles until the next Queen was crowned, though I knew they would not take the request as graciously as I meant it.

I left Isadore at her tent, which was always erected beside mine, trussed up with barely enough slack to comfortably eat dinner. After many nights of her staring into a few of the soldiers' eyes until they were blushing and stammering, or worse, terrified, she'd taken her meals there. Not at my request, but because the last time she had done it, Anali had embarrassed her by asking, voice as cool as anything, "Tell me, does the attention you get from bothering my soldiers adequately fill the void left by your inability to command a circus of fools at Court, Princess Isadore?"

Isa had turned such an angry puce, her green eyes full of venom, before she took hold of herself and smiled warmly, falsely at Anali. After that night, though, Isa took her supper alone.

Tonight I sat between Aketo and Kelis. Ten other soldiers sat on battered cushions around us. We were still waiting for Falun. After our talk, he'd gone to call back the scouts. A skilled tracker, Falun directly commanded them and set out to go scouting hours before dawn each day. It was Falun who'd found the rise of stone outcrops that hid Orai.

Kelis recounted a tale of how she'd become betrothed to a fey noblewoman and two weeks later fled her home under . . . dubious circumstances. Kelis, bloodkin and five years my senior, was rangy and coltish with dark eyes and copper waves hanging loose that reflected light like actual metal, and her stories were always engrossing, if a bit unlikely.

Aketo's knee pressed against mine and that single point of contact made my whole body flush. Perhaps it was that I knew what his skin felt like without layers of clothing between us—smooth, warm, and full of perfect angles well worth exploring. Or maybe because that knowledge was not enough.

Though Aketo slept often in my tent, the physical intimacy between us had stalled. And it was driving me mad.

After the great embarrassment on my nameday, when Aketo had rebuffed my request to sneak up to my rooms and sleep together, I resolved to let him set the pace.

And yet little touches like this threatened to upend my self-control.

Across the fire, Anali inclined her head, her gaze focused beyond me. I glanced back to see Falun making his way through the tents.

I stood, thankful for the reprieve. Watched to see if he held any grudge from our earlier argument.

Once again, I was struck by the changes in him. In a mere six weeks, the youthful softness of his face had been shorn away, leaving him lean and sharp. A deep tan complemented his hair, which was more gold than crimson today. With his hair unbound, Falun might have looked radiant, if not for the bruised circles beneath his eyes and the wan, humorless smile he gave me.

With a bow slung over his shoulder and two more guinea fowl held in one hand, he bore little resemblance to the courtly soldier he'd been in Ternain. He reminded me of Baccha, I realized with a sharp pang of longing I immediately smothered.

I returned his smile hesitantly and he nodded, eyes unfocused. I felt a stab of guilt at the way that our early conversation ended, but I was right. Baccha was an immortal being. I wasn't going to waste time worrying about him when he was probably on his way to betray me. The Tribe held Baccha's leash and his loyalty, and if they decided I was their enemy, even with my khimaer blood, there was nothing I could do about it now.

Once greetings were exchanged, and Falun settled in, Anali cleared her throat and gave me a pointed look.

Just as you practiced, I reminded myself, trying to work moisture into my suddenly dry mouth. "It's been two days since we arrived in Orai. And in that time, we have watched and waited for the people of this village to reveal their secrets. All that waiting has yielded little information on who or what dwells in the walled estate. So, I propose we change our tack. I say we go inside. Tomorrow morning."

A murmur rose at my words and Malto let out a whoop of delight. Thank the Gods I wasn't the only one who had tired of this tiptoeing about the Plain. I spoke over the rising din, "We do this together and so I want us all to determine the best way to get inside."

I sat down as the first suggestions were thrown out. Anali held up a hand and everyone fell silent. "If we must go in blind, our plan must account for opposition inside. If King Lei's family still lives there, they will not appreciate us breaking into their home. Even," she added, "if you are their kin, Princess."

The use of my title continued to make my skin itch. Whatever I was—kidnapper, traitor, or rebel—I'd left *Princess* behind.

"I can climb the wall and open the gate from the inside," I said quietly. "So that we won't need to mount an assault on my father's home. We go in as quietly as possible."

"No," Anali protested.

"Why not? I'm the only one who is sure to survive if I go in first."

"You can be captured and overwhelmed as easily as anyone else."

"I hardly believe my father's family will ransom me to my mother. And even then, as long as Isadore is in chains, I can't be killed. Give me a better reason, one that outweighs my assured survival."

"Oh, you'd like another reason besides that you are our Princess? The very reason we are here?"

I smothered a groan. Didn't she see that was why I needed to do this? "We have to put that aside for now. We're equals in this. You saw what happened when Falun shot my sister. Whoever lives inside the wall, they won't be able to kill me. If I can use the Entwining to make sure the rest of you are safe, we have to rely on it. Especially when I set our course here."

"What of a distraction?" Falun asked. "While Eva climbs, we'll draw the attention of whoever is inside elsewhere?"

"Where, then?" Anali mused, voice gone soft. As if she was actually considering my plan. "How will we distract them when they're either hiding or don't want to be seen?"

"We demand entry at the main entrance," Falun continued. Ever my partner and coconspirator. "If no one is inside, then we have no one to worry about but a few villagers. If King Lei's family still dwells there, they will answer or they will not. But they'll certainly wonder who has the nerve to make demands of them. They'll at least take a look."

My smile widened as the plan took shape in my mind. "This is how we'll do it."

Everyone—Anali and Falun, a grinning Malto and sharp-eyed Kelis, and Aketo, his eyes rimmed with worry—leaned forward. Their faces were glossy beneath the moon's silver light, their expressions just discernible.

Will they trust you? Should they trust you? I thought, words perched on my tongue.

All fell silent as I explained.

✺ CHAPTER 3 ✺

Eva

IT TOOK AN hour to iron out all the details, after which I went straight to one of the three steaming tents at the south end of the camp.

These were a lucky find in Dahn. Malto had grown up one of thirty grandchildren of Elbir Usam, an elder of the largest and most distinguished of the bloodkin nomad families. With his family, Malto had crossed the Plain as a child and even traversed the Deadened Jungle. A contingent of the Usam family had hosted us in their wagons while we were in Dahn, and we bought the tents from them for much less than they were worth. The bloodkin used the steaming tents whenever they crossed lands like the Plain and Kremir where there was little water to bathe with. Inside, a small copper brazier held warm coals, over which water was poured to create the steam. The inner canvas of each tent was treated with animal fat to make it impervious to moisture, trapping the vapors inside.

I lingered inside for nearly an hour, contemplating what I would say to Aketo. Eventually, though, Kelis tapped on the tent flaps to tell me that it was time for her shift in the night watch. Meaning she would have to escort me to my tent first.

I met her outside, still shrugging into a fresh cotton shift.

The sky above us was velvety black, and a waning sickle moon offered scant light. As we walked through the forest of tents, I massaged my right shoulder, looser, but still sore with overuse.

"At Asrodei, when someone is determined to work themselves ragged for the sake of working themselves ragged, we send them to the ice baths after," Kelis said, all studied nonchalance as she fingered the slim knife at her waist. She still wore her bloodletting knife despite being far from Ternain. "Have you been?"

"Of course," I said with a smile that was quickly replaced with a grimace as I recalled the baths. Anali sent me to the long bathing chamber in the Fort's infirmary just twice. Enduring tubs full of ice was part treatment and part punishment. Both times, I had snuck from my bed to practice swordplay by moonlight and had woken too sore to make a proper effort in my lessons. After the bath, instead of returning to the Sandpits, I had to cut bandages for the apprentice healers all afternoon.

"You've worked yourself to the bone each day for a week."

"And I suppose you and Anali must be trying to find some way to stop me."

Kelis stopped, her usually ruffled hair slicked back in a knot. Dark eyes surveyed me. "You're a grown woman, Your Highness. It isn't my job or the Captain's to stop you from being foolish. That's your job now. I only wanted to ask why."

Perhaps it was the darkness that made me feel safe enough to share the truth. Or maybe it was the clarity of Kelis's eyes and the lack of judgment there. "I'm not sparring mindlessly.

I'm trying to . . . find the bottom of this new strength. I'm testing my limits before someone else has a chance to test them."

"Aye," Kelis said. "I understand. You seek control."

Her words landed true. There was one person I could control, and thus depend on—myself. Not my family, not Baccha. There were limits to how much I could trust everyone now, even my friends.

When we were close enough to my tent to see Aketo waiting outside it, staring up at the stars, Kelis slowed.

I inclined my head, taking this momentary pause to draw a deep breath.

"If I may offer advice, Your Highness?"

I crossed my arms, glancing sidelong at Aketo's lean form. "As long as you start calling me by my name, so be it."

Kelis snorted. "If you truly want to learn your limitations, you must train your body alongside your magick. Good night, Eva."

With that, she disappeared behind a nearby tent and faded into the night.

I was glad she'd gone, or else I might have confessed that I hadn't used magick since I changed. Kelis was almost too easy to talk with.

When I reached Aketo, he lifted two buckets. "I told Anali we would go to the well tonight."

The well lay about a mile east of camp. During the day, men and women balancing stoneware jars on their heads and hips walked the winding dirt path that led from Orai to the aged well. Its position indicated the town had once been larger, but now the wildness of the Plain butted up against it.

We were silent as ghosts, neither of us eager to talk. Once we reached the well, Aketo turned to me, his expression careful.

Orai's well was red clay elaborately carved to look like a tree stump growing from the earth. Roughhewn stone plinths held up a bucket and chain. Broken pottery littered the yellow grass that grew waist high.

When we first arrived here, I had noticed that, around the well, grass grew through patches of paving stones. I had a feeling ruins of a once-larger town were buried beneath the dirt. Few noble Ladies would have chosen such an isolated place as their homestead. I wondered why our family settled here.

I opened my mouth, but Aketo held up a hand. "I have to tell you something first." Before I could relax, he rushed on. "The first time we met, you asked me why I enlisted and why I'd come to Ternain and I told you part of the truth. There were other things I hid."

"What?" For a moment, I thought I'd heard him wrong. "You mean the affair?"

The one between my father and his mother.

This time it was Aketo who sputtered in confusion. "All this time you've known?"

"Not exactly." I blew out a breath. "I wondered at Asrodei. When he spoke of her, I knew there was more to their relationship than friendship, but then he died and I . . . How else would you two have grown close?"

"Ah," Aketo breathed. "Well, no, that isn't what I was talking about. But yes, they did love each other."

I tensed, bracing for resentment toward my father for keeping yet another secret. But it didn't come. Instead I was glad to know he'd been loved in those years of exile. I had worried he spent all his time buried in work during his self-imposed exile in Asrodei.

"What is it, then?" I said, taking a moment to stare up at

him. In the moonlit night, his horns towered high above us. His brows were drawn together, but his mouth was soft, the barest hint of fang pressing into his bottom lip.

Aketo's gaze slid from mine, glancing up at the sky, before he met my eyes again. "First let me tell you about my home. It's a three-day climb up the mountain, and even then you might march right past Sher n'Cai during Far Winter, when its limestone and marble towers blend in with the snow. At the top of the highest tower, you can see Dracolan mountain villages roosting on the cliffs of the A'Nir like rooks in an aerie. In High Summer, wildflowers fill every valley until the land is like a patchwork quilt."

"It sounds beautiful." I cringed even as the words left my mouth. No matter how lovely the view from atop the mountain, the Enclosure was still a cage.

When I lived at Asrodei, my father refused to take me on any of his trips to the Enclosure. After the first few years of being denied, I stopped asking. Now I wondered if Papa had kept me away to preserve his secret. Maintaining the lie that he was human might've been difficult, but he should have taken me.

Aketo shook his head, nostrils flaring. "It is. And yet Sher n' Cai is a ruin. A castle left to rot for a thousand years before . . . the Usurpress"—my ancestor Raina the First—"sent us there. It's a lonesome place, as if the fey who'd abandoned it all those centuries ago left the very bricks of the castle in mourning. It is all these things, but mostly a cage, one that grows more dangerous with each day."

"I don't understand." What had changed?

"Five years ago, the previous Governess, General Ameela Nafi, retired and the Queen appointed General Throllo Sareen. Together they decided that General Nafi had taken too soft an approach. Ameela Nafi was my mother's long-time friend, and when they worked together, our population swelled. Lord Sareen on the other hand did not believe the khimaer should have any leadership. He believes once given a taste of power, we will only long for more." Aketo's smile was knife sharp, his laugh dark as bitter kaffe. "The Queen gave Sareen complete control of the Enclosure, and after that came all the rules. The first was that we were not allowed to leave the castle grounds under any circumstances, even though hunting allows us to survive the meager rations the military provides. The last one announced just before I left was a new curfew—an hour past sundown."

"How are the rule breakers punished?" I asked, already bracing myself for the answer.

"The first offense is house arrest. The second is public lashing. And the third is hanging."

My thoughts slowed to a trickle as I tried to take in his words. Surely not. I want to protest, but I know Aketo wouldn't lie. "My father knew this?"

"The King tried to stop Throllo, but he answered only to the Queen."

My hands curled into fists. I'd met General Sareen once before when his battalion was called to Asrodei for my father's once-yearly gathering of all the Generals of the Queen's Army. Usually Throllo skipped the meeting, but Mother had called for everyone's presence because she would be attending. I remember Throllo Sareen only because he was one of the few Generals who deferred to Mother, and not his King and Lord Commander. He'd reminded me of an oversize raptor. Tall, with dark teak skin, and the flinty, darting eyes of a predator.

The only time the cruel line of his mouth had curved was

when he bowed to Mother. And the oily smile he'd given her had not been any improvement.

"I didn't know," I mumbled uselessly. Even though a scream gathered in my chest. Why, why hadn't my father told me any of this? If he wanted me to fight for the khimaer, why keep me in the dark?

A muscle flexed in Aketo's jaw. "As I said, the situation is dire. That is why I joined the Queen's Army. Not just for the chance to leave the Enclosure, but so that I could go to Ternain and attend Court. My mother hoped that I would find allies there. And I did believe you were my best chance in find anyone sympathetic."

It must have been so frustrating then when my actions— first fleeing the capital for Asrodei before my nameday, and then leaving again afterward—had kept him from seeking any allies.

"I was naïve when I left my home," Aketo continued. "First I thought Throllo was an outlier and that most humans were like the King and General Nafi. I thought there was a way to fix this without rebellion. But by the time I reached Ternain, I had spent four months training at Fort Asrodei. By then I knew how wrong I was. The noble-born soldiers were determined that I knew my place as a khimaer. As a *beast*. When I met you, I was afraid you would be another disappointment."

"And once you knew me, why didn't you tell me then?"

He stepped close until we stood less than a foot apart and extended a hand, expression plaintive. "You were a bit busy running for your life at the time, Eva."

At this I laughed without mirth. I stepped forward, taking his fingers in mine. "I understand."

Still he frowned down at me, suspicious. "How reasonable of you."

I canted my head and offered my most convincing smile. "I can be reasonable."

"You can," he allowed, "but I can tell you're still upset."

Not so convincing, then.

I didn't know why I even bothered. He would know, with his ability to sense the emotions of everyone near him. And Aketo was quite determined about taking note of mine, most especially when I was keen on doing just the opposite.

Of course he sensed the sudden sadness in me. Knowing he'd held this in for so long made my eyes burn with unshed tears. Because I should have asked. I should have begged him every night to talk of his home and his family. But I'd spent the last months focused solely on my problems without worrying about him.

I rose up on my toes, aiming for his mouth, but I could only reach his throat and so I kissed him there. "I'm not upset with you."

"Not even about hiding the affair?" Aketo murmured into my hair.

"Not even that. I swear it." I stepped back. "We should finish and return to camp."

Aketo caught my arm as I turned to retrieve the buckets. "Wait, what did you want to talk about?"

Wind snaked through the underbrush, making music as it joined the chittering chorus of night bugs. I folded my arms, skin pebbling from the cold and the loss of Aketo's warmth. "It's altogether possible no one lives in that place. My father's family could have abandoned it a long time ago. I figured if I can't find out my father's plans here, then the next best chance is asking the woman he trusted more than most. If it's even possible to sneak into the Enclosure."

Aketo's loose, inky hair fell forward till only his mouth was left visible. "It can be done. I know a way."

"Good." If we failed tomorrow or if Papa's family were all ghosts like him. "And since Isa's no closer to agreeing to a truce, we should see what can be done about Throllo."

"Thank you."

"No more hiding anything. I will swear the same. There has to be absolute truth between us. We have to trust each other completely or this won't work."

Our fingers laced together. Aketo kissed the back of my hand. "I promise."

His eyes did not leave mine as I kissed his hand and repeated the vow.

We retrieved the buckets and strode to the well. We fell into easy silence as we worked to fill them and made our way back to camp.

✦

The next morning I woke well before the sun crested the horizon.

I dressed quickly, methodically strapping on all the supplies and weapons I'd laid out last night, and stumbled from my tent, mind still bleary with sleep. At the sight of Aketo seated by the smoldering remains of last night's cook fire, I smiled.

I filled one of the camp's battered copper kettles and set it atop the coals. I plopped down across from Aketo, picking through the dwindling sachets of tea.

At the first flicker of Aketo's gaze, I flushed. Along with my sword, a narrow dagger stuffed into my boot, and a throwing-knife belt that I'd repurposed to store a set of climbing spikes, I was well-prepared for our scouting mission. But the single curved short sword belted at Aketo's waist made me feel ridiculous.

"Sleep well?" Aketo grinned, his voice on the edge of laughter.

After we returned to camp last night, Aketo came to my tent. A few minutes later, Kelis had come to check that I'd returned to camp, shocking the both of us. Kelis's guffaws chased him from my tent, shirtless. She woke half the camp with her laughter.

I bit my lip. My sleep had been blissfully dreamless, which meant no nightmares. "Like the dead. And you?"

Before Aketo could answer, Falun stepped out from behind one of the nearby tents. The kettle began whistling as he sat down at my right side. We sipped our tea in silence and left camp just as the sun peeked above the horizon.

As we walked, the warm, writhing buzz of Falun's glamour spread over my skin. I looked to him and Aketo to see its effect; their features flickered in and out of focus, bodies seemingly as insubstantial as smoke.

Soon we reached the village's edge. Orai still slept, the shades drawn and windows shuttered, but I knew the shepherd girls would be up tending their meager flock soon.

Before then, I needed to see the wall of the estate up close. No one was willing to go forward with my plan unless I was absolutely certain I could climb the wall.

By the time we reached the ocher wall, the sun was just beginning to peek over the horizon. The four-sided wall rose over a hundred feet high, and each limestone brick was engraved with a different figure—women and men mostly, but also strange animals I had no name for. Water drakes crowned with antlers, winged lions with lashing reptilian tails, and massive saddled lizards with feathered chests. The people etched onto the bricks weren't only khimaer as I first suspected. There were fanged bloodkin and willowy fey—a few even possessed wings.

It was a tribute to ancient Myre.

Papa's family must have lived here for a millenium. An offshoot of the Red River once ran through the Plain, and in those years, thousands made their home on its banks, at peace with the animals who called this place home.

Papa's home hadn't been erected in this lifeless village. It was built when this land bloomed and teemed with life.

I traced a fox-faced woman, filled with the same frustration from yesterday. *Why didn't my father bring me here when he had the chance?*

Aketo's hands were clenched, his gold eyes glossy with unshed tears. "It was hard to believe any khimaer families could have escaped the Enclosures. Until now."

I ached at the bitterness in his voice. Here Papa's family was safe, while Aketo's family and the people he was honor-bound to protect went hungry and were killed.

If this frustrated him, what would the khimaer in Sher n'Cai think of me, coddled in the Palace most of my life?

"Can you sense anyone near us?" I asked.

Falun tipped his head, smelling the air. After both assured me we were well and truly alone, I leaned into the wall, fingers seeking the joints between the bricks.

About halfway up the wall, there was a row of triangular arrow slits. They were my goal. I wanted to take a look inside one and see the dwelling and grounds within.

"Remember, Eva. The glamour will only stretch so far. Past a hundred paces, anyone will be able to see you."

Falun's magick—a soft fuzz around my skin I'd stopped noticing—flexed as if in response to his words.

"I understand." Best guess, the arrow slits were about a hundred paces high. I wouldn't take long.

I took a deep breath and began. First I peeled off my boots, which, having been caked with grit for weeks, were neither light enough nor supple enough to climb in. Then I pulled one of the climbing spikes from my belt and clenched it between my teeth. Though I was loath to use them now and risk defacing the carvings, I'd be a fool to depend only on my hands.

One thing I'd learned from first climbing trees in the gardens of the Palace, and eventually ascending its marble walls, was that every climb is about calm.

You kept a clear head or you made mistakes and fell on your ass.

Even keeping that in mind, the sheer wall of the estate made me nervous. At ten feet, my palms were slick. At fifty, my claws driven so deeply into the stone that my fingertips bled, I looked down at Falun and Aketo. They wavered in and out of sight like motes of dust, the glamour warping my vision, and for the first time I wondered if these walls might just be too high, too sheer for me.

At sixty, panting and every inch of my skin damp with sweat, I drove the first spike into the wall and grasped a second, stretching to my full length as I hauled my body up and up.

Using the picks as proper footholds, I moved quickly, knowing the steel wouldn't hold my weight very long. When I was within arm's reach of the arrow slits, I heard Aketo and Falun shouting below.

I must have gone out of range for Falun's magick. No matter. I was close now.

Balanced on a single foot, I hissed as my hand caught the edge of the narrow window, the rough stone drawing blood. Groaning, I dragged myself up until I was even with the window.

I tried to force it open, but suddenly the window swung outward, slamming hard against my claws and ruining my grip.

I caught a brief glimpse of a feminine face—dark hair braided to her scalp in florid patterns and eyes with a core of blazing crimson—her expression turning sharply from confusion to horror. Her hand shot out, reaching for me, but it was too late.

A scream escaped my mouth, but the wind snatched it away.

I forgot my sister and all my assurances that the Entwining would keep me safe. All I knew was that if I reached the ground, I would die.

Instinct sent me barreling into my mindscape, searching for magick. My thoughts quested inward until I stood at the lake of magick in my mind. It defied all logic—in the past, seeking my mindscape was slow and awkward, but not anymore. In an instant, I was diving into the lake's dark waters, kicking toward the bottom, but panic seized me as I realized there was nothing here to help me. No magick of blood or bone could slow my descent.

At once I could feel the sun on my face, the wind yanking at my clothes, sensed the ground rushing, rushing, rushing toward me—and in the same instant, I felt the cool, dark water slipping over my skin as I kicked up, past glowing blood magick, and shot through the water to find golden light filling the air, gold like the sun on my face.

I knew instinctively what it was: my khimaer magick.

My fingertips slipped into the golden light, and searing heat tore through me. It was the same mind-ending pain from when I'd broken the binding on my magick, but only for the space of a breath before a new warmth enveloped me.

A warmth of creation and remaking.

A hoarse scream brought me back to my body. Not my voice, but Aketo's, yelling and too close. Too soon the ground was rushing up to meet me.

A whimper escaped my mouth and I shut my eyes. There was a strain in my back and a strange gust of wind that seemed to lift me aloft.

Then I struck the ground and did not feel anything at all.

⚜ CHAPTER 4 ⚜

Baccha

BACCHA, FIRST OF his name, last of his kind, tipped back a
cloudy glass, savoring the bitter dregs.

It was a foul brew—a blend of kaffe and whiskey and a splash
of ewe's milk, flavored with cinnamon—that these northerners
called firemilk.

The rest of his meal, a steaming plate of eggs, pork belly,
and peppered lentils, had gone fast.

Truth was, he'd always preferred the cuisine in southern
Myre, but the Sister Citadel boasted the best inns and serving
halls in the Queendom. In all the centuries he'd been visiting
the Loom, it had never disappointed him.

The inn had changed little, likely because in all that time
the innkeeper remained the same. Various panels of wood covered the walls—from blackwood to pale, buttery teak—each
carved with eerily lifelike renderings of plants. Creeping vines
and flowering trees and more. Even the wood of the floor was
carved from a great baobab tree, though that was hardly discernible in the tight space.

Baccha set down his glass and began counting.

Not the sweat-soured humans and fey crowding the bar. Not even the piles of sawdust where men had emptied their stomachs last night. And not the women manning stalls in each corner of the room. Dressed in bright cotton dresses of burnt orange and rose, they cut fruit for the inn's guests to go along with their breakfast.

No, Baccha counted seconds. Partly because it was a welcome distraction from the headache throbbing at the base of his skull, and partly because he was curious. How long would it take the near deity who ran this establishment to notice him?

Just thirty-two passed before someone tapped his back.

He looked up to find one of the barmaids, her eyes the green of the sea. Her skin was tawny, a pale brown shade, and auburn coils were like the sun rising behind her delicate face.

She was a pretty one, the sharp points of her ears marking her fey.

Baccha finished off that last bit of his drink and pounded his chest to relieve the sudden need to heave up a lung.

"Aunt Lyse will see you now," the barmaid said with a cool smile. Her eyes held a hint of frustration. Likely put there because she could not see through his glamour and Aunt Lyse, owner of this establishment, would not have any interest in the plain human guise he currently wore.

For the most part, seeing through glamour was a matter of strength of will and magick. (Baccha had long believed all matters of magick came down to strength of will.) Few fey had lived long enough to develop the skill required to unravel his glamour.

Aunt Lyse was one of those who could.

Baccha rose to his full height, peeling off layers of glamour like tatters of a gossamer cloak. He'd been slouching for weeks, hidden behind a nondescript face whose features he adjusted each morning. At the subtle widening of the young woman's eyes and the color rising in her cheeks, Baccha loosed a sigh. If nothing else, his face could be relied upon to rouse desire.

Now that he'd reached the Citadel ahead of any rumors about Eva and her sister, or himself, he could afford to show his true form. And Aunt Lyse would take insult if he appeared before her with any face but his own.

A couple people in the morning rush noticed his transformation, and those who did glared in confusion, not recognition.

That news of what happened, now six weeks ago, had not reached the Citadel chilled him. Not that he wanted rumors chasing him or her across the Queendom. But if the Queen had hidden news of her missing daughters, or worse, they'd been caught before the news had any reason to spread, there had to be some sort of calculation behind it.

Like hiding the King's and Princess's true heritage.

Or perhaps that the throne now lacked an heir with both its Princesses missing.

Baccha focused again on the waitress, who surveyed him with a veiled expression. "I am Saras, my Lord. I will bring you to our Aunt."

Baccha chuckled. Lyse and her apprentices believed that she was kin to all fey, but unlike most who came to see *their* Aunt, Baccha was her actual flesh and blood.

He followed behind Saras's gently swaying stroll. As they walked through the dining room toward the steamy and perhaps even more crowded kitchen, Saras piled empty glasses and stoneware platters on a small tray balanced atop a single palm. By the time they reached the large sink in the kitchen, the towering dishes rose higher than Baccha's height. Balance and grace were a particular quality of the fey, and a reflection of their latent potential for violence.

A strength some fey went to great lengths to hide, consciously or unconsciously, working to distance themselves from the khimaer humans despised.

It made it easier for humans to believe the fey were not a threat, and to ignore the fey's centuries of kinship with khimaer. An unspoken rule had risen up in the wake of the Great War: They had to guard their greater magicks from human eyes, lest the humans decided they too needed to be caged. Bloodkin avoided feeding around humans for the same reason.

Saras paid him little attention as they left the kitchens. She padded up a service staircase he knew led to the permanent dwellings in the inn.

It seemed his display had been a waste of time. Saras no more recognized him than had the thousands of Myreans he'd encountered on this trip south. He would have to ask Aunt Lyse to start telling more of his old adventures.

That even one of Aunt Lyse's acolytes did not know his face stung—a strange discomfort he should have gotten used to by now. But wanting history to forget your existence was altogether different from actually experiencing the fulfillment of that wish.

His stories portrayed him more charitably than he deserved. Really, history was like warped glass. The truth of him was hidden behind several heavily redacted tales that painted him as wild and wicked—but still a hero.

He was not a hero. All his attempts at heroism eventually

failed when his true nature—chaotic, cunning, and violent—was given any opportunity to take the reins.

The carvings continued through every hallway Saras led him down. Even the wood panels of the service quarters were inscribed by hand, etched with lacy patterns not unlike the embroidery decorating the hemlines of every woman in the Citadel. A few panels looked older than the rest, depicting scenes that seemed pulled right out of his memory. Fey with diadems perched on pointed ears riding beside khimaer with jeweled horns, all astride *pixen*, the changeling steeds that fled Myre after the Great War.

At the stirring of a familiar ache in his chest, Baccha focused on the gentle bounce of Saras's hair. Finally she stopped before a plain door with a strange window in the center—two crescent moons back to back like open wings.

"She is expecting you," Saras said with a bow. A tight smile danced across her lips as she straightened. "Should your visit to the Citadel last longer than a day, give any of the others my name and I will assist you in whatever you require."

"My visit will be woefully short." It would end as soon as this meeting was over. His headache, that gnawing pain that meant Moriya was calling him home, demanded haste. He'd only stopped here for a quick favor. "But you have my thanks."

She gave him a warm look that made clear what sort of assistance she was offering. Even if he had planned on spending more time here, he would have declined. The women and girls Lyse took in, taught, and employed were not to be trifled with, in bed or otherwise. Lyse chose them not only because of their unusual magickal skill, but also because of traumas in their lives. Baccha did not offer the sort of stability they deserved.

He pushed open the door and stepped inside.

The first thing he noticed was the smell. Wet earth and musky loam and sweet nectar from a dozen different flowers. Wind, sweet and unfettered, ruffled the leaves of a hundred different plants, and the air tasted of rain.

There was only one window—small and circular—at the back of the room. Yet all these plants survived—no, thrived—because of the woman who sat in the room's center.

She rested upon a wicker chair, the wood thoroughly intertwined with vines and dozens of small crimson flowers in full bloom.

Braids like ropes of woven gold hung to the ground and pooled at her feet. She wore a jade dress in the Citadel's fashion—heavily embroidered and cinched at the waist by a wide, embossed leather belt, with a billowing skirt. Most of the women of the Citadel wore at least one knife tucked into a pocket on their belt, but she was unarmed.

Her skin was the same flawless deep bronze as her mother's, but that hair marked Lyse as his get. Lyse was his last living descendant and great-grandchild. His only legacy not marred with grief.

But she was more than just his family.

Had Lyse been born during his age, she would have been called Godling. In the age that preceded his, perhaps a Goddess.

But in this time, she was known as Aunt Lyse, the most powerful fey alive. And besides himself, he was fairly certain she was the oldest, at nearly two hundred years old.

Lyse was not ageless like Baccha, suspended in youth; she wore her age proudly. A faint tracery of lines shown on skin pulled taut over a high forehead and full cheeks.

Heart-shaped lips spread to a wide smile as Baccha dropped to one knee. "You honor me, Lyse of the Sisters."

"Rise and join me, Great-Father," Lyse said, mirth in her brown eyes. "It is you who honors me. I did not think you would have a chance to visit on the way north."

He did as she requested. He'd first missed the chair beside Lyse's, because it was similarly enmeshed with flora. But neither the plants nor Lyse seemed to care when he sat atop it. Perhaps the small affinity he had for the earth gave him some advantage, because the leaves and petals peeled back, making room before he could crush them.

"As this trip was not ordered by the Mother, I have more say in how I spend my time." That and he was stalling, afraid to face Moriya after so flagrantly disobeying her.

"Imagine my surprise, catching your scent in this morning. It has been more than a hundred years since your last visit."

"I'm sorry, my dear. The Mother's orders were quite explicit. I was to reach the capital as soon as possible."

Lyse took this in with a slow blink. Though she was raised in the Ilbani Citadel until age nineteen, her mother sent her north to find Baccha when her magick seemed too unwieldy a beast to tame. Lyse had found him, and the Tribe. She'd spent the next forty years there, learning from him and the Elderi, as well as becoming fiercely devoted to their cause. "And your orders now are less strict?"

"Just marginally less demanding than usual. And I figured while I still have a mind to think clearly, I had to visit my great-child." About a week after he left Ternain, he'd felt that familiar pull that meant Moriya wanted him home. It began small, a near-imperceptible tightness in the back of his head, but now he wished he'd requested a second drink before leaving the dining hall. Still it was less painful than in years past when he'd been called back to the mountains.

Lyse's brow furrowed, clearly doubtful about his intentions. "And why is that?"

"I need to beg a favor of you, Aunt Lyse. I am sure Moriya must've told you she sent me to Ternain. Do you care to hear my story of what happened there?"

So he began to tell Lyse about the last months of High Summer, and Eva's nameday, and the unmistakable scent of ancient magick that wafted from her skin as she glowed like a sunburst and changed.

And how for the briefest moment, the oaths binding him weighed like chains around his neck. Just as they did whenever Moriya and the previous Mothers of the Tribe ordered him about. He recognized the scent of Eva's magick the moment she shifted.

The oldest magick of all. Queen's magick.

Gods, a half-human girl with Queen's magick. Oh, how the Elderi would rage and quake at that news.

When he finished, Lyse's eyes had brightened to a pale brown. Her hands were clasped in her lap and her lips moved silently, savoring the story.

This was why he'd come to Lyse. Her gifts of earth magick were certainly the most powerful magick she possessed, but at her heart, Lyse was a story spinner. One whose words had a way of catching fire. What fell from her lips to her acolytes who spread it around the common areas of the inn *stuck*.

If Eva ever found out he'd done this, she'd likely try to skin him alive. But he knew the power in a story—and since no one else was inclined to tell Eva's, he would make sure the world knew.

"Will you tell the story of Myre's future Queen, Lyse?"

A smile cracked her face. "Ah, but just because she has the magick does not mean she will be recognized as Queen."

"Who better to unify us?"

Lyse's gaze cooled. "Unity is not our goal, Great-Father. It is freedom for all Myre's people."

Baccha resisted the urge to groan. Idealism made his teeth ache. "Moriya will see the practicality in this. A girl who is both human and khimaer, a girl who already has a strong claim to the throne."

Lyse squinted at him. "And when you were in the South, did you receive any . . . news?"

Unease crept over Baccha's skin. Lyse's voice was like water rolling over smooth stones, but he caught her hesitation. Her worry.

"No, I passed reports through an apprentice in the Temple. I never received any replies." Typical of Moriya, who would never share her exact plans with him.

"I'm so sorry to tell you this, but Moriya is dead. She was shot in a raid a few months ago. The wound didn't kill her, but she took ill on the journey home. A fever claimed her the night they returned to Ariban."

Over the roaring in his ears, Baccha heard one thing: *A few months ago.*

Meaning Moriya had died when he was still in Ternain, solely focused on the Princess.

"I could have saved her," Baccha said, stomach turning over and over. "If she hadn't sent me back to Myre."

He was going to sick up. He had finally found a young woman of khimaer blood to put on the throne. Baccha's oaths were clear: He would work to see to the Tribe's ends until he helped another khimaer Queen gain the throne. Making sure Eva made it to the throne was the only way he could gain his freedom and give Moriya, and every other khimaer, back what he'd taken when he betrayed them.

Shame tore through him, deep and black as poison.

"Even if she hadn't sent you there," Lyse said gently, "you wouldn't have been anywhere near the Tribe to save Moriya."

Right. He'd been roaming Dracol aimlessly for decades when he could have been on Ariban with his friend.

Another stab of guilt and disgust at himself. Like he needed more of *that* to carry around. Baccha glowered at Aunt Lyse, but felt a fool when she looked back at him, expression tender. "Great-Father, I know you and the Mother were close, but if what you say about Princess Eva is true, Moriya was right to send you away."

He swallowed down his anger and buried his grief deep inside, where he kept the pain of outliving so very many. He refused to speak to his great-child with an uncivil tongue, because she did not deserve it.

Once he'd schooled himself to some calm, Baccha asked, "Who have the Elderi chosen to lead?"

"Moriya's girl child is Mother of the Tribe now. She inherited her mother's gifts."

He tried to recall the girl's name, but couldn't. That explained the weaker pull on him this time. She was inexperienced. Moriya probably hadn't gotten a chance to teach her to invoke the blood oath. "A child the Elderi don't yet trust won't be any help to me."

Most of the thirteen Elderi, the council that governed the Tribe alongside the Mother, hated him on principle and still blamed him for the war. They would reject Eva simply because he believed in her.

Lyse watched him, lips pursed. It was not the stare of grandchild to elder, but of a woman grown to a child. It gave his aged heart the strangest twinge to know, despite all his failings, he still had kin who would protect him. He wondered, not for the first time, whether the difference in his and Lyse's nature had matured her into a being with wisdom beyond him. He was ageless and ever-roaming—and static. She had lived long and would continue to; she had made a home here. She had grown and changed.

She grasped his hand. "If the Elderi do not yet trust Ysai, I am sure she will be in need of an ally. Through her, you can persuade the Elderi to choose your Princess as their champion. And pray that Eva will master her gifts without you. That may be the only thing that convinces the Tribe."

"Right," Baccha said. He'd wanted Moriya to be the one to remove his oaths, but her daughter would do. And if he could not give his old friend the gift of returning to Myre, then he could do so for her daughter.

Baccha started to climb out of his seat, but suddenly recalled why he'd come in the first place. "Have you thought on my request, Lyse?" he asked, still hopeful.

"Well," Lyse said after a beat, "it is a good story. One that deserves to be told and heard. A Rival Heir choosing mercy over the throne. Many will call it impossible or a fantasy, but they will listen."

At her agreement, he said the formal words: "Aunt Lyse of the Sisters, will you speak for me?"

She nodded, her honeyed brown eyes aglow. "I will,

Great-Father, great Hunter. I will speak for you and for Princess Eva and of the Great War. Change comes and with it, so shall the truth."

"You have my gratitude, as ever." Baccha stood and kissed Aunt Lyse's brow. If he wanted to make it to Ariban before the snows began, he'd have to beg a favor of an ancient, immortal friend. "Tell me, Lyse. Have you been in the mountains lately?"

"If you're asking about that irascible old horse of yours, you will find him waiting in Ydara's Pass," Lyse said, favoring her ancestor with a broad smile. "The creature doesn't let a sunrise pass without attempting to take another bite out of the sun."

⇜ CHAPTER 5 ⇝

Ysai

THE NIGHT WAS cold and lonely, and Ysai wanted a bath.

Her neck muscles ached, pinched together from too many hours reading by lamplight last night, and her racing thoughts would have welcomed warm, enveloping peace. But there were no bathing tubs in the camp beneath Mount Ariban. The nearest village with an inn was a country away.

In the Roune Lands there were few such comforts. No taverns or inns, only armored strongholds and heavily guarded camps and roving bands of thieves and slavers and rocky, lifeless dirt.

Ysai now led one of those bands, though the Tribe did its thieving in the South, in Myre, the country where once they might've ruled. They were exiles, long forgotten by their homeland and plotting to seize something greater than any thief had the right to set their eyes upon.

A throne.

There was a tap at the tent flap. Ysai called for whoever it was to enter, teeth already set to grinding.

The opening of the tent offered only scant predawn light. Ysai, always a poor sleeper, usually woke shortly after dawn, but she'd already been up for an hour, poring over her mother's notes.

Arsa, one of the Elderi, ducked into the tent, bent low, though her horns still scraped the top of the tent, and silently began to pour tea. It was the last of the Myrean mint and bloodberry taken in their most recent run south through the A'Nir.

Arsa sat and took one sip from a battered blue porcelain cup, candlelight flickering over the snowy feathers on her arms, and lifted her chin. The khimaer woman looked very much like a crane, crowned with white antlers, her eyes shaded the red of a sunrise. Her snowfall wings were tipped in black and tucked behind her. "A third missive came just moments ago."

Ysai's jaw tightened. Like every Elderi in the Tribe, Arsa did not speak Ysai's title easily. "Tell me."

"It is as Moriya reported." Arsa left off her title again and Ysai's smirk at the slight caused the woman to twitch. "The capital is truly in turmoil following the King's death. Our eyes in the Temple confirm the Hunter returned to Ternain with the girl following the King's murder and both left the city in the night following her nameday—separately. They say the crown is trying to keep news of her departure quiet, but the other"— Arsa's mouth twisted—"Princess has disappeared."

The porcelain cup in Ysai's clawed hand shattered. Silently cursing her temper, she dropped the ruined pieces into a nearby rag and wiped the spilled tea from her hand before asking, "All of our eyes in the capital confirm this?"

Arsa nodded. "The crown is trying to keep it quiet, but apparently several thousand soldiers are searching the country for them."

Gods damn it. The Hunter had always strained the bonds of his oath—her mother had told her the stories, of how he'd stayed far from the Tribe for the last century, hiding in the magickless country to the west—but this, aiding one of their Princesses, was beyond belief. They should have known he would be too weak to do what was necessary. He must have learned that the girl was half khimaer.

A fact Ysai had only stumbled upon late one night scouring her Mother's notes on the royal family. That the King was a member of a family of khimaer hidden in Myre was a detail her mother had declined to share with the Elderi. Ysai couldn't be sure if Moriya had withheld the information from Baccha and the Elderi so that he could discover it himself, or because she wanted nothing to do with the girl.

It did not matter—she had been raised as a human. She was still a Usurper.

Ysai might have considered accepting the girl or, at the very least, using her, but for the fact that she possessed the magick of Raina the First. Blood and marrow magick—violence incarnate.

The first words Ysai read as a child were accounts of the Great War. She knew of Raina's betrayal, and the slaughter that followed, before she was five. She'd read of horns torn from dead bodies and worn as trophies by human soldiers, and of blood still alive with magick soaking the earth.

Ysai's dreams had been drenched in that blood in the month since her mother's death and she made that promise. The thought of another person who possessed blood and marrow magick sitting upon the throne sickened Ysai.

That the Hunter had aided her, just as he'd assisted Raina in her treachery, made her pulse thrum with rage.

Arsa handed Ysai a bone tube, the sort used on messenger birds. "There is more . . . Mother."

Ysai pulled a rolled length of parchment from the bone, pleased to find the wax sealing it was unbroken. Lately Arsa and the rest of the Elderi had taken . . . liberties they would have never attempted when Moriya was the Mother of the Tribe.

Ysai's thumbnail slid across the top, cracking the seal. Her eyes widened at the character inscribed on the paper in red ink. A series of loops, winding like a river, crossed by a harsh line in the middle. Few knew the Godling language outside of this camp, and even then only the Elderi and Ysai could read it.

Per your request, I journey home. Its translation was simple. Even without a signature, she knew who'd written it. Lord Baccha's scent was distinct—wild, ancient, and unafraid. Even though she had only met him a few times in passing, she couldn't have mistaken it. Yet threaded through it, she could smell faint winter roses. How strange to find her mother's scent among his.

Relief flooded Ysai. Now she could be certain all those nights pouring out her blood into a scrying glass and calling the Hunter's name had been worth the effort. She'd found her Mother's notes on controlling Lord Baccha's blood oath infuriatingly vague. Just one terse line: *Blood will call him and blood will compel him.*

But apparently it had worked.

"Where did this come from?" Ysai snapped. "When?"

"A golden eagle winged through the camp at dawn." Arsa's white feathers rippled in agitation.

"Was it spelled? Selini may be able to trace its origins in the South if so. I'd like to know where our wayward Hunter sent this from. He could stroll through the gate at sundown."

"*His* messages are never spelled, but by the markings on its leg, it's from the Sister Citadel." Seeing the confusion in Ysai's eyes, Arsa offered a smug, closed-lip smile. "Godling magick is a strange thing, the Hunter's strangest of all. The creatures who bear his messages never have any magickal residue. They seem to have flown here of their own accord, which is impossible of course."

With the layers of warding and charms around the camp, no one should have been able to find, let alone enter the camp. Animals avoided their wards just as much as people did.

Ysai fought off a sigh. Another detail of the Hunter's nature her mother hadn't gotten the chance to share in her final, feverish night alive.

Ysai tried not to resent her mother's absence. It wasn't Moriya's fault a Myrean crossbow bolt had taken her in the shoulder. Nor was she to blame for the fever that set in a week later. Or that no amount of healing had been able to fight the fever that burned through her mother like a brush fire.

But that certainly did not make leading the Tribe and the Elderi any easier. All the women in their line were descended from the last khimaer Queen, and many in the Tribe considered them nearly sacred. But the Elderi considered her a child who should be led, rather than lead. A few of the Elderi, Arsa included, were old enough to recall the years after the rebellion, when the horned were hunted down and caged like animals.

As daughter of the previous Mother, and the only one with the Queen's magick that made Moriya so valuable to their cause, every member of the Tribe had known Ysai would one day assume leadership.

They just thought that time would come in a handful of decades, when Ysai was deemed mature. Not at twenty, before Moriya had even begun training her.

Ysai did not have the luxury of grieving her mother's sudden death in seclusion, as tradition mandated. Instead Arsa, loyal to Moriya despite her apprehensions about Ysai's ability to lead, had taken Ysai under her wing. To prepare her to lead and also, Ysai was certain from their first meeting, in the hope of one day controlling her.

It had not taken the woman long to give up on the second pursuit—hence the tension between them. Ysai at least gave her credit for that.

The real reason Ysai still had lapses in her knowledge of the Hunter was because Arsa and the rest of the Elderi enjoyed holding tight to information as a tool of control. Luckily one thing her mother had made sure to teach her from birth was to never be a pawn.

So Ysai allowed Arsa to see the disdain in her stare.

Let the Elderi ferret away their secrets. She would not beg for more details of the Tribe's uneasy bargain with the Hunter. "Very well, then. If Baccha's note is truly from the Sister Citadel, he could be here in days. Expand the rangers' circuit south and send Enki and Iriki to Ydara's Pass to watch for Lord Baccha. Tell the rest of the Elderi we meet at midday."

Enki and Iriki were just a few years older than Ysai's twenty years. The twins, her mother's nephew and niece, were loyal to her. Per Baccha's note, he was on the way here now. If the Hunter came by way of the pass, which was most likely, as it was the safest way into the mountains from Myre, they would notify her first.

But the Tribe's rangers, who searched the mountain for intruders each day, would report to the Elderi first.

No matter how many mornings Ysai woke before dawn

to ride through the A'Nir with them, she had not yet gained their favor.

Understanding her dismissal, Arsa inclined her head. "As you will"—Ysai arched an eyebrow and the older khimaer quickly added—"Mother."

Before Arsa ducked out of the tent, Ysai held up a finger. "Oh, Arsa, one last thing. Would you have Ashé saddle Hawk? I assume the meeting will take up most of the rest of the day. I need to make my rounds first."

Through the shadows, Ysai saw the rage that flickered across Arsa's avian face. "Would you like me to accompany you?"

Arsa often took wing when Ysai left the relative safety of the camp for the foothills around their valley, trailing her from above.

"No need. I'll ask Farrad."

When the tent flaps fell behind Arsa's feathered backside, Ysai snorted.

That last order had been petty, but it was no less than Arsa deserved, the way she'd savored telling Ysai about the *mysteries* of Godling magick. One of her great-mothers in generations past had been a Godling. All the Elderi and their descendants, Ysai included, could trace their line to such power.

Among the many pages of notes her mother had left, the instructions on dealing with Baccha were at least simple. She just needed blood and the Hunter would be hers to command.

As long as the Elderi did not undercut her authority at every turn.

There lay the greatest danger. That one of the Elderi would use the Hunter as a tool to ruin her plan.

A reckless plan that required the entire Tribe to venture far south into their homeland for the first time in centuries.

A plan the Hunter might have been instrumental in, had he not become distracted in Ternain. Her mother had devised the plot in the weeks before her death, and Ysai had built upon it.

She'd made the mistake of telling the Elderi when their contacts in the capital sent news of King Lei's death. Ysai had believed the timing was perfect—they could take advantage of the power vacuum in the army. But when the Elderi protested at their lack of resources in Myre and decided they could make no more moves until they saw a clear path to the throne, she knew she'd miscalculated. And worse, damaged their confidence in her irrevocably.

She would use the Hunter to reverse that damage, some-how, and she'd need his help to chart a new path. And be rid of the human Queen and her daughters for good.

Perhaps she could use his weakness for humans against him. His connection to the descendant of the Usurpress, Raina, would pose a threat, depending on where his loyalties lay. If Baccha thought to put Princess Eva above the Tribe, Ysai would simply have to compel his every move. Let him convince this Princess they would back her for the crown and then, once they held the capital, steal the throne right from under her.

It was exactly what they deserved. Humans had stolen their country and caged their people. They were not to be trusted.

The Tribe would not bow to a human Queen. Not now. Not ever.

Ysai gathered the broken shards of her cup and left her tent, the image of a throne she'd never once seen held bright in her mind's eye.

❧ CHAPTER 6 ❧

Aketo

HE TRIED TO make sense of the last minute.

He kept replaying it over and over in his head. Stuck in a loop in his memory even while he leveled his sword at the horned man and seemingly human woman who'd come rushing toward them from a door that swung open just ten feet away.

A door so neatly hidden in the estate's high walls that none of them noticed it before Eva began her climb. Or after she fell.

He'd reacted first, leaping to his feet as Falun cupped Eva's face with shaking hands and pressed an ear to her chest, listening for her heartbeat.

She was alive.

Aketo could still sense *her*. Echoing silence and distant pain that made his stomach knot. Her pain had to be immense for him to still sense it while she was unconscious. He had no doubt Eva's tether to her sister was the only thing that was keeping her alive.

If he could speak, he would've told Falun all this. But as it was, unsheathing his sword and leveling it at the khimaer man and the presumably human woman while ignoring Eva's spreading blood required all his concentration.

Unbidden, his thoughts circled back again.

First there were the shouts from Falun as Eva's glamour peeled away, revealing her, claws driven into the wall, perched on one foot as she clung to a window. Then Eva was tumbling head over foot. And for a moment, she was suspended in an aura of viscous golden light—or possibly magick, he wasn't sure—then he saw what he thought to be a white cloak unfurl from her back.

But no.

As the cloak flew wide, he realized it wasn't fabric at all, but something much more inexplicable—long, slender bones that, between one gasp and the next, grew muscle and sinew and, finally, stunningly, dark, lustrous feathers.

All of this within the span of a few breaths where a scream shredded his throat, because she was still falling, too fast for them to catch her. Even as her wings spread wide, trying futilely to slow her descent, he knew it was too late.

When she did strike the ground, the cry from her lips was punctuated by the sharp cracks of those newly made—grown or created?—bones.

The memory of that sound threatened to upend his stomach.

But his sword arm remained steady, directed at the space between the woman and the man. Closer now—for they had not stopped when he drew his blade—he could see the khi-maer man's legs were furred and tapered to graceful hooves.

They were clothed both richly and practically, in vibrant silk tunics, the collars thick with embroidery, and supple calfskin boots that curled over their knees. Golden hoop earrings decorated the shells of their ears, along with fat diamond earrings dangling from their right earlobes. Both had skin of the same deep complexion and were nearly as tall as he was, but that was where the similarities ended.

The woman's eyes dominated her face, wide-set above high cheekbones. Their color immediately reminded Aketo of Eva's; the brown at the edges and bright flash of crimson around her pupil like a fire in the night.

She was long and lean, with the sort of bearing he'd come to recognize at Court. Her spine stiff, shoulders tossed back, and chin lifted. There was something in that posture that said, *I expect the world to bend to my will.* Eva and her sister often wielded it to the same effect.

The sword at her hip seemed to be her only weapon. Aketo noted distantly that her hands were trembling, and despite her stance, the primary feelings were disoriented confusion and dread.

The man's face, like much of the rest of him, was broad. His arms and legs were as thick around as tree trunks, and he carried no sword, only two half-moon axes strapped to his back. White tattoos like forking, thorny branches began at his hairline and wrapped around his cheeks. His hair hung past his shoulders in locs, and white ram's horns curled back from his brow. Heavy eyebrows drawn down over hazel eyes were his only sign of worry.

"Who are you?" Aketo snapped.

The man lifted both hands in a placating gesture. "We don't have any quarrel with you."

"Glad to hear it. But I have a quarrel with you. You came from up there, yes?" Using his sword, he pointed at the high window where Eva had fallen. He felt a surge of guilt from the woman.

"We don't want trouble with you," the woman said. "Please let us help her."

A snarl ripped from Aketo's throat as she tried to step around him.

"Please," she repeated. Her guilt swelled as her eyes slid to Eva again. "It was an accident."

The man took a tentative step, trying to get around him.

Aketo was already in motion, sword whistling as it cleaved the air. To their credit, both danced back. The woman's entire countenance changed the moment Aketo attacked. In one clean movement, she drew her own sword. She bared her teeth as their blades met.

"Stop," the man bellowed, his voice grinding in Aketo's ears. *"Enough."*

His voice seemed to vibrate down to Aketo's very bones. He slumped as all his strength suddenly faltered. His sword clattered to the ground, and a beat later, the woman's blade fell. She managed to keep ahold of its hilt, but from the acrid resentment wafting from her skin, she had just as little choice in the matter.

Khimaer born with the ability to command others by the power of their voices were called speakers. In centuries past, khimaer born with such a gift always became members of the Queen's Elderi Council, for even nobles couldn't ignore their words.

"Speaker," Aketo said. Still dizzy with the pressure of the man's magick, it took him a moment to form words. "You will have to keep up those commands if you expect me to let you approach her."

"It is you who came here," the woman said.

"And it is you two who still haven't introduced yourselves or given me one reason not to believe one of you *threw* her off that wall." He hadn't seen much of anything from the ground, but without Eva to give an account, he needed to be sure these two were not their enemies.

The woman's gasp and the horrified looks the two exchanged—and most especially, the feelings that preceded both—reassured Aketo enough that he didn't point his sword at them again.

"My name is Lady Lirra and this is Osir. I am the Lady of this House. It was my mistake that caused the young woman to fall. If you can guarantee she will be safely healed, we will return to our home. If not, please let me bring her inside."

"Are you the King's family?" Aketo asked.

Their expressions, open with concern and worry just a moment ago, closed off instantly.

Aketo shrugged, faking nonchalance. "I just thought you should know. That's his daughter you nearly killed."

"Please," Osir said, with the same echo in his voice from earlier, though less severe. "We can explain everything inside. She will be safe with us."

Aketo felt the sureness of his sincerity. Neither seemed to be a liar and he believed Lirra's assurances that this had been an accident, but that barely soothed him. Whether by design or not, they'd perfectly trapped Eva.

No one at their camp would be able to heal so much damage. Before the door banged open, he'd been considering which one of Orai's few small buildings to knock on first in search of a proper healer. The rough combat healing one of the soldiers knew would not be sufficient for this. There was no one at their camp who could save her, which was partly Aketo's fault. He'd been the one to let the Hunter go in Ternain, giving Baccha a day's head start before Eva ever knew her dear friend had fled.

He'd apologized for it more than once, but Eva wouldn't hear it. *It is not your fault he can't be trusted.*

But in moments like this, Aketo wondered whether he'd done the right thing, keeping Baccha's secrets.

He drew in a breath. His mouth was dry as sand; his head pounded. All their discordant emotions made it difficult to think. "You will swear on your family's behalf?"

"I swear on my behalf," Lirra said, cool-eyed as a snake. Her semblance of calm could not hide what Aketo sensed: fear and loathing and regret. No human tattoos laced her skin. He wondered what magick lurked within her. "The Princess will be safe in our home."

He glanced back at Falun, who stood over Eva with an arrow nocked and pointed at Osir. The fey's anguish crawled over Aketo's skin like fire ants. Falun's panic twined with Aketo's, but instead of blocking it out, he drew on the feeling.

He rolled his shoulders back, smoothing and sharpening their fear until rage shone bright on his face. He retrieved his fallen sword and sheathed it. "We will come, but make no mistake. If any of you intend her harm, if this is a ruse or a trap, or if your healer should fail, we will show no mercy."

Falun practically bared his teeth at Aketo when he instructed him to take Eva's legs.

"Should we be moving her?" the fey asked, his voice on the edge of the growl. His gaze tracked Lady Lirra, and by the coldness in his gaze, he was plotting her death.

"We have no choice," Aketo said, crouching behind Eva. This was his first true look at her: at the blood splattering her bronze skin, crimson droplets like flecks of paint in her hair; and the wings, shattered and bloodied. The outer feathers were dark as sable, but paled to dark gold where the wings met her back. The lustrous plumage continued up her shoulders and neck, almost like a collar. He could tell by the boneless splay of her legs, moving her now would only make the pain and injuries worse.

She was a dream turned suddenly, and terribly, to a nightmare.

Steeling himself, he gathered her upper body in his. He had no choice but to breathe the sweet scent of her blood. Wildflowers, smoke, and bitter oranges drizzled with honey. Perhaps if he'd been raised by his father, who was bloodkin, he would not be so horrified at the way his stomach twisted with hunger.

But he'd grown up with only khimaer; their noses wrinkled at any sign of his fleeting desire to drink blood.

With Eva cradled between him and Falun, Osir ushered them to the teakwood door.

Aketo didn't worry about intimidating the pair. They weren't the sort to be impressed by the gnashing of teeth. Instead he listened to the steady thump of their heartbeats and, at every stutter, scanned their expressions.

If they did have more treachery in mind, he saw no indication. Still he sketched out a vague plan as they walked, Eva's breath coming in flinching, labored gasps.

It would have to be the man, Osir, first. They would crush his throat. Aketo had kin who were speakers, the sound of their voices able to drown out any resistance instantly.

As soon as Falun walked through the doorway, it slammed shut behind them. Aketo took in the dim brick-lined hallway they'd entered. The ceiling was at least fifty feet high, lit by hanging copper lamps too far up to brighten this place. Still, the fires within them cast shards of starlight upon a gleaming jet floor. There were more carvings on the inner walls, each more florid than the next. Etchings of grand leafless branches climbing the walls reminded him of ghosts.

They arrived at another nondescript door, unadorned but for a single flowing palm-size character he recognized immediately. It was twin to the symbol on the sword Eva was gifted by her father months ago with Khimaerani on its hilt. Old noble khimaer families used these symbols, *iktar*, to denote their surname.

Nbaltir. A royal name and a dead one, or so he'd thought then.

However living in hiding might have broken these people, against all odds they were still alive.

The woman stepped around them and heaved the door open. Airy sunlight filled the corridor, turning dust motes to fireflies.

A tree-lined path opened up beyond the doors, paved with flagstones smoothed by time. Above, the branches intertwined, creating a canopy dotted with fluted yellow blossoms. Some part of him wondered how flowers bloomed here, when life did not easily thrive on the Arym Plain, but mostly he did not care.

"Welcome to Nbaltir, our home," Osir said as the doors swung shut behind them. "This way."

In the distance Aketo finally glimpsed the huge red-stone building that must have been their home. Its design was similar to the *akelae* he'd seen in Ternain—the single-story homes that opened to a central courtyard—yet was built on a much grander scale. Part homestead and part palace, it was four stories and all hard angles and columns, but for its central domed ceiling and two towering pillars tipped in spires of gold.

Broad acacia trees dotted the grounds around the home, blackbirds and azure thrushes winging through their upmost branches. There were tilled and untilled fields behind the home and a small herd of spotted goats roamed the viridescent grasses.

With no time to stop and admire, Aketo was glad when Osir continued forward, leading them down the path until they came to the home's marble facade.

A kind-faced khimaer woman stood before wide, unadorned doors. Her face fell when she caught sight of them, her amber eyes assessing and tight. She looked at least twenty years his senior and was petite. Narrow shoulders curved inward beneath white-and-black wings held tight to her back. Her face was a seamless blend of human and owl, with amber eyes and a pert nose above a sharp beak.

He nearly stumbled with relief as she rushed forward, chattering in rapid Khimaeran, "Oh, you fools! What has happened? What have you done?"

Falun, still wary, inched back at her sudden approach and Aketo remembered the fey likely did not speak Khimaeran. "Are you the healer?" Aketo asked, switching to Common.

She nodded emphatically. "Yes, I am Tavan. Please come inside."

Tavan led them through a tiled walkway and into a courtyard with broken paving stones that crunched beneath their feet. After a few sharp turns, they reached a healing chamber.

In short order, Tavan had them set Eva down on the bed in the center of the room—"Slowly, slowly," she barked, wings twitching with impatience—and sent Osir and Lirra from the room.

"I will let one of you remain," the healer chirped. "But you must be able to keep a cool head and assist me."

"You stay," Aketo said, turning to Falun. With the sensations of Eva's pain still ringing in his head, he could barely think.

Falun shook his head. "No, I'll go to the camp and return with everyone." To Tavan he said, "Will your . . . friends let me back in again?"

"Not friends, they are my kin, which is infinitely worse." Tavan's feathers fluffed in annoyance. "Yes. Lirra will let you in."

He and Falun shared a long look before the fey stepped out of the room. It wasn't hard to decipher. *Protect her.*

He remembered his promise to Baccha to keep Eva safe. So far he had failed spectacularly. He wouldn't fail her again.

Tavan's hands dropped to her hips, her fingertips somehow already tinged crimson. "How is she alive?"

Aketo rounded on the woman. Wasn't it her job to know that? "I think you could give me a better explanation than any I'd offer."

"She *should* be dead. From the fall, the shock of shifting so abruptly, the internal damage. She should not still draw breath and yet she lives. Her pulse is strong. Tell me why."

"There is a spell tethering her life to her sister's," Aketo said. "It is called an Entwining."

"Hmm." Tavan nodded, eyes fluttering closed. "I can sense many . . . tethers, as it were. I will keep my healing away from her mind. That seems prudent considering the possible magickal complications."

Aketo flushed. He didn't know how healing magick worked, except that it did, but he could hardly believe Tavan could sense his attachment to Eva.

Tavan made a clicking noise with her beak. "Hurry now. First we must reknit her spine."

✦

By the time Aketo left the healing chamber, and the healer Tavan, he was clinging to the last of his patience by his fingernails, and his entire body ached from quelling the nausea each time the owl woman reset one of Eva's bones. Every single time, Eva's pain had hit him like a wave of nausea.

Before he left, Tavan explained that Eva might not wake for a week. He imagined that if Eva had heard the prognosis, she would have let out a stream of curses wicked enough to make even Falun's floppy hair coil. He supposed there was some irony in the Entwining spell saving both Eva's and Isadore's lives now. She was alive when she should have been dead. She would have laughed at that with the bitter mirth he'd first fallen for, a shield against the old sorrows and resentments.

He understood arming oneself. His calm was as much camouflage as anything else.

He was grateful for Tavan, truly, and requested that she not let anyone enter the healing chamber without him. Falun had not yet returned, so he went in search of Osir and Lirra. Aketo could sense the residue of their emotions—from Osir there was only increasing unease and from Lirra, more worry—and followed the faint pulse of their emotions until he reached another courtyard.

Unlike the first yard he'd walked through in their home, this one was well maintained. Paved with blue-and-pink half-moon tiles was a reflecting pool at its center. Before it lay a circle of high-backed wicker chairs. It seemed like the sort of place where audiences used to be held at a minor court.

There Osir and Lirra sat beside each other, arguing furiously.

The former looked up first at his approach, his penetrating gaze heavy with worry. "How is she?"

"She will heal." He quelled his frustration, imbuing his voice with calm. "My name is Aketo Jahmar. Introduce yourselves. Formally, please."

Osir's eyes widened, but he bowed his head in acquiesce. "I am Osir Nbaltir. This is my eldest sister, Lady Lirra. She leads us."

"Who else is included in this *us*?" Aketo asked, tone placid.

Osir seemed to wilt at this inquiry. "Just the three of us. The rest of our family is either dead or scattered across the Queendom, in hiding."

"Just," Lirra added, "as you should be."

Aketo's eyes narrowed as he turned to her. "Speak plainly. Please."

She inclined her head in an act of deference that surprised Aketo. "Very well, Prince. Yes, I do recognize your name. We get little news here, but always have kept an eye on our fellow noble khimaer."

Aketo nearly pointed out that King Lei had done more than keep an eye on them, but decided against it.

"Last year, my uncle, who you know as Lei, wrote to us. He said that he believed someone had discovered our . . . secret heritage. He wanted us all to flee Orai for good and hide in the mountains up north until his daughter was crowned. Tavan, Osir, and I stayed to care for our home and Orai. Everyone else left shortly after."

"Why you three?"

"Because I would not leave and Osir will not leave without me. Tavan stayed, in her words, to keep an eye on us. Besides, there is nowhere safe for them. They cannot pass."

Aketo fell into one of the seats across from the two. "How is it you manage to pass as human, Lady? How did the King?"

Lirra sighed. "First you must understand: Our family has stayed in hiding for one reason alone. So that one day we would be able to infiltrate Ternain's noble class and get close enough to the throne to . . . take it. Which meant that any infant born into this family who looked just a bit more human than khimaer had their horns cut."

The nausea he'd smothered in the healing chamber rose back up again. Such violence, and enacted on babies too young to even know what was being taken from them. He looked, trying to see any scarring around Lirra's hairline.

She caught him searching. "You won't find any signs of it. Skilled healing can hide a great deal. I was born winged, but because my face was human enough and there were no other signs of my heritage besides my horns, they were . . . done away with." At his look of revulsion, her eyes darkened. "Don't mourn for me, Prince. It is a reasonable price to pay for our people's freedom."

"It isn't reasonable, Lady." Aketo cast his voice low and rubbed his temples. "None of this is."

The King must have seen this violence for what it was, as he'd found another way to keep Eva's true form from being revealed. Binding Eva's magick had also been a violence, but not so traumatic and permanent as this.

Aketo couldn't hide his disgust, but he did smother his pity. Lirra did not want it and he could give her that at least. "What happened on the wall? Eva was climbing, she seemed secure, and then . . . she just fell."

"I heard you all, outside. And when one of you began to climb the wall, I rushed upstairs and I shoved open the window, hoping to dislodge whatever intruders had come. I expected another soldier. I didn't think to find a young woman. And as soon as I saw her, I knew I'd made a mistake, but it was too late," Lirra explained, staring down at her folded hands before glaring up at Aketo, both plaintive and defiant. "We thought you were soldiers. Had Evalina just come to our doors and knocked—"

"We *did*. Others in our company, soldiers loyal to the Princess, knocked the first day we—"

"Bah," Lirra cut in. "They all had the look of soldiers. Just like that other one. Just," she decided, plainly scanning him from his horns to his boots, "as you do, Prince."

Aketo would have sensed the cool disdain in her tone without the rush of disappointment he felt swell inside Lirra when she considered him. Aketo surprised himself by laughing. "Lady, I have more reasons than you to despise the Queen's Army. I did not join its ranks with pleasure. But since it is the reason I'm here with Eva now, I'd appreciate if you reserved your judgment."

Osir gave Lirra a pointed look, after which the Lady of the House bowed her head. "You're right. Doubtless you've sacrificed much being away from your family. My apologies."

She paused and then went on. "I *am* sorry, for the whole of it. We've been hiding for decades and I was afraid to see the small peace we have here broken."

For Aketo the play of her emotions conveyed more than her words ever could. Her defiance was wrapped up in a great deal of protectiveness for this place and her family. She'd believed she was defending them and her guilt left her raw, frustrated, and lashing out at him.

"Tell me," Osir said, the timbre of his voice like distant thunder, "has our cousin ever shifted before?"

Aketo shook his head. On the night of Eva's nameday,

she'd broken the binding on her magick, revealing her true self. That night he'd been too dazed from blood loss and Isadore's magick to realize what the transformation *meant*. But Baccha had understood.

When Aketo had visited the Hunter's room the following morning, Baccha had been cryptic about the Tribe and finding Eva a teacher. In the weeks after, Aketo mulled over the conversation once a day. *Why,* he'd wondered, *should Baccha worry about Eva harnessing more magick when she'd already beaten Isadore with just human magick?*

It didn't make any sense until he started to think on the old stories his grandmother used to tell. About the Tribe and its Elderi Council, waiting in the mountains until a rightful khimaer woman was ready to take back the throne.

Before the Great War, before Aketo's ancestors was forced into Enclosures, before the Tribe fled north into the mountains, that same Elderi Council had two roles. The first was to help the khimaer Queens govern Myre, and the second was to choose the next Queen. They selected candidates from each generation of nobly born khimaer young women, because they had the same gift in common: the ability to shapeshift.

Back then they called it Queen's magick, or Mother's magick, because it was the power wielded by Khimaerani herself: the first khimaer and Mother of their kind, whom their various forms reflected.

How shocking that Eva could possess the hated magick of her ancestor and the gift they held most sacred. Some part of him had not thought it possible, even after he'd figured. She was still half human, and Queen's magick was the one ability that no human could command.

His granna, Amina, had only the smallest gift, the ability to change her coloring and slightly alter her features. What Eva had done would have been well beyond her skill.

But shapeshifting was a strange magick because, unlike any other magicks Aketo knew, its power waned in those not chosen to take the throne. And in whoever was crowned, their shapeshifting strengthened until the next generation was born. Then even the Queen lost her command of her gift, marking the time for a new Queen to be chosen.

"I don't think she knew she could," Aketo replied. He wouldn't tell them about her nameday; if Eva wanted to share that night with them, it was her story to tell.

Lirra sighed through her nose. "Well, at least that is one good thing to come of this. Terrible as this is, at least she will have awakened her power."

"Don't you let Eva hear you say that. She will not thank you for any of this."

"I should hope not," Lirra shot back. "I only pray she will forgive me."

For Eva's sake, he wished she would; she had few kin left. "Are we safe here? Have others come searching for you here?"

"Not yet, but I am sure they will," Lirra said. "Especially now that you've come."

"She had no choice but to come here. The King told her nothing, nothing of you or her heritage. She needs answers from you."

"And we will give them," Osir said, his locs swinging as he nodded.

"But I won't lie," Lirra said, and the weight of her gaze and sheer force of her worry made Aketo's head begin aching again. "I am certain we're all in danger of being found here, and I'm not sure what we will do if that happens."

Aketo had nothing to say to that, because she was right.

Osir nodded, expression grave. "I can show you to your rooms. We'll make space for the rest of your companions as well."

"No need. I'll stay with the Princess until she wakes," Aketo said, fighting back a yawn as he stood.

Lirra's eyes narrowed, but when she spoke, her tone was light. "What exactly is the nature of your relationship with the Princess?"

"We are allies," he breathed. *Allies* was too small a word for what they were, but it was true on its face. So why it made his stomach twist, he couldn't say.

Suddenly Aketo was entirely too exhausted to continue this conversation. Instead he turned on his heel and began to retrace his steps.

As he walked, Aketo thought back to the first and only time he tried to bring up Eva's khimaer magick.

Two weeks after they left Ternain, when they'd hired a ship, *Silversong*, he'd come knocking on the cabin Eva was sharing with Falun, when the fey replaced him on the ship's deck to keep watch. They'd feared betrayal from the flinty-eyed sailors on those first few days aboard.

He'd tried to broach the subject of Baccha, and Eva had ignored him, her attention focused solely on sharpening a dagger. "We should at least talk about it."

"Talk about what?" she'd asked, distracted.

"What Baccha told me the night he left. Eva, he implied your magick—"

"I don't want to talk about magick," she'd bit out, each word edged like the blade she was honing. "I can feel something new inside, like a second pulse, but I need a break from magick.

Whatever my family can tell me, I'll listen, but for now . . ."

She'd trailed off, sheathed the dagger, and stood to lace her fingers through his. Then she'd kissed him too thoroughly for him to think of anything but the warmth of her lips, and he dropped it.

Now he wondered whether he should have pushed her. Maybe if he had, Eva would have known what to do when she fell. He hated his magick in that moment, making him feel every bit of her terror when he could do nothing. He would not forget how the feeling had swelled inside him, blotting out every other thought. Worse was that, the moment before Eva's body struck the ground, her fear had turned to acceptance.

When he replaced Tavan in the seat at Eva's bedside, Eva's expression was smooth.

Yet still he felt the faint aura of pain radiating from her mind.

When Aketo was younger, he thought if he could just squint and stare long enough, he would be able to *see* emotions instead of feeling them. He thought if he could see them, he would escape having to *feel* what others felt.

But that was fantasy. Some emotions struck him as songs or flavors, or a certain rhythm and pulse to the air. None of that changed the very nature of his magick, which was to draw in emotions like they were his sustenance.

Jaw clenched, he grasped Eva's hand and gathered her pain into his limbs. She would hate him if she knew how often compulsion drove him to do this. Drinking in small amounts of her, and everyone else's, darkest emotions because instinct drove him to comfort.

But at least he could let her heal in peace.

↬ CHAPTER 7 ↫

Eva

I WOKE IN a field ablaze with crimson, persimmon, canary-yellow blossoms, their petals coated in iridescent droplets of dew. Around the field, great trees with vast trunks grew high into the sky so that only the silhouette of their leaves above was visible, blurring out all detail.

I sat up, the flowers' fragrant nectar coating my tongue, and did not know where I was. An indigo sky made incandescent by a sea of flickering stars showed through the canopy of branches, but there was no moon that I could see, nor sun.

The chitter and click of insects filled the air, as well as bird-song and deeper, sharper calls that surely belonged to larger beasts.

For a long moment, I lay still, feeling the velvet petals crushed beneath my hands and thinking nothing at all. My mind was a void, offering no knowledge of where I was or why or *how*.

I took a breath, smelling the air, and finally stood, feet bare in the dirt. Wind lashed through the trees, causing my skin to pebble. And though horns still adorned my brow, my hands had changed back. My nails, though still long, were soft and useless compared with the bone-hard claws I'd become accustomed to.

My feet weren't alone in their nakedness. I was nude from the top of my head to my toes, but as soon as I thought it, raw silk glided against my skin. I jumped as a simple rose-pink dress materialized around my body, falling to my ankles.

I took a step and well-tooled leather sandals laced my ankles. I was in my mindscape, then. In this place where my magick lived, the rules and laws of nature and creation shifted to suit the occasion. I'd avoided this place—and my magick—as a rule since leaving Ternain, and Baccha's departure, half afraid of encountering him here and half terrified I'd never see him again. Or worse, that when I did, whatever new orders the Tribe laid upon him would make us enemies.

Now I had the where, but the why and how still escaped me. When I closed my eyes, all I could remember was the vague impression of a woman's face twisted in anger; the more I tried to think back, panic filled my chest like an expanding balloon. No matter how much I thought *return*—just as Baccha had commanded during my first visit to this place—nothing happened. So I walked until I reached the tree line. I caught the distant gurgle of rushing water and pressed forward, ears straining.

It could only be Baccha's river. And if I could find that, I might be able to find my lake and figure out a way back into my body.

Leaves lashed my skin as I kicked into a sprint and I slowly understood that this was not the forest I knew from other ventures into the mindscape. For one, the heat and damp made my mind spin, and vines thick as arms twined around the trees.

Soon I was lost, as sounds of the jungle rang in my ears.

The harsh cries of golden monkeys, croaking toads, and singing birds sounded warped and hollow, like the howls of ghosts. All of it drowned out the soft gurgle of water.

I wandered so long that I nearly forgot what I was searching for . . . until I heard the river again. In a few breathless bounds, I stood at the banks of a wide river, the water so clear I could see jewel-tone fish and silvery eels at the bottom.

Now that I'd left the trees behind, the roar of the water was so great I couldn't believe I hadn't heard it before. Another trick of magick and the peculiarity of this place perhaps.

A certain hair-raising scent in the air—blood, musk, and the unidentifiable quality that was only *Baccha's*—brought on acute longing and rage. Useless, lying fey bastard. He could have at least told me he was leaving after my nameday, but he had passed the message along through Aketo like a coward. After everything we'd endured, survived, and all the magick he taught me, he disappeared without even a word.

Missing him was a terrible waste of time, but he was the only person who knew about this place and might help me. Even if he was lost in the Roune Lands, the river and his scent were proof enough that the coalescence held strong. Months had passed since our first meeting and it was hard to believe I'd ever agreed to enmesh Baccha's magick and his mind with mine. Our ability to communicate through the bond the coalescence created had drawn us so close. I hated that I missed his presence in my head and the emotions that flowed between us.

I screamed Baccha's name until my throat was raw and finally dove into the river. He would have to come then.

The moment my body touched the water, the world around me changed.

Suddenly I sat astride a massive stallion. Whiplike shadows wafted from its glossy black coat. Snowdrifts tall as buildings rose around us. The horse eased along a narrow ledge, but it showed no signs of fear from the height.

The beast whickered and looked back at me, eyes rolling. Something about it tickled at my memory, but I was sure I'd remember if I'd ever seen Baccha riding a horse like this.

"What is it, old man?" a dark voice asked. I watched as pale, elegant hands adjusted their hold on the reins. Gold and black rings adorned the fingers. And legs much longer than mine were clad in well-worn leather trousers and boots with gold tooling.

I'd jumped through the river and into Baccha's mind.

What is happening? I tried to speak, but the only sound that escaped me—the me that was somehow Baccha—was a croak of surprise.

The moment I noticed, Baccha seemed to as well. He— *we*—drew rein. He cocked his head.

And what are you doing here? Baccha's musical voice echoed in my mind, his mirth and annoyance apparent.

Believe me, I'd be elsewhere if I could. Something has happened to me but I—

Our gaze lifted, scanning the horizon. Jagged cliffs rose around us, eating the sky. What I could see of it, though, was deep violet where it wasn't filled with black clouds. There was no one and nothing in sight beyond the mountains. So he was going north, then. Back to the Tribe, but by order, or choice? *Where are you?*

Aloud Baccha tutted. "Oh, no, I won't have you chasing me down. I'll return to you soon enough. When I can. If I can."

I need your help, Baccha. Come with me into the mindscape. I'm stuck—

"Sorry, love, I'm a bit busy now." He reached out and patted the horse's neck. My screaming filled both of our heads. He was not *busy*. He was mounting a cliff in the middle of nowhere on some otherworldly beast. He was—

Stay alive, Baccha's voice whispered through my mind and then he thrust me out—back into the river. I opened my eyes to find I was standing waist-deep in water by the river's edge. I pulled myself from the water and, exhausted by the mud sucking at my feet, lay on my side in the dirt.

Well and truly trapped. Though at least I wasn't dead.

⇜ CHAPTER 8 ⇝

Aketo

AKETO STOOD IN the hallway outside the healing chamber, watching Anali and Lady Lirra attempt a civil conversation.

They were like two cats just perched on the edge of violence, but he doubted they would come to an actual argument. The Captain's pride wouldn't stand for such a breach in decorum. Lady Lirra had welcomed them into her home, and fed them. They had to respect her.

A few minutes earlier, Tavan had come by to check on Eva's progress. Two days had passed and Eva still hadn't woken. Though her body was completely healed, Tavan insisted her mind was still tender. Tavan's assessment must have passed right in and out of Lirra's ears, because she asked if there was a way to wake her, just in case they had to leave at a moment's notice.

When the healer admitted that it was possible, Lirra had exuded such relief that Aketo was stunned. She maintained a strong appearance, but her anxiety had increased tenfold in the past days.

Though Aketo, Osir, Falun, and the rest of the scouts searched the Plain for Queen's Army soldiers before dawn every morning, it still wasn't enough for Lady Lirra.

Now she was making demands. "Send a few of your best scouts out onto the Plain. Not a few miles like you usually do." They went quite a bit farther than a *few*. "Far enough that we can be certain your arrival has not drawn attention."

Leaning against the wall opposite Aketo, the Captain studied Lirra. "Do you truly believe we're in danger? Immediate danger, mind you, the kind that necessitates me risking soldiers who don't know how to survive on the Arym Plain."

"Those most magically gifted would be safe," Lirra said. "Predators on the Plain have a gift for sniffing out magick and learn to avoid it."

"I'll consider it, but for now we'll wait and watch to see if anything changes. You said there was something else you wanted to speak about?"

"Yes"—Lirra's mouth tightened, as if she tasted something foul—"I spoke to one of your soldiers yesterday. She said your . . . prisoner has been returning her food untouched. We all heard her crowing at dawn. I'm surprised she can find the energy."

Aketo snorted. "Don't expect thanks from her. It's not as if she's here by choice."

Kelis, newly assigned to keep an eye on Isadore, had told him the same thing in passing. This morning Isadore had demanded to see Eva, but Anali refused, citing Eva's incapacitation. He knew they all expected him to deal with Isadore, but he couldn't leave Eva's side to placate her sister. Isadore would only continue such a stunt if it served her, which was exactly why he'd decided to pay her no mind.

"I only brought it up," Lirra began through clenched teeth, "to ask you if there is something you plan to do about it. I would not want the Princess to think I am starving her sister. No reason to engender more ill will."

Anali's normally gray eyes darkened to obsidian, stark against the dense fringe of her white eyelashes. The annoyance in her gaze was unmistakable. "Ah, so you'll shove someone off a wall, but draw the line at starvation. I'm sure Eva will appreciate the distinction."

Even Aketo felt a thrill. Most of the time, the Captain kept her emotions on a tight leash, and right now her rage and sense of duty balanced on a dagger's edge. Lady Lirra's explanation of what happened when Eva climbed the wall had not satisfied Anali. Aketo suspected she would hold a grudge even if Eva forgave the Lady of the House.

"I certainly hope she will," Lirra murmured, her tone light.

He stepped between them as Anali pushed off the wall. Despite her casual act, Lirra's hand curled around her belt knife the moment Anali shifted.

"I will check on her," Aketo said, already regretting it.

It was a short walk to the bedroom where Isadore was being kept. Eva's family only used the eastern wing of their home; the west had been boarded up after King Lei's letter. The halls were decorated with mosaics or hung with tapestries that reminded him of his granna's loom and the legends she wove into blankets for the Enclosure's children.

Each weaving was a precious work of art. He and Dthazi found flowers that grew on the side of the mountain, and his mother did the work of dyeing and spinning the wool.

He couldn't believe it had been six months since he last saw them all. His mother and granna, his aunts, his brother,

Dthazi. For their sake, he prayed Eva would wake soon and that she hadn't changed her mind about going to Sher n'Cai.

Kelis waited outside the room, picking her nails with a bloodletting knife. The bloodkin guard's elongated canines flashed when she spoke. "I would feign surprise, but I suppose there's no point in faking with you."

He shook his head. "No, not really." Indeed she wasn't shocked at all, but pleased, and prickly with annoyance.

"I've never known a noble so inclined to help when asked," she said. Her skin was flushed and she looked more vital and radiant than usual; likely she'd fed from one of the guards. He'd offered to let her feed from his wrist early on in the trip, but she'd never taken him up on the offer, explaining that she preferred to drink from women. He understood; though bloodkin didn't consider feeding sexual, it was very intimate.

"It must be my lowborn half, then."

"Doubtful," she muttered. "Rodrick is not so kindhearted."

Aketo wondered if he should take that as an insult.

He forgot sometimes that his father was well-known among the bloodkin, for being one of their few ambassadors and staying in the Queen's good graces. When Aketo visited with him in Ternain, he'd lived in a modest akelae at the edge of the bloodkin sector. It seemed every room of his father's home was crowded with twenty people all looking forward to meeting his son, the Prince. Aketo was sure he'd offended every last one of them by declining dozens of proffered goblets of blood and wine.

"Make certain you aren't too kind to her," Kelis said when he moved to the door. "She'll not return the sentiment."

He nearly parroted his mother's words, *No one deserves kindness, and that is enough reason to give it.* Instead he grimaced, pulled open the door, and stepped inside.

It was a narrow bedroom, with an unmade daybed heaped with cushions and rumpled linens. The only other piece of furniture in the room was a small table with a washbasin on top. An untouched tray of grilled flatbread and a bowl of goat stew sat beside it.

Isadore knelt on a shearling pillow beneath the window with its shutters thrown wide. He could only see her back as she peered through it. She wore little more than a linen shift that showed off her too-sharp shoulder blades, and the frothy mass of her golden hair was piled atop her head haphazardly.

He took in the way the cotton hung from her body, and the shackles loose around her wrists. She'd been getting thinner and thinner without them noticing.

"If you've come because you're worried, save it," Isadore said without turning. "If you've come to do anything but bring me to my sister, go."

He didn't step any closer. She was particular about personal space and the distance would have been necessary either way. He was a man and she was a woman with her arms bound. He would be cagey under such circumstances, and women lived with even greater fears.

He'd grown up with too many soldiers and knew too well what men liked to do when a woman was made vulnerable.

"I can't take you to Eva."

She turned to him, eyes narrowed to slits. Isa had the kind of fine-boned face that even when giving her most baleful glare, she was still beautiful. "Then go."

"If that's what you want, I will. But no one else will even entertain the notion, no matter how long you go without eating." He paused to wait for her answer. When she said nothing, he continued. "How can I when I'm not sure if you will hurt her?"

"I don't even know what happened to her. No one will tell me a thing, besides that she is hurt."

"Are you so concerned?" Last week she had made an off-hand comment about choosing a dress for her coronation. He'd let it pass by without comment, not sure she'd even registered that to speak of that ceremony was to imagine a world where Eva was dead.

Once he naïvely believed Eva's mercy would change Isadore. In all their conversations he expected at least some regret from her—about kidnapping him or stabbing him or attempting to kill her sister—but for someone to regret, they had to feel what they'd done was wrong. And Isadore did not.

"I won't hurt her," Isadore said, blinking those bottle-green eyes and playing at innocence. "What would be the point? If I killed Eva, one of you would be free to do away with me, and then we'd both be dead."

Aketo turned, prepared to leave. "I can't trust you if that's the only reason you won't hurt her. Pitching this tantrum, not eating . . . when you would just as soon slit her throat if we all woke up in Ternain tomorrow. It isn't about her. It's about you getting what you want."

"I don't know what you two expect from me. It's me or Eva. That is how it is. That's what our lives have always been."

"It doesn't have to be anymore, Isadore. And you know that."

"For *now*. Should I temporarily convince Eva I still love her, and when everything changes back to the way it was, simply forget?"

"You could choose to remember. You could decide that everything won't go back to the way it was."

"You're too old to be this naïve. You have my oath that I won't hurt her as long as we stay here, on the Plain."

"At least tell me why you want to see her. If you're still so set on being enemies, then I don't understand."

"I'm not allowed to worry after my sister?"

"It just doesn't make sense, Isa," Aketo said, his magick questing after her emotions, which were slippery and hard to get a clear sense of most times. There was genuine worry but also anger. Isadore had a well of untapped rage that clung to her always; it made him wary now.

"Must it? It doesn't make sense that she's kept me alive all this time, but she has. And it doesn't make sense that she still wants to be sisters, but she does." A seed of resentment bubbled up through the swelling tide of her emotions. "I can at least repay her for that by making sure my sister is well. Does that sound ridiculous? Maybe it does, but I still want to see her. Now."

It did actually. It was clear Isadore wanted to shut Eva out, but somehow Eva had gotten into her head.

After a long moment of wondering if he was making a mistake—maybe Isa's magick had wormed through his thoughts while he was distracted—he opened the door again. "I'll wait for you to dress outside. And before we go, you have to eat."

Upon leaving the room, it was immediately clear Kelis had listened in on their conversation. He sensed her distress and sadness.

Aketo sat down to wait on the floor beside her. Kelis gave his hand a squeeze. "Too kind by half, Prince."

He gave no reply, too busy reconsidering kindness. Here he

was, trying to mend the rip in Eva and Isa's relationship, losing himself in this human world.

He remembered Isadore's face when she stabbed him. Her twisting rage and black sorrow and insidious magick had made his bones ache for days afterward. He didn't know if helping them was fighting against his own interests.

He wanted to believe in Eva's dream of peace between them, and their mutual survival, but he doubted Isadore would stop wanting the throne. Eva wouldn't change her mind either. Much as she struggled with the weight of the crown, he knew she wanted to be Queen just as fiercely as her sister. She feared wanting it.

He was afraid that Eva's being khimaer through blood, but not upbringing, outlook, and . . . soul was still not enough. Not what his khimaer deserved anyway. But that was the thing about deserving. No one merited justice, not really.

Theirs was not a world of weights and scales, but of blood and dust and conquest.

✺ CHAPTER 9 ✺

Isadore

THE SKIN AROUND Isadore's left wrist was beginning to bleed. Just a few drops beading like jewels on her skin. As this was just a minor inconvenience within a sea of discontent, she didn't bother mentioning it to Aketo or Eva's Captain, Anali.

The khimaer woman watched her the way a hawk might stare down a field mouse. Or a field mouse glare at a smaller, even weaker beast. Power rippled off the woman like a fine perfume, and she was a striking beauty—all that flawless deep skin contrasting starkly with her white braids and horns dangling with gold chains. And though the woman was over fifteen years older than Isa, few signs of her age showed on her face. The image of the Captain as a mouse brought a brief smile to Isa's lips.

On another day Isadore would have smiled at the woman, revealed all her teeth, and whispered the idea into her mind that perhaps they were sharp enough to shred flesh. She might let the *click-clack* of her teeth, suddenly wolfish, rattle in Anali's ears. After a few of years of observing the woman by Eva's side, Isa knew she wasn't easily rattled. But Isa's magick could disarm even the most hardened soldiers. That is, if she wasn't wearing these infernal shackles.

Scaring the woman wouldn't be worth the splitting headache and nausea for hours afterward. Instead Isa wiped the blood on the hem of one of Eva's cast-off dresses that fell just past her knees and said nothing.

These people tolerated her presence only because Eva had decided her prisoner must be treated fairly. All of this was an effort to get Isa to soften toward her sister and agree to this crackbrained truce. Still Isa didn't want to push her luck. Who knew how long her sister would be . . . incapacitated. Whatever that meant. She still knew nothing, only that her sister had been grievously injured. Her friends weren't panicked, which was a good sign, yet they seemed on edge, which was not.

On the way here, she'd tried to pry information out of Aketo, but he hadn't taken any bait, lost in his thoughts.

She'd considered spelling the soldier guarding her this morning, but using persuasive magick took too much out of her. The magick-dampening shackles made catching hold of any real power near impossible. She learned that lesson the hard way.

What Eva believed was an attempt at escape had in actuality been Isa's test of how much magick she could wield while wearing the shackles. The moment she used persuasive magick on Eva, pain had lanced through her head, like claws of flame, shredding and burning her thoughts to ash. She was only half conscious of riding away. When Falun's arrow pierced her shoulder, she'd been thankful for something to distract her from the agony in her head.

In the weeks since, Isa hadn't figured out a way around the pain, though she had accepted it. The only magick she could manage was a bit of glamour. She used just enough to stabilize her appearance and maintain the face and carefully refined features they'd all seen at Court. It hardly required power at all. Fey cast glamour as easily as breathing, even half fey like Isa.

Even that small use of glamour left her with a near-constant headache. But she endured it. If Eva learned the truth, that Isa had been hiding all these years too, Eva would see Isa for the hypocrite she was. And hate her all over again.

Unfortunately the few bites of food she'd eaten after Aketo demanded it weren't enough to quell the pain, but she couldn't force down more. Her appetite would not return.

Since Isa had woken six weeks ago, astride a horse she did not recognize and bound to her sister, her tongue bloated as a dead fish, everything tasted of ash and her own mistakes.

Mistakes she couldn't blame on Eva. It wasn't her sister's fault she'd accepted her mother's mad idea to kidnap Prince Aketo. It had seemed wise at the time to get things over with as soon as possible. The most terrible bit in particular—murdering her sister—had to be done quickly. When Eva returned to Court after years at Asrodei, her mother had been sure to warn Isa each day: *Your sister is dangerous. She will kill you the first moment she has a chance.*

Isa, having spent the years her sister was away stewing in hate for how easily Eva abandoned her, had believed every word. And some part of her still believed it, despite all evidence otherwise.

The moment Isa had come of age, she wanted nothing more than the contest of Rival Heirs to be over and done. Not for Eva's life to be ended, but for the worst thing Isa would ever do to be past her.

Anali's crisp voice brought Isa back to the tiled corridor

outside the healing chamber. ". . . go inside, you may not touch her," the Captain was saying. Isa had missed the first part of her speech. "You may notice some . . . changes in the Princess, but don't be alarmed. She will be well. She is just healing."

Isa swallowed drily. "She's unconscious?"

Anali's gaze flicked to Aketo, eyebrows raised in surprise. "You didn't tell her."

Aketo shrugged. He'd been unusually quiet on the walk here, worried, unlike the calm he almost always exuded.

"Eva fell as she was climbing the walls to this place," Anali said.

"Fell? My sister?" Eva was like a cat, all power and grace and surety. The very first time Isa taught Eva to climb a tree, Eva had beaten her to the pinnacle branches. Soon she learned to balance on the thinnest of branches even when they swayed beneath her. When she was eleven and Eva nine—the best climbing ages, for they were light and lithe as lizards, not afraid to muck up their nails or scab a knee—Eva had shimmied up one of the columns in the Throne Room. Their father had to beg her for an hour to get down.

"She lost her grip, when a window in the wall opened," Aketo clarified. Slowly, like he expected Isa to react poorly, and in such a placating tone that Isa wanted to scream. "It was an accident. One of the people who live here thought we were soldiers."

"She—Papa's family? They hurt her?" Isa's jaw tightened. "Who?"

"It was an *accident*," Aketo repeated.

Anali gave a minute shake of her head. "You've quite a range I'd never appreciated before, Princess Isadore. Imagine being offended that one of Eva's kin might accidentally harm her, when you've already tried to kill her. One would think you'd approve of the effort."

Without sparing Isa another glance, the Captain entered the room. Isa gathered her shock and followed the woman inside.

It took Isadore a long, breathless moment to understand what she was seeing.

Eva lay upon a large bed in the center of the room. A half-moon window rose above the headboard, its shutters thrown open so that sunlight danced across her face. Shelves took up the walls on either side. The left were filled entirely with cotton bandages and ecru towels. The opposite shelves were lined with glazed pots of the poultices and ointments healers used to aid their magick.

From what Isa could see of her sister, she *looked* hale, her expression serene, though her face needed washing. What she couldn't quite understand was what the great brown-and-gold . . . thing beneath her was. At first glance, Isa nearly took it for a pelt, the way it softly hugged Eva's body, curled almost protectively around her. But, no, as she stepped closer, she saw the material wasn't fur but feathers.

Isa rushed toward the bed, ignoring Anali's groan of disapproval.

Eva had changed again. She'd grown wings. In her flight from the wall perhaps? Was this some sort of shapeshifting khimaer magick? Had she inherited this from Papa? The old bitterness about Eva's wondrous magick threatened to rise up as she stroked a hand over the feathers.

She held her breath as Eva twitched. The movement was so small that Isa wouldn't have noticed it, if not for the strange *tug* she felt at her center.

That subtle pull reminded her of Eva's nameday ball and the

Entwining spell. After the Sorceryn had woven their threads of magick around them, there had been a moment where the residue of the spell hung heavy in the air and Isa realized she was tied tightly to her sister. She understood then that their lives were one until she killed Eva and severed the cord. Or Eva killed her.

She'd prayed not to feel that strange tug between them again. But now, here it was again. She didn't want to be any closer to Eva; Isa was certain probing at this connection could only cause more problems.

She ignored the strange pull and was satisfied when the feeling faded. "What is wrong with her? Why doesn't she wake?"

"It's some sort of shock," Aketo started, making Isadore jump. She hadn't noticed him follow her inside. "Many of her bones were broken, but her body has completely healed. When she fell, she shifted. It was such a huge change that it must have sent her into this state. We believe she will wake soon."

"And who gave this opinion? I'd like to see them. Please." She folded her arms and rose to her full height, managing to glare down at Aketo and Anali, though both were taller than her.

"You're in no position to make demands, Isadore," Aketo said softly, sadly. She wanted to shake him out of this sudden onset of sorrow. Shake both him and Anali, staring at her like she was mad.

Maybe she was. Seeing Eva so changed, Isa felt like her skin was peeling back, freeing all the feelings she needed to keep hidden.

"Of that I am well aware," she sighed.

She stalked to the back corner of the room, where a pitcher of water rested. She tested the temperature—it was warmed by the sun, as she'd hoped—and wet a towel. There was a round cake of lavender soap beside the basin. Isa gathered it, the pitcher, and a few more towels and returned to the bed. It was difficult, maneuvering with the shackles. The loose chain that connected her wrists banged noisily against the stoneware.

She had to step around Aketo, who gawked at her, but halted when Anali's hand fell on her shoulder.

"What are you doing?"

"What you've failed to do," Isadore snapped. She waited, pinned beneath the Captain's glistening eyes. She hoped Anali would not cry. She was supposed to be tougher than this. "Please. If you would like to check me for any makeshift weapons, do it now, but after I am going to wash my sister's face."

Anali stepped aside. "You have my permission this once."

They let her work in silence.

She made sure to be gentle, afraid Eva would stir and trigger the connection she felt earlier, their lifeline. She even worked some of the water into the curls fanned out behind Eva's head, cringing as flakes of dried blood came away in her hands.

Each of the towels was pink-tinged and smelled faintly of copper when she'd finished. She went back to the sink and cleansed her hands. Finally she asked, "Who stays with her? I know you must have someone outside her door, but who stays in here? In case she wakes up?"

"I do," Aketo said. He'd gone to lean against the shelves with all the potions. "And Falun."

"Let me." The words were out too quick to regret them. *You've a foolish tongue, Isa,* Mama had once said. *Make sure you can control it or I'll have it plucked out.*

Isa shivered at the memory. Her mother had pinched beneath her chin, her lacquered nails digging into the tender flesh. She'd drawn Isa up until she was balanced on her toes.

"Absolutely not," Anali said from the doorway. Shadows obscured her face, but Isa could imagine it: smoky eyes dark with disapproval, her mouth puckered around disgust.

"Why not?" She knew the answer. Why beg them, why ask for anything? She was letting herself forget that she was a prisoner. As trapped as Eva was stuck in her bed.

"Because you are the only weapon here that can kill her." Anali took a tremulous breath. Quivering, Isa suspected, with rage. "Because I do not trust you and will not until Eva does what she should have done weeks ago."

"How is it," Isa murmured, "that you fault me for doing what needed to be done, and yet don't blame her for failing to do the same?"

"A soft heart is not the best trait in a Queen, but mercy I can stand behind. She was trying to save you. *You* were trying to kill her." She gestured to the door. "If you eat, you can return in the morning. But you two cannot be alone."

"I wouldn't kill my sister in her sleep. I'm not a coward."

"No, you were just brave enough to kidnap her friend and use him as bait." Anali pointed to the door. "Go before I change my mind."

Isa hesitated, but before she could begin another argument, Anali murmured, "I'll not ask you again, girl."

Aketo took Isa by the arm and practically dragged her from the room.

✦

The following morning, Isa was back at her window, watching the ultramarine sky. The only time she'd ever seen a sky so intensely blue was in the South, just moments after dawn. Only the horizon over the Kremir Sands rivaled it.

Yesterday she'd spotted a crow flying from one of the rooftops. It wasn't marked by the messenger crows' characteristic white bills, but Isa had seen men spell ordinary carrion crows, pigeons, and even sparrows. Only ravens were impossible to command.

She'd hoped it was a message. That someone had seen them all ride through town and spotted her.

She wasn't too hopeful, though. Who would extend their network of spies here, unless they were here for another reason? Like keeping an eye on King Lei's . . . her father's family.

She had passed within eyeshot of a family member on the way back to her room yesterday. He was a great hulking man with velvety antlers and hooved feet, but he looked right through Isa, as if she didn't exist.

They had little interest in her. Which was perfectly fine, because she wasn't keen to get to know them, besides learning who caused the *accident*. She wanted to make that one pay—a sentiment she had no business harboring, considering she had no opportunity to do so and Aketo swore it had been an accident. (On the way back to her rooms yesterday, she'd asked no short of ten times and he would not waver.)

The difficulty was that Isa wanted—needed—to do *something*. She needed to know what was next. She couldn't escape until they left the Plain, and even then she'd have to choose the right moment. And somehow, she'd have to get Eva to take off these shackles first. The only way she saw to get that done was agreeing to this truce.

It was near midday when Aketo knocked on her door. She knew it was him, because Kelis, the bloodkin soldier who'd

124

been assigned to watch her door, would have simply come inside. The woman only communicated through sucking her teeth and dramatic sighs. Isadore almost respected the frankness of her disdain. At least her gaze did not skitter from Isa's every time their eyes caught, like the rest of theirs did.

The door swung wide and the Prince's horns barely cleared the doorway as he stepped inside. Aketo carried a tray of sliced fruit and more flatbreads, drizzled with honey and mango paste. A steaming pot of tea completed the array, and she prayed it was strong. In Ternain, she had kaffe every morning before Court.

Wordlessly he set it down on the floor beside her spot at the window and returned to lean against the doorjamb. His face was lined with exhaustion. Black curls spilled over his shoulders, ebon horns gleaming thanks to the sun. "Whenever you are ready, let me know."

"Well?" Isa demanded. "Is her condition the same?"

She gathered her hair in a knot to one side, furtively peering at the dark blond strands. Her glamour was an illusion that worked even on her eyes. She had a mind to let it fall away bit by bit, till everyone could see the true color—light brown shot through with gold.

Aketo nodded. "I would let you know if something changed."

"And what of yours? Are you still in the same foul mood?" She took her first sip of tea and scorched her tongue, gulping it down.

His eyebrows rose—barely a crack in his armor—as he studied her. "No. I'm in an even fouler temper."

"Well done. I wasn't sure you had darker depths. I worried you and Eva wouldn't have anything in common. You know, blood magick and all. She can be a bit gloomy, prone to wallow in her pain."

He turned to stare at her, more bemused than angry. "Did you ever learn to enjoy others' company without picking at them?"

Isa shrugged. "It's in my nature to manipulate."

Picking, as he termed it, helped her know where all the tender places were—the pinch points. The anxieties and fears she could mold to her advantage. It was what she was made to do. She only had practical knowledge of light magick. It was nothing compared with her true gift, its rush and power.

Persuasion.

"How early on did you decide that?"

"Before my tattooing." Back when she'd investigated each time magick crackled beneath her skin. Magick had come to Isa early and often. She remembered the first time she'd ensnared a friend's mind accidentally and the first time she'd done it on purpose. All before her ninth nameday. She barely understood what she was doing, and was lucky she'd never damaged anyone's mind from her childhood fumbling.

She'd loved magick for as long as she could remember and had always yearned for more. Eva may have feared her power, but Isa wanted it—a real weapon. Her persuasion magick had its limits after all. You could not simply persuade someone to fall over dead. But with blood magick, no one would defy her without fear for their life.

With power like her sister's she would be safe.

"Being human, this may be difficult for you to accept, but magick doesn't determine our nature. It's just . . . a gift, not a manifestation of your soul."

She considered correcting him—half human—but it

would be unkind to dump her secrets in his lap and ask him to hold them. Isa wasn't sure he even believed what he was saying. Of course magick reflected the person. She bit into a ripe berry and, briefly struck speechless, groaned as the tart sweetness burst on her tongue. "And what about you, peacemaker? You can't believe that your magick hasn't shaped you."

"It has, but I could just as easily use my magick to incite violence or lust or fear. I choose not to, because of who I am, not because of the magick."

"So you say. If you sense everyone's emotions, I would guess peace is in your best interest. Wouldn't it get noisy"—she tapped her temple—"up there if everyone was constantly enraged?"

"Yes, but—"

Isa shook her head; her thoughts had carried back to yesterday. "Why are we staying here? What are Eva's plans once we leave?"

"I think it's better for me not to tell you that." He dragged a hand through his hair, rumpling the curls.

"Why? I can't escape."

"Because," he said, pinching the bridge of his nose, "I don't want you to disappoint me."

Isa stared at him, willing his words to make sense. How could her reaction to Eva's plans disappoint *Aketo?* Unless Eva's plans were all about him and they intended to go north, into the mountains to the Enclosure.

Suddenly she understood perfectly. "You know, you've never asked me what I think of the Enclosures."

The flat look Aketo gave her made Isa want to squirm. He'd never asked her, but she'd never asked about his home. Of course he'd expected disappointment. He inclined his head, gold eyes flashing like coins, waiting. "I shouldn't be surprised you were quick to understand."

"Eva and Lei left when I was fourteen. Old enough that he made sure I knew right from wrong," Isa said, pausing to pick at a loose thread on her hem. "When we were young, we took a long trip to the Kremir. We stayed at one of the strongholds at the edge of the desert, Adonsai, for a week. Mother and Lei went to the Enclosure for a few days at the end of the trip. Lei wanted me to come, but Mother said Eva was too young to go, and I had to watch her while they were gone. Adonsai was different from Ternain. The only khimaer person I knew before that trip was Mirabel, but much of the staff at the stronghold was like "—she caught herself about to say *me*—"you.""

"Khimaer and bloodkin?" Aketo asked, head tilted as he studied her.

"Of mixed blood," Isa clarified, hoping Aketo didn't notice the heat rising in her cheeks.

He cringed at the description. "I prefer *ashini*." Isa frowned, not recognizing the Khimaeran word, and Aketo explained, "It's shortened from a longer phrase, *ashini dapa ʒahare*. 'Blessed with countless kin.' "

Isa tested the word on her tongue. It sounded better than her terms, which always made Isa think of the Palace kitchens and the head cook's recipe book. It only took Aketo's new phrase for her to realize it had never sat right. She didn't feel like one part of her was human and the other half was fey.

She felt like neither and both all at once.

"I asked my father," Isa said, barely noticing she'd forgotten to call Lei by his name, "and he explained that in the regions far from the capital, the lines between fey, human, bloodkin, and even khimaer aren't always so clear. He said I ought to imagine what Myre might've been like without the war."

At the time, Isa thought he was referring only to her and Eva, and their future as Rival Heirs. Without the war, they wouldn't be Princesses, because they were human. Without the war, they wouldn't have to try to kill each other. In hindsight, though, it was clear Lei must have known what she would soon come to understand: She was half fey.

It was months later in that very year that Isa began her lessons with the Sorceryn and discovered that what she thought was human magick, was really glamour. She could make the palace guards see her as a plain servant girl, which was useful for sneaking about. And if she conjured an image of her mother's glossy blond hair strongly enough in her mind, no one could tell that she was unchanged beneath the glamour. Human courtiers would coo and sigh as they pawed at her hair, captivated by the idea that she looked more and more like her mother every day.

What Lei had actually been asking was for Isa to imagine a world where she, human and fey, did not feel out of place.

"My fath—" This time she caught herself. "King Lei was always asking questions like that. I think it was because he didn't want our future limited by what we thought Myre was supposed to be. He wanted us to imagine what Myre could be if we changed it."

Relief softened the frown on Aketo's face. "And what changes do you plan to make?"

"A great many, once I take the *throne*," Isa said, chin lifted, because she did have plans. Vague ones that called for a slow release of khimaer from the Enclosures. A proposal she might actually get the Queen's Council to agree to if her mother had no say. "Laws can't be changed overnight."

The disdain in his glance was enough to make Isa squirm

anew. "So you say. But Queen Raina did not wait for the law to change before she stole our throne and country from us. I am less interested in laws than keeping my family safe."

"What are you two planning?"

Aketo shrugged and did not answer.

"Whatever it is, your family won't be safe if you bring the Queen's Army down on all the khimaer who live in the Enclosures, Aketo. You'd be wise to include me in on your plans."

So, she did not add, *that I might use them to my advantage* and *keep you from getting yourselves killed.*

The look he gave her told Isa everything she already knew: She was a prisoner and would not be privy to their schemes. He glanced again at the tray of food that sat mostly untouched.

When she finished half the meal he brought, they set off. Aketo took them on a different route today, crossing through two open courtyards—one beautifully appointed, the other in disrepair—before they reached a hallway she recognized.

One side of the hall was stone, and the opposite wall lined with carved arabesques. The midday sun cast floral patterns upon the marble floors.

They took another turn and nearly ran headlong into a tall, regal-looking woman Isa had never seen.

Isa did not recognize her, but knew she must have been one of Eva's cousins.

She was a handsome woman, perhaps ten or fifteen years their senior, with a long neck and dark brown irises with a shade of Eva's fire around her pupils. The shape of her eyes, downturned in the inner corner, made Isa think of their father.

Eva's father. Not Isa's, not anymore. But it didn't feel right to call him anything else.

She nodded at Aketo as she passed, and though the woman's

eyes clung to Isadore's back, she said nothing. These cousins must have known she wasn't Lei's actual daughter. Just the bastard child their real kin, Eva, would have to kill.

The rejection stung, but Isa beat down the feeling. They weren't *really* her family; their opinion mattered little.

When they reached the healing chamber, Isa was panting with the effort of keeping up with Aketo's long stride.

She didn't wait to catch her breath, but went right inside.

Falun sat on an oak stool at Eva's bedside, and when he looked up to find her, he was not pleased.

As ever Falun looked as lush as a painting—the bright ruby and crimson of his hair was stark against his light brown skin, and his eyes were like ocean glass. He'd matured in the last few months and the last of his boyish thinness had filled out. His fine-boned face had taken on a more masculine tilt, and his hair, braided in a complex style, did little to soften the effect of his sharp jawline and the hollows beneath his cheeks.

They hadn't spoken once in the last six weeks. Falun hated her for obvious reasons, so instead of picking at him, she nodded and crossed the room. With a noise of disgust, Falun left. Isadore tried to feel nothing, but she couldn't ignore the ache in her chest. She'd chosen Falun for her Court before Eva even met him. She remembered when Falun and Lady Jessypha moved to Court and how lovely Falun had been with his toasted-almond skin, glossy carmine hair cut just beneath his chin, and the manners of an experienced courtier.

"I'll return shortly," Aketo murmured as he followed Falun out the door. When it swung shut behind him, Isa was frozen in place. Had this been a thoughtless mistake, or did he intentionally give her this time?

When Isa approached the bed, she found Eva looked just

the same. Her corkscrew curls sprung up in a dozen different directions, but her face was serene.

Like yesterday, Isadore cleaned Eva's face and then sat down on the stool Falun had abandoned. She watched Eva, taking in the spiraling curl of her horns, the splayed wings.

Isa could slip away now—crawl through the window and test her fortune with the village—but she felt rooted to the floor. In the last two weeks, Eva had spent most of their time together talking *at* Isadore about peace, family, and how little they had left. She insisted she'd brought Isadore along only to fix everything between them.

Isa didn't believe her then and she didn't want to now. Eva brought her along to torture her, to make her feel weak. Yes, she loved her sister, but part of her still hated Eva. It had started when Eva left her alone with only their mother and Kitsina, Isa's nursemaid, for comfort. She couldn't forgive Eva for refusing to answer the hundreds of letters Isa sent to Asrodei while she was away. That hate had only deepened when Eva returned to Court, constantly reminding Isa how quickly love could turn. She'd held tightly to that hate too long to release it just because her sister had been hurt.

And yet, here she was, begging Aketo and Anali for scraps of time at her sister's bedside. She was being foolish; she needed to guard herself against Eva, not get any closer. Or it would be impossible when the world—when Court—finally caught up to them and they were back at each other's throats.

She remembered the night of Eva's nameday in flashes of clarity and chaos. Isa couldn't recall what she'd been thinking when her sister nearly slew her, only that she needed Eva to see that while she'd gone to study with soldiers, Isadore had become strong too. Hard as bone.

But it had been a different face in her mind's eye that night, one much older and fairer. All the anger Isa believed she'd been storing up for Eva was really focused on their mother. She'd set them on this path. Lilith was the one who told Isa that she was destined to one day murder her sister. She'd only been six at the time.

Isa risked touching the wings. Eva shuddered, breath escaping in a dry rasp. Isa felt that tug at her center again, but instead of ignoring it, as she had earlier, she pulled on the cord of magick connecting them.

When nothing happened, she yanked on it once more.

Eva suddenly coughed, half rising from the bed with the force of it.

Isadore gave one last jerk. Eva's eyes flew open as she continued to cough and retch. Isa went to get a cup of water and pressed it into her sister's hands.

Eva blinked at her, uncomprehending, before taking a sip. "Isa? I thought . . ." Then Eva shook her head back and forth hard enough that it made Isadore cringe.

"I'll get—I'll get—"

The rest of her words were lost as the door banged open. Aketo stood in the doorway, mouth open. Others were crowded behind him, but Isa couldn't make out their faces beyond Falun. Eva's eyes went round as they all flooded into the room. As the last came inside, Eva let out a keen of panic.

Isa tried to speak, to warn them not to overwhelm her, but it was too late.

In one movement, Eva leaped to a crouch on the bed. Her wings flared wide behind her as she stared down at the woman, at her final guest. It was the cousin Isa had passed earlier in the hallway.

Eva bared her teeth and growled, "Who are you?"

CHAPTER 10

Baccha

FOR TWO DAYS following Eva's strange appearance in his head, Baccha looked over his shoulder each time the wind screamed. He felt watched, and worried she would return and demand answers.

But he couldn't expend too much thought on Eva, because he and Meya—his old horse and oldest friend—were picking their way through Ydara's Pass. A task that required all his concentration.

Despite having crossed from Myre to the Roune Lands to Dracol in a hundred different ways, he never underestimated the mountains where he was born. The jagged cliffs of the Ydara—a high rift of earth split by the Red River flowing south—required all his attention. It would be easy to get disoriented here, fall from one of these high bluffs, and be deserted in a place that seemed like the very edge of the world entirely.

This high, the air was thin and each exhalation released a puff of white vapor.

Most people who left Myre for the North traversed the pass

by boat, but on water there was no way to catch the scent of the Tribe's heavy warding. He might very well sail right past the path to Ariban, the mountain the Tribe called home.

Because of those worries, he missed the telltale frisson to the air that meant he and Meya had made it beyond Ydara and into the Tribe's territory. All four wards were set in concentric circles, with twenty miles between them. They were designed by the fey of the Tribe—with his help—to sew deep aversion in anyone in the area.

Half a day later, Baccha rode through the second warding and his skin grew tight and itchy. Meya snorted and stomped his hooves, tendrils of black and blue shadows rising off his skin like steam.

Baccha made camp that night and set off early again in the morning, when sunlight danced through the clouds. The next day, snow began to fall—fat, wet clumps that soaked into his clothes—and building a fire to dry himself was impossible. When they reached the third warding after riding for days through dense forest, Baccha knew something was wrong. Tribe sentries patrolled the wards and chased down anyone who came close to their home on Ariban. But as the Hunter rode through the final ward, instead of the clap of hoofbeats he expected to greet him, there was only stillness. Even the wind fell silent. No creatures stirred, no pine boughs snapped.

"An ambush," he muttered. "Brilliant."

The back of his neck prickled and Baccha turned, directing Meya with his knees. A delicate face peeked out from behind one of the trees. He caught a flash of white hair and drew two throwing knives.

One blade caught between his teeth, he and Meya spun, searching for their would-be attackers.

Then a young woman stepped out from behind a massive pine, its branches heavy with snow. Her hair was bone white and fell to her waist in dense coils and curls. Her skin was a deep chestnut, and proud, ice-white horns sprung from her brow.

She smiled at Baccha and he began to feel sluggish the longer he stared into her glittering black eyes. He knew that smile but not the face. Still he knew the woman that had once bore it was gone from this world. This was her daughter.

"You're Moriya's girl," he called. Even his tongue felt thick in his mouth. "I've returned—"

Another young woman appeared beside her, armed with a bow trained on his horse. A boy slunk from the trees to stand behind them, softly caressing his ax handle. They looked to be twins, and both were no more than sixteen years, but that was no reason to relax. Children raised in the Tribe went on their first raids at the border at thirteen, and began weapons training much earlier than that. *Shit.*

He might survive an arrow through the neck, but Meya, older than even Baccha, might not.

Moriya's daughter guided her horse forward, one hand outstretched. She cut a small nick in her finger, and all Baccha could do was watch as her blood dripped into the earth. He knew this moment was his only opportunity. Just the scent of her bloodline—wildfire, magick, burnt clove—weakened his resolve, but he could still resist, as long as he hadn't yet ingested it.

"Baccha, Lord Hunter." The girl dismounted in one fluid movement, as if she were born on a saddle and rarely left it. A smirk gave way to a shallow bow in his direction. "I am Ysai, new Mother of the Tribe, and I order you not to resist me."

Baccha tasted blood before he noticed he was biting the

inside of his cheek, hard. At least it was his. "Why would I resist you, Mother? This is my home."

She returned the knife to a pocket, and accepted a tin cup from one her companions. She held her finger over the cup until three fat drops of blood spilled into it. In five long strides, her hand was pressed to Meya's tangled mane. She held up the cup and Baccha accepted it.

She waited until he downed it to answer. "I am arresting you for treason and assisting the Usurpers."

He dismounted and knelt in the snow, pressing his forehead to wet ground. *Shit.*

Baccha could feel Ysai watching him from the saddle as he stumbled forward, wrists tied to the young man's horse. She called the two Iriki and Enki, but Baccha wasn't yet sure who was who. Or how he'd find a way out of this situation.

He could barely manage his usual swagger, yanked forward as Ysai suddenly kicked her horse into a canter and the pair of twins shadowing her followed.

Treason.

It was a fascinating accusation. One that had only been leveled in his direction once before. He'd certainly been guilty then of aiding Raina and beginning the destruction of the Myre he used to know.

He'd paid for it, though, and was still paying. Unbidden, his thoughts circled back over a hundred years, to the first Mother of the Tribe who set these oaths upon him. *Right your wrongs, Hunter. See a khimaer Queen crowned and we will free you. Until then, you'll pay back your debt by working toward our ends.*

Baccha had done just that in Ternain, but of course they wouldn't see it that way. He should have known this was a possibility. Before Moriya called him back to the Tribe, little over a year ago, he'd strayed for decades. For all those years he'd spent abroad—first in Dracol, then the Isles, and even farther, to an island off the coast of a vast empire on the other side of the Silvern Sea—most of his allies in the Tribe had passed away.

The Elderi who had been raised to the eldership during his time away thought little of him. Only Moriya believed in trusting him with this critical mission. And as Mother of the Tribe, her word had been enough of an endorsement to send him south with ten bags of gold and one task: Seek out the humans' destruction.

He'd known the Elderi wouldn't take well to all he'd done. Moriya had instructed him to stay away from the human Queen and her daughters, and he'd broken that rule quite spectacularly. Still he hadn't expected them to call him a traitor. He returned exactly to prevent the Tribe from deciding Eva was their enemy. All this for a woman of just twenty to bring him to his knees with a few drops of blood and a handful of words.

He could feel his ancient rage welling like blood from a deep puncture wound. He despised being compelled. Moriya only invoked his oath on ceremonial occasions. They'd traded correspondence over a fifty-year friendship. She accepted his need to wander free—to live—and longed for the same thing. But her obligation to her people, and then the birth of her daughter, kept her trapped in the shadow of a mountain. Plotting, planning, and thieving all her life.

He knew he was merely a tool to the Tribe, their dog commanded to follow whatever rules they demanded, but a friend holding his leash had eased the chafing around his soul. Moriya had always understood that he wanted to avoid returning to Myre, where all his greatest sins and failures drove destructive fissures through the fabric of the past.

If he could repair those cracks, right the wrongs, he could be rid of his oaths, and leave Myre and the Tribe behind for good.

In peace.

At an order from Ysai, riding at the rear, the horses sped up again and Baccha began to run in earnest as the land sloped downward, the craggy, shrub-peppered switchbacks leading down to the valley. The usual path down the mountain was well-worn from centuries of Tribe members dwelling here.

Baccha called, "We follow an unusual path, Mother."

He heard Ysai shifting her weight in the saddle, likely deciding whether to answer. On the wind, he caught a brief exhalation of breath and spoke quickly to cut her off—"Mother, I beg of you, come forward so I can hear you."

Then came another sigh and a murmured command to her horse and the *clomp-clomp-clomp* of her horse galloping forward.

The Hunter's eyes widened as Ysai pulled up beside him. Her horse reared, a great Kremiri stallion from the sandy coast, its hooves striking the air mere inches from Baccha's skull.

"We take a longer path to camp, Hunter, so that you and I can discuss your excursion in the South before I present you to the Elderi."

Baccha grinned, understanding clicking into place. Ysai had reason to use him and clearly wanted to control how his return was received by the Tribe.

So what was her goal?

A young, fresh leader suddenly come into power in the role

her mother filled for more than half a century? It had to be strength she sought and sure-footing with the Elderi, the council that ruled the Tribe alongside the Mother.

She wanted power—and would need it if she hoped to command the dozen century-old khimaer that made up the Elderi Council.

"What is it you'd like to know?" Baccha asked.

Ysai just stared at him, blinking slowly. "We will arrive at our first destination shortly."

She shook her head, her snow-white hair floating around her shoulders like a cloud, and snapped her reins. "Until then, enjoy the ride."

Clods of mud struck Baccha in the chest as she rode forward to join the others.

All riding together, he noticed their similarity. They all wore shearling-lined leather. Ysai in tall boots similar to the pair her mother favored—buttery-brown calfskin laced up to mid-thigh. Both young women wore cream woolen tights beneath a vibrant coat, made from woven cords of wool. Ysai's was a bracing icy blue and green.

The twins were just as striking, with glittering green eyes with the vertical pupils of a cat, and pointy fox ears beside ram's horns. Both wore their thick, kinky hair in braids down to their waists.

Baccha could barely sense Meya following at a distance. When the young male twin approached with a rope to restrain the beast, Baccha cautioned that Meya would not consent to constraints. The boy hadn't heeded the warning, but did wisely back away seconds later as black smoke rose from Meya's flesh. He might've told them that Meya had once taken a bite out of the sun and, ever since, he'd been afire inside.

As he ran, Baccha used a thread of the Wind to keep pace with the horses. He doubted his magick would have stirred had it not been in service to Ysai's first order to follow them.

Eventually the trees thickened the deeper they rode into the valley. Baccha could smell the great wealth of magick just a handful of miles away.

His captors drew rein before a cave mouth and dismounted. In unison all three turned to watch him, eyes slit against the cool wind gusting through the trees.

Baccha did not banish the Wind immediately, instead letting it dance about his shoulders. Tendrils of blond hair snaked through the air like a krakai's tentacles.

Ysai frowned and barked, "Retrieve the Hunter."

She walked into the cave without a backward glance.

"What are you called?" Baccha asked when the youth approached.

"I am Enki," he answered, and set to cutting the rope around Baccha's wrists.

Enki stared briefly at the dried blood painting Baccha from palm to forearm, and the already-healed abrasions beneath. Its source was a deep scratch from one of the trees as he ran, a scratch that had already healed. Strangely Baccha had hardly noticed the pain. He suspected his mind was too full of magick, the coalescence with Eva, and so very many memories for certain sensations to penetrate his thoughts.

It was a troubling consideration.

Enki held the edge of a long knife to Baccha's neck. Only briefly did he let himself imagine striking the fellow. But there was no use in that with Ysai and her accursed blood so near. All killing these two would do is anger the girl he would need in the coming weeks.

He needed to lead with charm, not violence.

So he pointed his chin toward the girl, who'd first busied herself with tying the horses to a young pine stripped of all but its upper boughs. That done, she strode toward the cave, watching Baccha with sharp eyes. "And your sister?"

Enki blinked once before answering. "You may call her Iriki. However, she may not answer."

Baccha tried again. "Can you tell me why your Mother believes I've betrayed the Tribe?"

In lieu of an answer, Enki grinned like a jackal and pointed to his sister. "Iriki will take you inside."

Baccha sighed as he picked his way across the sopping ground. He stepped lightly, avoiding melting piles of snow, even though his boots were already soaked through. These two would have been perfect members of the Hunt in centuries past. Ysai too. They moved silently across the ground and had a bloodthirsty look about them.

The foxlike girl led Baccha into the cave. Snowmelt dripped down the walls. They followed the scent of a fire, Iriki ducking around the stalactites. The stone growths winked away as Baccha reached them, clearing a path—an effect of old Godling magick Baccha barely understood—but if Iriki noticed, she was unimpressed.

After a while the cave tunnel opened to a clear pool. Ysai sat on its banks, atop shearling-lined blankets, brass lamps arrayed around her. A well-used meeting place, then, smart to have a place away from the Elderi.

Ysai sat with a delicate teacup balanced on one palm, the other hand extended in invitation. A wet smear of red on the cup's lip caught the firelight. Baccha took in the small, satisfied smile on her lips with sinking dread.

"I suppose that's mine?" Baccha asked, trying to keep his voice light.

"Join me, be welcome, and tell me only the truth, Lord Hunter." She held out the cup.

"And if I decline?" The power in her first command had waned enough for Baccha to start dreading the next. "You don't have to compel me to answer your questions. You'll recall I answered your request to come home without complaint."

"You also flouted my mother's orders on your mission in Ternain. I've no doubt you told more than a few lies while you were there and may have gotten used to such subterfuge," Ysai said. "Drink up."

Baccha inclined his head. "Fair enough."

He settled down across from her and took the cup, watching the firelight reflected in her black eyes. He tipped his head back and drank. "You know, your mother only ordered me about when she had to. She found it a drain on her magick otherwise. Your blood is valuable—you should not waste it so."

Ysai canted her head. "Interesting. Tell me about the Usurpress, Hunter."

Her orders smothered the flip comment Baccha wanted to make. "Raina was born to the first generation of humans gifted—"

"Tch." Ysai held up a hand. "You know who I mean."

"If you require absolute truth, Mother, then you must speak in terms we both agree upon," Baccha murmured, voice devoid of amusement.

"The Princess, then," Ysai said, waving a beringed hand. The glossy, bone-white claws curling over her fingertips reminded Baccha of his first meeting with Eva.

She'd recalled the story of one of his first missions for the khimaer Queens. Where he'd chased down a fey man obsessed with cutting off the hands of beautiful maidens.

"When I arrived in Ternain, per your mother's request, I hid my presence with the help of two of our contacts. I lived for weeks in the library of the Temple, leaving only by night to learn of the rumors in the city. I had no plans to go to Court."

In fact, Baccha had spent nearly every minute of his seclusion wondering exactly how he was meant to break the humans' dynasty while barely catching one glimpse of them. He'd been busy discussing such with Sarou when the young librarian was whisked away by an apprentice.

He listened in on their hushed conversation, noting the mention of a "noble" guest. He hadn't made a conscious attempt to lure the Princess to his lair. Moriya and the Elderi's rule not to seek the Killeens held him in place. He'd let his scent drift through the library's stacks days before, hoping to lure an Auguri or a Sorceryn he could mine for Ternain gossip. Sarou had no mind for it.

Baccha had been shocked when Eva and Falun stumbled upon him, and further knocked off-balance when Eva's scent dragged him centuries into the past. He'd tried to maintain his air of being perfectly at ease, but he was overwhelmed. When he shut his eyes, there was only Raina's face—pale, sharp, fire of ambition in her eyes.

This Princess was entirely different, her confidence edged in worry. Still she was warm and entirely too trusting. He was immediately charmed by Eva's knowledge of his oldest legends, and her beautiful guard, who rightly did not trust Baccha at all.

"How did you meet, then?" Ysai asked, drawing Baccha back to the present.

"She found me in the library. I did not reveal my identity—she guessed and knew of my history with Raina," Baccha answered.

Ysai watched him over the rim of a teacup, steam rising from the top, eyes tight with distrust. "Our contacts in the South sent word that you moved into the palace to . . . instruct Eva?" She said the name like a curse. "Why is that? When the Elderi wisely instructed you to stay away from Court, why go right to the humans' den?"

"There were rumors when I arrived in Ternain, about the young Princess who spent her last years away from the capital. Her older sister was, and still is, favored to become the True Heir. There was already a divide between these Princesses and the Queen. I sought to sow further chaos."

"By arming one with the magick that broke us in the first place?" she asked in a voice like smoke. "What else am I to view that as but betrayal?"

Beneath her anger and with her blood working its magick, Baccha felt his will shrinking inside him. When said that way, he couldn't defend his decision.

Except that no part of his lessons with Eva felt like arming an enemy, but of course they would see it that way. They thought Eva was human, in line for a stolen throne.

No matter that he hadn't taught Eva any of blood magick's darker workings. He'd gifted her with magick that could kill a few men at a time, not hundreds like Raina.

"I believed I found the key to breaking the humans' rule. And I was proven right in the end." Baccha sat back, watching rage flicker across Ysai's face. "Eva is part khimaer."

"Raised by humans," she spat. At Baccha's noise of protest, she held up a hand. "Excuse me, a human who has just discovered she is khimaer, but knows nothing of our culture, of being khimaer. That is our solution?"

Baccha's mouth fell open. She already knew? Did the Elderi? "How did you know?"

"I saw it in my mother's notes. I don't know how she knew, but I haven't yet shared it with the rest."

A fact Baccha tucked away to use to his advantage later. "A khimaer Queen is still our goal, if you recall. Her presence on the throne will immediately invalidate the Enclosures. A Queen cannot lock her own people away."

"Considering the girl is human, I'm sure she will find a way to do just that."

"She is our ally, Ysai . . . Mother."

"The throne is earned. Even you know that. And," she added, "you know as well as I do that no half-human girl will have what it takes."

Baccha thanked the dreaming God that Ysai did not inquire any further about Eva's magick, or else he'd have to reveal that this half-human girl had exactly what they were looking for. He wasn't going to tell her just so she could forbid him from sharing it with the rest of the Tribe. It was clear Ysai hated humans, and with good reason, but he couldn't let that bias disrupt his plan to see Eva crowned.

"Then test her. I know we deserve a Queen who has earned her place the right way."

"If you intended testing," Ysai shot back, "why not bring the girl?"

"It's unlikely that I could have persuaded her to come here without breaking our sacred trust. No outsiders, ever, remember, Mother Ysai?" He smiled and it was not a kindly expression. "Not to mention I highly doubt the Elderi would welcome a host of human soldiers in Ariban."

"What makes you believe this girl is our path to freedom?"

"I traveled to Asrodei with the Princess months ago. I was able to see the number of soldiers in the Queen's Army. With thirty thousand soldiers stationed there and double that number stationed at the Dracolan border. Ninety thousand soldiers lay between us and Ternain. War cannot be our path, Mother." He paused, letting his words sink in. "It isn't only that I believe Eva is the best candidate for the next Queen. I also believe this moment, this time, is the best opportunity we will ever have. Following Eva, supporting her, is the only path that does not lead to our slaughter. Or require another century of planning. This is a chance we have to take."

Ysai leaned away, apparently having heard quite enough. "Lucky for us, I disagree. Your judgment doomed us in the past. Forgive me if I cannot trust it now."

"Your mother did." Soon as the words leaped from his tongue, he knew he'd made a mistake.

"Well," she said, "my mother is dead, and maybe she would have entertained your schemes. But I will not surrender the throne to another human. Never again."

"Who will be the Queen, then? Unfortunately," he said, a mirthless smile on his lips, "you cannot. When you became the Mother of the Tribe, you forswore the throne. One of the Tribe who has never set foot in Myre?"

Ysai flushed but covered it with a shrug. "There will be a girl with Queen's magick living in one of the Enclosures. Perhaps more than one. They can be the next Queen. The Elderi and I will find them."

"That's your plan, then?" Baccha asked. He already knew the answer. There was a new intensity to Ysai's gaze. She was working up to something more.

She sighed in acquiescence. "Fine, I will tell you. You're a part of it, so I might as well. Finding a candidate for the throne is but one part of my plan. A year ago, after you left, my mother sent two spies south. They will find at least one potential Queen. The rest, well, I must depend on the discord in the South, so I can at least thank you for that."

Baccha gasped, "You plan to go into Myre!"

Really this was perfect. The most difficult part of his plan would be persuading any Elderi to step foot into Myre. Each Elderi swore to never return to their homeland unless the khimaer had a sure path to freedom.

It was meant to protect the race, for they knew if they failed, they all would die. And worse, the khimaer still dwelling in the Enclosures would pay in flesh and blood.

"I swore to my mother that I would see us *home*." Ysai's gaze jerked from his, blinking rapidly. When she faced him again, her eyes were wet with unshed tears. "It's as you said. No other time has the Queendom been so vulnerable. While the Queen chases around her daughters, we will strike— freeing the khimaer before we claim the capital."

"And how will you do that without being slaughtered? What about the Queen? The Rival Heirs?"

Her expression shifted suddenly, from grief for her mother to a broad, hungry smile. In the firelight, her silver hair glowed and light flashed off her pale white horns.

"That is where you come in, Hunter." She dragged one sharp nail across her wrist until blood welled. She held it over his cup again and glared until Baccha tipped back his head.

"Now tell me the exact nature of your relationship with Princess Eva."

With his will locked away in a box in the far reaches of his mind, Baccha leaned in close and explained.

❧ CHAPTER 11 ☙

Eva

I WALKED THE lakeshore in my mindscape. Every ten steps, the still water bubbled and frothed until it belched up magick.

I couldn't be sure how much time passed while the weapons in my blood magick arsenal made themselves known to me. First arrows pulsing with crimson effulgence shot from the depths like jumping fish. Then daggers slim as spindles, and perfect for throwing.

The marrow magick was stranger: animal skeletons danced along the top of the water, snapping their teeth and creating a rattling music when they moved. Each was silhouetted in silver-white light that made my pulse race and drew me back into the memory of my first lesson in marrow magick. The night Baccha and I hunted down the antelope, I severed the poor beast's horns to harness its speed and animal instincts, and they'd glistened with the same hazy luminescence. Marrow magick was no less brutal than its counterpart, and this lurid display upon the waves only further emphasized that.

No matter how many times I crossed the shore, only red and white magick emerged.

Blood and Marrow.

All this magick at my disposal without fresh blood or bones to call them forth.

I'd been ignoring my magick and my mindscape with near-religious fervor for the last six weeks. It only occurred to me now that I was stuck here, but clearly breaking the binding had changed things. While I'd hid from my magick—expecting another burden when whatever khimaer gift I'd inherited emerged—my mindscape had flourished. Alongside the lake and the river that appeared when my magick and Baccha's coalesced, there was a balmy jungle and fields of flowers.

There was no rest to be had in this place. My first and last attempt at sleep had failed. Every time I shut my eyes, I woke in a different corner of the jungle, the trees blurring around me. I couldn't recall why I'd made my way to the lake, but my feet were leaden, caked in mud up to my shins. It seemed I'd been walking along the shore for hours.

Or days.

Or years.

No matter how long I walked, the khimaer magick I'd been dreading discovering never showed itself.

I contemplated another glimpse into Baccha's head, but I felt safe near the lake. When it grew dark, I lay beneath the heavy boughs of the encroaching jungle, as close to the shore as possible, watching a sky that had no moon, just thousands of stars.

But all of that ended when I felt a sudden yank on my center. I stumbled forward, arms slapping at the water as my knees sunk into the waves. I gasped as the pull came again, dragging me deeper into the water.

I fought the pull for a moment longer, but gave in to it when my chest began to ache from lack of air. I gasped, expecting to be choked by a mouthful of silt and water.

Instead I drew in a sharp breath and opened my eyes to find Isa's staring at me. With a shriek, I shrunk from her. My throat was dry as the Kremir Sands in High Summer, and each breath set my chest ablaze. I tried to take in my surroundings. I didn't recognize where I was, but it was a sick room by the looks of it.

"I'm not going to hurt you," Isa murmured, brows raised in apprehension. Gold hair fell in wilted ringlets around her face. The color of her hair was darker than I'd ever seen it, and her eyes a touch more hazel. She offered a glass of water and I snatched it from her. "How do you feel?"

Before I could form words or ask her what I was doing here—and what was *she* was doing unrestrained at my bedside—the door crashed open.

Aketo stood in the doorway, staring like he'd seen a ghost. Then Falun forced his way past and Anali followed him. A large khimaer man I didn't recognize ducked in behind her. He looked back, whispering something to the tall, stately woman who walked in his shadow.

Her hair was braided to her scalp, and her eyes were dark brown with a core of red at the center. A flame in the darkness.

I recognized her, the only image I remembered from my time in the mindscape. Fear throbbed in my chest like a fetid wound.

I jumped into a crouch. The air behind me made a sound like it was cut with a knife, but I only had eyes for this woman.

"Who are you?" I asked even as pain shot through my body. Saliva filled my mouth, but I swallowed back the nausea and bared my teeth.

The woman paled when she met my gaze. "I am the Lady of this House. Lady Lirra . . . Your Highness. Your father, Lei, was my uncle."

"I know you," I breathed. Spots danced behind my eyes. "I know you. How can I know you, when I do not know where I am?"

Lirra bowed her head. "You recognize me because it's my fault you're here. Forgive me, Evalina. I thought you were soldiers, trying to break into our home."

I drew in a deep breath, trying to quell the fear that had risen at the sight of her. Her words flipped a switch in my mind, and a memory snapped into place. A woman's face carved in shock and dismay as I lost my grip on the wall I'd been struggling to climb. My body tumbling head over foot, heart in my throat. Terror that had dragged me into the vastness of my mind before I hit the ground.

I'd been certain of my death in the moments before I struck the ground.

But in my panic, I hadn't accounted for my sister and the string Sorceryn tied around our souls. The Entwining kept me from dying in an accident or by another's hand. It was chilling to realize we'd both be dead by now without the spell. On my nameday I'd resented being tied to Isa in any way, and now it had saved my life.

"Well, you weren't wrong." I cringed at my voice, thin and reedy. Much of the water in the glass Isa gave me had spilled when I jumped to my feet. I took a long swallow, finishing it off. "My guard is full of soldiers and I have come for information on my father. But, Lady, why would you expect the Queen's army to come searching for you?"

The only soldiers who would have reason to come here were those searching for me.

"You wouldn't think it, but rumors travel, even here. They say Lei was killed at Fort Asrodei. You never suspected that some of them betrayed him?"

I had briefly, but eventually discarded the idea. No Myrean General would hire a band of Dracolan assassins; they would use trusted soldiers or do the job themselves. "I killed one of those assassins myself," I murmured. "I can assure you, they weren't soldiers."

Lirra's eyes flared, but that was her only sign of surprise. "I am sorry to learn that and sorry we are meeting for the first time under these circumstances. Lei should have brought you here . . . before."

Though her voice was stiff, I suspected this was what amounted to warmth for Lady Lirra. I could see the slight similarities in her face and my father's—the high, full cheekbones, the slope of their noses, and the warm brown skin we all shared.

I glanced toward Aketo, who hardly reacted to our exchange. Beside him, Anali and Falun both stood in silence, staring at me, mouths ajar.

"What?" I snapped, unnerved by their silence.

Isa, still beside me, heaved a sigh. She pointed at the bed and shot back, "Eva, you are so thick. Look *down*."

I did.

My feet floated a few inches above the bed.

Except, no, I wasn't floating. I was hovering, bobbing slightly with every movement I made.

I felt them then. The muscles of my back straining as wings . . . my wings lifted me up into the air.

My . . . wings.

The moment I understood what was happening, and *tried* to keep my body aloft, I fell. I screamed as my knees crashed into the foot of the bed, reaching out blindly. Isa, standing closest, caught one of my arms.

She eased me back onto my bottom and drew even closer, green eyes glaring at me. "Calm down," she ordered. "You're fine."

Before I could get out a word, Isa looked up at Aketo and Anali, and pointed at Lady Lirra and the khimaer fellow. "Get them out of here. You need to talk without an audience."

When the door shut behind Lirra and the man I could only assume was another distant relative, Anali rounded on Isadore. "Away. Stand against the wall until I'm sure what we'll do with you."

"What?" Isa and I said together.

"Are you ready to swear you won't harm your sister, Princess Isadore?" the Captain said, thumb stroking the hilt of her belt knife. Eyes white as salt bore into Isa's, and to her credit, my sister did not shrink. Her chin lifted and her hands curled into fists.

"I—" Her eyes darted toward me. "I'm sorry, I can't."

"Apologizing now, are we?" I laughed, voice rising in pitch.

She backed away until she lay flush against the wall, arms folded across her chest. "I would not harm you while you are incapacitated, all right? That I can promise. Imagine the embarrassment."

"Banran the Second?" I guessed. The third Queen in our line had earned her place by murdering her elder sister in her sleep. Despite a peaceful and fortuitous reign, because of her cowardice, history did not hold her in high regard.

Isa nodded, though her eyes didn't meet mine. She must have forgotten about Banran when she decided to kidnap Aketo on my nameday.

I turned to my friends. My skin pebbled as the feathers of my wings brushed against the bed. I shivered violently, but shook my head when Aketo stepped forward. "What happened to me? I remember climbing and being pushed, but . . . what is this?"

"When you fell, you . . . shifted." Aketo tugged at a tendril of hair that had escaped his braid. "You grew wings, but it was too late. When you hit the ground . . . we thought you were gone. That's when those two showed up—your cousins, Lady Lirra and Osir. They had a healer inside. We had no other choice but to bring you in. Tavan, she's another cousin of yours; she healed you right away, but then you didn't stir for days . . . How *did* you wake up?"

I swallowed. I didn't remember this transformation. I did recall reaching for magick and praying something would save me, while knowing neither blood nor marrow magick could save me from the fall. I must have lost consciousness in those final moments, because I would hope to remember growing great wings. "I have no idea. I just felt a pull and I . . . woke up."

Isa, from her spot in the corner, shifted her weight and stared fixedly at the jars of salve on a nearby shelf.

I managed an awkward crawl to the edge of the bed and ignored Aketo's outstretched hand as I slid off the edge. My knees buckled, but I stayed on my feet. The wings—my wings tucked against my back, the tips brushing the floor. It was dizzying, these new sensations of feathers against the wood floor. "Can someone send for the healer? Tavan, was it? I need a mirror."

I shut my eyes, overwhelmed and slightly nauseated. Could I change back?

"What is *this*, Anali? Aketo?" I asked, gesturing behind my back.

"You should sit," Anali chided.

"I am fine and I want to get used to being on my feet. We can't stay here forever." My eyes met Aketo's. I hadn't forgotten about his home and what we intended to do there.

My chest ached and sweat beaded on my lip. The air in here was warm and damp. "I want to move."

I needed out of this room. Anali, Aketo, and Falun hesitated, but none stopped me as I began walking, haltingly at first, but gaining strength with each step. I felt stiff and . . . strange, but the only pain was in my sore knees.

I pushed open the door and was glad to see my *cousins* had seen fit to give us privacy. They were nowhere to be found.

"Let's go," I called. "All three of you, please."

That *please* seemed to snap them of their spell. Anali took my arm, while Aketo walked on my other side. Falun's cinnamon eyebrows were drawn together in worry as he walked beside Isadore.

"What is this? Do many khimaer shapeshift?"

"No, not many. Not anymore," Anali explained. "Do you know how our Queens were chosen?"

"Baccha told me the elders chose from daughters of the noble families."

"Yes, that is true," Anali continued, "but not all daughters were considered for the throne. Before the Great War, only those who carried the seed of Khimaerani's power—the ability to shapeshift—became our Princesses."

Baccha had also shared the story of Khimaerani, the first khimaer and Goddess, born on the banks of the Red River, and her lover, Safiron, the first fey. She was the only deity sacred to khimaer—known simply as the Mother—and in Baccha's tale, her body had been ever shifting and changing.

"Three or four girls," Anali continued, "were born in a generation, and that chosen few competed for the throne in trials to prove their wisdom, magickal prowess, and skill in combat. The oldest and most respected khimaer, the Elderi, oversaw the trials and chose the Queen they thought most suited to rule Myre. And when that Queen was crowned, her ability to shift grew stronger as the other Princesses' gifts waned. But in the years since the Great War, shapeshifters have become rare because most of our noble families died."

"My mother didn't inherit the gift, though my grand-mama can still change her face and coloring," Aketo added, scratching at his beard. "It's a sacred ability, Eva. Chosen by the Mother herself. Few khimaer would accept a woman who could not shift as Queen. In the past, each Queen was carved into the Ivory Throne in her favored form."

I gasped. I'd traced those women with my chubby fingers as a child. "Do you think my father planned this?"

"He might've hoped, Eva, but no magick is guaranteed. But he must have realized when you were born and decided to bind your power."

I stopped and pulled my arm from Anali. I massaged my temples, reminding myself to breathe slowly, but my heartbeat drummed in my ears. "I don't want this."

"What?" Anali asked.

"*A sacred ability?*" I said, repeating Aketo's description. Couldn't they see that this was another burden? "Blood and marrow magick, and now this? I don't want it, Anali."

On the opposite side of the corridor, Isa scoffed and muttered something.

"What was that?" I said, rounding on her.

"Nothing, just marveling at your wondrous power like the rest of them," my sister said drily.

"I didn't ask for this, Isa." My hands tightened to fists.

"I know," she said. "That's what makes this so nauseating. You have power. More than most of us can ever dream of, and you want to cry about it?"

I stepped toward her, but Anali held up a hand. "Eva, Princess Isadore, please. We have much to discuss. Whether or not you want this power, it is yours now, Eva. And you can decide what to do with it." She folded her arms and leaned against the wall. "You can return to Ternain now if you want. Adopt a human guise and even the word of your sister won't be enough to convince the Court you are khimaer."

She meant return to hiding. I glanced at Isa, hoping to gauge her reaction to the idea, but her face was as smooth as glass. If she was expecting me to give up my hope of peace between us, she would be disappointed.

"No." I didn't look away from Isa. "I don't want to hide anymore. I won't lie about who I am."

Anali's narrowed eyes swung from me to Isa and back again. "Well then, we must decide what's next. It has been four days, and nearly three weeks on the Plain. We're at risk here, with nowhere to hide."

I drew a steadying breath. "I've a mind to go farther north, to Sher n'Cai."

Anali frowned. "The Enclosure? I suppose it's a fine place to hide—the Queen won't think to search for us in a cage—but it's crawling with soldiers who might recognize anyone in the guard."

"We're not going to hide." I almost forgot I hadn't told her about my plan. "Did you know the General who governs the Northern Enclosure hangs khimaer? Did you know Mother allows it?"

Anali's mouth twisted with disgust. "Throllo is a vile brute. Your father nearly killed the man on two occasions if what I've heard is true. But the General is a favorite of the Queen's and he resisted acting against him."

My smile was more of a grimace. "Well. We're rebels now. I've stolen my sister and forsaken my duty to the crown. Now that I have this free time, until my mother catches up to us, I want to use it for something good. We're going to do what my father wouldn't. Kill General Sareen and liberate Sher n'Cai."

"Don't you worry staging a rebellion will attract the attention of the Queen?" Falun asked.

Suddenly I could feel Isadore's stare on the back of my neck. I should have sent her away, but maybe showing her some measure of confidence might help her trust me. "Not if we're careful, Fal. Not if we're smart."

Falun cleared his throat. "It's too dangerous. There are twenty of us, ten of whom might not want to go to the Enclosure. How are we to take over the force of two hundred soldiers at Sher n'Cai? And forgive me, but if we soldiers are captured by the General, he'll be free to hang us."

Silence fell.

The nightmare I'd been having, about hanging bodies of soldiers, my friends. I was walking them into a death trap.

"Lieutenant," Aketo began, voice cool, "what do you know of the force of khimaer soldiers in Sher n'Cai? Suppose each of us is five of the grunts stationed there, I can rally at least two hundred trained khimaer."

Falun's cheeks darkened. "My apologies, Prince. I only meant to suggest the wisdom in lying low. Especially now that Eva is injured."

"I am well, or at least I will be soon!"

Falun stepped wide around my new . . . limbs. The tips of the longest feathers dragged against the marble floor. My previous reality crashed into the current one at the sight of them. I was keenly aware of each sensation. As I breathed, the muscles of my back and wings flexed in turn. And I felt this strange lightness in my step.

I had *changed*. Again.

"We'll have to give everyone a choice. I won't force anyone to go, but I think we should do this. Unless you can think of anything else worth doing? I've given up almost any chance of becoming Queen. I'd like to do something with the freedom that has been given to us."

Anali pulled me into a tight hug. "Yes, you're right. Thank you."

I flushed, not at all deserving of her praise. "Thank your Prince for advocating for your . . . for our people."

Anali and Aketo embraced. Falun took my hand, and though he still look worried, the smile he offered warmed me.

"There is something else. When I was unconscious, I was trapped in my mindscape."

Anali, Aketo, and Falun exchanged confused looks. I realized then none of them were human and as such likely had no idea what I was talking about. "It's where my magick lives.

Just . . . all you need to know is that it's the place in my mind where my connection to Baccha is strongest. While I was there I looked into his mind. Fal, he's safe in the North, somewhere in the mountains."

As usual, Baccha hadn't been very forthcoming, but it wasn't difficult to deduce where he was headed.

I relayed the story Baccha had told me about the Tribe hidden in the cliffs of the A'Nir and Baccha's betrayal over a century ago: how he brought Raina into the Palace and she killed the last khimaer Queen, sparking a war that left khimaer caged and humans in power above everyone else. He'd been repaying that debt by seeing to the Tribe's interests across the realm.

"I can only assume he's in the mountains to seek out the Tribe, and who knows what that could bring? They ordered him to destroy the Killeen line the last time, so whenever we see him again, our interests may not align."

"What will you do about it?" Falun asked.

"There's little I can do, except keep an eye on him." My stomach gave a lurch. There was so much to do and learn, and soon. Apparently walking down the hall had been too much for me. The nausea I'd been fighting since I first woke was no longer content to be ignored. "I need to return to the room, though. I think I'm going to be sick."

I spat up in a potted palm around the corner and was relegated to my bed for the rest of the day.

Osir came to introduce himself, along with the healer, Tavan, who insisted I do nothing but eat fruit and lean strips of lamb, drink several pots of tea, and sleep. The strength of will in her eyes reminded me of Mirabel. And just like my old nursemaid, she seemed to believe stuffing me full of food would be the only way to recover and I didn't mount any protest.

I asked her a dozen questions about flying—could she teach me?—and Khimaerani's gift—who was the last in our family to possess it?—but Tavan wouldn't answer, repeating that I needed rest. When I ignored that and continued to pester her, she left and returned five minutes later with a book. Then Tavan swept out of the room, with curt instructions to her nephew to follow.

Aketo returned Isadore to her bedchamber and Falun went to run drills with the soldiers, until only Anali remained. She sat in a chair at my left, boots propped up on the bed.

We'd been picking at the heaping tray of food Osir brought for nearly an hour. I was pleasantly full and drowsy, trying to direct my thoughts only to the things I had a hope in understanding.

I held up a bright blue piece of *mazi* fruit cut into a star. "This place is strange. Who do you suppose cut this so carefully? And how does it grow here?"

"I daresay everything about the last few days has been strange," Anali agreed. "They say there is an offshoot of the Red River that runs beneath the land here. Wait till you see the trees outside. There are giraffes and flocks of birds who only nest here. It seems your father's family really was blessed by the Mother. And I'm told Lirra handles all the food. I've sent soldiers to help her every morning, but she sends them away. Strange, irascible creature, that woman."

"I'll meet with them first thing tomorrow."

"Aye, I know."

"What do you think of them? Of Papa's family hiding out here while so many others suffered."

"I am glad they survived." Anali shrugged. "If Lei had never become King, neither of us would be here. I don't begrudge them staying safe, much as I wish they could have done more. If you're right about Lord Baccha, then the Tribe has done the same and I'm sure they have more resources than one family afraid of being exposed."

"He should have told me."

I expected Anali to defend my father as always, but she nodded. "Yes, he should have told all of us."

I turned my attention to the book Tavan had left at the foot of the bed. It was longer than my forearm and nearly as wide. On the front a symbol was inscribed in gold, an exact match to the iktar inscribed on the sword Papa gave me last year. The symbols, used to represent khimaer names, were the last vestige of an ancient language that predated Khimaeran.

I remembered how Aketo had seen it inscribed on the blade, and thought the name this iktar represented, Nbaltir, was a dead one. But it wasn't dead, just in hiding. That sword was my father's first and only clue to the truth about us. And I had missed it.

I traced the sloping lines of the iktar. *Nbaltir*, my new family name. I would gladly drop Killeen in favor of it, if only I could go into hiding like they had. For a moment I imagined a future where Aketo, Anali, Falun, and I traveled across Myre like ghosts, freeing khimaer until we had a host of ghosts. No, not ghosts but hunters ourselves.

If we could remain free, would I even want to return to the throne?

I opened the book and found an illustration of a vast baobab tree. Its branches reached up into an inky-blue sky.

I turned the page and scanned the words. It was written in Khimaeran, a list of names and dates from centuries before the Great War.

"I think it's a book of the family lineage."

"Keep going," Anali urged. "There's likely a family history near the back. All the noble families used to maintain libraries and employed archivists to keep their histories. The Nbaltir library may still be intact."

I flipped forward a couple hundred pages until the list of names ended. I gasped at the strange letters flowing across the page in even more florid designs than even the iktar. I held it up to Anali. "Do you know this language?"

"I've seen it before, but no." Anali traced one of the letters and I suddenly knew where I'd seen something like it. In the passages beneath my bedchamber in the Queen's Palace. The words inscribed in those halls were written in whatever this was. Baccha might know it.

I turned a few pages and the words switched back to Khimaeran, but a strange dialect I could barely follow. I would need paper and a quill to work this out.

More to do.

I sat back in bed, holding the heavy tome up close to my face, trying to parse some meaning. Eventually I fell asleep and for once my dreams weren't blood drenched. Instead they were filled with the flapping of wings and a sweet autumn wind carrying me far from here.

❧ CHAPTER 12 ❧

Eva

". . . I DO NOT see how that will be a problem, Osir." Lirra's voice wafted through the open doorway.

I drew up short and grabbed Anali's arm before she could step into the room.

It was a few hours past dawn and I was late to the meeting with my cousins. Even though I woke to predawn light filtering through the thin linen shades in the sick room, I'd fallen into studying the book. Anali had brought sheets of parchment, a pen, and a little pot of blue ink sometime in the night.

I spent the morning translating the first few sentences of the family history before suddenly remembering the meeting. I found someone had laid out clothing at the foot of my bed. Perhaps it was Tavan, since I didn't recognize the knee-length saffron tunic embroidered with sapphire swallows and matching, slim-cut pants.

The tunic took some time to get on. It closed in front with a row of tiny pearl buttons, but was fashioned with slits for the wings. I nearly left my room to ask for help a dozen times while trying to ease my wings into the shirt. I imagined how Mirabel would cackle if she saw me, panting and sweating as I feebly twitched my wings.

I tried not to think on the strangeness of having wings. Tried and failed miserably.

But I was glad I hadn't gone for help once I finally got it on. Now that I was used to living without a body servant, I did not want to ask one of the guards, or Mother forbid, my sister, for help now.

A pair of soft-soled and very supple calfskin boots were also by the door. When I slipped them on, they molded to my feet like a second skin.

Anali came to get me only after Tavan sent word. By then I was slurping down a cup of tea gone cold hours ago and wrapping up a few crescent-shaped buns in a cloth napkin to take with me.

Now standing before the door, I held a finger to my lips and waited to see what else they would say.

"Will you really leave this place?" Osir's rich voice rang out clear as a bell.

"We're duty bound now that they've come here," Lirra said softly.

Anali grabbed my hand and hauled us both into the room, muttering about the impropriety of eavesdropping.

Osir and Lirra sat on one side of a long oak table that looked like it had once been roughhewn, but softened by years of use. In the center, there was a rendering of the Nbaltir iktar inset with moonstone.

Tavan sat at the other end of the table, warming her hands on a steaming mug of tea. Her owl-like face was capped with a crest of dark brown feathers and her clothing fashioned to accommodate her wings. She gave a bright smile as she rose from her seat and offered a deep bow.

"Tavan, please do not do that! I should be bowing to you for saving me. And thank you for these by the way," I said, tugging at the sleeves of the tunic.

"Thank Osir," Tavan said. "He has some skill with a needle."

"Oh, I didn't realize," I said, face heating. "My apologies for my lateness, Lady Lirra. And many thanks to you, Osir. They are lovely."

"No thanks are necessary," he boomed, holding up his hands. I tried not to laugh at the thought of his plate-size hands holding a needle or working a loom. "I can make adjustments to the rest of your things if you decide to keep this form."

I joined them at the table and chose a seat evenly between Tavan and Lirra, with Anali beside me.

"I . . . don't yet know how to change back." And then I didn't have the first idea of what form I would take when I could shift at will. "Until my . . . fall, I didn't know about this magick. My father never told me of you. I did not find out we were khimaer until weeks after he passed, I'm afraid."

The head of our House looked softer than yesterday, her unbraided hair falling in crinkles around her face. She wore a floor-sweeping skirt of palest yellow and a beaded shawl draped over her shoulders. She was at least ten years my senior, but carried herself like an even older woman.

"That will come," Lirra said, by way of greeting. "Good morn, little Evalina."

"Good morn, my Lady," I said slowly. Was that genuine affection I heard in her voice, or what she thought I wanted to hear? "You have my thanks for hosting my friends. I will cover any cost incurred, of course."

Lirra leaned forward, her palms flat on the table and a small journal rested beside her. "You must have many questions."

I did have questions—about magick and history and the whys and hows of pretending to be human all this time—but I knew where I wanted to start. "Please, Lady, will you tell me about my father?"

"When I was ten, Lei left to join the Queen's Army. I remember the day especially because he crafted an illusion for us in one of the courtyards, depicting the human Court he hoped to infiltrate." Lirra's nostrils flared as she studied my face. "He rarely visited for fear of being followed, but the last time was three years ago. Our grandmama, your namesake, had died suddenly without ever meeting you. He and my mother, the Lady of our House at the time, fought about it. My mother demanded Lei tell you the truth and bring you to Orai so you could be one of us properly. So you could shape your future, and not be a pawn of the humans in the South. Lei said that once you knew, you wouldn't be content to hide. And it would only become harder to keep this secret once you knew the truth."

He was right. I would have loathed being trapped in the capital even more. He had barely gotten me to return to Ternain from Asrodei. I would have abandoned my life as Princess without a second thought. "What do you mean, become one of you properly?"

She exchanged a look with Osir and Tavan before explaining, "We all spend a year in the North, usually at fifteen or sixteen."

I sucked in a gasp. It couldn't be. "North? With the Tribe?"

This time it was the three of them who gasped. "You know of the Tribe?"

"Yes, I . . . My nursemaid, Mirabel, told me of the rumors," I lied. I didn't want to explain Baccha to them just yet. "But why? What does the Tribe have to do with our family?"

"They teach some of us the old ways and train us. We aren't the only khimaer in hiding across Myre, just the only nobles. Many of us in hiding spend time with the Tribe in our youth. Your father, of course, did not go."

Lirra paused, drumming her nails against the table. "You've noticed I appear human. Just like your father." I nodded. "The few children who are born in this family who can mostly pass as human have their horns severed and healed to show no scars."

I flinched, but Lirra rushed right on as if it wasn't worth lingering on. "Instead of going to train with the Tribe, Lei joined the Queen's Army. He didn't have any plan but hoped to find a way to fix the seemingly insurmountable divisions in the Queendom. You," she continued, "were the result. After he made the fool mistake of falling in love with that terrible Queen and adopting her bastard child as his own, she became pregnant with you, and Lei found his solution. Another daughter. A part-khimaer Rival Heir who could become Queen without any humans knowing the truth."

My stomach roiled. *His solution.*

I would have done anything to hear my father's voice again. I wanted him back so I could properly direct the rage building inside.

"Well, my father was right to believe I wouldn't have wanted to hide." Not for long at least. "They would have hanged me for a demon Queen if I waited to reveal my form once I was on the throne."

If Isadore and I fought again for the crown—and I hoped we would not—I wanted everyone in Myre to know who I really was. They would need to know that my crowning would come with as much change as Raina's had.

"If you don't mind me asking, Princess Eva," Osir said. His long locs were braided back away from his face, emphasizing his heavy brow and the antlers that jutted out a foot in each direction. "What will you do then? About the throne?"

I could feel even Anali staring at me as I sought an answer. "I'm not ready to claim the throne just yet, though if I do, I will have to take it as a khimaer woman, which presents a number of problems I hardly want to think about. Right now I have this new magick I need to work out. Since my mother can't crown anyone while we're both away, until I am ready, I want to do some good with the little freedom I have. Have you ever been to the Enclosures?"

All three shook their heads. I continued, "Neither have I, but we would like to help those in Sher n'Cai, where Prince Aketo grew up. He saved my life a few times; I need to return the favor and make sure his family is safe."

"What about the Queen? Surely news of your actions will reach her eventually," Tavan asked, rising from her seat to pace around the table. Her stride was so light, wings flaring and retracting with every step, that it looked like she was floating.

"We'll come to that when we come to it." I shrugged. It wasn't a matter of if my mother caught up to us, but when she did. I imagined it would not go well. "We leave as soon as I am healed. Will you join me?"

Tavan and Osir both turned to Lirra, who gave a solemn nod. "We've sacrificed much for the chance to change this Queendom. We will journey north. It is time we witness the fate we escaped." She inclined her head and then slipped into Khimaeran in a rolling accent much like Aketo's: "Now to begin your lessons. Tell me, can you speak the Mother's tongue?"

"I can. My nursemaid began teaching me when I was six," I replied in Khimaeran.

"Good," Lirra chirped, "you can, however poorly, speak it."

"Unbelievable," I said.

She feigned a look of innocence. "What? You said you wanted to take the throne as a khimaer woman. How will you if Tavan and I do not teach you?"

"Can you teach me about my magick? The shapeshifting?" That was all I had a mind to learn just now.

"I don't know much, but my grandmama had a touch of the gift"—her gaze slid to the thin book at her side—"all she did learn, she found in this."

She held out the book, which I could now see was bound in twine. "It belonged to a Nbaltir Queen who died fifty years before the Great War. Her name was Assani."

I tried to handle it lightly but the delicate parchment crinkled at my touch. I ran a finger over the barely perceptible words written on the front: *On Mutable Flesh*.

I flipped open the first page to find a detailed sketch of a khimaer woman with golden eagle wings, proud spiraled horns, and hooved feet. Notes surrounded the sketch, and I held the book close to my face, but the words were too small and crowded.

"Do you have a magnifying glass?" I asked, nose an inch from the page. Sarou, my friend and apprentice at the Auguri library, would have scolded me for treating such an old text so cavalierly.

"I can show you to the library later," Osir said. I smiled in thanks and he returned it with an even brighter grin. "It is my favorite place in our home—"

"Even so," Lirra cut in, "there is more to learn than just magick, Eva. The history alone will take us weeks."

"Let us wait, then," Tavan said. "The Princess will have other things to do today. I need to assess whether she needs any additional healing, and we need to begin preparing for this journey."

"Just one last thing, Princess Eva," Lirra added as I began to rise.

Much as I wanted to leave the table, her eyes had a weight to them. I felt pinned to my seat. "Yes, Lady Lirra?"

"Forgive me for asking, but what is the nature of your relationship with the Prince? You seem quite close."

"We are allies." My fingers were wrapped around the ornate carvings of my chair, digging into the wood. "Why is it your concern?"

"I only wanted to offer a warning. Be sure you two don't grow too close before you decide whether you want him as your King. When we go to the Enclosure, and everyone sees you together, that is what they will see. A khimaer Queen and King is a powerful notion for all of us." She gave an elegant, stately shake of her shoulders, but her eyes were gentle. "Be sure he is what you want, or else your desire might get wrapped up in the hopes of others."

"I'll thank you to trust me to keep my own counsel where my . . . *desires* are involved. I still have my sister to contend with before I can take the throne or marry."

"Contend with?" She waved a hand in the air, swatting like Isa were a pest we all needed to be rid of. "You may as well kill her now."

"*No,*" I said.

Anali laid a hand on my arm. "She has a point, Eva. If you kill Isa now, we don't have to risk the lives that will be lost in a rebellion at Sher n'Cai. The throne would be yours. You can change the Enclosure laws without spilling any blood."

"Yes, and then start a war of succession that could end in another civil war. Even if we do this carefully, you know as much as I do that most of the courtiers will refuse to crown me on the grounds of Papa's blood. They'd kill to keep me from it, afraid freeing khimaer will mean they have to return their stolen wealth."

"There is no law against a khimaer claiming the throne, Eva. They were too arrogant to consider writing it in, assuming khimaer would forever remain far beneath humans. If we return to Ternain with your sister's body, they will be forced to name you the True Heir."

I shook my head, my pulse thudding in my fingertips. Even if all that did work, there was no telling what my mother would do if I returned to Ternain with Isa's dead body. "It's not happening, Anali. I'm not ready to kill her, and even if I was, it wouldn't be wise to start with such treachery. If Isadore and I fight again, it will be before an audience."

"And will you be able to kill her then?" Lirra pressed.

"Yes." I stared at them, daring Lirra or Anali to call me the liar I was.

Anali nodded, and after glares from Osir and Tavan, Lirra did the same.

I swept from the room, the precious pages of Queen Assani's

On Mutable Flesh held lightly to my chest, as the true answer to Lirra's question clanged through me.

Would I be able to kill Isa? I wasn't so certain I could.

✦

"This doesn't make any sense," I said, furiously stirring the cup of tea that had long since gone cold.

I read the line from Assani's journal again. *Harness the light within; it will show the limits of your shift.*

What *light within?*

So far her notes had offered little explanation in how to use my shapeshifting magick. It was filled with detailed sketches of every animal she encountered—their claws, wings, and the like— seemingly in order to adapt those features to aid in her shape- shifting. Which was helpful in its way. I could imagine that if I had been raised with the knowledge that I would one day wield this gift, I would have done much the same. I would have exper- imented endlessly with various forms until I found the right fit.

Instead I was trapped with wings I did not know how to use and no closer to finding a way to get rid of them. Tavan had offered to teach me how to fly, and I was beginning to think a lesson with her would have done me more good than the past hours toiling away to translate Assani's notes.

"None of this makes any sense," I repeated. And I desper- ately wanted it to. Never had I felt such fervor studying blood magick. All those lessons had been filled with dread. Although the potential mistakes I might make with this gift worried me, I did *want* to know. My frustration did not detract from my awe. What a gift I had been given. What a blessing from the Mother to choose exactly what form you wanted to be.

I traced the rendering of Assani beneath the words. Auburn ears peeked out from long, beaded braids hanging to her waist, and a spiny, reptilian tail curled around her body.

"That explains why you've been stuck on the same page for hours now," a voice called from the other end of the library. Falun spoke again without turning his attention from a tapestry depicting a pair of ancient fey and khimaer allies crossing the Red River. Each held a sword and walked hand in hand. Allies or lovers or both.

Two days had passed since I had woken and I spent most of them here. The library at Nbaltir was an eight-sided room with a glass ceiling just ten steps away from the kitchen, where Tavan and Lirra spent most of their time. Every morning I entered to find a fresh cup of tea, flatbread dripping with butter and garlic, and a plate of eggs—Osir had taken me on a tour last night where I met the hens supplying the estate. Whatever else I thought about my new family, they had lived entirely self-sufficiently within these walls. It was admirable, the skills and crafts they'd developed to make life here comfortable. Yet the necessity of such isolation made me sick to my stomach.

Through the glass ceiling, one could see the pinks and golds of the sunset, which accented the heavy gilt work on every bookshelf and most of the other furniture within the room. A table long enough to seat twenty held an older, more ornate version of the family history Tavan had given me. A basket in the corner was heaped with vibrant blankets, woven by my cousin's hand. Osir kept a small garden of flowers and herbs to dye the wool from their small flock of sheep.

I sat wrapped in one up to my chin, wings hanging uselessly over a low-backed chair. I'd found stools or sometimes just sitting on the floor was more comfortable, since most chairs were not built to accommodate wings.

Osir, Anali, Aketo, and the rest of the soldiers had left before dawn to scout the Plain far beyond the village to see if we were being followed or watched. I was glad to have the two of them out of my hair. When I had my first Khimaeran lessons with Lirra yesterday, Aketo, Tavan, and Anali had found reasons to loiter around the library. All of them except Aketo couldn't help but offer corrections whenever I made a mistake. It was maddening. Even Aketo had to leave the room to keep from laughing at my enraged expression.

"Come here," I said to Fal.

"I swear this one looks just like Baccha," Falun murmured, more to himself than to me.

"It's not Baccha." Not enough violence to depict any tale from Baccha's past. "Could be his brother or his great-father."

Falun shrugged and, after another long look at the tapestry, joined me at the table.

I showed him the passage, the sketch, and my translation written on a long sheet of vellum. "What do you think?"

The fey tongue was similar to Khimaeran, both having roots in the language of the Godlings. Though I'd always found Faeyin much more opaque and full of bizarre rules, I would take any input.

"I can't say for certain, but this word here, *ibasi*. There is a similar fey word, but I would translate it as 'seize' or 'to capture.'"

Capture the light within.

I wrote it down, though it offered very little in the way of illuminating the phrase's meaning.

"I'm surprised you haven't tried to ask him yet," Falun said, avoiding my narrowing gaze.

"Why am I not surprised you've found another reason to direct our conversation toward Baccha."

Falun's pointed ears went pink. "Forgive me for offering advice," he said with a sniff. "I'm going to get a headache if I have to watch you glare at the same three pages for another hour."

Falun wasn't wrong, but the last time I asked Baccha for help, he'd abandoned me to the forest of my mind without a second thought. I didn't want to beg him for help again.

"The last time I went into my mindscape, I was stuck for days." And I still had no explanation for why I'd been pulled from my mindscape. I needed to go see Isa and ask her what happened before I woke up.

"Because you were healing. You're better now, or so you said earlier."

"And you were the one who said we couldn't trust him."

"We can't," he said. "But you can still use him."

Baccha might help, if he didn't immediately throw me out of his head. And I did want to know what he was up to in the mountains.

"Very well. It is worth a try."

"I knew you'd see wisdom," he said. "Just don't stay too long or I am dumping that tea on your head."

"You're braiding my hair after this," I added. I should've asked him to help me tame the matted disaster on top of my head hours ago.

"Gods, I was wondering when you'd ask," he snorted.

I rolled my eyes, but sat back down. I shut my eyes and fell into the yawning chasm of my mind.

≈ CHAPTER 13 ≈

Baccha

THE LAST TIME Baccha had swaggered into the camp at Ariban, he'd been walking off a bender that started in the King's City, the capital of Dracol.

He remembered sitting in a tavern, talking up the matron who owned the place, Delu. He'd been wearing a human guise, using glamour to round his ears and soften his features. He was too vain to do anything about his hair, but he wore it braided and muted his magick.

He'd wound a lock of Delu's hair around one finger. Her complexion was darker than most in Dracol, and she had smoky eyes he found soothing. Delu murmured, "Sora ohai, ne?"

He enjoyed the clipped Dracolan accent, was charmed by the frank way all Dracolans spoke. But what he liked most about Delu was that she had no need to take their months-long flirtation beyond just that.

Baccha leaned in, but felt a sudden yank at his center accompanied by a sharp punch of pain that nearly upended his stomach. He hardly remembered extricating himself from Delu, just rising unsteadily from his seat and snatching a bottle of white liquor from the bar.

Drinking, Baccha found, helped clear the pain long enough for him stagger back to his apartment high in the city's structure. And though he did not enjoy the scorch of liquor on his throat, it numbed him enough. He barely lasted an hour more in King's City with the pain driving him to flee. He stayed only long enough to pack his things, say a few goodbyes, and summon Meya to beg for a ride through the A'Nir. The ancient beast was the only horse Baccha trusted to ride through these mountains quickly.

He drank his way south, replenishing his supply in the few mountain villages on the way. It never did completely dull the pain in his center. Every morning he woke up clutching his stomach, certain someone had stabbed him in the night.

Only in his few bouts of lucidity did he stop to wonder exactly why Moriya was calling him home after all these years.

The journey took two weeks, and by the time he found his way to the camp, he must have looked haggard and probably reeked of alcohol.

This time Baccha walked through the garden of stripped trees surrounding the camp with his arms bound. Tin and wood animal charms hung from the bare branches, creating an eerie music every time the wind blew. Magick charged the air, making him feel slightly light-headed.

His head was beginning to ache. Not to mention the pain in his back—something about the slumped shoulders caused by his bound wrists made his lower back sting something serious.

Ysai had tied the rope wrapped around his wrists to her saddle and divided her attention between tracking a path through the barren trees and glowering at Baccha.

She suspected he wasn't telling her all he knew about Eva, but by the end of their strange, blood-fueled interrogation, Baccha could tell that compelling him had drained her strength. Truth was, he had managed to hold back a few key details about the Princess. By the time she recognized her mistake in not asking all he knew about Eva, it was too late. Ysai never thought to ask about Eva's power, assuming she only possessed human magick. He understood why Ysai avoided the subject—the marrow and blood magick that Eva had inherited from Raina was still a source of fear to many here. The Elderi never let them forget all the atrocities humans committed during the war, including the thousands killed when Raina's magick was let loose on entire battlefields.

The most important detail he left out about the *Usurper* was that this part human possessed their rarest magick. The same magick Ysai had inherited from a long line of khimaer nobility. She'd not given any physical indications that she could shift, but Baccha could scent it on her nonetheless—wild and ancient magick.

How Eva would cringe to hear Ysai call her *that*. Technically every human noble had taken lands and titles they had no right to. They were all Usurpers.

He was afraid Ysai would never see Eva as anything but human. Eva would need the Elderi. Reintegrating khimaer into Myre would not be an easy task; she would have to work to earn the loyalty of the khimaer in Myre *and* the Tribe. Freedom wouldn't be enough. Humans would have to find some way to return some portion of what had been stolen. He supposed Aketo and Captain Anali could help her in that to a certain degree, but the work would be hers.

Or she would fail as Queen.

His best chance at uniting Eva and the Tribe lay with the Elderi, but he saw a slim chance of making Ysai's plan work to his advantage.

If he could convince the young Mother of the Tribe he was indeed loyal, he might be able to play her long enough to get Eva on the throne.

He flashed a smile in her direction. "Mother, I notice the air smells of smoke and myrrh, and the charms"—he pointed at a carving of a pouncing leopard hanging from the nearest branch—"are of predators. Do you suspect raiders in the region?"

The Elderi created these charms to ward off any potential enemies, and the children of the Tribe climbed up the trees weekly to hang them.

"Many bands roam these mountains. When they test our boundaries, we deal with it," she answered stiffly.

"My wolves can patrol the mountain"—he paused, grin brightening just a tick—"with your permission, of course."

Ysai favored him with a rare smile. "Is this your attempt to roam free and escape south?"

Within a moment of concentration, he'd summoned five wolves. Moon, a white she-wolf with brown eyes, was, like all the apparitions that lived inside him, a double to one of the mountain wolves that had raised him from birth. She nuzzled his knuckles and nipped at his fingertips. "They can roam quite far without me, Mother."

Finally this, of all his stunts, had the desired effect. Iriki leaned forward in her saddle, the tufts of her orange ears twitching happily, and let out a decidedly canine yip in greeting.

The wolves all danced around Baccha's knees until he nodded, and then as one they all ran to Iriki's horse. Enki swung out of his saddle and practically cooed as the wolves nipped at his hands and sniffed him.

This close to Baccha, they would feel nearly corporeal, yet the farther from him they ran, they would become more and more like ghosts.

Ysai simply blinked at the beasts, though her expression did reveal a hint of delight when one of the wolves, a grizzled old boy named Brushfire, licked and then nibbled her boot.

"I will let you know if we have need of more surveillance," she said.

Baccha called his wolves back into himself, each fading into nothing where they had stood, and he continued walking until they came to a wall of trees bound together with twine and mud and painted white. An arch was carved out of the center, leading to a wide road of packed dirt. Two women and three men stood out front, each armed with dual axes or a set of half-moon short swords called *iveki*.

The tallest of the group, a bronze-skinned woman with broad shoulders, the forelegs of a lion, and golden eagle wings, approached.

Ysai dismounted and unwound the rope, then none too gently hauled Baccha forward. "Onyi, the Lord Hunter is to be my guest until we meet with the Elderi tonight. Please take him to my tent and leave someone to keep an eye on him."

"Yes, Mother," Onyi murmured, taking hold of Baccha's leash. "Shall I keep him tied up?"

Ysai stroked her chin, gaze moving from the road before her, then to Baccha, and back again. "You can untie him for now, but don't linger in the camp. His return may cause some stir, but this day is important. I'm sure our Hunter doesn't want to be a distraction."

"I serve at your bequest," Baccha said, bowing slightly, though his jaw was tightly clenched. He knew he deserved to serve the Tribe, and all khimaer, and would continue serving until he found a way to return them to the throne.

Yet it did chafe. Here he was a servant. He missed Myre, where he could still be a source of wonder—a legend. Eva had thought so much of him, until she learned the truth.

He would earn back her regard and gain Ysai as an ally of sorts. Somehow.

He swore it to himself as he walked past row after row of tents as big as houses.

Somehow.

✦

The Elderi gathered in the only permanent building in the entire camp: a clay dome structure with a single chamber, its floor hollowed out to fit circular rows of seats padded with throws and furs. It had no name; it didn't require one. It was simply the place where the Elderi met each morning. Or whenever something of note happened in the camp.

Such as Baccha's sudden return to Ariban, in the Mother's possession no less.

It wasn't until Baccha was escorted into the meeting hall and bade to sit on the single stool at its center that he realized this was a trial of some sort. However informal, he had been escorted in with his wrists still bound. All thirteen Elderi watched him furtively. A few eyes glittered with open malice, and the few elders he'd called friends in decades past would not meet his stare.

They exemplified the array of forms found in the khimaer

tribes. The Great War had made dividing and marrying according to tribe nearly impossible for khimaer in the Enclosures, but the bloodlines that had become enmeshed in the South were still strong in the Tribe. Winged *chalam* khimaer sat beside raven-feathered *nixin* who, like Eva's Captain, had skin of the richest brown and hair as white as snow.

"Lord Hunter," called Eramin, a bull-snouted Elderi with ram's horns and tufts of white hair sprouting from bovine ears. He inclined his head to Ysai, seated in the center of the elders, many of whom were more than thrice her age. Eramin was the oldest of the elder council. "The Mother has called us to hear you account for your behavior in the South."

How many times had he been in similar situations? He'd been taken before local rulers or Queens dozens of times and been accused—often rightly—of any number of treacheries.

Somehow the dread that filled him now was sharper than ever before. This meeting would determine much more than Baccha's fate.

"I will account for all my perceived misdeeds, but first may I ask why I am being treated as a prisoner?"

"Because you aided the Usurpers," Ysai said.

"May I ask one more question, then?" Baccha murmured. Before his request could be denied, he went on. "Did you know when Moriya sent me south that the Princess and King Lei were khimaer?"

Silence was all he got in return. Baccha smiled. Not the wolfish grin he was known for. Instead he offered a tight-lipped smile that showed exactly what Baccha thought of Moriya and them for withholding that knowledge when he was sent on the mission. "I admit I have trouble believing a family of khimaer managed to hide in Myre for all these years without any of your help. I've pondered this as I made my way north to make my report. How would they ensure their bloodline remained strong?"

Finally the striking, red-eyed Elderi seated to Ysai's right, Arsa, spoke: "We know of a few families hiding in Myre. The Nbaltir family were once invited to join us here, but wanted to remain in Myre. Instead their children may train here for some years."

"Did you know the King was from that family when you sent me to Ternain?"

This time it was Ysai who answered: "Moriya only learned of the King's true identity shortly after you left."

How could she have stumbled upon that secret here? His bafflement must have shown on his face, because Ysai added, "She learned this from one of our sources in Ternain. You remember Sarou?" Baccha nodded; the library apprentice had been his only companion until Eva came along. "Apparently the Sorceryn archive even their correspondence. She found an old letter from the King to a long-dead Sorceryn. It was all coded, of course, but she noted the strange symbol the King wrote alongside his name."

"An iktar?" Baccha assumed the King must have felt certain no one in the capital would recognize the language. The letter must have been written years and years ago, when the King was still certain his identity was well hidden.

Ysai nodded. "Indeed. Moriya recognized it as the symbol of one of the families the Tribe has been in loose contact with."

"Did Sarou share this with anyone besides Moriya?" Baccha asked. "The Princess believes whoever killed him must have learned that the King was khimaer. This could be how they dis- covered the truth."

Ysai shook her head. "Unlikely, but I suppose it is possible. However, the King's death is not why we are here, Hunter."

"You're right, Mother Ysai, but I don't understand why I am sitting here. I aided a khimaer Princess in danger of being killed."

"What you learned later does not absolve you from forsaking your commands," Ysai said with a sniff. "She is still a human, and though my mother believed you had learned from your past mistakes, I am not so sure."

"Forgive me, Mother Ysai. I admit when I began to suspect the truth, I became protective. Forgive me for believing the Princess would be a useful ally."

How kind of you, a feminine voice whispered through his mind. Eva might as well have spoken right into his ear for as clearly as he could hear her. *What is this? Are you a prisoner?*

Baccha made an effort to school his face. *Doing a little spying again?*

"Your treachery may yet prove useful," Ysai said, rising from her seat to look at the Elderi. "Lord Baccha can attest to the unrest in the South. We cannot wait here forever. We must act now and make plans to take the capital."

Since you won't tell me anything, what else am I to do? You made it to the Tribe, then? Who is Mother Ysai?

Baccha opened his mouth, preparing to reply to the words in his head. Ysai's sharp look shocked him back to his senses. *Sorry, a bit busy here.*

"You are right," he said, offering a smile that faded beneath her glare. "Following the King's death, the Queen has turned her attention on Dracol. Both Rival Heirs are missing from the capital." He'd barely finished speaking before the Elderi began arguing among themselves. Baccha tried to keep track of the different sides, but it was difficult with Eva's voice buzzing in his ear.

Baccha, what is going on here? He could feel her agitation seeping through the bond. *You are going to bring them south?*

I am doing this for you. Unless I'm wrong and you already have a bevy of allies.

How Eva had managed to convey a snort of laughter through the bond, Baccha could not say. *Somehow I doubt this is just about me, Baccha.*

Fair enough, Princess, he thought with a shrug. Baccha knew he should explain the whole of his plan to help her and free himself, but he would sound just as self-serving as she already thought. *Just watch.*

His attention was drawn back to the bickering Elderi by Ysai's glare.

Eva's presence in his head reminded Baccha there was one last thing he wanted to share. *Tell me, Eva, have you shifted yet?*

Her shock suffused through the bond. *So you knew. Thanks for sharing that with me. Bastard.*

I can hear you, Princess.

Good.

Before their mental exchange could devolve into more bickering, Baccha held up a hand. "There is one thing you should all know that I learned in the South. It may soothe your misgivings about returning to Myre."

Ysai quieted the Elderi. "Yes, Lord Hunter. What is it?"

Baccha gave her a wolfish smile. "Against all odds, the *human* Princess I aided in the South possesses Khimaerani's gift."

The look of betrayal on Ysai's face sent genuine fear skating down Baccha's spine. It promised revenge.

"What?" Ysai's voice was quiet but it snapped through the room like a whip. "What proof do you have, Hunter?"

He could still sense Eva, like a tight bundle of energy buzzing at the back of his neck.

Baccha shrugged, fighting to keep the smile from his face. "You are free to compel me with my oath, Mother. I wouldn't have thought it possible either. Very few khimaer of mixed heritage ever inherited the ability to shapeshift, but I speak the truth."

Ysai gave a sharp jerk of her head. "She may be khimaer by blood, but she is human in nature. She possesses the accursed magick that slaughtered thousands of our people. She was raised in a den of violence and treachery."

"How can she be blamed for the magick she was born with?" Baccha countered. "It is not her fault that, instead of telling her the truth, the King isolated her."

"Khimaerani will provide a Queen for us at one of the Enclosures. This changes nothing."

"Come now, Mother Ysai. It changes quite a lot," said Eramin, the Elderi who had begun Baccha's questioning. "If what the Hunter says is true, Khimaerani already has provided. I am not so keen to turn away her blessing."

"Yes," Baccha said, flashing Eramin a grateful smile. "Now a young woman chosen by Khimaerani is closer to the Ivory Throne than in centuries and you have the chance to aid her. You *all* can guide her and make certain she is khimaer in more than blood alone. And you have a responsibility to keep her from being killed."

"I think I will compel the truth from you, Hunter." Ysai gathered her white skirts in one hand and stalked forward. "This may yet be another scheme of yours, another betrayal."

"I"—Baccha rose from his stool and held out his bound hands—"am no freer to betray you than I am to walk out of this camp. And you are not free to ignore this. I was there the day Princess Oyani fled north with her Elderi Council. Everyone swore by their blood and magick to retake the throne the moment a path to it was clear. Khimaerani has laid this path before us. You have to take it."

"Lord Hunter, didn't you also swear to obey the orders of every woman who would lead this Tribe?"

Baccha nodded, jaw clenched.

"Good, then you should leave the ordering about to me." She pointed to the two guards standing at the steps leading out of the meeting chamber. "Take Lord Baccha to the cages. We need to discuss this alone."

It was only when the guards hauled him up the steps did Baccha realize Eva had finally fled from his mind.

CHAPTER 14

Eva

I OPENED MY eyes to find the room still spinning and leaned forward till my head rested comfortably between my knees. I had vastly underestimated just how dizzying it would be to jump from here, into my mindscape, then into Baccha's head, and *back*.

"Are you all right?" Falun asked, reaching for my hand. "Is Baccha . . . ?"

"I'm fine," I groaned. "Baccha is well enough."

Despite his bonds, he was unharmed from what I could tell. Then again Baccha could heal almost any wound, so there were any number of possibilities. Though I did not think these Elderi would harm him. I had skimmed through Baccha's thoughts, surprised to find the council that chose Queens in the past was attempting to do so again.

"Well enough? You don't sound so certain. Where is he, then?"

"He's exactly where I told you he would be." I paused to

sit up and so that I could look into Fal's eyes. "But it's not by choice. He's their prisoner, because he helped me."

Falun scoffed. "Don't feel too bad. I'm sure he can escape whenever he'd like."

"Possibly," I agreed, "though I believe their leader has some power over him."

I told him about the strange, large chamber and the Elderi. Even in Baccha's mind, I could sense the weight of their collective wisdom and power. Then there had been the girl, the one they called *Mother Ysai*, who couldn't have been more than a few years older than me. The young khimaer woman was lovely, with bronze skin and silver hair. Short, black-tipped claws curled over her fingertips and she had no obvious animal aspects, yet something about her had struck me. I couldn't dispel the image of her face, the glossy black eyes full of violence, and her sharp chin.

She was clearly their leader, but her words didn't hold as much weight with the Elderi as they should have if the way they'd argued was any indication.

And then there had been Baccha, who when bade to reveal all he had learned in Ternain, had instead chosen to advocate for me. Baccha, who was still my friend.

I hesitated at telling Falun about the last thing I had heard before I returned to my mindscape. *Take Lord Baccha to the cages.*

Guilt writhed in my gut. Whatever else he'd done, Baccha hadn't chosen the Tribe over me. He remained my ally, despite his abrupt disappearance after my nameday. All the anger I'd clung to so tightly now curdled in my stomach.

"I still don't understand how he knew about the shapeshifting. Or why he didn't tell me."

"You remember how he is. Too full of secrets to know when truth will serve him best," Fal said. "And Baccha is a tough one. He will be fine."

"He wants to bring them south, to help us. If he succeeds . . ." I trailed off, remembering the vengeance in Ysai's eyes when Baccha revealed my khimaer gift. Even worse was the venom with which she described marrow and blood magick. Her words were painfully familiar; I'd been directing the same hateful thoughts at myself for years.

"Then we'll have another ally," Falun replied. "And maybe someone to help us in Sher n'Cai. This is a good thing, Eva."

"Yes, you're right. I'll check on him again tonight," I said. In truth I should have shared my plans with Baccha when I was in his mind, but I'd been unable to think of anything but the strange scene playing out.

The beat of several sets of footsteps sounded outside. After a sharp rap on the door, I called for them to enter.

Osir, Anali, Aketo, and Kelis spilled into the library, the latter giving me a fanged grin.

"Guess what we saw?" She collapsed into a chair across from Falun. "Osir took us to a watering hole far east of Orai. Hundreds of animals all drinking from one place, yet when I attempted to partake, you would not believe how they scattered."

"Likely because you smell like a predator," I said, nodding at the bloodletting knife at her waist.

She shrugged. "True enough. I did not know elephants still lived on the Plain."

"You saw elephants?" I wish I could have gone with them. "Well, your day has been significantly more eventful than mine. I did not even know elephants ventured this far north."

"Less and less do every year," Osir said. "They will return to the marshlands in the South as soon as the weather grows cold. Hundreds used to cross the river every spring. But now that cities line the riverbanks, it is harder for them to find a place to wade across."

When the rest joined us at the table, I stood. "I am going to see if Lirra needs help with supper." I pointed my chin at Falun. "You can tell Anali about your fool idea and see what she thinks. Excuse me."

Aketo and Anali both began to speak, but I left the room before anyone could attempt to stop me.

Lirra let me help fold buttery sweet dough into pastries shaped like the sun and moon while she took stock of their food stores and salted meats. Lirra gauged they would have at least three weeks of food—enough to get them off the Plain and into the mountains. After an hour of baking, she shooed me out, complaining about having to sweep up feathers.

When I left, Aketo waited outside. He leaned against a tiled wall, arms folded with one ankle crossed over the other, his eyes shut. The moment I brushed past him, they flew open. "Hello, Princess."

I rolled my eyes and began walking, nowhere particular in mind. "Prince."

Aketo fell into step with me and I did not bother to hide my inspection of him. His boots were caked in the yellow-brown dirt of the Plain, and like me, he wore one of Osir's creations: a wide-collared cream tunic with gold-and-crimson embroidery down the sleeves and the matching low-slung pants. Two short swords hung from his belt, along with a hollowed-out horn Osir had given him for calling across the Plain.

"May I ask where you are going?"

"Back to my room."

"How about a walk outside?" He caught my hand, lacing our fingers together.

I nodded and let Aketo lead us to one of the outdoor courtyards, where one wayward goat was gnawing on a wicker chair. We walked over the worn-down tiles, stepping lightly to avoid those especially in need of repair.

Beyond the courtyard lay a field of such viridescent grass that, when we first toured the grounds, I had been certain it was some sort of illusion. Like that day, I let go of Aketo's hand and knelt to feel the blades of grass on my palm. I took off my slippers and sat, enjoying the cool ground beneath my feet.

Aketo joined me. "What's wrong?"

I glanced to the side to find Aketo watching me with a small smile. "I went to my mindscape to check on Baccha."

"And? How's the ancient one?"

I smirked. I'd have to call Baccha that the next time we spoke. "He's a prisoner of sorts, but fine. And trying to convince the Tribe I'm worth trusting."

I quickly relayed Baccha's meeting with the Tribe's elders.

He smiled slightly. "A Queen needs her Elderi."

"I am not yet that." I shook my head. "I may never be that. Besides, I would rather build a khimaer council from those who have suffered in this Queendom, not ones who abandoned it."

"Even so, should we leave Baccha as their prisoner? If we tried to find him, the Tribe could return with us."

"He doesn't seem to want or need any help." From the tone of Baccha's thoughts, he had everything well in hand.

"Hmm, sounds like a bull-headed girl I know," Aketo teased.

I gave him a shove. I was not stubborn. Or at least I was not as stubborn as Baccha. "It's better we focus on Myre, and not those hiding outside its borders."

"Right," he breathed. "We are planning a rebellion sure to bring the army down on our heads."

I lay back in the grass, wings spread out beneath me, and stared up at the endless azure sky. "Must we talk of our doomed future?"

Aketo leaned over and kissed my throat. "Is there anything else you want to discuss?"

Warmth spilled over every inch of my skin as he breathed the words into my neck. "I . . . I don't think so."

"Good," he whispered. I couldn't help my sigh of disappointment as he climbed to his feet and held out a hand. "There is something I want to show you."

We walked farther onto the grounds, passing the small pond where most of the animals gathered. Then past the copse of tall acacia trees where three towering giraffes regarded us with little interest as they reached for the leaves on the uppermost branches.

Until finally we stopped at an untilled field with sparse Plain grass up to our waists. "I should have begun teaching you this as soon as I learned you were khimaer. But we've had little opportunity and . . ."

And the one time Aketo had joined me to spar since we arrived in Orai, we'd ended up arguing about Isadore, and neither of us was inclined to try again until now.

"Taught me what?"

He removed his sword belt. "The true potential of your

body. I'm sure you've noticed an increase in stamina since the binding broke." I'd been spending my afternoons exploring that new endurance before I fell. "I am going to show you how to run."

"What—" I began, but he took off, sprinting across the field.

He blurred, seeming to fly through the grass. I blinked just once, and when I opened my eyes, my mouth fell open. I squinted, and sure enough, he was all the way across the field, grinning.

He ran back and this time I concentrated until I could track him with my eye. "What the hell was that? I've never seen you move that fast."

Even Baccha only moved with such speed in rare circumstances.

"We call it *cashina*, or true speed. All khimaer, and fey for that matter, are significantly quicker than humans. I noticed you harnessed a small amount of that speed sometimes when we fought, but it didn't occur to me that you were harnessing cashina."

"How?" I wiped my sweating palms on my thighs. This explained that endless well of energy within.

"It's a simple matter of concentration. First clear your mind of any errant thought."

And how exactly was I to accomplish that? When I glared at him, Aketo laughed. "You might try finding the music first."

So I shut my eyes and listened to the wind knifing through the high grass. Beyond that, I heard the faint grunts and huffs of the animals nearby and the steady rhythm of Aketo's breathing.

"Good," he murmured. "Now open your eyes. Find a point

to focus on. That will keep you from becoming disoriented the first few times."

Across the grass, I spied a flowering bush with fuchsia blooms. One slightly wilted flower rose higher than the rest. "Can I try now?"

"You'll want to keep your wings tucked as close as possible."

I did as he instructed, my back aching as I drew in the wings.

I took one step, holding the image of the flower foremost in my mind, then another.

And then I felt it, a fierce buzzing in my limbs, and with the next step, I shot forward. My feet ghosted over the grass like I was an apparition. I felt nothing but the wind fighting against my speed.

I tore through it and in another blink, I could see the bush, just a few steps away. But I was moving too quick to stop, so instead I leaped over the bush and expanded my wings. As I'd hoped, catching the air slowed my momentum until I fell and rolled head over foot a few times.

I lay there in the dirt, heart racing. No, not racing—singing—begging for the chance to do that again.

Aketo was there when I finally climbed to my feet. "Oh Gods, how could you wait this long to teach me this?"

"That was good. Only marginally embarrassing, but for your first run, a good showing. Eventually you'll reach my speed, but that could take weeks of training."

Oh absolutely *not*. "I'll match your speed today."

Aketo, frowning, drawled, "And how do you plan on doing that?"

"Easy," I said, giving him the slow, vicious smile I had learned from Baccha. "I'm going to chase you."

Aketo eased back a step and I followed, matching his long

stride. "Really? You sure that's a good idea? We haven't sparred in weeks and I won't hold back with you any longer."

My mouth hung ajar as I realized he'd been holding back this magnificent speed every time we'd fought.

"Well," I said, glaring up into his gilded eyes, "let's see how we both fare against each other when neither of us is holding back anything."

Faster than I could blink, Aketo bent forward until his mouth was less than an inch from mine. "Fine. See if you can catch me."

Then he kissed me.

Aketo's soft lips moved against mine, gentle and yet demanding, deepening the kiss until I gasped. It was not the quick brush of his lips earlier. This was a true kiss. This felt like the honeyed sun spilling over my bare skin.

So confident and assured, this Prince. And I liked it.

My fingers curled around his neck, sliding down the cool strip of scales hidden beneath his hair. He said something unintelligible, words vibrating against my lips, my tongue.

I pulled back. "What?"

"Pray you catch me," Aketo said, laughter in his eyes.

With a growl, I reached out to take hold of his collar. But it was too late. He winked as if to say *too slow* and fled in a burst of speed that sent up clouds of golden dirt.

"You better pray I don't," I yelled, and took off after him.

✥ CHAPTER 15 ✥

Aketo

THE SUN SAT low in the east the following morning when Osir turned to Aketo. "So . . . allies, you said?"

In the midst of pulling the breakfast Lady Lirra had packed them before the sun rose an hour ago out of his pack, Aketo ignored the probing question.

His fingers closed around the warm cotton sack just as his stomach growled, angry with him for missing supper last night. Yesterday he and Eva had run around the Nbaltir lands until the sun set. By the time they'd stopped chasing each other, both exhausted and lightly bruised, they'd lain in a patch of blue-violet flowers and promptly fell asleep.

A waxing gibbous moon was overhead when Osir and Anali found them, hours after everyone else met for supper. Aketo went with Eva to the kitchens to see whether any food was left. When they got there, Lirra was up to her elbows in soap. Although the Lady of the House had greeted Eva warmly enough, the look she'd slid his way when the Princess wasn't looking . . . He'd decided, empty stomach or not, he'd make himself scarce.

No one said anything, but the particular tenor of the household's agitation made it apparent they all believed he and Eva had been up to something few allies engaged in.

Aketo folded back the warm cloth wrapping the meat pie and took a large bite. Filled with sweet peppers, well-seasoned goat, and rich egg yolks, this pie, like all Lirra's cooking, was among the very best he'd had since leaving Sher n'Cai. He hoped she would agree to take over the cooking when they journeyed north.

He handed the man the other pie and could feel his curiosity like a finger tapping on the back of Aketo's neck. He finally met Osir's penetrating gaze.

What business of theirs was it if they were more than allies? he wanted to ask.

Aketo's silence stretched and Osir sighed. "Well, I won't press you. I daresay with your gift, you're more likely to know what you're doing to the rest of us." He tapped the side of his head.

Aketo snorted. Feeling emotion wasn't the same as understanding it. "I wish it was that simple, Osir. Most of the time, I don't know what I'm doing."

Not even remotely.

Lami khimaer, the serpentine tribe, were known to be wise because of their ability to sense and influence emotion, and Aketo's mother exemplified that more than most. But Aketo knew his mother wasn't wise simply just because she could sense others' emotions, but because she acknowledged those feelings weren't something you should trifle with.

"Well, you two seem close."

Before he could think better of it, he told Osir about the night of Eva's nameday and the courtship gift he had given her, a pendant with a jewel that shifted colors.

"Does she still wear the gift? Did you ask if she regrets it?"

"Yes. No, but—" Aketo shook his head. He'd felt her regret that night at the well. Regret and uncertainty and worry that made his teeth ache. "I worry it was too soon."

"Ah, I see. You know what she feels, but you do not *understand* her feelings because you haven't spoken with her. You two have not yet learned to be vulnerable with each other."

Aketo began to protest. They had been through a lot in Asrodei and Ternain. They'd saved each other's lives more than once.

Osir continued, oblivious. "It is a simple enough thing to fix. You need only begin by being honest with her."

"What if telling her the truth is breaking my promise to someone else?" He still hadn't told Eva everything about his mother and the King.

"You needn't worry about revealing your every secret. Start small. One truth exchanged for another. It is more important you learn to be honest with your heart. Your fears, what you desire. Share your heart with her; she will share hers in return."

"You sound like my mother," Aketo grunted.

"A high compliment if all you say about her is true," Osir murmured, smiling lightly. He was the only one of Eva's family to ask about life in the Enclosure. "If you can believe it, Tavan and Lirra are not the easiest to live with. And before Lei's warning, nearly two dozen more members of our family used to live here. I had to learn to break up arguments without using my voice." Aketo hadn't heard Osir use his speaking magick once since their first meeting. "And that earning someone's trust is easiest when you first give it."

"I know that," Aketo snapped, surprised to find he was suddenly annoyed with the speaker's advice. He shouldn't have had to explain something so simple. Aketo *knew* that, knew as well that he was holding back with Eva. That was why they hadn't slept together. He wasn't afraid he would change his mind, but that she would.

And then he would have to live with her regret, even if she never expressed it openly.

He needed her to see him as he truly was, in his home, with the family he loved. Yet he hadn't realized until now that the distance between them was more than just the physical lines he wasn't willing to cross. He'd let his secrets become an excuse not to be open with her about everything else.

Aketo was about to offer an apology at his tone, but suddenly surprise shot through Osir like an arrow.

"Get low," he breathed, eyes narrowed as he glared at something to the west.

Without hesitation, Aketo lowered his body to the ground. They had been crouched at the foot of a rock outcrop since daybreak. Luckily the waist-high grasses hid them well.

Osir's eyes must have been sharper than Aketo's, because he could not see anything. He pulled out the eyeglass Eva let him borrow and scanned the horizon. First all he could see were the dark silhouettes of trees and craggy brush and more rock outcrops. Until movement in the west drew his eye.

Then he understood exactly what—no, who—he was seeing and a chill spread over his skin.

There were just three men that he could see. Their white

uniforms glowed like firelight, reflecting the fiery sunrise, but what struck Aketo as even more important were the masks each man wore.

He rose to a crouch. "We have to get back to Nbaltir. Now."

✦

Aketo's journey outside Sher n'Cai began about ten months ago. The last of the winter snows had just come and gone, and his father had written him to ask whether he would leave the Enclosure this year.

His father, Rodrick Sylea, was the bloodkin ambassador to the crown and one of the leaders of the bloodkin's informal power structure in Ternain. Rodrick's family had settled there after the Great War and, unlike most bloodkin families given to traveling the realm, remained for the next two centuries. Yet like many bloodkin youths, once he came of age, he'd joined a bloodkin caravan to travel every inch of Myre. Rodrick and Daischa, Aketo's mother, had met when that clan came to Sher n'Cai. Of the few merchants that bothered to travel so far north to trade with them, all were bloodkin.

Back then visitors were allowed to linger for extended stays in the Enclosures, but after months in the mountains, the blood-kin traders planned to leave. On the eve of Rodrick's departure, Daischa learned she was pregnant. As his mother told it, a year after Aketo was born, Rodrick returned to the Enclosure to demand his son accompany him to Ternain. He wasn't allowed; all khimaer born in the Enclosures must remain there. So instead his father became ambassador in the hopes of negotiating for Aketo's freedom. He still took the months-long journey from Ternain to the mountains every year.

His father rarely pressed him on anything, but in the half year since Aketo had turned seventeen, each letter from his father mentioned leaving his home. Aketo kept most of the details of life in Sher n'Cai to himself, most especially the new curfew set by General Sareen, the army veteran who governed their home. Yet without ever asking Aketo what he wanted, Rodrick assumed he would leave the Enclosure. Aketo noticed how Rodrick avoided mention of the military he would have to join in exchange for his freedom.

A number of his father's kin served in the Queen's Army, and Aketo had known a number of mixed khimaer who left Sher n'Cai to join them. Yet the path of a common soldier held little appeal to Aketo.

Escape wasn't reason enough to swear fealty to a Queen he despised. Even if her military would afford him every opportunity . . . it would be a lie. He would never condemn the others who'd been willing to tell that lie in order to escape. But he loved his home, despite its being a cage.

For better or worse, Sher n'Cai was their home. Anywhere else he traveled, he would always be an outsider.

He had needed to do *something*, though. Dthazi was the first son; he led their secret khimaer force alongside their cousin Yayazi and would take over Daischa's place as their leader one day.

Aketo was the second son, second Prince. The expectations placed upon him were different, but no less demanding. He was to find his purpose in a calling, a passion that would honor every gift Khimaerani had given him as well as serve his family.

The khimaer in the Enclosures were trapped, beaten, and killed, all for rules not even a child would be expected to follow.

Bowing to the Queen while his family was still here would not serve them well.

He wrote back to his father: He would stay in Sher n'Cai for now and serve by teaching the children. If nothing else stirred passion in him, making sure the young learned the song of the earth was noble enough.

Then, a week later, he woke to the news that three men, one his cousin, had not returned to their homes at sundown. Daischa asked her sons to see if the men were locked in the cages Throllo kept outside his stronghold. Instead of using the dungeons in the basement of the manor, he cruelly subjected his prisoners to the harsh northern climate.

Even though the General had agreed to notify Daischa a day in advance of executions and provide documentation of the accused crimes, Aketo had been sick to his stomach as they sprinted downslope. When they stopped before the manor's stone gate and saw the three men hanging from nooses, he vomited.

Then, worse, one of the soldiers manning the gate began to joke that the General should start keeping trophies.

"Maybe," he'd said, "we should untie the bodies and take their horns. Throllo loves surprises."

A strange roaring filled Aketo's ears and he took two steps forward, gaze locked on the sword on the hip of the nearest soldier. His brother's hand dropped onto his shoulder and Dthazi's magick poured out from him and took hold. Icy calm blew through the air on a phantom wind. The purity of the feeling captured Aketo's mind just as soundly as it ensnared the soldiers'.

Dthazi questioned them while Aketo could only stand there, completely severed from his rage. Powerless.

In the floating peace, his mind still raced. He was grateful his brother stopped him. Ten soldiers manned the gate; they could not stand against them and survive. But mostly he seethed with loathing, not only for the soldiers but also for himself. What could he do here? Accept the murder of his kin and people as routine, or resist and in doing so consent to be killed himself?

Despite his brother's requests to see the General, Throllo never emerged from the manor.

He understood finally that the khimaer who left Sher n'Cai to become soldiers hadn't done so merely to escape. They'd done so to regain some measure of power, however small.

He could justify swallowing poison if it yielded power. If it sickened him to serve the Queen, it would be worth it if he could rise in the military ranks and find a way to destroy Throllo.

It would have been easier to approach one of the soldiers with his intentions. But every khimaer he knew that joined the army had made the pledge to the Queen's Army before the General, and Aketo didn't think he could look Throllo in the eye without attempting to murder him.

That night, after the bodies were buried and prayed over, Aketo stole a horse from the soldiers' barracks and led it through the caves surrounding Sher n'Cai. He took what little food his mother had to spare, a handful of their family's dwindling jewels, an aged map, and a letter from his mother addressed to the King.

It took him two months to reach Fort Asrodei. He survived by riding at night, keeping wide of every village and stealing eggs and vegetables from the few farms he passed.

When he rode into sight of the military fort, half-starved and more than a little delirious, his requests to see the King were ignored. They put him in magick-dampening shackles and left him in a cell for two days until the King was notified there was a Prince in his dungeons.

In the following weeks, Aketo regained his strength and began training with the rest of the recently enlisted soldiers. He sat through lectures offered by the Generals in residence. He watched and listened to the humans. The King forced General Sareen to honor the earlier agreement with Daischa, indicating that she had to be notified of any hangings, but that incensed Aketo more than it soothed him. In months the man might very well change his mind again on a whim. And besides, what good was notifying his mother if she could not petition for their lives?

By the time summer was on the horizon, Aketo was restless and angry that he'd left. He went to the King and asked to rescind his vows.

Instead, the King showed him a sketch on his desk. His daughter, he explained, needed more soldiers in her guard. His daughter, the King had assured him, would be interested to know why he left Sher n'Cai. And he implied more than once that his daughter would be sympathetic to khimaer in the Enclosures.

Aketo had heard from others in passing that the Princess used to live in Asrodei; she was well-known among the soldiers. He didn't put much stock in the power of the Princess's curiosity, though, in the short term. If the King's word wasn't enough to sway the Queen, he doubted she could do more. But guarding Evalina would take him to Ternain, where he would see his father, meet his extended bloodkin family, and go to Court. And if the Princess did become Queen in the future, even better if he could come to trust her.

Aketo agreed, even though the few months at Asrodei did

not leave him confident any of these humans, save the King, could be trusted.

The following days, while he waited to join a larger party of soldiers to travel south, might've passed easily if not for the arrival of five thousand soldiers. Fort Asrodei had always been busy, much busier than he was used to, but overnight it went from comfortable to tight, to near to bursting.

With them came a host of new higher-ups and Generals. The King insisted Aketo be introduced to each one. He'd been called on to serve watered wine and kaffe in meetings and to display his skill with a blade. Most wondered why he hadn't been assigned to a battalion, and when King Lei told them his plans, several tried to sway him.

Of the half-dozen khimaer soldiers he'd met since fleeing the Enclosure, each was assigned to a special force within their battalion. Every army unit included one large group of soldiers led by one General, known as the First, and another much smaller force led by another General, called the Second. The Second's elite band of ten to thirty soldiers were chosen for their skill in combat magick.

Aketo barely remembered the names of the First Generals, who for the most part were older men and women who'd gained their status through nobility. The Second Generals, though, had each stuck in his mind because they were younger and each walked around with an animal mask strapped to their back. Everyone called them by the animal masks they wore—hyena, leopard, monkey, and boar.

The one General who had recruited him most insistently was Second Almar Mateen, the Jackal. The man had tattoos of stones and crystals on his arms, and Aketo sensed the might of his earth magick before he ever saw the man fight. When he did finally see Mateen journey to the fighting pits, the man's abilities had chilled him.

While his opponents drew their swords, Mateen would simply crouch and dig his hands into the dirt. Before they could attack, they would find the ground pulled up from under them or erupting shards of sand as hard as stone.

The men he'd spied in the distance wore jackal masks.

As he and Osir ran, Aketo imagined the Plain's rocky dirt was coalescing into magick-honed blades of stone beneath his feet.

❧ CHAPTER 16 ❧

Isa

A MUFFLED EXCHANGE outside her door was Isa's only warning before the bedchamber door swung open. Eva stood in the doorway, but for a moment, Isa didn't recognize her.

She couldn't reconcile this new Eva—pronged horns spiraling back from her brow and wings dappled gold and bronze—with the mental image of her little sister.

It was only when Eva took a step inside and Isa could see her sister's eyes, still that fiery orange, that both images resolved into one.

Eva's determined expression faltered as she scanned the room. "Isa?"

"I'm over here," Isa said, feigning indifference, though she'd been anticipating this. In fact, she'd been waiting since being dismissed shortly after Eva woke up.

Isa sat in the far corner of the room, curled up on a cushion beneath the window, trying not to pick at a loose thread on her shirt. She didn't bother to rise, expecting Eva would join her soon enough.

She'd woken up a few hours ago to find a large stack of clothing folded neatly outside her door. Unlike the castoffs from Eva she'd worn for the last six weeks, these actually fit. There were long tunics with touches of embroidery, soft leggings, three gauzy overskirts, and a woolen cloak, all in the jewel tones Isa favored.

The clothing wasn't up to her usual standard, but Isa found she didn't care. As much as she missed her weekly trips to Mistress Al'Meera, the fey seamstress who made all Isa's clothing, she was more than grateful for these few pieces than any gown. She'd been annoyed to find her eyes smarting as she inspected each piece, so pleased to have something of her own again.

The tears were mortifying, and she'd been furious at Eva all over again, for bringing her here. This promise of a truce seemed like a trap to Isa, one that offered no real solution. What would they do when Eva and Aketo's plans to liberate the Enclosure drew their Mother's attention? Lilith would kill the khimaer they freed out of spite and still demand Eva's death.

Across the room, Eva hesitated near the doorway. Isa rolled her eyes but smiled with genuine fondness. She was the same worry-filled girl Isa remembered, no matter her physical changes.

"Are you going to join me or just stand there?" Isa called.

Eva sighed, but walked around the bed to stare down at Isa. "Good morning. I didn't realize you were speaking to me now."

Her sister was wearing clothes of a similar cut, but in pale buttery yellow that set off Eva's blood-orange eyes. A fringed shawl was wrapped around her neck, and her hair was freshly braided in a complex design. Isa guessed it was Falun's work, because Eva could never manage something so intricate.

Isa folded her arms and returned Eva's frank look with a glare of her own. "We spoke plenty a few days ago."

"True, but I assumed you had a different set of rules for your incapacitated sister. Now that I am well enough"—Eva paused, sitting down across from Isa—"I thought you might've changed your mind."

"Doesn't seem like much of a point to that now," Isa said, still worrying at that loose thread.

At her words, Eva perked up, the beginnings of a relieved smile on her lips. "So you've finally seen the wisdom of a truce."

"I wish I saw the wisdom in it. The law is the law, Eva. We can't simply ignore that."

"Why not? If the law has us trapped as you say, what happens if we refuse?"

Isa lifted one shoulder. "When neither of us takes the throne, a war of succession will begin and that could kill thousands."

"I didn't say we'd leave the throne empty. What's to keep us from choosing? What's to keep the Court and Queen's Council from finding another way to pick?"

"Mother won't have it, Eva, not with this stunt you pulled, not knowing—" Isa swallowed up the words before she could said something foolish. "She'll find some way to force our hand. How will you feel when she kills Aketo to force your hand?"

"Like you kidnapped him to force my hand?" Eva stood, her hands trembling. "Not knowing what exactly, Isa?"

When Isa said nothing, her sister began to pace in a tight circle. "You never said who told you about Papa being khimaer."

"It doesn't matter," Isa said. She finally yanked the thread and was rewarded with a long run in the finely woven fabric. "I doubt they are the only ones who know."

Eva's mouth fell open and Isa could practically see the understanding forming in her gaze. "Just tell me, Isa. I'll forgive everything if you just tell me this. *Please.*"

The desperation in Eva's voice made Isa want to flee. "Forgive me? And what about me forgiving you?"

"What would you have to forgive me for? You're the one who tried to kill me almost half a dozen times by now. First when you chased me from Ternain when we were children, then the assassins when I returned, and on my nameday."

"I swore to you, I had nothing to do with any assassins. And I didn't *chase* you away from anything. You left *me* in Ternain, remember? So happy to run off and play soldier with Papa that you didn't once write me. I sent dozens of letters and you ignored every one." Isa absolutely hated the whining in her voice, but it wasn't fair. Eva's insistence on victimhood always made Isa into a villain.

Isa's memories of the fight that led to Eva's departure from Ternain were hazy. Isa wasn't trying to kill Eva. Since their parents wouldn't, she had tried telling her sister the truth about the Rival Heirs. She wanted Eva to know she should fight and let go of her fear of magick. But Eva had been so full of fear.

Eva stumbled back like she'd been struck. "You're right. But only about the letters. Can't you understand why I didn't want to speak to you? You told Mother I used my magick to hurt you. I had to leave, to get away from her."

Isa climbed to her feet, tired of looking up at Eva. "I did no such thing. Why would I? Mother has always so been so paranoid about marrow and blood magick. I knew she would keep us apart if she believed you were using it."

"Mother"—Eva's mouth twisted, like the word tasted

sour—"she said you confessed I'd been using my magick. She said I couldn't be around you anymore, that it was too dangerous."

"So quick to believe I would betray you."

"I was a scared child, Isa."

"So was I. And you left me there with Mother and Kitsina." Eva had seen firsthand how Isa's fey nursemaid was more liable to strike her than dispense any kindnesses. As children they had spent most of their time supervised by Mirabel for that very reason. "You knew how they were and you left me."

Eva hung her head, shame filling her eyes. "Mother adores you."

"Adores me so much she ignored Papa for years when he told her about Kitsina. Adores me so much she wants me to be her exact copy."

"Why are you still defending Mother, then?" Eva snapped. "It was Mother, wasn't it? She told you Papa was khimaer, didn't she?"

Because I'm no better than her, Isa thought.

It was Isa who'd learned the truth about her father and sister, and let years of resentment convince her they were the villains for lying to everyone at Court. Meanwhile she'd been doing the very same. Even though her mother flew into a rage anytime Isa asked about the identity of her real father, Isa knew the truth. She was half fey, and her mother would never let her reveal that fact publicly. Whether it was from the shame of bearing a child out of wedlock or the shame of having a fey child when the Killeen line had remained purely human for eight generations, Isa didn't know.

When she found out Eva and Lei were khimaer, she'd hated them for sharing this secret. They'd had each other, and Isa had always been alone. Since she couldn't punish herself, she would punish and loathe them the very way she despised herself.

She knew she could have turned that frustration toward the Court and the Great War that had sewn division between humans, fey, khimaer, and bloodkin. But she wanted to hurt her sister so much, and all it took was some gentle prodding from the Queen. *Why wait for her to become stronger and steal your rightful seat on the throne?*

How Isa had swelled, hearing those words. Now they made her feel sick. A stolen throne was a vile birthright.

If Eva found out Isa was fey, there would be no forgiveness.

Isa crossed the room and sat down on the edge of her bed. She folded her arms across her chest. "Is this why you came here? To argue as we usually do?"

Eva slowed her pacing and leaned against the wall. "No. I came for two reasons. First to ask you about the day in the healing chamber. I wondered what might've woken me up since you were the only one in the room. Did you notice anything?"

Isa's awareness shifted; she was still staring back at her sister, but now she could feel the magickal connection between them, as firm as a rope around her waist.

Eva's hand flew to her stomach, confusion plain on her face.

"I only noticed it when you were incapacitated. Some sort of effect of the Entwining, I think." Isa thought if she could *see* the connection, it would've glowed like the ribbons of magick the Sorceryn had woven around them during the spell.

"I bet it would feel terrible"—Eva's eyes narrowed and Isa felt that strange tugging around her midsection—"severing this. It's almost as if they want this to be as painful as possible."

"It will be terrible either way," Isa muttered. "You said there was a second reason?"

"Oh, right. Lirra and Tavan have started packing their food stores since we are to leave soon. Would you like to help?"

Isa held up her wrists, still bound in the magick-dampening shackles. "In these?"

"I'd hoped you'd agree to the truce, so I brought this." Eva held up a key that Isa recognized from when she was freed from her chains to bathe.

"And if I haven't yet decided?" Isa asked when her sister approached.

"Then, I suppose," Eva said, sliding the key into a slot on one side of the shackles, "this is temporary."

❧ CHAPTER 17 ❧

Aketo

HAVING ONLY TAKEN a few bites of breakfast earlier and after an hour of running back to Nbaltir, Aketo's stomach ground against his spine, begging him to fill it.

But he shoved the hunger to the back of his mind, practically vibrating with impatience as Osir fiddled with the lock on the outer door hidden in the wall. At true speed, Osir, with his hooved feet, was just a bit faster than Aketo and had beaten him to the village.

His mind was a tangle, trying to decide how long it would take the Jackal and his soldiers to reach Orai and how soon they could depart. There was no way to know if the First General and the rest of the battalion were with them, which was a terrible prospect. In either event, they needed to get far from here.

As far as possible and quickly.

He didn't realize he was muttering to himself until Osir's gaze slid from the lock in his plate-size hand to stare in his direction. "All right there, Prince?"

He fought to maintain his usual calm. "Yes. Just thinking."

A second later the lock clicked. With a murmured apology, Aketo shouldered past Osir and ran until he found Anali and Falun sharpening their weapons. His distress must have been apparent, because both followed.

"What did you see?"

Aketo shook his head; there was no time to explain. "Soldiers on the Plain."

Not easily troubled, Anali sheathed the curved dagger in her hand. "Gather the guard," she instructed Falun, and turned to Aketo, her salt-white eyes alight with fire. "Who?"

"Almar Mateen's forces."

Anali's stunned silence meant she knew exactly who the Second General was.

They found Eva, Lirra, Tavan, and, most surprisingly, Isadore in the kitchens. Eva and Isa both sat at the gnarled wooden table in the center of the kitchen, while Lirra stood over them, overseeing them wrap up salted goat and fresh fruits in roughspun cloth. Behind them, Tavan's beak clicked happily as she stoked the fire of the massive clay stove at the back of the kitchen.

Eva's smile slipped from her face as she took in his expression. "What happened?"

Aketo loosed a breath. "We saw soldiers on the Plain wearing masks."

Eva cursed. Her right hand flexed, and twitched toward where she usually wore her sword, dread and panic flickering through her. Her eyes scanned the kitchen and Aketo would've sworn she was searching for a weapon.

"How close?" Eva asked. "Did you recognize them?"

"No more than thirty miles from here. They could be here by late afternoon. They wore jackal masks."

"The Earthbreaker?" She spat another curse. "Of course my mother sent Mateen after us. He was the first ever given the title of Second General. One of my father's personal recruits."

"They are coming from the east," Anali said. "It's possible they were stationed at the border, and are simply passing through the Arym Plain on the way to Asrodei, but . . ." The Captain trailed off, shaking her head.

"No," Eva said. "They'd be farther east in that case. They're searching for this village, looking for us. We knew coming here was a risk. We're lucky this is our first encounter with the Queen's Army. I'm surprised we've evaded them so far."

Anali murmured, "Another blessing from the Mother."

Eva stared down at her inked and clawed hands for a long moment before nodding. "Yes, a blessing."

Tavan had begun dousing the fire in the stove at the first mention of the soldiers, and clicked her beak in agreement. *"Elelai."*

The word meant "noble, or chosen," in Khimaeran.

"So I was right," Lirra said, though she did not feel glad of it. Her emotions were a thorny blend of regret and mourning and excitement. "You shouldn't have come."

"It doesn't matter now. Even if we are captured, I won't regret coming here. But now we have to leave."

They started for the door, but Lirra stood near the stove, staring down at the tile floor. "You will come with us, won't you?" Eva asked.

She nodded. "I must see what food we can travel with. You all go on. There is much to do and little time to get it done."

It didn't take long to gather everyone. The thirteen members of the guard, not including Aketo, Falun, and the Captain, were lined up in the back of the library. Some had already begun arming themselves and the rest fidgeted, longing for the calming grip of a sword hilt. Tavan and Osir sat on silk-backed settees on the other end of the room, speaking softly. Only Aketo sensed the anxiety emanating from them like acrid smoke. Theirs was a deeper fear than the rest of the soldiers felt. Aketo was shocked to find no sense of resentment from the two.

Eva's arrival had upset their quiet life here. Even if they did manage to return to Nbaltir one day, it would be ransacked by the soldiers passing through.

Aketo leaned against the door, the best place to watch everyone in the room. A headache pulsed at the back of his head. The tension and agitation and fear in the room were like layers of thick perfume, each new essence overwhelming. His magick writhed eagerly, pushing him to use it. He wanted to soothe them, not just for their sakes but his.

Eva sat atop the long table in the center of the circular chamber, legs folded beneath her and wings fanned out on the table behind her. At her side rested an old map of Myre. Her hair was woven into dozens of braids of varying sizes, and pinned up so the woven stands framed her face. The beams of light filtering through the glass ceiling turned her horns to a glossy black, like shards of obsidian. And in Osir's well-made but home-spun clothes, she looked far different from the girl he'd met in Ternain.

Still that noble Princess lay beneath the changes—in the straight line of her spine, her shoulders thrown back, and her sedate expression.

Isadore eyed Eva from the corner opposite the door. Aketo

was surprised to find she wasn't wearing shackles, but he hadn't had time to ask Eva about it. Isa had a glower for everyone who dared glance in her direction. She was all prickly agitation and, Aketo noted unhappily, practically buzzing with anticipation.

It hadn't occurred to him until now that this would be the perfect opportunity for Isa to escape. Like they needed another thing to worry about.

"We don't have much time," Eva began. "I know you've all heard that as I speak, General Mateen and his Jackals are nearby, searching for Orai and my family's home. I doubt he's brought an entire battalion onto the Plain, but even so, we need to travel far from here, and fast."

She slid off the table and moved the papers off the map. Before the guard filed in, she, Tavan, and Anali had pored over it, searching for their next stop. "There is a town directly north of here called Pagra. Anali tells me there are ruins of an ancient Godling Temple outside its walls. We'll regroup there and make our next plans."

"Why north?" Kelis asked, her cool tone effectively masking the suspicion the young bloodkin felt. "Why not back toward the coast? We'll encounter more and more soldiers the closer we get to the border."

"Our ultimate goal, for now, is in the North," Eva said slowly. Last night Eva told Aketo that she planned to tell the guard about Sher n'Cai, but now, with the threat of capture, hiding their true destination would be prudent. "I know we risk more soldiers, but it's a risk I'm willing to take. However, I will not force you to gamble your lives. You should know that my plans will put me in direct opposition with the crown and the Queen's Army. That is why I want to offer you all the opportunity to leave."

Almost everyone began talking at once. Only Anali remained silent, watching the soldiers under her command take this in.

Eva looked to Anali. "I am grateful for every sacrifice you have made for me. You have risked much for me, and in exchange, I refuse to risk your lives. From today on, you are no longer renegade soldiers in the Queen's Army. If you follow me north, let it be your choice alone."

Eva's gaze swept the room, hesitating on her sister, before finally settling on Aketo. The tone of Eva's emotions was so distinct it stood apart from the storm of tension. Her doubt and uncertainty as cold as spreading frost. Aketo gave what he hoped was a reassuring nod. This was the right thing. Her guard deserved to know what they would face if they stayed with her.

Undercurrents of relief and suspicion left him worrying how many would join them on the journey to Pagra, and then up into the mountains. Many, he suspected, would chart a new path.

Eva took a shaky breath, fists clenching and unclenching at her waist. "It's settled, then. Be ready to leave in an hour."

When the door fell shut behind the last guard, Eva, once leaning against the table, slid to the floor and dropped her head into her hands.

Even though his magick was attuned to her emotions, it took a moment to realize, beneath Eva's laughter, she was crying.

~ CHAPTER 18 ~

Eva

NOT EVEN A third of my guard remained when we gathered out front an hour later. My cousins, their packs heavy with the food we'd been packing away this morning, were there, but from the guard, only Anali, Aketo, Falun, and Kelis remained. I'd watched from a window in my bedchamber as twelve of them left together, traveling south. Maybe I should have felt betrayed, but I was relieved. The fewer lives that depended on me, the better.

Unlike most days on the Arym Plain, the sky above was a flat gray. Outside of Orai, aside from the occasional jut of a large outcrop, dry golden grasses stretched on for miles. The land was almost completely flat, though the distant shadow of mountains rose far, far in the west.

I wore my saddlebag on my back, below the apex of my wings, and it served as a reminder to keep them tucked in. I'd hardly had time to get used to a new set of limbs, marvelous as they might one day be. This run would finally test the limits of my newfound strength. Already the muscles of my back were too tight, a sign of cramps to come.

Isa's bags, once hiked high up on her shoulders, now hung askew. I had decided not to replace her shackles, but I was wondering whether I would eventually regret it. I saw the way Isa's eyes scanned the horizon, hopeful in a way I hadn't seen in months.

We stopped at the well outside the village to fill our water skins. Aketo was already stretching and jogging in place to warm up his limbs. We set off the same way we had begun traveling the Plain, switching back and forth between a jog and a walk.

✦

Aketo set our pace, just as he and Anali had when we first traded our horses for tents in Dahn and started onto the Plain.

Those first days of walking and running on and off had been grueling on our bodies, but once my blisters healed a week later, I came to enjoy it. The grassland stretched on forever; and eventually there came a point in every run where the pain of pushing my body retreated and my thoughts simply fell away. One moment I would beg to stop and set up camp for the night, and the next there was nothing but the slap of my boots on the dirt and the sun on my face.

This time, though, there was no peace.

It was impossible to resist the voice in my mind, urging me to turn around, certain Mateen's Jackals were already on our heels. After an hour, every muscle from the back of my thighs up to my shoulders burned, and looking over my shoulder every few minutes only made the pain worse.

Late in the afternoon, after we'd been traveling for four hours, the grass grew sparse until there was only rocky, lifeless dirt. More outcrops dotted the land, though these rose higher than the outcrops near Orai. It looked like there had once been hills here, but some giant had come to shatter and break the earth apart, and these jutting bits were all that remained.

As the sun was setting, we came across three outcrops clumped together with only one narrow entrance. Another blessing from the Mother, or simply luck.

Anali squeezed inside first and I followed not two hands' width behind her. There was a surprising amount of space inside, enough for us all to sleep comfortably.

Lirra, Tavan, and Isa joined us. Then came Osir and Aketo guarding our backs. I drew in the cool air. I spared a moment to yank off my bags and sword belt, and lay facedown in the dirt, wings spread over my back like a blanket.

Moving as little as possible, I eased off my boots and accepted the dried peppered goat Lirra proffered. Aketo's offer to stay awake while we rested was the last thing I heard before I fell asleep.

The worried voice still whispered in my mind when I woke hours later to find the once-rocky dirt had been transformed into the finest sand, and my sister was gone.

I rolled onto my back, struggling to find my footing as the sand sucked at my feet. I froze, wondering if this was a nightmare. But I heard Aketo stirring a few feet away.

The air reeked of magick. Wood smoke and sandalwood; sugared buns and gardenias.

That second scent I recognized; Isa's magick had always smelled of sweets. But the rest? The rocky ground beneath us had been transmuted into sand while we slept. I scooped up a handful of the sand, holding it up to the moonlight streaming through the small opening in the rock above. It glittered black and silver—magick. It had to be the Earthbreaker, the Jackal. Mateen.

I stood, counting the rest of the sleeping bodies. I spotted Falun, his crimson hair peeking out from his blankets, Anali, and my new family, their bedrolls set slightly apart from the rest of us. Kelis sat with her back propped up against one wall of the rock outcrop, snoring slightly.

I crawled over to Aketo just as he sat up. "Eva?"

"Isa's gone, but still close. Her bag is still here. I can sense her magick. Who is supposed to be on guard?" I breathed.

"I passed the guard off to Kelis when night fell," he said, voice still groggy with sleep.

I felt around until I found my boots and yanked them on. My sword was half buried in the sand and I used it to push myself to my feet.

Aketo began quietly rousing the others, while I approached the seam in the rock.

Outside, Isa stood before a man kneeling with one fist pressed into the dirt. Where he touched the ground, black sand flowed in a narrow path, winding around Isa's feet and into the rock outcrop, bare inches from where I stood.

Such fine control.

The General's face was cast in shadow, but I recognized the locs spilling across his shoulder and the mask at his side. Its narrow snout hung open, showing off silver-capped teeth and a lolling, leathery tongue.

I couldn't hear a word of what they said, but I eased my blade from its scabbard. The bone hilt carved with Khimaerani's likeness was wrapped in buttery leather, but it felt no less at home in my hand.

Isa cupped Mateen's cheek, nails digging in faintly. But I could tell she wasn't in control of the situation.

Before I could begin to think of a plan, Isa turned and called, "Come on out, Eva. It seems you've been caught."

☙ CHAPTER 19 ❧

Isa

THE WIND SANG through the fissures in the rock like howling wraiths. The sound reminded Isa of the whirling branches of the Deadened Forest that had terrified her as a child.

Waking up in the circle of rock outcrops felt a bit like finding herself in the belly of a mountain. It took Isa a long moment to recall exactly where she was and why. In the dark, walls of stone seemed to close in on her, but she stared up at the stars until her memory settled. They were fleeing again, which seemed to be Eva's solution for everything.

Isa climbed out of her bedroll and spied Kelis, snoring and half slumped against wall of jagged rock, a sheathed dagger clasped loosely in one hand.

Using her magick to keep the bloodkin woman from stirring, Isa tucked the knife into her belt just in case. Eva might've removed those wretched shackles, but she had not armed her. Everyone else in their party was armed to the teeth and the distinction served as a reminder: Isa, still a prisoner.

Intending to relieve herself, she went still when she heard

laughter coming from outside, and crawled to the widest seam in the rock outcrop.

She didn't dare look out. It would've been foolish to consider anything but the obvious—the Second General had caught up to them during the night.

She waited until eventually two voices sounded again, one sedate and masculine and the other melodic and feminine with a southerner's lilt to her accent.

"Do you know . . . smoke them out? If we . . . the Queen will have our heads," the higher voice said.

"Hush, Sala," the other replied. ". . . this doesn't wake them, a small tremor will do."

A sound like grinding stone reached Isa's ears. She clutched the wall of stone as the ground slid beneath her feet.

She stepped out of the rock outcrop and slipped, tumbling forward in the sand. Her heart thumped in her chest. *Shit*.

This was her chance and she was already spoiling it. If that little trick of turning the hard ground to sand didn't wake everyone, she could use her magick to persuade Mateen to take her away from here, and leave the rest of them alone. If she couldn't persuade the General to leave Eva behind, well . . . How could Isa be blamed for that? What else could she be expected to do? Remain a prisoner and accept Eva's truce?

What happened when Eva changed her mind? Even Aketo would turn on her eventually. She stood in the way of their freedom—their history—and Isa didn't blame them for choosing Eva. But she still had to choose herself.

She managed to keep her footing and took in the sight before her. Spheres of magickal light bobbed in the air, illuminating the clearing where a good thirty men fanned out behind the one Isa assumed was Mateen and his companion. All but those two wore their masks. She'd been nursing the small hope to find the Captain of her guard among Mateen's battalion, but there was no sign of anyone but these Jackals.

She sensed the net of each of their minds. Isa's magick sense was something between seeing and feeling. She saw the will of every person she encountered. There was a certain vibration in the air around everyone's head—her Sorceryn tutors called it an aura—and when she conjured her magick, touching one of the many symbols on her arms, her mind could reach out and grasp those nets. It would only require a featherlight touch to supplant one of these soldiers' will with her own.

But ensnaring thirty minds, not including the man and the young woman standing less than twenty feet away, wouldn't be an easy matter. These men were all skilled and Gods only knew what magick they possessed.

The young woman that Isa had heard speak stood behind a kneeling man. Her skin was a flawless golden brown and her dark hair was done up in hundreds of narrow braids cascading over her shoulders. Isa noted the bandolier of throwing knives slung over one shoulder and the bow strapped to her back.

The man did not look up when Isa approached. His shirt-sleeves were folded back, displaying tattoos of rock forma-tions and gems rendered so vividly on his dark skin that they seemed to glitter in the moonlight. His iron will was like barbed prongs around his aura. This was a mind that did not like to be changed. It wouldn't be a problem for Isa, though. Many at Court were much the same. She'd learned to make her mind sharp as an arrow and deft as a Palace seamstress.

"Are you General Mateen?" Isa asked, casting her voice in a whisper.

The man finally lifted his chin, offering a smile cool enough to make Isa's entire body tense. But when he spoke, it was to his companion. "Is this her? The elder heir?"

Isa was pleased. At least now that he'd blatantly ignored and disrespected her, she would feel no guilt at ensnaring him. "I am, General," Isa said.

Only when the young woman cocked her head, studying Isa, did Isa remember she wore no glamour. A storm of racing thoughts left her holding her breath: Should she conjure the guise she wore at Court now? Lighten her hair and sharpen her nose and make her eye such a vivid green they would not look away? But no, she couldn't, not when they were staring right at her.

"Forgive us, Your Highness. Our battalion has been stationed north of the river for as long as I can remember . . . until recently we had little cause to visit the capital."

Isa smothered the bone-melting relief she felt at the woman's words. Of course they wouldn't recognize the minor changes in her appearance. The elite forces of the second battalions were never stationed in Ternain. They kept to the Myre-Dracol border, where they'd be most valuable.

"There is nothing to forgive, General Mateen and . . . what is your name?" Isa asked sweetly. Neither noticed as Isa stroked a finger down the thorny vines tattooed on her wrists. Her magick always felt like fire under her skin; the blossoming warmth burned on the edge of painful, but she loved it. To Isa, that pain came with freedom and power.

She extended her mental fingertips to the woman, loosening the soldier's tongue.

"I am Lieutenant Sala. We've come to"—she hesitated, glancing behind Isa to where the rest of her party still slept— "to help you, Princess Isadore."

Isa sensed this was only half truth.

"How did you find us? I thought I would never return south." She let a quaver creep into her voice as she drew deeply upon her magick. No more than a powerless noble.

General Mateen listened to their exchange with waning interest. He still knelt, hand buried in the sand, staring beyond her into the rock outcrops.

All of it made little sense. If they'd come for Isa, why did the General take no interest in her?

Sala's eyes had gone blank and her smile was lifeless and wan. Her mind firmly in Isa's grip now, the Lieutenant pulled a gold-and-green enamel ring from her pocket. "The Queen gave me this. I've been tracking you for weeks."

She snatched it from the woman's palm. A tracker . . . Isa eyed Sala, searching for signs of fey blood, and sure enough her ears were slightly pointed. As far as she knew, only the fey could track one person across hundreds of miles.

At this, Mateen finally stood. He squinted at Sala, taking note of the Lieutenant's vacant expression. His gaze swung back to Isa and the hand curled round one wrist, the finger stroking a tattoo of a serpent. Isa arched an eyebrow, daring him to order her to stop.

Instead he barked a laugh that made her skin crawl. "Sala, stand with the others. Princess Isadore and I need to have a talk."

Sala, mind still foggy from Isa's intrusion, walked back without a parting word.

Magick still roaring beneath her skin, Isa turned her focus to Mateen, who would still not grant her the dignity of rising to greet her.

"I am pleased to find you unharmed, Your Highness. The Queen warned us, any injury to you—before or after we retrieved you—would be repaid in kind."

Retrieved. The word made her stomach knot up. Like she was a toy or a trinket.

Still she sensed subterfuge through the General's will. His thoughts were a thicket too intricate for Isa to untangle—no matter how hard she tried, her magick could not grant her that ability—but the longer she probed at his mind, the more confused she felt. Could it be that they weren't here for her at all?

"What else did my mother's orders specify?" Isa asked. She needed a way into his mind.

Isa summoned the magick within her, that which required no tattoos to trigger, and appeared to *change*. Her hair, a mess of unruly gold curls, now looked like the silvery blond of her mother's coloring, and her skin took on the radiance of the sun, glowing with inner light.

And it was all false. Glamour did not change one physically, but instead cast an illusion so strong, only a fey of higher skill could penetrate it. And Isa had made sure she was strong, testing herself first against her fey nursemaid, Kitsina, and then against the fey nobles of the Court.

She heard the gasps of the nearby soldiers, and even Mateen's mouth fell open as she cloaked herself in glamour. Isa took two long steps forward to cup his cheek. Touch wasn't necessary for her magick, but it did make it easier to keep hold of a mind once it was in her thrall.

Remain still, she commanded, and all resistance left his body.

It would be foolish not to at least consider commanding him to take her back to the capital, no matter what his intentions were. She'd be wise to tell the General to capture them all. They would make it back to Ternain in a few months, even quicker if they hired a ship to sail down the coast and up through the River. After that, she would be named True Heir. And in a few years, Isa could persuade Mother to step down and she finally would take her seat upon the throne.

But betraying Eva like this? Marching back to the capital with her death in mind? She and Eva were closer to understanding each other than they'd been since they were children. Even though there wasn't exactly peace between them, Isa wanted to hold on to whatever this was for as long as she could.

You were ready to kill Eva just months ago, she reminded herself. Now was not the time to become queasy over bloodshed. It was the nature of the crown. As her mother was quick to remind her, our throne is draped in blood, whether the rest of the Court sees it or not.

But try as Isa might, the young woman who'd captured her sister's lover in order to kill her . . . That version of Isadore was harder and harder to hold on to the more time she spent outside of Ternain. The plan to capture Prince Aketo wasn't even hers at the start. And it didn't help that her memories of that night were hazy. Isa's only clear memories of her sister's nameday were the Entwining spell and Eva's transformation.

Several soldiers had unsheathed their blades and pointed them at her, but none dared approach. Yet.

Isa's eyes fell shut as she sought the magickal connection she and Eva had created during the Entwining and gave it a great yank.

When she opened her eyes again, Mateen glared up at Isa. Her concentration must have slipped, and though her command still held his body, his mind writhed in her grip like a fish on land.

"Why are you here?"

Before Mateen could answer, the air began to crackle with unspent magick.

It shouldn't have been possible for him to conjure any magick while she held him in place, but the ground beneath her feet quavered. There was that small tremor he'd mentioned earlier. Now that the soldiers could taste the magick on the wind, she would be facing down dozens of blades if she couldn't regain control of this situation.

General Mateen's eyes darted past her, widening.

Isa looked behind her. Whatever had drawn his attention, she couldn't see anything through the narrow seam in the rock. There was no way to know whether her attempt at waking Eva worked, but she suspected her and Mateen's combined efforts meant everyone was awake. Nonetheless she drawled, "Come on out, Eva. It seems you've been caught."

Isa sagged when Anali, Falun, and then her sister emerged, sword in hand, with Aketo following close behind her. The Captain's face was murder, and she held a short sword in either hand. Falun immediately eased an arrow from a quiver on his back and pointed it in Isa and Mateen's direction.

When she caught her sister's gaze, the look of disappointment in Eva's eyes was so familiar. Isa scanned Eva's mental net. Disappointment warred with a desire to protect Isa from this situation she'd found herself in. Eva already believed Isa had betrayed them.

It burned Isa up inside, even though she'd been considering just that.

While Mateen's Jackals had pointed their weapons in Isa's direction, they seemed unsure whom to point them at now. The whine of bowstrings pulling taut filled the air.

"What are our orders, General?" Lieutenant Sala called.

General Mateen began to tremble, fighting her still. She held to Mateen with dwindling magick, well aware he would break her hold if this went on much longer. She needed to draw more magick with her tattoos, but losing contact with his skin at this point would sever their connection.

Tell them to lay their weapons down, she commanded, but she met a wall of magick, roiling power, and will. A vein throbbed in Mateen's neck as he managed a minute shake of his head. "I'll not let you use me as a puppet, girl. Release me and you will find we are not your enemy."

Isa exchanged a glance with Eva, and at her sister's sharp nod, she backed away from the General and let her magick ebb away.

Anali, Fal, and Aketo charged forward in an instant, moving faster than her eye could track. When the Prince reached Isa, he shoved her behind his back and said, "You and Eva will run with Kelis and the rest. We'll hold them off."

"Hold off *thirty* soldiers?"

"We don't have many options here," Aketo replied tersely.

Behind them Mateen held up a hand. "Wait. We are here for the Princess. We intend you no harm, but if you insist on a fight, we can do that as well."

Eva walked forward until she stood at Isa's side. Isa could sense the soldier's shock at the sight of Eva. Mateen's gaze swept from the horns atop her head to the wings flared out behind her.

Isa registered the unsheathed sword in Eva's right hand just a moment before Eva drew the naked blade across her opposite palm. Eva groaned as blood welled, but the glare she gave Mateen did not waver.

A sigh hissed out between Eva's teeth as luminous crimson magick dripped from her palms to envelop the long, curved blade of her sword. Blood magick licked at the air like a living flame. "If you hope to take my sister back to Ternain, we do insist on a fight, General."

"I should have been more specific." He made a sharp gesture behind his back and the soldiers lowered their weapons. Then Mateen surprised them all by bowing deeply. "We are here for you, Princess Evalina."

CHAPTER 20

Eva

I DIDN'T WANT to trust him.

Even when General Mateen invited us to join him at their camp and presented a letter written in Papa's economical script, listing the five Queen's Army Generals I could trust to remain loyal to him in the event of his death, I couldn't shake my distrust. The letter was dated less than a week before his death, and an inexplicable surge of wrath made me want to crumple the letter.

Papa had written this when we were together at Asrodei; he could have just told me. I was beginning to accept I might never forgive him for all these secrets.

When Mateen's soldiers unmasked themselves, I noted that besides a few fey, most, including Mateen, were human. I saw the way they assessed my body. Their eyes flew wide at the sight of my horns, claws, and wings. I could hear the words none dared express: *monster, beast.*

I lifted my chin, threw my shoulders back, and stared down any whose gazes lingered too long.

Kelis emerged from the rock outcrop where she'd remained to watch over my cousins. All three followed behind her, clearly not pleased to find themselves among a company of soldiers. Lady Lirra took in the scene while palming her belt knife, Tavan twitched in that avian way of hers, and even steady Osir checked the leather straps around his shoulders that held vicious half-moon axes.

The General stood in front of me, waiting for a response to the letter and his declaration. He was a large man, towering above me by well over a foot. "Explain it all to me, Mateen. How did you come to have my sister's signet ring? The only way that I can think of is that my mother gave it to you, which flies in the face of your supposed loyalty to my father. And why the tricks with your magick?"

"At the end of High Summer, the Queen called our entire battalion, the first and the second, to Ternain. A few weeks after that, I was summoned before the Queen. She asked if I could be discreet and said she needed us to track Princess Isadore, because you had kidnapped her. She said we were to tell Isadore that she was to kill you before we returned to Ternain." Despite the General's crisp, matter-of-fact tone, my mother's cruelty once again hit me like a slap. Mateen went on. "She also told me about the King's true heritage, and made it clear I wasn't to share that truth with anyone. I could tell she only told me to denigrate Lei."

"And I am to take your presence here as proof it did not work?"

"Yes," he said, tucking a few stray locs behind one ear. "I decided to track Princess Isadore, not to bring her back, but to offer you our allegiance."

"Why? All of your people are prepared to do this?"

"I never would have joined the Queen's Army without King Lei. He recruited me when I was a teenager, using my magick, believe it or not, to pick pockets in the streets of a coastal town far west of here."

I squinted up at him, trying to imagine the street child he must have been. Picking pockets with earth magick?

Mateen surprised me with a warm chuckle. "Little distracts a rich man from his coin purse as thoroughly as the ground shifting beneath his feet."

That brought a fleeting smile to my lips. "What about the other half of your battalion? I see only Jackals here; where is the First General and his forces?"

"The First General is stationed just to the west of the Arym Plain, waiting for us to capture you and return. I did not share my intentions with the General; I'm afraid he's a Queen's man." That was unfortunate. Mateen's Jackals boasted a bevy of magickal gifts, but we could have used the sheer might of the First General's soldiers.

I glanced past Mateen and saw Isa, still glowing with unnatural beauty. As soon as Mateen had given me the letter, she had retreated. But now the understanding that I had been forcing to the back of my mind reared up again. I could ignore it no longer.

"Please excuse me, General." I offered him a tight smile. "I need to speak with my sister."

I stalked past Mateen and grabbed Isa's arm, hauling her away from listening ears.

When I let go, she rubbed at her skin where my claws had scratched her. I found I did not care.

"What do you think you're—" Isa started, but I cut her off.

"Did you not think I would notice?" How could I have been such a fool all this time, ignoring what was right in front of me? "You aren't in my head right now, and yet, look at you."

Isa's brows knit together. "What?"

"You're wearing glamour, Isa," I said, punctuating each word with a shove to her chest.

Each time I'd noticed Isa's darker curls, I'd just attributed the difference to the lack of potions and paints of the capital. Plenty of women at Court lightened and straightened their hair. Isa was no different, or so I'd believed.

I remembered the day I brought Baccha to Court. Isa had flexed her beauty then, as always, but I'd been under the thrall of her persuasive magick then. I'd assumed she was using her gift to convince everyone she was even lovelier than usual.

But it was apparent now I'd been wrong. No magickal fog was pulled over my mind. This was glamour.

"Stop. That," Isa spat, returning my aggression with a push that had me skidding back in the sand. "So now you know. I'm a liar and a hypocrite." She cast out a hand, at the soldiers and everyone else watching our exchange. "Here's your audience, Eva. Kill me now, expose Mother for letting the Court believe I was Lei's daughter. Bring your host of soldiers and Generals and take back the throne."

A noise of disgust escaped me. "I don't want to kill you. Did you know I killed five people last year? I didn't want to, but I had to protect myself. That's why I refuse to let the Rival Heirdom force my hand. That's why you're here. I've had enough of death. I just want the truth."

"Well, here you go," Isa said, lowering her voice so that

only we could hear. "I am half fey and don't ask who my father is, because Mother refused to tell me."

My heart thudded in my chest. "Oh, Isa, then why were you so angry at us? At Papa?"

Her appearance flickered and returned to what must have been her actual self. Her hair now a mess of golden-brown curls, freckles sprayed across her nose and cheeks, and her face overall softer than the one I'd gotten used to. "I was jealous. In my mind, you two shared a secret I'd been hiding since I was old enough to know what glamour was. You were always so close. I thought you'd been conspiring against me all along and I hated you both for it."

I shut my eyes for a moment, trying to make sense of her words. I'd always envied the bond between Isa and our mother so much, it never occurred to me that Isa might feel the same. I was so tired. I could've lain down in the sand right then and fallen asleep for a year.

And yet an entire crowd of people waited for me to decide what I would do. I could feel everyone's eyes on me; the waiting was like a cloying perfume in the air.

I turned from my sister and walked back to where the General stood, speaking quietly with one of his soldiers, a brown-skinned, younger woman with pointed fey ears.

Truth was, as much as I was reeling, Mateen's appearance, and apparent loyalty, changed little, except to give us a real chance of surviving a rebellion at Sher n'Cai. His Jackals' skill in battle and magick might be the edge that granted us a victory. And I had a notion to seek out the rest of the Generals in my father's letter. If they joined us at Sher n'Cai, I might actually be able to mount a force against the rest of the army when they came to root out rebellion.

"Mateen, you say you're still loyal to my father. Well, I'm going to give you a chance to prove it. We go north, to Sher n'Cai. I hope General Sareen is no friend of yours."

Mateen rocked back on his heels. I couldn't decide if he was impressed at my boldness or troubled. After a moment, though, he nodded. "We go where you command."

"And you have no problem following the commands of a khimaer?"

"Well, I didn't know it at the time, but I've been following the commands of a khimaer for nearly two decades. I don't see why that should change now."

I just prayed at least some of his colleagues felt the same.

- II -
QUEEN
OF
REBELS

Many scholars say the khimaer planned for rebellion the moment they surrendered in the First War. Others theorize that the human rulers' unforgiving laws forced their hand. One truth we know for certain: there was no avoiding insurrection. The khimaer will never consent to human rule.

—From *Killeen: The Cobalt Dagger of Myre*,
by Kreshi Isomar

CHAPTER 21

Baccha

"YOU LIED TO me," Ysai growled in lieu of a proper greeting. She shoved a cup of tea across the rickety table between them.

He'd been forced to sleep in the "cages" in the back of camp for the past four days. The cubes, made from woven strips of teakwood and packed mud, were only half his height. He'd been folded up on himself, contemplating kicking out one of the sides, so at least he could lie flat, when Ysai finally retrieved him. She said nothing as she undid the latch holding the cage shut. When Baccha half crawled and slithered out of the cursed little box, she'd surveyed him with a curling lip.

The indignity of it all might've infuriated a younger version of Baccha, but right now, he was just glad to be smelling something other than mud, sour sweat, and piss. Besides, he'd once been locked in a pine chest and left in a citrus grove for three months by a fellow magickian wanting to test the limits of his immortality. This was only a minor annoyance compared with that.

When Ysai walked away, Baccha knew he was to follow. They

went to her hideaway cave, where they'd first spoken at length.

"What a lovely surprise," Baccha said, settling down on a tree stump that passed as seating here. "Good morn to you, Mother Ysai. How can I, a lowly Hunter, be of service?"

She held up an empty tin cup, opened a small wound in her palm, and bled into it. She pushed it toward him with one clawed finger. Baccha hadn't noticed the claws the last time he'd seen her, but he'd noticed she favored small shifts in her form. One day when she visited his cell, she would have large fox ears, the next, long canine teeth poking out of her lips or a tufted tail lashing the air. A very tasteful, if curious, use of Khimaerani's power that made Baccha want to know the young Mother of the Tribe more.

"Drink."

"You know, Moriya used to brew me a cup of tea to make this a little more pleasant. Have the Elderi come to a decision yet?" Baccha said, stalling as he stared down at the swirling crimson liquid. "It has been several days now. I would've expected my news would make things much easier for you."

"Oh, is that why you waited so long to reveal it?"

He offered her a toothy grin. "Helping you is exactly why I waited, Ysai. I know you wouldn't have believed that we needed her without some . . . convincing."

"Drink," Ysai repeated, and Baccha followed the order, tossing back the contents of his cup.

"Why did you come here?" she asked as the coppery liquid slid down his throat.

As ever, it loosened his tongue. He answered honestly, "To ask Moriya to teach Eva how to wield Khimaerani's magick, and to request the Elderi's help in making Eva into the next Queen. So I can be freed from my oaths."

That last bit, he wished he could have held back. Baccha cringed at the light of victory in Ysai's storm-cloud eyes. "Just as I thought. This is all about your selfishness."

Baccha shrugged. "You may call me whatever you like, Ysai, but this is about righting my wrongs and fulfilling my duties as servant to the Tribe."

"Mother Ysai," she corrected absently. "It doesn't matter now. The Elderi have decided we will find your Princess and test her. And when she fails, you will be the one to slit her throat."

Baccha wasn't chilled by the threat. It was the same one she'd made before. "Perhaps I forgot to share this, but the Sorceryn placed quite a nasty spell on Eva and her sister. Because of it, Eva can't be killed by me or anyone but her sister."

Ysai smiled like a cat with a canary trapped behind her teeth. "Then you, Lord Hunter, shall endeavor to break that spell. Lucky for me, you are known to be gifted in a number of magicks."

Ysai rose from her seat as if she had said something of little consequence, nostrils flaring. "You should wash up. There is a stream nearby. We leave in two days. You are free to roam the camp until then."

"But where are we going?"

She cocked her head. "I told the Elderi you would lead us to the Princess. I hope you are able to find her. Else we will be forced to make other plans."

Baccha didn't doubt that if he couldn't offer Eva's exact location, Ysai would use that as an excuse to forgo the testing. If she got it in her mind to go to the Southern Enclosure first—a journey that could take at least six months during Far Winter—Baccha might miss the succession entirely.

Break a Sorceryn spell. See a khimaer girl to the throne. Be free of his oaths. If he accomplished those feats, he would make sure Aunt Lyse wrote a song about his most legendary accomplishments yet.

As she was leaving, Ysai called back to him. "One last thing, Hunter. You should have asked my mother more about our magick. Your Princess shouldn't need my help. The gift comes to you one way or another. And you'd best hope it has come to her, or she'll fail the testing."

At that, he offered a silent prayer to Khimaerani on Eva's behalf. But there was nothing he could do about Eva's magick or lack thereof now.

Once Ysai was out of earshot, Baccha climbed to his feet, muttering his oldest and most emphatic curse. He would wash his aged bones and then search for Eva. It could not be so difficult. She'd stepped right into his head. He shouldn't have any difficulty waltzing into hers.

He summoned his wolves, instructing them to find the stream Ysai mentioned. He wasn't going to stumble around this mountain searching for hours. And he needed an excuse to expend all the magick that had built up in the last days. He'd forgotten the headaches that plagued him when he went without using magick.

A brown-and-white-speckled whelp returned a few minutes later and herded him out of the cave, happily prancing through the snowdrifts and nudging him with her snout. The narrow stream was covered with an inch of ice that Baccha melted by calling a warm Wind from the South. The Wind wasn't near hot enough to make the icy water bearable, but Baccha, having grown up on a mountain like this, couldn't complain. It was deep enough to cover his shoulders, little silver-and-brown fish darting around his ankles. He found an abandoned cake of soap and a bucket on the shore.

Baccha washed up and laundered his clothes, calling for more Wind to dry them both. Once he'd dressed, he made sure no one was nearby and settled down on a large rock.

Eyes shut, Baccha's mind stepped into the Wind.

Well, he didn't *step* exactly, but it felt like that. Like his mind had undone its tether to his body so that it could be carried on the Wind. For the first years of the life, being carried away on the Wind was the only way he came in contact with other people. From a mountaintop not far from here, he'd let his mind wander for hours, venturing to the South, where fey built great kingdoms, calling upon the elements to carve out cities in the highlands.

As he'd done before, he coasted on a chill Far Winter gale, flying south. Seeking Eva's scent.

The truth was that not all scents were unique to one person. Certainly, some particular combinations of smells might only belong to one person, but more often than not, one had to look beyond the various aromas and discern the true essence beneath.

When Baccha first caught Eva's scent—untamed ferocity, blood oranges, and ancient power—he thought he must have been mistaken. She was far too close.

He'd expected to find her much farther south. What could she be doing in the mountains near the border?

It occurred to Baccha that he should have asked Eva what exactly she was up to the last time he checked in on her.

Baccha followed the faint scent, seeing through the Wind's eyes until he reached a sizable camp, just over the Dracolan border, not a hundred leagues from where Baccha currently sat.

Dozens of men and women in soldier white—perfect camouflage for Far Winter in the A'Nir—sat around cook fires.

He spotted Falun at one, stoking the flames with a belt knife, while the young woman sitting next to him plucked feathers from a quail.

Baccha continued his search, winging through the trees around the camp, before he came to an abrupt stop. At the center of the camp, there was a long table with two maps spread across it. One depicted the A'Nir with marked trails through mountain passes and the other he did not recognize, showing the layout of a strange city. Eva leaned over the first map, shifting an enamel paperweight. He read the words on her lips: "Sher n'Cai."

Aketo and the Captain of her guard, Anali, stood on either side of the Princess, all three watching as an older man with a jackal mask hooked to his belt gestured at the second map.

Eva looked up, scanning the tree line, with nostrils flaring. *Scenting the air.*

It had never occurred to the Hunter once in his hundreds of years that his scent was likely carried on the Wind. Fool that he was.

Baccha's eyes flew open, and he found himself sitting by the stream, legs folded up beneath him. He fought to make sense of what he'd seen—Eva in the mountains, in the company of soldiers, scouring maps, and intent on the Enclosure. But there couldn't have been more than forty people in the camp. Not a force large enough to mount an insurrection.

Did Eva have nerve enough to try to spark a rebellion?

A slow smile spread across Baccha's face. The Elderi would want to know about this and, he hoped, help. He climbed to his feet and made for the camp.

❧ CHAPTER 22 ❧

Isadore

AMONG ALL THE indignities Isadore had suffered since becoming and unbecoming her sister's prisoner, stumbling through knee-deep snowdrifts in ill-fitting boots, while Eva and Aketo worked together to guide them up a mountain, their making eyes at each other whenever the other wasn't looking was absolutely the worst.

It had taken two weeks to reach the mountains and two more after that to reach the base of the one where the Enclosure perched. Journeying with General Mateen and his soldiers made for much smoother travel than their first months on the run. The battalion had plenty of extra horses—Isa had quite missed riding—and they broke camp each morning with quick efficiency.

Isa was surprised she'd even been invited on today's excursion. When Aketo came to her tent yesterday to ask her to come on this trek up the mountain, she'd immediately said yes. They were to look for a cave that served as a secret entrance to the Enclosure. Only a small group would actually sneak into the

Sher n'Cai. The rest would wait in the mountains until they decided to strike at the General who governed Sher n'Cai. Isa didn't want to be left with soldiers she barely knew. And a small, buried voice inside wanted to know whether a chance still existed for peace—no, love—between her and Eva.

So far it seemed like the answer to that was a resounding no. In the days after they fled from Orai, Eva hadn't demanded Isa return to wearing the shackles, but Isa didn't see it as an act of goodwill. It was more likely she'd forgotten, spending her days bent over maps with the General, Anali, and Aketo. Eva had all but ignored Isa since finding out that she was fey, and Isa didn't know what to make of it. Eva was still dead set against their fight to the death, but beyond that, who knew what their future would hold?

Every morning Isa woke up dreaming of escape, but where would she go? A week ago, they had passed through a small mountain village to trade their horses for the supplies required to traverse the mountains. She could have fled then, but it wouldn't have been difficult to track her. The few roads this far north were muddy because of the snows. Traveling alone from the A'Nir to Ternain would have been difficult in any case, but alone and with soldiers chasing her? Impossible.

When they met on the outskirts of camp at dawn, Eva greeted everyone warmly. She embraced Anali, Falun, the trio of Eva's family from the Arym Plain, and even Kelis, who'd only come along because she was assigned to watch over Isa. Then her eyes slid right off Isa as if she weren't there.

Isa reminded herself indifference was certainly a better reaction to the revelation that she was fey than she deserved.

The sun was right overhead now and Isa was beginning to regret the choice to come along. The ground was soggy with moldering leaves and melting snow. Mountains rose on every side. And despite the shearling-lined blanket wrapped around Isa, held in place with a wide belt, and a pair of thick leather gloves, she could not quell her shivering.

She watched Eva and Aketo, their heads bent together as they discussed the route, with growing resentment. It served as a perfect reminder to Isa just how infuriating it was that Eva believed she'd been so deprived of love, all because of their mother. Eva might not see it, but she had the love of this boy and she'd had the love of the Lord Hunter before his strange disappearance.

Isa had never been in love. By now she was certain she'd never have a chance to learn the soft contours of the emotion. There had been dozens of affairs of convenience—and curiosity. Scullery maids and courtiers and even a soldier in her guard. She had kissed countless young men and women. Yet she'd never felt any love from them—only hunger and much of it not focused on her, but on her power. Even when she tugged at their emotions, she couldn't conjure love where it did not exist.

Isa did not look forward to the hours without any sun, trapped with Eva and Aketo sorting through their emotions while Anali rubbed her sword hilt anytime she caught Isa's gaze. The Captain had not come to trust Isa. In fact, the woman seemed to take the removal of her shackles weeks ago as an excuse to keep one hawkish eye on her at all times.

Osir, Lady Lirra, and Tavan didn't seem to have any interest in knowing her. That Lei had been her father her entire life did not matter to them. Only Kelis was easy to be around, as she never projected outright hostility. If Isa could concentrate on her magick and keeping her footing in the snow, she might have tugged at the bloodkin woman's aura until Kelis walked beside her. Instead Isa trailed behind them all, stopping occasionally to adjust her too-tight boots.

Isa shuddered violently as wet clumps of snow began to fall. Twenty or so feet ahead, Eva and Aketo had stopped. Isa hiked up her thick tights and jogged a few steps to catch up with them. She gritted her teeth as the blisters on her toes protested such vigorous movement.

"Why have we stopped?" Isa asked, her breath fogged in the frigid air.

Like Isa, Eva was used to the heat of the South. A scarf Isa suspected belonged to the Prince was wrapped around Eva's head, yet she trembled, shifting her weight from foot to foot to keep warm. Slight amusement softened the annoyance in Eva's expression. "Aketo is lost."

Isa was surprised Eva had even answered her.

"I am not lost," Aketo protested. "The cave entrance is difficult to find for a reason. I expected we'd come upon it an hour ago, but we must be close now." Snowflakes covered Aketo's curls, but he was at ease in the cold. "We can continue as one or split up."

"Separating seems a bit reckless, all things considered," Isa said. From the eyebrows raised in her direction, her input clearly was not wanted, but she refused to care. Aketo had promised them warm beds when they made it through the caves.

"Princess Isadore is right," one of Eva's cousins, Osir, murmured in his rich baritone. Snow was gathering on his antlers and Isa fought down a laugh at the sight of it. "We could easily become lost in this."

"A fair point." Anali sighed. "And yet, we waste time and risk being caught out here the longer we search."

Eva nodded. "Agreed."

"I'm with Kelis," Isa cut in.

Once again every head swung her way. Eva was first to react, her expression caught between annoyance and mild curiosity. Her gaze shifted to the bloodkin woman. Wondering, perhaps, if Isa was interested in her. "Very well. Anali, Aketo, and I will continue north; Osir, Lirra, and Tavan will venture farther west; and Falun will go with you two to retrace where we have already searched, if that is all right with *all* of you."

Falun glared at Eva—since the beginning of their trek up the mountain, he'd avoided Isa like she carried the plague—but after smoothing away a grimace, he offered no complaints.

"I've no problem with holding the Princess's leash," Kelis said with a grin, her fangs flashing in the sunlight.

Isa rolled her eyes. She *had* briefly entertained the idea of flirting with Kelis, but then recalled some courtier explaining that bloodkin liked to drink from their partners. Much as her recent experiences had done to show her how little she knew about bloodkin and khimaer, she was not quite ready to investigate whether that rumor was true.

Aketo taught them a birdcall to use in case they found the cave and they agreed to meet back here in an hour.

Despite Kelis's cheek, the woman did not care to hold on to Isa's leash very tightly—that or she rightly guessed Isadore was too smart to take her chances with the mountains—because after a while of tracking their path back through the snow, she and Falun let Isa slow until she trailed far behind them.

Ahead of her, Falun helped Kelis climb over a massive fallen tree. When Isa came to it, she sat, swearing she would stop just long enough for her blisters to cease their pulses of pain in time with her heartbeat. All she wanted was a big platter of moon and sun pastries from the palace kitchens and a steaming pot of tea. The cold made her thoughts sluggish and strange.

She heard Kelis in the distance calling for her to hurry. Falun replied, and though Isa couldn't quite catch his words, she doubted they were kind.

How long was she going to stay on this course? Long enough to sate her curiosity about the Enclosure at least. She would need to escape at some point. This strained silence could only last so long, until everyone realized she was the lone barrier keeping her sister—her powerful, *blessed* sister—from the throne. The goal of escaping her sister felt less and less pressing every day. Ternain seemed so far from here, and for a moment, Isa imagined what if would be like if her fate was not chained to the throne.

She pictured Myre's salt-crusted northern coast again. She could march north until she forgot Princess Isadore had ever existed. Lord Baccha said he'd lived in Dracol for years; maybe she could forget herself there too. If Baccha had managed to hide his identity, surely she could.

When Isa first heard the crunch of boots on snow behind her, she assumed it was Kelis and Falun, circling back to retrieve her. "Come to collect me?"

She climbed to her feet, wincing as the pain in her feet began again in earnest. She heard a sharp intake of breath behind her and froze. Had a soldier caught onto their trail?

Three things struck Isadore as she in turn gasped: Kelis was far beyond her sight now, she was armed with only a single dagger, and she was completely alone.

Remembering the Entwining loosened some of the tightness in her chest. Her life, at least, was not in danger. But there were so many other things to consider.

Isa unsheathed her dagger—the same one she'd taken from Kelis many weeks ago—and spun, words racing out of her mouth. "Before you decide to attack me, know you will regret it. I am no easy meat."

"And why would I have need to attack you?" a deep, masculine voice whispered through the trees in a way that made Isa's skin crawl. *Magick.*

Isa's mouth went dry as a young man stepped out from behind one of the trees. He was beautiful and utterly foreign.

He was obviously khimaer. Velvety white antlers sprang from his brow, each of the prongs decorated with a slightly different gold ring. Long thick mahogany curls, the texture even denser than Eva's, spilled down his back and softened his sharp jawline and high cheekbones. His lips, full and downturned as he and Isa inspected each other, needed no softening. His skin was light brown; the warm undertone in his skin was complemented by threads of burnished gold in his hair and cinnamon freckles on the bridge of his nose. It looked as though his eyes—their color like sunlight on clover honey—were lined dramatically in kohl to make them seem more catlike.

He wore a sleeveless vest lined with matted shearling, which would have been shocking were it not completely overshadowed by the tawny fur covering his arms. So perhaps it wasn't kohl at all.

As he stepped forward, Isa realized that his bearing and bone structure immediately reminded her of Aketo. Tension eased from her so suddenly that she stumbled across the fallen tree and fell right on her ass.

"I know who you are," she said. She'd asked Aketo about his older brother once; she couldn't quite remember his name, and yet . . . she was certain.

"I doubt that," he said slowly. His accent had a way of rounding each syllable so that it took her a moment to understand. "How would a human girl come to know me? Which reminds me, how does a human girl come to be here, of all places?"

Part of Isa wanted to protest. She was not human, or at least not *only* human. But the stronger part of her, the part that had discovered the truth about her being a bastard long before her mother ever told her, still liked to keep that information shoved into the furthest reaches of her consciousness. She feared if she thought too long on it, there would be no stopping her from falling apart.

"I know you are Aketo's brother and a Prince," Isa said, squinting against the sunlight that framed his body. "I know you knew my father. I even know what you must be here to guard."

In one smooth movement, the Prince pulled a long-handled knife from his belt. She noted the tail undulating in the air behind him. A lion must have been the animal he shared flesh with. Aketo's features clearly favored that of a snake, but perhaps they had different fathers.

He pointed the knife at her, though there was still enough distance between them that it was barely a threat. "Get up."

"I must kindly ask you to lower that," Isa said through gritted teeth. She lifted her dagger, pointing it in his direction. "I can make threats too."

He glanced at her weapon like it was of little concern. "My brother is far from here in the South. I do not know how you came to know his name, but—"

"Your brother fled from Ternain when he aided my sister in my capture." She reached for his mental net, but found it nearly impenetrable. Just as Aketo's mind had always given her trouble, the desires and dreams floating around this boy's head weren't hers to toy with. "Or has the news not reached you this far north?"

He pointed again with the knife. "Get up. I don't know who you are, but no human should tread this path."

Isa's fine control on her anger snapped. What was the danger really?

In three long strides, she came within a hand's length of the blade. Isa's thin arms were covered in pale scars from learning to fight with knives when she was younger, so she had no fear of a naked blade. She reached for the hilt, but he caught her wrist. "I asked you to stop pointing this at me."

This close, he was lovelier than she first thought. His leonine eyes seemed to glow as he stared at her.

"Who are you?"

She switched to Khimaeran, hoping that would make him listen. "Have you ignored every word I've said? My name is Isadore. Your brother and my beloved sister, Evalina, are somewhere nearby. He went south, as you say, to guard her."

He cocked his head, his smile edged in laughter. "I speak Common perfectly fine. Your Khimaeran is abysmal."

"Do you just *listen* poorly, then?" she asked, baring her teeth to outmatch his wickedness. "I am telling the truth, Princeling."

His nostrils flared at *Princeling*, but he finally relented. He dropped her arm and took a step backward as if fearing retribution. The blade rasped as he eased it back into its scabbard.

"Finally," Isa said, rubbing at the spot below her wrist where his warmth still lingered. He'd been careful to keep a tight grip, but it was not painful. "Aketo told me your name but I can't quite re—"

"Dthazi," he said, still watching her warily. "Are you truly her, then? Princess Isadore?"

D-thazi. She wanted to roll the name around on her tongue a few times to get the feel of it, but refused to give him the satisfaction.

"What, unimpressed?"

"Not . . . unimpressed. I am simply wondering why it is you are still alive if it is as you say. If you are indeed Princess Evalina's prisoner, why hasn't she killed you yet?"

Well, that was one way to state it plainly. "If I could understand every decision my sister does or does not make, I doubt I would be here. You're free to ask her when they finally get around to searching for me."

"Or you could be lying. Maybe you aren't lost. Maybe you escaped."

"Or maybe my sister was too weak to kill me and granting me freedom is the only way to assuage her guilt for ever considering it."

That was Isa's best theory at this point. Few things were more powerful than a guilty conscience, especially when one needs to believe in their personal goodness.

Isa rarely let herself feel guilty over the things she'd done. Her mother taught her early on that being good did not get you what you wanted. Only being ruthless could ensure that.

"Then I should do her a favor and kill you, as I have no such weakness."

Isa shrugged, eyes sliding past him and into the trees. When *would* they search for her? "You are welcome to try, though I'll warn you. If it were that easy, I assure you I would be long dead by now."

"So you say." His voice did that spine-tingling thing where

it seemed to move with the wind as it blew through the trees. "And you are quite good at feigning fearlessness, but I can hear your heartbeat from here and it tells a different story."

She leveled a flat look in his direction. It wasn't fear that made her pulse race, but his beauty. She pulled off her scarf—despite the cold, sweat dripped down her back—and lifted her chin, suppressing a shudder as a snowflake landed on her bare neck. "Do your worst."

Dthazi stepped toward her, but the sound of snow crunching underfoot sent them both flying apart, hands grasping for weapons.

Isa noted with some amusement that Dthazi took a half step, positioning himself in front of her. A second later Aketo came crashing through the trees, arms open, a smile so wide it seemed to split his face in two. He slipped into Khimaeran, speaking too quickly for Isa to understand much.

Then the two young men were embracing, both wiping away tears of joy and relief.

Their joy struck Isa the most profoundly. It was like looking at the sun, their mental auras too bright with happiness to stare. Kelis and Anali followed Aketo through the trees, Eva on their heels. When her sister caught sight of the brothers together, her face softened. But just like Isa, she could watch for only a moment before looking away, and joined Isa.

She shifted uneasily, eyes flitting to Isa and away again, until she finally whispered, eyes on Aketo and Dthazi, who were still embracing, "Hard to imagine that."

Isa laughed because she'd been thinking the same thing. This display of familial affection should have been normal to them, yet it was anything but. Once Isa had hoped that when Eva returned to Court, they would have such a reunion, but that was before Eva spent those years away ignoring every letter Isa sent.

Isa and her sister looked on and it was with some comfort that Isa noticed Eva felt just as awkward as she did.

"Kelis and Falun lost track of you?" Eva asked. Worry that this was some attempt at an escape rolled off Eva's skin, mingling with anger at her guards.

Isa shrugged, trying and failing to smother her annoyance. "I fell behind and I sat down to rest my feet. I told you I would go to Sher n'Cai, Eva. I am not going to slip away in the night."

Eva sighed. "I know. I believe you. I want to, but . . ."

Isa understood the feeling. She wasn't quite ready to abandon her distrust either. "How about I let you know the next time I am planning a betrayal."

Eva smirked. "Isn't a defining aspect of betrayal that it comes by surprise?"

"I suppose I should rescind that offer, then," Isa said, shaking off the snow settling in her hair and cowl. She was back to her natural golden curls and she didn't miss how Eva's eyes tightened at the sight.

"Why, Isa? Did Mother . . . make you use glamour?" Eva asked, voice soft. This was a conversation for their ears only.

"She never forced me to do anything," Isa whispered. "Is it so surprising? I always wanted to be just like her."

"I always thought you wanted to be like yourself. I never thought . . ." Eva shook her head. "Your true face is a high price to pay to be like Mother."

If Isa had any Gods to pray to, she would have thanked them when the boys broke apart, cutting their conversation short.

Dthazi punched Aketo in the gut. "That is for leaving without telling me."

Seeking retribution, Aketo grabbed his brother's antlers and flipped him onto his back. Dthazi swept Aketo's feet out from under him and pinned him almost casually. "Don't tell me you've been away so long you think you can best me now."

"Unlike you, brother, I never underestimate my opponents." He escaped Dthazi handily and pulled his brother to his feet. "Please let me introduce you. This is Princess Evalina and Princess Isadore." He added, with a significant look, "Lei's daughters."

Isa wanted to protest, but she held her tongue, because the words felt like truth.

⚙ CHAPTER 23 ⚙

Eva

AKETO AND DTHAZI chattered in Khimaeran as the two led us to the cave mouth. Kelis and Falun had come looking for Isa and found us all, and Isa didn't bother to hide her grin while I chastened them. Anali had circled back to collect my cousins, and after greetings were exchanged, Dthazi took the lead.

After about five minutes of walking we reached the entrance. The ground around the opening was free of all vegetation, but what I thought were massive pillars of ice dripping from the top of the cave turned out to be vines with fat white flowers and rubbery leaves I had never seen before.

Ice coated the petals, but their sweet, almost fruity scent filled the air. I reached out to grab one of the flowers, frost melting beneath my fingertips. "How?"

"The land doesn't always play by the season's rules in the North," Aketo explained.

"Our great-mother says it's because Myre's ancient and strangest magicks retreated into the mountains after the Great War," Dthazi added, smiling at the disbelief in our eyes.

"Even in deepest winter, some flowers never stop blooming."

"Come on," Aketo said, pulling back the vines so they could duck inside.

It was warmer inside the cave, but only just. Ice crusted the walls near the entrance, and beneath the frost, the gray stone glittered faintly, as if it were embedded with jewels.

The deeper into the cave they got, the more pronounced the glittering became until the walls actually glowed, lighting their path forward. When Osir asked Dthazi about the light, he explained that old fey magick made the crystal embedded deep in the stone light their path. Out of respect for the ancient fey and Godlings who had built this place and made a network of these caves, they didn't question the strange intricacies of Sher n'Cai. They simply counted them as a blessing from Khimaerani that after centuries the magick still held. I wondered if Baccha would know anything about it, but the city that had once been here might've already fallen by the time he was born. He'd said he grew up in isolation.

Isa and I walked beside each other, but we barely spoke. It required all my concentration to follow Dthazi and Aketo's conversation, but I certainly wouldn't have had anything to say to her otherwise. In the weeks since we left the Arym Plain, I had thought of a hundred different things to say to my sister, yet every time I tried to speak to her, some other need presented itself. I happily took on any minor task to distract me from her and the potential fallout from rebellion.

Isa frowned at the brothers' backs as we scooted around a massive stalagmite bursting through the ground, a geyser of stone. I stumbled and Isa caught my hand before I could slip.

I looked to Aketo and Dthazi. "Do you want me to translate?"

Isa lifted her chin, ever the Princess, even with her nose pink-tipped and dripping from the cold. "I can understand . . . most of it."

"You can speak Khimaeran?"

Color rose in Isa's cheeks. "Before Papa left, he made sure my Sorceryn tutors knew to keep up my lessons. Even if the palace instructors wouldn't. I can hear it better than I speak it."

My chest tightened, surging with love and longing, and I blinked away sudden tears, which was still the usual response at any mention of my father.

"I'm sorry," I said, even though I wasn't exactly sure what I was apologizing for. Maybe it was because we had left her to fend for herself. Of course, Isa had been swept up in Mother's spell. What else did I expect? Isa's entire persona at Court was an imitation of how the Queen ran it, with a seamless blend of charm and cruelty that kept her in control.

"Don't be." Isa sniffed.

We made our way around small frozen pools of water and every so often passed more vines and moss peeking through seams in the stone, still verdant and blooming despite the lack of sun.

After an hour of walking, we came to a fork, one path leading into a pool of water. No crystals lit the path to that surface, so you couldn't tell whether it was a small pond like the rest we'd passed, or a vast lake. I stared into the dark waves, reminded of my mindscape, but when a long, milky-white tail arced through the placid surface, I careened back.

Suddenly Aketo was there, wrapping an arm around my waist, guiding me away from the lake. I hadn't realized it, but I'd drifted much closer to its edge than I should have. A few more steps and I would have fallen right in.

"*Shit,*" I breathed. "What was that?"

"Nothing to worry us," he said, giving my hand a squeeze. "An old thing that just wants to be left alone, most likely."

We took the other path, but it didn't lead to more caves. The walls had been sheared down and polished until perfectly smooth, and instead of more stone underfoot, thick, springy moss carpeted the floor. This tunnel had to have been created with magick.

We reached the end of the tunnel, marked by a round door with three interlocking rings, but Aketo stopped. "We're going to wait here for a few hours. This tunnel opens to a road and, at the end of it, the stairway up to the Aerie. It's too public for us to climb them by daylight."

"The Aerie?" Isa asked when we'd settled down on the mossy floor.

I'd forgotten she hadn't been in our countless meetings with General Mateen, where Aketo explained the layout of the Enclosure.

"Sher n'Cai is made up of three main parts: General Sareen's manor and the grounds where the soldiers live; the town outside of it where we are supposed to live; and the Aerie, high up on the mountain, where we actually live. Years before I was born, we left the town and moved up into the Aerie. Over the years, it became its own village. And it keeps the soldiers from breathing down our necks all the time."

"Why is that?" Isa asked, looking at Dthazi.

His full lips pressed flat into a thin line while he gave Isa a look that would've made me squirm. It wasn't a heated look. It seemed more like he was deciding if she deserved an answer. Deciding if she actually cared. I would've bet he was at least as discerning as Aketo, if not more.

My sister gave him a simpering smile, and cocked her head, waiting.

"The only way up to the Aerie is by a set of narrow, very steep steps carved into mountain," Dthazi explained. "Throllo only sends the soldiers up once a week for inspections." His gaze slid to me. "You still haven't told me what you're doing here. Aren't you two supposed to be at each other's necks by now? What about the throne?"

"It's a long story, but as to why we're here . . . we've come to rid you of a problem," I said. "When you say the word *rebellion*, Dthazi, what do you hear?"

"I hear war drums and singing," he said, offering a grim smile. "What would you say if I told you I was already planning one?"

"Glad to hear it. We can offer some aid." I told him how we'd come to travel in the company of the now-rogue Second General and his small but powerful squadron. "Each one is worth at least three regular soldiers. Aketo tells me the same is true of your force here."

Dthazi hung his head. "Ah, I'd hoped you'd say each one was worth ten. Considering Throllo just had another two hundred soldiers transferred here, I'm afraid we are still quite outnumbered."

❋

We finished off the last of the dried meat and I tried to rest, but couldn't fall asleep. The mood had shifted with Dthazi's revelation. Aketo had estimated no more than two or three hundred soldiers were stationed at Sher n'Cai, so this changed everything. Anali ordered Kelis to return to General Mateen and inform him there might be more patrols crawling these mountains than we'd expected.

When night fell, Aketo and Dthazi rolled back the door to the tunnel. They waited until their eyes had adjusted to the thin light. After Dthazi returned from a check for any nearby patrols, we left the caves behind and finally stepped into Sher n'Cai.

The air was dry and crisp, but apart from the cliff faces that rose up on every side, we could've been walking on any street in Myre. Except that everything was made from the same pale limestone. Simple, single-story homes with tiled roofs lined the narrow, abandoned road we stepped out into.

I looked up to see a sickle moon peeking out behind two craggy mountains, striped with ocher dirt and patches of forest where there was no snow. The moon looked close enough to reach out and touch, like a double-ended dagger I would've tucked into my belt.

At Dthazi's instruction, we jogged up the road, keeping low. I was aware just how exposed we were. All it would take was one errant soldier looking on, and we would be caught. But it was a short run to the steps, which were just as I imagined. Like the stairs that winded up the side of Asrodei, there was no railing, only an open side to a sheer drop. If one fell spectacularly enough, they could go sliding down the side of the mountain.

I nearly turned back to the cave. I would return when I learned to use my wings properly, I promised. This was just the motivation I needed, and the irony of that fact didn't escape me. Avoid my fear of heights by learning to fly? Ridiculous.

I wasn't ashamed to clutch Aketo's hand the entire way up, counting each of the nearly two hundred steps. The climb was almost completely vertical, but every time my gaze strayed to the edge of the steps, he squeezed my hand and pulled me up to the next ledge.

We finally reached the zenith, a new layer of sweat cooling on my skin. I stood frozen for a long moment, a gasp on my lips.

The glowing crystals from the cave walls were embedded in the flagstones, lighting the way up a street. Small houses lined one side of the street, many stacked on top of each other like creo tiles, each facade painted a different color.

On the other side, just before the ledge of the mountain that held the Aerie fell away, tall, thin trees with silvery bark and chartreuse leaves clung to finger-width branches in cloudlike clumps. More of those flowering vines clung to the roofs of the Aerie's small homes, along with strands of dried flowers hanging in every window. Though it was still bracingly cold, only an inch of snow had accumulated on the trees. It made little sense that the flowers still bloomed in the midst of winter, further evidence that Sher n'Cai was brimming with old magicks.

It was beautiful.

As we walked down the Aerie's single street, khimaer spilled out of their homes, calling warm greetings to their Princes. As late as it was, I was surprised to find so many still up and about, but Dthazi explained that as soldiers rarely came up here, the Aerie still hummed with activity late into the night. In the town below, their movement was so restricted by General Sareen's rules that they made all they could of nights in the Aerie. Faint sounds of music spilling from doorways and open windows reminded me of the Patch. I ducked my head, but besides a few nods and some pointed looks at Aketo's fingers laced through mine, no one recognized me. Isa was too busy studying the Aerie to even notice the people.

We came to the last two houses on the street. The first was the color of sea foam with a stone path leading right up to the door. A young woman, who looked a good five years older than me, watched them from the porch. Like the khimaer we'd already passed, she wore layered and heavily embroidered clothing, along with a thick woolen cloak wrapped around her shoulders. Hundreds of narrow golden brown braids hung down her back, dotted with glossy beads. Ram's horns framed a broad face, dominated by wide-set amber eyes. A sharp, almost-masculine jawline made her even more striking, and like Dthazi's lion eyes, her eyes were rimmed in black.

"Dthazi, this is what you've been busy with all evening?" she called before jogging down the path toward them. A tail that ended with a tuft of sienna fur twitched in the air behind her. For a moment, I wondered if she was Dthazi's wife, but no, they looked too similar. Family, then.

Aketo's hand slipped from mine as he moved to greet her. He folded her into a tight hug and Dthazi, taller and wider than the both of them, joined their embrace, wrapping an arm around each of their shoulders.

The young woman pulled back, eying Aketo like he was an apparition. "What are you doing here? Why didn't you send word you were done playing soldier for the humans?"

She spoke in Khimaeran, but thanks to Lirra's lessons, I could follow her words with little difficulty. A flush warmed my face. *Playing soldier.* Was that what he'd been doing?

"Hush, a few of those humans are still with me," Aketo replied mildly. "Sending word could have endangered us, and from what I can recall, you *like* surprises."

She lifted her chin, sniffing the air. "I smell no humans. You know I'd never mistake their reek."

Aketo flinched but stepped away from the woman to wave a hand in my direction.

"Eva, Isa," Aketo said. "May I introduce you to my cousin Yayazi? She commands our force here alongside my brother."

Yayazi flashed a grin, revealing a set of canines longer and sharper than even Baccha's teeth. "Call me Yaya."

I gave her what I hoped was a warm smile and replied in Khimaeran, "Good to meet you."

"You forgot to mention, brother, that's *Princess* Evalina and *Princess* Isadore," Dthazi said.

For some reason, this prompted Isa to glare up at him. Dthazi simply smiled sweetly in response.

Yaya's demeanor shifted, now watching us with blatant suspicion. "Is that so."

"It is a long story, there is much to explain. But first, I'd like to see my mother," Aketo said, pointing his chin toward the last house on the street, unique only because no one stood out front.

Two more homes were stacked on top of it, accessible through ladder rungs up one side of the structure. Aketo took my hand again and started in the direction of the house, but Dthazi stopped him.

"Mama will want to see Eva alone first," he said, and turned to Isa. "And you as well."

I tried to catch Aketo's eye but his hand slipped out of my grip and he was too intently studying the horizon for me to read anything.

Isa and I approached the front door, and I knocked. A feminine voice called, "Come on inside. Please."

I pushed open the door, unsure of what to expect. A beautiful woman leaned against a round table in the back of the room. Curling impala horns, just like Aketo's, spiraled up from her brow. She wore a simple green silk dress, banded at the waist, and her glossy sable hair was woven into two long plaits. Like Aketo's, gold and black scales stretched from her shoulders down to her wrists, where they met chestnut skin.

A sleeping toddler rested on her hip, one of the braids clutched in its small brown hands.

I stopped moving. Stopped thinking of anything but those small brown fists.

When I tried to speak, to introduce myself, words failed me.

Daischa straightened and took a few tentative steps closer, one arm propping up the child, the other hand pressed against the child's brow.

She stopped within arm's reach, frowning at my frozen expression. "My, you two are lovelier than Lei could ever convey."

Daischa followed my gaze to her hand on the toddler, and explained, "He is a fussy boy. By his age, Aketo and Dthazi slept so easily. Self-soothing is how we first test out our gift." She shifted the infant to her opposite hip, and wouldn't meet my eyes as she continued. "But I'm afraid Otho will take after his father."

Otho.

She gestured to the table behind her. "Please sit. We don't want to make my other boys wait too long. And . . ." Her voice trailed off for a moment, eyes going unfocused, before her gaze settled on me again, her lips twisting into a wry smile. "Aketo worries I will mishandle this."

"Mishandle what?" Isa asked.

Daischa sighed, a tinge of regret in her tone. "I apologize for being so abrupt, but I find frankness and honesty is the best approach in delicate matters. You may or may not know that your father was my lover for the last four years. I must assume, from the look on Eva's face, she's already guessed that Otho is your brother."

There was a long pause. Isa's face betrayed nothing of her emotion. There were no trembling lips, no shining eyes. Only words just above a whisper and the beginnings of a pivot that would see her running out the door: "Lei isn't—wasn't my father. Not truly."

Daischa reached out to catch Isa's arm. "Princess Isadore, please. Lei told me stories of both of you. Your place is here with your sister and brother."

As soon as Daischa's hand left Otho's forehead, he woke, head peeking out from behind his mother's arm. He couldn't have been more than a year old, but his eyes were bright and steady as they found my face. Beautiful, perfect brown eyes.

Tears slid down my cheeks as it all fell into place.

My father's eyes. I thought I would never see them again.

❧ CHAPTER 24 ❧

Eva

A FEW HOURS later, it was nearly midnight and I still sat at Daischa's table, unable to eat even one more bite of food, watching Aketo bounce Otho on his knee. The little white nubs of his horns peeked out from a cloud of springy coils as Aketo tickled his cloven feet.

With a small shock, I realized the dimples flashing with Otho's every smile were just like mine.

Our brother. The words felt strange. Did it change anything between Aketo and me? Should it?

Daischa had welcomed Lirra into her kitchen and together they whipped up several dishes. Roasted pheasant over golden rice, grilled fish from a lake in the mountains, a peppery stew that left my brow damp with sweat, and more. Given the scarcity of food and supplies in the Enclosure, Anali insisted Daischa accept much of the rations we'd gotten from General Mateen.

When the rest had come inside, I still hadn't recovered from my shock. Daischa had handed Otho off to Aketo and set in front of me a steaming mug of tea, and "a little something extra" to take the edge off. I was grateful to have something to do with my hands.

Otho wailed at first sight of Aketo, then cooed and gargled, and hadn't tolerated anyone else holding him since, yanking at his gold earrings and pawing at his face. I'd never seen Aketo laugh so hard. Joy radiated off everyone in Daischa's family and it wasn't just me who squirmed in the face of it.

Isa gulped down her tea so quickly she had to have scalded her throat, and she watched Otho furtively, expression shifting between wonder and anguish. I wanted to say something to her, but I had no notion of what would help.

I was still supposed to be angry with her, but I couldn't hold on to the feeling while watching Otho's wide-eyed wonderment. I wanted to tell her that we could forget every terrible thing between us, but then I remembered that she still hadn't told me who revealed Papa's secret. She still couldn't or wouldn't condemn Mother.

Aketo, noticing my attention, looked up, his smile slipping for a moment. He frowned and climbed to his feet and slid into the seat next to me.

"Otho," Aketo murmured, "have you met Eva?"

The child followed his brother's gaze. Unsure of what exactly to do—how did one communicate with an infant?—I waved a hand. Otho's gaze immediately locked onto my gold signet ring.

His chubby fingers reached for it, and I slipped it off, handing it over to him. He immediately put it right to his lips.

"Uh-oh," Aketo cooed, hooking a finger into Otho's mouth to extricate the jewelry. "She needs that."

Otho threw his head back and let out a cry of outrage, but quickly settled when Aketo gave him a wooden spoon. "Do you want to hold him? I understand if it's . . . too soon."

I shook my head. "I don't know how. There are never babies at Court."

"Here," he said, holding out Otho until I was forced to grab his waist. "He can sit up now, so there is no particular secret to it."

Otho settled into my lap, curious fingers grasping at my clothes. He tried stretching to his full height to reach my horns, but when I held him close, he noticed my wings. With a wet gasp, he grasped at the feathers at the apex of my wings, and despite my best efforts he climbed halfway over my shoulder.

I jumped, squirming at the touch. Few people had touched my wings and I still was not used to it. I pulled Otho back down to my lap.

"Are you all right?" Aketo whispered.

"I *should* be angry with you."

"I know. I'm surprised you haven't thrashed me yet."

"I understood when I saw him. Throllo knows about him, doesn't he? That's why Papa couldn't remove him. The news would get out and my mother . . ." There was no telling what this information would make her do.

"I thought you would think I was mad. Here I was kissing you, *courting* you, but I couldn't share this secret. I didn't know if you would hate me or my mother."

"Has anyone who's ever met your mother hated her?"

He snorted. "Admittedly no." He looked at my neck, searching for the pendant. It was tucked into my shirt and I yanked it out.

"It doesn't change anything for us. It does, though, make me worry about what we're planning. What if we fail? The Queen might try to harm your mother, or worse."

I wanted to believe she wouldn't care—she had no reason

to. Her marriage to my father had been loveless for quite some time, and she'd had more than a few lovers who were known to the Court. But I'd come to expect cruelty from my mother. This was the same vengeful creature who had chased me from Ternain with her lies about my magick and inherent wickedness.

"Mother would never harm a child," Isa said. I hadn't realized she was listening in on our conversation, but at the mention of Lilith, she shifted to glare at me.

"I'm glad you're so certain of that," I snapped. "But she hurt both of us when we were just children. Maybe you're misremembering."

Isadore rose from the table and stormed out. I started to follow her, but Dthazi waved me off. "I'll make sure she doesn't wander too far."

Otho began to cry, great hiccupping wails that drew Daischa. "I'm sorry," I mumbled.

"Don't worry. He needs his bed," she said, rubbing small circles in Otho's back. "You take Eva for a walk"—she directed at Aketo—"I will get everyone here settled in for the night."

When we stepped outside, I gulped down the night air. "Did you still live with your mother before you left?"

Aketo pointed up at the homes above Daischa's, one painted red, the uppermost golden yellow. "When I came of age, I moved up there. My brother lives in the yellow one."

I nodded. We hadn't discussed sleeping arrangements yet, but I couldn't wait to get a look at where Aketo called home. There at least we could have some privacy for the first time. Canvas tents didn't offer much seclusion.

"What do you want to see?" Aketo asked.

I approached the line of trees, looking between the

branches. The rest of the Enclosure spilled out beneath the ledge. Even though it was night, the crystals embedded in the stonework and the moon above lit everything in a silvery-lavender glow.

Finally, I could see the towering wall of limestone that blocked out the rest of the world beyond Sher n'Cai. The fine hairs on the back of my neck lifted at the sight at the top of the wall. It was covered in massive shards of glass that reflected the moonlight, designed to make climbing up and over those walls lethal.

The Aerie sat on a shelf of stone carved out of the mountain, so that from up here you could see the empty town directly below. There was a market at its center. Rows of stalls were covered in black-and-ivory cloth, and even from here I could see piles of broken pottery and sacks of grain. There were three streets of nearly identical single-story homes, whitewashed with peaked roofs of white tiles. The only source of color was the green ropes of vines climbing up the walls, a sharp contrast to the colorfully painted homes in the Aerie.

Past the market stretched a swath of yellowed grass with a wooden mechanism I couldn't quite make out at its center and what looked to be a high wall of marble, beyond which I could only assume sat General Sareen's manor.

"So the steps are the only way *up* to the Aerie?"

I felt the heat of his body against my wings a moment before he spoke. "Do you see the vacant stores below?"

I nodded. A row of the larger buildings with large plate windows caked in grime, these roofs at least were flat. And not more than a fifty-foot drop from the ledge where they stood. I threw Aketo an incredulous look. "Seriously? You jump down?"

"Dthazi did it first," he said, laughter in his eyes. "I couldn't let him one-up me."

"Is it safe?" I couldn't see any soldiers from here, but that didn't mean much.

"The soldiers sleep in the barracks near the manor. At this hour none should be in town. As long as we stay together, we'll be fine," Aketo said, taking my hand.

"You remember my aversion to heights, yes?" I said, taking a long stride back from the edge. My mind flashed to the memory of falling in Orai and my palms were suddenly damp. "Is there another way?"

"Yes, though it's no easier than this." He pointed west, where the Aerie's ledge dropped off. One building stood taller than the rest. "The drop down to that rooftop is less than twenty feet. The problem is we'll have to climb across a tangle of tree roots to get to where we can jump . . . and you'll recall there's snow on the ground. The roots will be slick with it, perhaps frozen."

That sounded more suited to my skills. "Can you manage it?" I asked, giving him an impish grin as I brandished my clawed fingers.

I tried not to think too hard on the last time I'd climbed up something treacherous. If Aketo said something would be hard, he was probably underplaying its difficulty, since he was great at most things. I refused to let one near-death among several stop me from something I love.

"I'm sure I'll be fine with you to look after me," Aketo said, his voice wry.

Together we inched over to the ledge, but instead of jumping down, Aketo showed me the roots that jutted out from the earth. Some of which were as thick around as my thigh. It had been years since I'd climbed up a tree, but unlike the easy-to-grip bark and moss on a tree trunk, these were smooth.

My mouth dried up as I counted the trees and their tangled root network. We'd only need to climb across the length of six of them, until we were directly above the tallest building. Aketo went first, testing the weight of the roots. I could hardly breathe as I followed him down. Beneath the tree roots, there was nothing and nowhere to place my feet. I drove my claws into the fleshy tuber I held on to and tried not to think of my dangling legs or what would happen if I lost my grip.

My eyes fluttered shut for a moment as I tried to think past the pounding in my heart.

"Eva," Aketo yelled, sounding panicked. "Open your eyes."

My eyes flew wide. The sight of him just a few feet away steadied me. "Sorry. Lost in thought."

"Come on, then," he said. "Aren't you supposed to be looking after me?"

"Right," I muttered.

We inched our way toward the rooftop, root by root. The only near fall came when Aketo lost his grip. I swallowed a shriek as he swung himself up with one arm and found a sturdier root.

When we reached the very last tree, which seemed to be clinging to the Aerie's ledge through sheer will as its knotty trunk protruded at a near horizontal angle, we used its branches to turn around so we'd actually see where we were falling. As one, we let go of the branches. A scream bloomed in my chest, but I smothered it as we fell through the air. The moment my feet hit the roof, I ducked into a roll. My momentum carried me head over foot a few times until I finally skidded to a stop, bones aching.

I climbed to my feet, grimacing at my raw hands. "This is what you and your brother did for fun?"

Aketo, brushing dirt from his knees, laughed. "How did you and Isa pass the time?"

"We climbed trees and snuck around the palace like two mice."

The building was too high to easily leap down, so we picked our way down rooftops until we reached a small, single-story shop. The jump down to the alley below was much less painful. It could have been any backstreet in Ternain, with debris in soggy puddles of melting snow.

We headed toward the market, which, Aketo explained, was shared by the khimaer and the soldiers in the Aerie. The soldiers traded coin for craftwork and repairs, and khimaer used that coin to trade for food.

We were just feet away from turning onto the main street, where the market sat, when we heard the first crunch of boots on icy snow.

We ducked under the eave of one of the houses, pressing our bodies flush against the limestone wall. My pulse thundered in my ears, but after a few long minutes, they passed without turning onto our street.

Once they were gone, I slid down the wall. "What would have happened if they caught us breaking curfew?"

"Flogging, most likely, for your first offense. If they discovered who you were . . . worse."

I stared up at him, unable to understand how he could be so calm. "Do you think it's like this in the Southern Enclosure? This bad?"

"Not in the same way, no, but I imagine similarly terrible," he said softly, like he was speaking to a child.

I didn't even mind, because I felt like one, wholly unprepared to make sense of this. Sher n'Cai was as beautiful as

Aketo had said, and they had made a true home in the Aerie, but they were still under siege. Constantly.

I had thought myself so brave sneaking from my rooms in the palace. That small act of rebellion had been so gratifying at the time, and now it felt completely hollow.

I dropped my head into my hands. "How can I . . . how can we fix this Queendom? The Rival Heirdom, the Enclosures, Court, it's all wrong."

"We start here and then figure the rest out as we go along." Aketo gently pulled at my wrists until I looked at him.

I kissed him, first each of his cheeks, then his eyes and his brow, until I made my way back down to his lips, whispering, "There's no one I trust more than you."

As I said it, I realized just how true it was. Aketo had kept so much from me, but with good reason. I trusted his heart and his empathy. I felt brave enough to ask the question I'd been working up to all night. Resting my chin on his shoulder, I said, "Where do they do it?"

Dread filled his voice. "Do what?"

"The killing. The beatings."

"Right outside the General's manor."

"Can I see?"

A muscle in Aketo's jaw flexed, but he agreed.

It wasn't safe to go any closer to the wall outside Throllo's home, but from atop one of the homes nearby, we would be able to see it.

"Stay low," Aketo commanded as we climbed up the back wall of one of the homes choked in vines. The sweet scent of the crushed white flowers filled the air, making my stomach turn. Once we reached the top, we had to cling to the roof tiles, lest we slipped right down the peaked roof.

I scanned the surrounding streets, but no patrols of soldiers ventured close by. We inched around to the front of the home and looked past the market's tents and into the patch of grass beyond it, where I could finally see the wooden structure clearly.

It was a gallows. Though three nooses swung in the night breeze, no bodies hung from the gibbet. I blew out a relieved breath, but my stomach gave another heave. A dozen feet from the gallows lay a rack made of heavily splintered wood with shackles attached to the top and bottom. Black stains that could only be long-dried blood covered it.

Saliva filled my mouth, a warning that I would be sick if I looked on much longer, but I could not stop staring. I imagined I could smell the reek of death from here, even though that was impossible.

When I shifted to look at Aketo, the wrath in his face stole my breath. "This is new. Usually he just hung them from the wall, but this . . ."

By some unspoken agreement, we climbed down. When I reached for Aketo's hand, it was fisted and trembling.

"This is why we're here," I reminded him. "He's not going to get away with this anymore." But Aketo's eyes were still on the gallows.

"We should head back to the Aerie," I said, a quaver in my voice.

"Yes, you're right," he said, his jaw clenched tight.

Aketo opened his mouth, but his words were swallowed as the sound of a scream pierced the night. I recognized my sister's voice instantly and took off running.

⫷ CHAPTER 25 ⫸

Isadore

IT WOULD HAVE been better if she could hate Daischa.

It would have been for the best if she had never come here at all.

Goodwill seeped from the woman's skin like perfume and it should have infuriated Isa. Daischa swept through her small home like it was a Court of her own making, ladling rice, pouring drinks, and refreshing tea, lithe as a dancer. She was stunning, but not like Mother, whose beauty seized you by the throat.

Instead Daischa carried an inner warmth that radiated with her every smile and affectionate touch. Every time Isa managed to work herself into a fury, it melted away when Daischa made her way around the table, asking a silent question with a touch of her fingers before she piled more food onto Isa's plate or refilled her cup.

She should have expected no less from the woman who raised Aketo. His sense of being perfectly at ease in his skin had always aggravated Isa, and clearly he'd learned it from her.

All of that had been nearly too much to bear, but when Eva

held Otho, without even considering that she might want to hold him, that she wanted to tell him her name or let him steal her jewelry for teething, she couldn't take it.

Unlike Eva, she was comfortable with babies. When she was young, the nursery in the Queen's Palace was one of the places Kitsina liked to visit when they weren't at Court.

Her sister, Kethra, was one the nursemaids there. She was Kitsina's diametric opposite, plump and pretty with eyes like the sky and chunky blond-streaked curls piled atop her head. Her pockets were always filled with candied fruit. Whenever they visited, Kethra let Isa cradle one of her charges while she and Kitsina shared Court gossip. Isa had loved the children's smells and their soft sounds, how their minds offered up no cruelty, only simple desires.

She left Daischa's home and began walking without any plan. It was reckless to wander a place she didn't know alone, but she hardly cared about anything, let alone what these people might think of her. She followed the trees for a while, her hands trailing through the soft leaves. A few people still milled about the street. She expected them to keep wide of her, and several did eye her with suspicion, but just as many approached her, inviting her to share the warmth of their stove. When Isa declined in stumbling Khimaeran, they smiled and corrected her pronunciations until she had it right.

One older woman, whose heart-shaped face was framed by ram's horns, had undone her scarf and wrapped it around Isa's neck. She'd tried to protest, but the woman waved her off, calling, "I won't need it in my bed, but you will need it in this cold."

Isa walked until she reached the steps leading down the mountain and sat down. She wasn't sure how long she sat before a shadow fell over her. "Thinking of walking all the way home? If so, you're going to want this."

She looked up just in time for a wool blanket to fall on top of her head.

Sputtering, Isa reached first for the tattoo of a white desert rose in the center of her forearm. Her magick quested outward, hoping to tie a string around his will.

But the magick would not take hold. It seemed to melt upon contact with his mental net. It was infuriating.

She threw off the blanket and jumped to her feet, slightly off-balance on the stairs, her arms pinwheeling.

Dthazi, smirking, offered a hand. "Easy there, hellcat."

She managed to steady herself without his help and sneered, "You're the one who looks like . . . like an overgrown mountain lion."

He grinned, flashing those long canines, and retrieved the fallen blanket. "Yes, I do rather look like a cat. Thank you for noticing. I will not bite—however, you look liable to take a chunk out of me right now."

She realized she was baring her teeth at him, and quickly smoothed her expression, taking the blanket from him and wrapping it around her. "Perhaps I will."

"Bah," he purred. An actual purr that left Isa staring at his lips. "You wouldn't attack head-on. I'll be safe until I turn my back on you."

"Best avoid that, then," Isa said, glancing past him back to the row of stacked-up homes. "You must know everyone who lives here."

He shrugged. "Yes."

"Doesn't that get exhausting? Where do you go to be alone?"

He squinted at her, assessing. "I'd show you, but you may

not like it. I noticed you didn't enjoy the trip through the caves, Princess Isadore."

Her mouth fell open. She thought she'd hidden it completely. Even Eva hadn't noticed. But she hadn't accounted for Aketo and Dthazi. Of course, both had probably sensed her rising anxiety the longer they stayed beneath the mountain. She couldn't get the thought of all that earth piled on top of them out of her head.

"It was just fine, thanks. And I assure you I can handle it," Isa said.

Dthazi held out a hand again and Isa looked at it, lip curling with annoyance. The leonine boy chuckled. "Very well, then."

They walked down the steps to Sher n'Cai. When Dthazi reached the foot of the stairs, he held up a hand for her to wait and darted into the street, disappearing in the darkness. Isa counted up to five hundred before he reappeared, grinning.

"Some of the soldiers like to drink and play creo in the abandoned houses." He held up a bottle of cloudy liquid. "We're in luck."

Gods, besides the spiked tea from Daischa, she hadn't had a real drink since Eva's nameday. She accepted the bottle from him once he'd taken a generous pull.

Isa put the bottle to her lips and tipped her head back. Fire licked down her throat, but she managed to keep the liquor down. "Lead the way."

They passed the bottle back and forth, retracing their way back to the same wide street that they'd first taken. They followed the wall of the Enclosure, Dthazi pointing out landmarks until they came to a seam in the wall.

Dthazi felt around until he found a particular brick, and the door to the tunnel swung open. "Who discovered the caves?"

Isa asked as they stepped inside. Like last time, it was significantly warmer inside the caves.

"I'm not certain. We've known about them for generations."

"And no one ever thought to leave?"

His lips twitched into a small smile. "And go where?"

"Right." Isa's cheeks heated as she reconsidered her ill-conceived suggestion. Dracol would not welcome them and it was a long journey through the mountains to the Roune Lands, if one could even make a life there. "Sorry."

"Don't worry about it," Dthazi said. "I used to ask my mother the same thing."

They stopped at the bend in the tunnel, one path leading deeper into the caves, and the other to the pool of dark water. Dthazi rubbed his chin, contemplating.

"Please don't tell me your secret hideaway is the same tunnel we sat in for hours earlier," Isa said, taking another generous gulp. Now that she was used to its efforts to peel the flesh from her throat, she could handle it.

Dthazi snorted, reclaiming the bottle. Instead of taking his share, he shoved the cork back in and pointed toward the dark cave with the lake. "No, it's not. It's just a bit farther." He continued forward until his booted feet rested inches from the placid water. "Can I trust your footing?"

Isa nodded, glad she'd accepted a third serving of flaky white fish from Daischa, but when she stepped into the cave, what had seemed like packed dirt was a slippery, muddy silt.

She set her jaw and took three long strides to meet Dthazi at the lake's edge. "So you come here to stare into the darkness," Isa joked.

Beyond the lake's edge, Isa spied a doorway at the other end of the cavern, lit by the same crystals all over the Enclosure. To get there, they would have to inch around the few feet of dirt surrounding the water and pray not to fall in.

"When Aketo turned sixteen, I dared him to bring me a rock from the bottom of that pool."

"And did he?"

"No, but he did find a rather unfriendly water snake."

"What happened?"

"He was fine other than a little bite. Our magick works almost as well on animals as it does with people," he said and then laughed. "But my mother tanned my hide for a week."

This time when Dthazi offered a hand, she took it. They began working their way around the lake, Isa keeping a sharp eye on the flat water in case they were visited by any hostile creatures.

"I noticed my brother avoided mention of how you came to ally with your sister," Dthazi said.

Isa stiffened. She'd noted he left out the events of the nameday, a lapse that could have only been for her benefit. Dthazi would not have brought her here if he knew that she'd commanded her guard to kidnap his brother. He would not have held her hand if he knew that four months ago, she'd used it to stab Aketo in the chest.

She sucked in a breath and the words spilled out of her like a torrent. "I tried to kill Eva on her nameday. She bested me, and instead of killing me as she should have, she fled Ternain with me as her prisoner."

"You don't seem like a prisoner." They were halfway around the lake now.

"I'm not exactly one. Before we came here, Eva asked me for a truce."

"And you agreed?"

291

"Not exactly."

Dthazi didn't respond as they'd finally reached the entrance. Water lapping at her toes, Isa followed him into a large round chamber. Unlike the rest of the caves, massive crystals embedded in the rock jutted out from the sheared-down walls. Amethyst and cloudy pink quartz, the pillars longer and thicker than her arms. And though cool air blew in through the doorway, it was warm as a summer evening.

"What was this place?" Alcoves were decorated with carved crystal reliefs of lithe figures in flowing garments, hands raised in supplication. Isa traced one sharp avian face, noting its tapered ears and the braids that draped its body like a cloak.

The next carving did not have fey ears, but a fox's ears, and instead of hands, flowering branches sprouted from its wrists. "Godlings . . . this place must be five hundred years old."

"Try millennia," he said, staring at the wide golden bowl resting atop a plinth in the center of the cavern.

Isa joined him, following his gaze to the center of the basin where two figures were etched into the metal. One she recognized immediately, Khimaerani, the first khimaer. Even if the Sorceryn and her palace tutors had intentionally neglected several aspects of Myre's history, Papa had shown the girls drawings of Khimaerani in the few books on ancient Myre in the Auguri library. The other figure, a masculine one, had long locs that seemed to dance in the lifelike sketch. His bone structure reminded her of Baccha, and somehow the artist who'd created this had conveyed the power of his gaze.

Isa gaped at Dthazi as he poured nearly half the bottle into the bowl and passed it to her. "Don't worry, it will be gone by morning. I once left dried flowers in here and somehow they were gone six hours later."

She felt warm all over, but not unpleasantly. More like she wanted to lie faceup in the dirt and forget the world outside existed.

"Every offering requires a prayer," Dthazi said, tapping her hand.

She blinked at the etching still visible through the liquid. Humans did not *pray* or set out offerings. The Godlings belonged to fey and khimaer; the Temple where they'd once been worshiped was the center of human learning and magick. "What did you ask for?"

"The same things I always ask for—safety for my brothers, joy for my mother." His antlers cast spiky shadows on the ceiling as he bowed his head. "Freedom for my people."

For clarity, Isa thought as she poured more in.

They sat down atop a pile of furs and wool blankets in one corner. Isa yanked off her boots and tucked her feet beneath her. They passed the now-dwindling supply of liquor back and forth.

"So you haven't agreed to a truce, but you haven't disagreed either, or else what would you still be doing here?" Dthazi asked.

"Eva thinks she is the only one of us with a moral compass," Isa said, knowing full well the drink had loosened her tongue. "I wanted to see the truth for myself. My . . . the Queen never visits the Enclosures. I think she likes to pretend they—you don't exist."

"And what do you think?"

Their eyes met. "I can see the beauty here, but when we walked through the Aerie, I skimmed the mind of every person we passed, and everyone, besides you and Daischa, held a bone-deep fear and impotence." It had chilled her, that dread so at odds with the warmth of their greetings. They were living in terror.

"What about the Queen? What will you tell her?"

She wished she could promise to repeat all that to her mother, but it wasn't that simple. When Lilith didn't want to deal with something, she either ignored Isa or attacked her, and unlike Eva, Isa had learned to navigate that as well as she could. She didn't say things that would displease her mother. The last time she said something out of turn at Court, voicing an opinion that was slightly different from the Queen's, she'd been confined to her rooms for a week.

Lilith never commanded her to stay in outright. She just stationed ten of her Queensguard outside Isa's rooms.

Isa's opinion would matter when she was Queen. Until then it was best not to cross her mother. "I'm not sure."

She didn't want to face it. When her mother found out Isa was here while they planned a rebellion, the punishment she'd dole out would not be pleasant.

"What's it like? At Court?"

She made a noise of disgust. "I used to love it." But then Eva returned, dredging up all the feelings of betrayal and loneliness Isa had felt at fourteen. She dove headfirst into the petty Court dramas to escape it, and longed to repay her sister in kind. But even the pliant minds of the young courtiers grew tedious, and hurting Eva wasn't enough.

No, she'd needed to *beat* Eva at the one thing that mattered. She hadn't even bothered to consider what she would do with the throne if she won it.

"You don't miss it all?" Dthazi pressed. "Not even a bit?"

"I miss Ternain." She missed the fey craftsfolk with shops lining the boulevards outside of the palace; the pools in High

Summer; her horse, Arrow; and the freedom to do as she pleased. But Court itself? Her friendships there were shallow enough to forget. She'd gotten so used to showing the Court a reflection of her mother that she couldn't form true bonds with any of the courtiers in her circle.

"You must have . . . what is it they're called? . . . Suitors?"

She nodded, grinning at his affectation of ignorance.

"You've got to have suitors chasing you around wherever you go."

"That is the most circuitous compliment I have ever received," Isa said, with a small giggle that turned into a hiccup. "But yes. There were many, and whenever I tried to let a rumor spread that I didn't want to marry until well after I was crowned, their attentions only seemed to increase."

"You don't sound as if you want to return."

"Wants—" Isa hiccupped again. She'd been about to repeat a phrase she'd heard from her mother a hundred times. *Wants and wishes are for children.*

"Come on," Dthazi said. "My mam will threaten me with the washing for a week if we stay out any longer."

They went back the way they came, and once they reached the entrance, Isa had a queasy feeling in her stomach. Chalking it up to the food and the drinking, she shouldered past Dthazi when he pushed open the door.

"Wait," he called in a sharp whisper. "Isa—"

She did not want to throw up in front of Dthazi, and darted for the nearest house. She heard the sound of laughter cut off abruptly and backpedaled, but it was too late.

Two men in soldier white stepped from behind the house. Both human, they could've been brothers, both of the same medium-brown complexion with neatly trimmed beards. The only difference she noticed was that one massaged the pommel of the sword at his belt, and the other actually had gone as far as to unsheathe a sinuous dagger. By their stumbling gait, they had been drinking.

The soldier who'd yet to draw his weapon drawled, "Who is this, Prince?" He spat Dthazi's title like a curse.

She felt Dthazi come up behind her, so close she could feel the heat of him on her back. "Let me handle this," he breathed into her ear.

Isa was already palming the thorny vines on her wrist— best for violently seizing someone's mind—magick surging beneath her skin. She grinned at the knife-wielding soldier as both came to a sudden stop.

Their eyes rolled like those of spooked horses, lips quivering as they fought to speak.

Isa spun on her heel and smirked up at him. Isa had inherited her mother's height, but she only came up to his chin. "What were you saying?"

He loosed a whistle. "That's a neat trick."

"What do we do?"

Dthazi dragged a hand across his face. "Unless that magick of yours can steal memories . . . knock them out and drag their bodies far from here?"

"It can't." *Unfortunately.* "That's good enough for me."

But when she turned around, her concentration slipped. Any other time, with a clear head, she would've been able to regain control of their minds. But one of the men was already lunging for Dthazi.

Isa didn't think as she stepped in front of him. A choked gasp escaped her as the dagger bit into her stomach, and when he yanked it out, the pain sent her every thought skittering away.

She sank to the ground and didn't see what happened next. Only heard the meaty crunch of weapons against flesh and bone.

Distantly she understood that she should hold the wound shut to try to stop the bleeding, but she curled up on her side, listening, wishing she'd offered a prayer up for their safety.

Soon the sound of more footfalls reached her ears. A panicked keen escaped her. But then Dthazi was crouching before her, gently rolling her onto her back. Flecks of blood dotted his cheeks in a macabre imitation of his freckles. "Can I take your pain?" Dthazi asked, voice so gentle that she wanted to remind him she couldn't be killed. Not by any hand but her sister's.

She nodded. His hand gripped hers and the pain almost immediately drained away.

Aketo's voice called for them to leave. She thought she was hallucinating when Eva appeared on her other side. "Can you walk?"

"If I must." Eva and Dthazi helped her to her feet. "What are you doing here?"

"We were in town too, and I heard you scream," she explained, eyes scanning the street.

Aketo emerged from the closest house, wiping bloodied hands on his thighs. "All right there, Isa?"

All that was left of the soldiers were two small puddles of blood. "What happened?" Isa asked.

"I killed them . . . it was all too fast, I had to." Dthazi switched to Khimaeran, spitting out a slew of curses Isa could barely parse.

Aketo spotted the fallen bottle of liquor and rounded on his brother, fuming. They began arguing, but Eva cut them off. "If we heard it, others will have too. We have to go. *Now.*"

❧ CHAPTER 26 ❧

Aketo

"WE SHOULD BE evacuating everyone to the caves now," Aketo said the following morning. "They could have already found the bodies. Throllo could be sending his men here as early as noon."

"What good will that do, brother?" Dthazi asked.

"It'll keep Throllo's men from gathering up the first people they find and hanging them for the killings." He glared at his brother. "You endangered everyone here with your recklessness, or have you forgotten?"

They gathered around his mother's kitchen: Eva, Dthazi, Anali, his cousin Yayazi, and Isa. Late last night, when they'd carried a bleeding Isa into the house, Tavan, who'd been sharing the extra room along with Lirra, healed her. Isa's hand still strayed to her stomach whenever she thought someone wasn't looking.

"Aye," Dthazi said, "I know."

The intention to hold off a week before attacking had been upended last night. They'd already decided they couldn't afford to wait to strike at Throllo. At dawn, they sent Falun to bring word to General Mateen, since he could use glamour to pass through the patrols unseen, and because he was the best tracker. Hopefully he could retrace their path down the mountain and guide them back to the hidden entrance to Sher n'Cai. Aketo hadn't even slept; after he'd settled Eva in his bedroom, he'd descended the steps once again an hour before sunrise with a jug of water to clear away the blood.

The original plan they'd conceived when traveling with Mateen had been fairly simple. While the khimaer force his brother commanded would storm the General's manor from within the Enclosure, Mateen's Jackals would use magick to rend a hole in the outer wall of the Enclosure. That way Throllo would have to divide his attention between dual assaults.

Aketo explained all this, but his brother had an even more devious plan in mind. "There's another way to split Throllo's forces—wait for the inspection." Aketo hadn't forgotten about the early mornings when near a hundred soldiers flooded the Aerie, inspecting their homes for weapons and any other signs they weren't the docile creatures who happily accepted his decrees. "The inspection is in two days. If we can trap a portion of the soldiers in the Aerie, we'll have the advantage. If we storm the General's manor while half his men are away and the rest are dealing with an unexpected attack, we'll have a real chance."

"That's risky," Eva added. "What if the bodies begin to smell? Surely they'll go searching when two men turn up missing?"

"I'd agree with you, Your Highness," Yaya said. "But General Sareen doesn't keep close tabs on his men. He's more likely to accuse them of desertion than assume any of us had anything to do with it."

Aketo wasn't so certain, but they were both more qualified to know Throllo's habits. "Do you have a count of how many soldiers are stationed here?"

"Seven hundred," Dthazi and Yaya said at once.

Dthazi's father and Yayazi's mother were siblings, and the three young cousins had been attached at the hip growing up. When Dthazi took over his father's place training the khimaer who wanted to learn to fight, he made it into a more formal force and tapped Yaya to lead beside him. Her bone-white antlers were decorated with tarnished gold rings connected by a spidery golden chain. A piece, Aketo knew, she'd inherited, like most of the jewelry here. The only khimaer with trinkets of significant value had family outside the Enclosure to send for such things.

"And how many of them come on these inspections?" Eva asked.

"A good hundred at least. If there have been more . . . violations of Throllo's rules than usual, he sends more."

Anali, massaging her temples, groaned. "You two are right, then. It's too great an advantage."

"We need some sort of plan to keep everyone in the Aerie safe until then. Just in case you're wrong about Throllo searching for his men. I agree with Aketo," Eva said, "we should evacuate tonight."

Isa, who hadn't spoken since the meeting began, surprised Dthazi by asking, "What if your forces went to the caves today? That way you could keep an eye on the steps up to the Aerie. Wouldn't that give you some warning if they move up the inspection? And everyone else can follow over the next days."

Dthazi exchanged a glance with Yaya. "That . . . could work." If they saw Throllo's men going up to the Aerie, they

300

could cut them off. If they forced the soldiers to fight on the steps, they could cut them down easily.

They sat there for another hour ironing out the details. Eva and Isa eventually retreated from the discussion. Daischa strong-armed Isa into grinding grain with a mortar and pestle, while Eva disappeared entirely.

When Dthazi, Yaya, and Daischa left to spread the news of what happened and their plan, Aketo climbed up to his house. He would have to make his way back down to the caves by nightfall to see if Falun and Mateen had returned, but until then, he needed to sleep.

His home wasn't much larger than the great room at his mother's. Just a stove at the back, a table he'd purloined from an abandoned house in town, a nubby rug that had seen better days, and a pallet of quilts in one corner.

He inched across the ledge that was technically the roof of his mother's house, and stepped inside.

Eva was inside, standing with her wings outstretched. They spanned half the length of the room, fading from gold near her shoulders to a deep luminous brown. The longest feathers fanned out like throwing knives. In one hand she held her sword and in the other that slim journal she'd been carrying around since they left Nbaltir.

Whenever she had a spare moment, and truthfully they had few, he found her poring over it. She slowly lowered and lifted her wings, creating a torrent of wind swirling around her. Aketo's eyes traced the line of her body, the proud horns and short curls at her brow twined around them.

"What in Khimaerani's name are you doing?" Aketo asked, ducking one of her wings. His hand brushed against an outstretched feather, and she jumped.

She lowered her sword, but her wings remained out-stretched. "Is this a mistake? We only have a few days to prepare."

"It's not ideal. Luckily most of the planning will be left to my brother and Yaya," Aketo said.

"Wouldn't it be better if we just hid during the inspection? We can attack another day."

He hesitated. He agreed, and yet Dthazi had been right. Aketo trusted their skill would outclass the soldiers. They were quicker, stronger, and had real belief in their freedom behind them. But seven hundred soldiers, compared with their paltry two hundred, was too great a deficit for skill to over-come without getting creative. "We risk Throllo's laws and his whims if we wait. What if, in a week, someone is caught breaking the curfew?"

"We were fools to go out last night. They were fools to—to go and get drunk." Eva finally tucked her wings in and set the book down on the table. "I should have kept an eye on Isa."

"To be fair, neither of us could have anticipated those two would get along," Aketo said, practically falling into a seat at the table. He tried to remember the last time he'd gotten a full night's rest.

"They were at each other's throats the first time we found them. The next time, there were two dead bodies. I don't even want to think of what will be next," Eva said. She flipped the other chair around—they were too high backed to accommo-date her wings—and sat. "Isa sneaking about with a khimaer Prince. What will Mother think of her?"

Aketo smiled. "Arguing is how Dthazi shows affection."

"And how do you?" Eva asked, the beginnings of a grin on her lips. "Show affection, that is?"

"Oh," Aketo began, tipping his chair back, "I'm even worse than he is. I just brood and teach you how to fight."

Grinning in earnest now, Eva said, "You do realize Anali was my instructor for years before you came along."

"I do. And thank goodness, else it would've taken much more to teach you."

She reached across the table, poised to flick his nose, but Aketo laced his fingers through hers instead.

"Very well," she said. "No more of the brooding, though. From either of us. It's up to us to keep our family safe."

"Speaking of that," Aketo said, "what do you think of asking Isa to keep an eye on Daischa and Otho when we attack the manor? Just in case."

Eva was silent for a long moment. "You trust her."

It was not a question, but he answered nonetheless. "Not in all things, but yes, in this, I do."

"All right, then," she said. "I'll do it. How is she . . . feeling about everything?"

He usually avoided sharing the emotions of others, but Eva needed to understand her sister. If they couldn't find it in them to communicate, this was the least he could do. "Overwhelmed, I think, and sad. But not as unhappy as she was on your nameday."

"Because she lost," Eva guessed.

"No, when we first met at the ball, she was upset."

They both fell silent, still hand in hand.

"You should go to sleep," Eva said a few minutes later when his eyes fell shut. She held up the journal. "And I should get back to this. I'll be more useful if I can shift at will."

He read the title. *On Mutable Flesh.* It had been written by a past Queen and ancestor of Eva's. "Does she explain how to shapeshift?"

"There are bits and pieces, but nothing explicit," Eva said.

"Maybe you're coming at this the wrong way," Aketo said, walking to the pallet. He lay on his back. "Our magick should be . . . instinctual. It may be that this is how one Queen experienced her gift. It could be different for you."

Eva rolled her eyes, but within, frustration warred with disbelief. "Why would Queen Assani have written this if not to understand Khimaerani's gift?"

Aketo shrugged. "She may have tried to unlock its every secret, but came up short. Or she just loved it so much that she wanted to write about it. I think you should try conjuring the need to shift. Imagine it in your mind. Something will resonate eventually."

"That's very helpful, Aketo." She stood at the edge of the blankets, glaring down at him.

"Apologies," Aketo said with a yawn. "You're welcome to join me, you know."

She crouched and gave him a chaste kiss. "I know. Rest well, Prince."

He was asleep before she made it to the door.

❧ CHAPTER 27 ❧

Eva

WE WERE GATHERING in the caves, hours before nightfall two days later, when Dthazi found me. I sat cross-legged on a quilt, fifty feet from the tunnel door that led out to Sher n'Cai. Aketo was next to me, mid-conversation with a youngish khimaer woman whose name I couldn't quite recall.

The two days had passed in a blur of introductions, meals around Daischa's kitchen table, and trying to persuade Otho to add my name to his short list of words.

Aketo, Dthazi, and I went back and forth from the Aerie to the caves nightly to speak with General Mateen, who was not at all pleased to find the timing of their plan accelerated. His squadron had taken shelter deeper in the cave network, and like us, when morning came, they would leave to attack.

Anali and Falun sat behind us, debating the merits of each dish Daischa had served last night. While most of the khimaer forces had already been in the caves for two days, we stayed in the Aerie, aiding in the evacuation. Most people simply went about their business in the market, and instead of returning to the Aerie, they'd waited for a gap in the soldiers' patrols to enter the caves. But the children and elders who couldn't easily navigate the steps, they helped. I hadn't even considered that to have the measure of freedom the Aerie offered, many were confined to it. The isolation was an additional layer of the terror Throllo had inflicted.

Yaya stood at the head of the tunnel armed with a bladed staff, listening for any movement outside. As Dthazi rightly predicted, General Sareen hadn't mounted any search for the dead soldiers, but a waiting hung in the air. Like we had forgotten something, but couldn't quite remember what.

Dthazi, who had been walking back and forth talking and laughing with everyone he passed, seemed the only one at ease. When he stopped in front of me, I'd expected a joke or sarcastic remark to his brother. But he folded his arms and looked down at me. "Let's see it, then. Your magick."

"Excuse me?" I asked. I was in the midst of oiling my sword, and we were supposed to be setting off soon. Now he wanted a display?

"Really, Dthazi?" Aketo groaned. "I told you she can handle herself."

"Psh, I'm not worried about that. Your bragging has me curious. Besides, would you expect a leader to go into battle without knowing all the weapons in his arsenal?"

"Fair enough," I muttered. Dthazi's booming voice had drawn stares, and my stomach lurched at all the attention. "What do you want to see? I can't exactly use my magick without a target."

"I see all those weapons inked on your arms," he offered.

At least he hadn't mentioned my khimaer magick. I had followed Aketo's advice, and all the picturing didn't manifest a thing.

I looked to Aketo, wishing that Baccha was here. It was easier to ask someone for blood when you knew they would heal immediately. "Do you mind?"

Aketo bit into his wrist and held it over my waiting palm. Soon as the blood touched my skin, I could taste the magick in the air.

I drew my sword and let the magick drip down my hands until it cloaked the blade. Dthazi made a noise of approval and went to touch the flickering crimson power, which moved like flame over the metal but produced no heat.

I inched the sword back from his curious fingers. "Don't. Unless you want to bleed from that hand."

Next I found the arrow on my forearm and, with the last of Aketo's blood, called forth the quiver of arrows I'd discovered while trapped in my mindscape, with only magick for company.

Unlike the blood magick I used in tandem with actual blades, these arrows were pure crimson power. When I drew an arrow from the quiver, it was as hot as blood and felt insubstantial in my hand.

"How will you use them without a bow?"

"Duck," I said with a grin, before I released the arrow.

I didn't throw it. I simply told it to stop at the tip of Dthazi's nose for a moment, before it arced around him and whizzed through the room. Pleased with Dthazi's frozen expression, I bade it to return to my hand. "If you want to know if they strike as hard as arrows, let me know."

I only noticed the cave had fallen silent when Dthazi let out a low whistle.

I looked around and found wide-eyed, fearful expressions staring back. Heat rose in my cheeks and I released the power and the quiver immediately disappeared. What had I been thinking, showing off blood magick like that? This was Raina's magick, the murderous gift that had won the war, resulting in a rebellion that left them trapped in the Enclosures.

"Brilliant, Eva," Aketo murmured, giving my hand a squeeze.

"I'm glad you fight with us," Dthazi said with a wink, his bright expression so at odds with the fear he must have felt spreading through the room. "Little sister."

He moved on to the next group of khimaer soldiers. Silence broken, the chatter throughout the rest of the tunnel began again.

I released the breath I'd been holding, and excused myself, intending to find my sister.

I made my way toward the caves deeper in the mountain, where the rest of the khimaer who wouldn't be fighting tomorrow were. Bedrolls were laid out beside the stalagmites jutting up from the cave floor. An elder woman sung a Khimaeran folk song, banging a hand drum against her hip. Children of various ages ran around the cave, playing.

Searching the crowd for Isa, I spotted Kelis's cap of red-brown waves first. At my request, Kelis was going to stay with this group when the fighting began tomorrow. I was glad of it, another eye on Isa, another sword to safeguard them all.

Behind Kelis, Isa sat on a wool blanket next to Daischa. Otho sat up between them, playing with a set of well-worn blocks. When he tried to shove one into his mouth, Isa gently took it from him.

At my approach, Daischa rose and gathered Otho into her arms. "I'll give you two some privacy."

Then she gave Isa a long, significant look I could not decipher. Isa returned it with a reluctant nod. Daischa, rope braids swinging, wandered over to the singing woman, leaving us alone.

"Can I sit?" I asked, awkward suddenly.

Isa lifted one shoulder in a half shrug. "Go ahead."

"How are you?"

"All things considered, not terrible." Isa smiled and it was not her usual radiant one, or the grin that was more a baring of teeth. It was wilted at the edges; she looked as tired as I felt. "Shouldn't you be off scheming?"

"There's nothing left to figure out. Either our plan works tomorrow or we fail. That's why I wanted to speak with you."

"Oh?" Isa cocked her head, curious.

"Aketo asked me if you would look after Daischa and Otho tomorrow, in case anything should go wrong and Throllo's men find these caves."

Isa's eyes narrowed. "Of course I will keep them safe."

"That isn't why *I* came, though. My request is a bit more significant. I want you to take them far from here if anyone attacks this place. Don't fight, just use your magick to get them out."

"You're that worried?" Isa asked, color draining from her face.

She'd been there during our first meeting about the rebellion. She knew the odds were stacks against us, as they always had been. "Seven hundred soldiers, Isa. Even if we divide them, if they overtake us at the manor, there will be no one to protect you all. Will you do it?"

Isa nodded, but she looked distracted.

"Isa, I need your promise. Even if after this, we end up back in Ternain at each other's necks, please keep them safe."

Our eyes met. Isa's bottle-green eyes were shiny with unshed tears. "All right. Yes. I promise. I'll keep them safe."

➳ ISA ➳

It shouldn't have been this easy, sneaking out of the cave.

She waited until night fell and impenetrable darkness blanketed the cavern. Once she was certain Kelis slept soundly, she reached into the woman's mind and tugged at her aura until Isa was certain she would not wake. Casting a glamour so that anyone whose eyes passed over her would see nothing, she picked her way through the cave. It was the same route she had followed with Aketo and Dthazi that first day in Sher n'Cai. It seemed impossible that only a few days had passed since then.

When she reached the tunnel where the khimaer force slept, she had to use more persuasive magick to make sure none were woken as she stepped over their sleeping bodies.

The only trouble came at the end of the tunnel, where Yayazi stood guard. The heavy slab of stone that served as an entrance to the cave system was firmly shut. Isa stood waiting, hoping a solution would come before morning, when Yaya bade one of her companions to open the door and do a routine check of the street.

Isa slipped out as soon as they rolled back the stone, heart thudding in her chest. Once she caught her breath, she walked through the town. She had taken note of the map of Sher n'Cai during the meeting the morning after she was stabbed and followed the streets that would bring her closer to General Sareen's manor.

When a soldier came stumbling out of an alley a dozen feet ahead, Isa had his mind in her grip in an instant. *Take me to the General,* she whispered into the man's mind. His face went slack but he nodded vigorously and led Isa away.

⇜ *EVA* ⇝

The first sign of something ill came at dawn.

Not a single Queen's Army soldier came to inspect the Aerie.

After a terse discussion between Dthazi and Yaya, it was decided we would have to go forward with the plan. They sent a soldier in search of Mateen to let him know Sareen might be aware we were coming. How Sareen had gotten wind of our plan, I couldn't fathom. Yaya promised she'd seen nothing out of order in the few soldiers who patrolled the street outside the cave that night.

There was no way to know, or any way to change it, so we set off as planned.

Dthazi led the first of three waves, heading for the General's manor. The second wave would follow us to the manor, and the third, which Yaya led, would remain at the caves in case of a possible ambush.

I wore one of the tunics from Osir, designed with slits at the back for my wings, and sleeves rolled up to my elbows, despite the cold. I barely felt the chill, though I did notice that my breath fogged the air.

We swept through the streets like specters. Held in a tight, V-shaped formation, with Dthazi at the helm. Aketo guarded his back, and behind him were five rows of men and women armed with longbows. Anali, Falun, and I were grouped together several rows beyond the bowmen. I could hardly keep an eye on Aketo. I'd tried to persuade Dthazi to let me in that first row of khimaer, but he'd refused. *You may be a skilled fighter, but you aren't a soldier. And I'd like to keep you hidden unless I need you.*

Whenever a new wave of fear crested within me, I grasped Falun's hand.

We encountered their first patrol, ten men who nearly blended into the whitewashed walls of the town in their soldier-white uniforms, not five minutes after leaving the tunnel. Easily handled in a hail of arrows. The first stirrings of guilt churned in my stomach, but then I remembered the gallows. The rack stained black with old blood.

But after that, we didn't pass any more patrolling soldiers. The streets were quiet. Even as we traveled closer and closer to the manor, it was deserted. A voice screamed in my head to beg them to turn back. But it wasn't up to me.

When we reached the market without confronting any soldiers, unease hung in the air like a cloying perfume. Dthazi held up a fist and we stopped.

"We knew something wasn't right when we left the caves. Well, this confirms it," he called. "Any other morning, this close to the manor, the streets would be crawling with soldiers. Onward."

We kept low and took off at a slow jog. Two more streets and we were one turn away from the manor. Icy sweat dripped down the back of my tunic, and my pulse seemed to vibrate in my bones.

Dthazi commanded three men to scout around the corner, to see how many defended the manor. When they returned, carrying news that no one was out front, that in fact the gate was open, I wanted to call the entire thing off.

But it wasn't my decision.

Dthazi raised his fist again and we left the street, fanning out around the gate.

This was my first true look at the place, and I could barely take it in. A high wall of the same limestone bricks that made up the rest of Sher n'Cai. Behind it rose a square, three-story house made from packed clay. Half of it was obscured by snow-capped trees at the base of the home and it butted up against the sloping edge of the mountain.

By all appearances, it was deserted. Yet we would've been fools to expect anything but an ambush was waiting for us behind that gate.

At Dthazi's signal, the sound of ringing metal pierced the air as we unsheathed our swords. Dthazi, who held a blade-tipped staff nearly his full height in his right hand, stamped it in the dirt. "Archers, nock. Remember, strike with magick first . . ."

At Dthazi's side, Aketo nodded to me. Our eyes met and I knew we would fight side by side, no matter what.

Dthazi gave a sharp whistle and we rushed for the gate. I could hardly think over the clamor of booted feet, hooved and clawed, and the clang of weapons. I tried to push past everyone ahead of me and reach Aketo, but no amount of shouldering could get me past men double my size.

But as soon as the first soldiers crossed the threshold of the gate, a crack as loud as thunder rent the air.

My thoughts turned to mud. Storm magick, my mother's magick. But I didn't smell the salt of the sea on the air. Instead there was a pungent scent of freshly turned dirt and wood smoke that left a metallic taste in the back of my throat.

It was Mateen's earth magick, and that sound must have been the Second General boring through the outer wall. Everyone around me slowed, but I pushed past them, shoving heedlessly until I reached Dthazi and Aketo.

Up ahead, fifty feet beyond the gate stood row after row of soldiers. The gleaming medals on their lapels brought an unbidden memory of my father in death, his every pin and honor soaked in blood.

I scanned them, getting a quick count. There couldn't have been more than three hundred. Where were the rest of the soldiers under Throllo's command?

Where was the General?

As soon as I stepped up beside Aketo and Dthazi, one soldier broke off from the rest and began to approach us. She was a middle-aged woman with her hair in knots, and though she walked with her hand on her sword, she did not draw it.

I glanced at Dthazi, who inclined his head as if to say, *You figure this out.* I lifted my sword. "Stop there. Where is your commander? Where is General Sareen?"

"The General fled in the night." The woman paused. "May I ask, Lady, who you are?"

Cold bled through me and roaring filled my ears. My mind presented an answer to all this. I had no reason to believe this was my sister's doing. And yet I knew in my bones. *Isa, what have you* done?

Saliva filled my mouth and I swallowed it down, forcing away the urge to sick up. "I am Princess Evalina Grace Killeen." Sounds of surprise from the assembled soldiers filled the air. The weight of their gazes felt like an anvil on my chest. "Tell me, do you plan to hold this place in General Sareen's stead?"

Three hundred still far outnumbered us, but Mateen was on the way. And without a real leader, they would eventually fall apart in a real clash.

Slowly the woman released the pommel of her sword. "I am just a Lieutenant, Your Highness. I speak only for myself, but I will not stand against you."

She knelt and bent her head to the ground. Several soldiers followed the gesture, but the rest looked confused and listless.

Somehow this display of submission infuriated me. I couldn't forget that some of these people had likely sat by while khimaer were hanged. Some might have even participated in the beatings. "Then go. Leave this place! Flee and never return."

As if they'd planned this from the beginning, a limestone wall at the opposite end of the courtyard collapsed in with a huge crash. A vast cloud of dust rose up in its wake, and when it cleared, General Mateen and his company, all in their jackal masks, stepped through the opening.

Throllo's soldiers scattered, and in the crush, it was apparent not all were as peaceful as the Lieutenant.

Dthazi stamped his spear into the dirt, calling for them to remain in formation, but as a hail of arrows flew in our direction, the formation shattered.

Lightning rent the sky, striking the ground where many of the human soldiers in white still stood. Then it became a battle in earnest.

Aketo and I stood back to back as half a dozen men rushed us. I darted forward, blade singing before it struck one in the chest. Blood sprayed, burning where it coated my hands, and I ignited.

Power swelled within me. The smell of magick was thick in

the air, but I felt invincible with blood magick coursing through me. The soldier nearest went down first, a flash of my blade opening a wound from neck to groin.

Sword lit with killing power, I spun, crimson magick leaping off the blade with every thrust. Soldiers ten feet away fell as the power met their flesh.

I lost sight of Aketo and Dthazi. Jackals battled the other soldiers alongside us and I was grateful for the masks, which were the only difference between the two groups, both clad in soldier white.

Then in the corner of my eye, I spied a sword aiming to sever my wing. I pictured it, my wing as it was now, and my back smooth and unadorned.

In a flash of golden light, I watched, gaping as the wing *unmade* itself. There was a sharp pain in my back, but that was it.

Just like that, my wings were gone.

One of the Jackals close to me lifted a hand into the air, their mask streaked with blood. Lightning struck from the sky, felling only the unmasked men and women in soldier white.

I cut down another woman with a wave of my sword. Each time I drew more blood, the power grew and grew until my skin felt too tight. But I was too drunk with power to be in awe.

I screamed, praying Aketo and Dthazi and any others nearby would know it was a warning. I gasped as jagged bolts of crimson blood magick emerged from my skin. Dozens of them hovered in the air around me, waiting for instructions.

A terrible, terrible thing I had unleashed. One of Raina's gifts Baccha had declined to show me. The first story I ever heard about Queen Raina the First was about her taking on an army at the shores of the Red River. A Queen of Marrow and Blood. At the time, it had terrified me. Now, though, I embraced the terror I'd become.

I was a maelstrom of blood and flesh. Girl of my nightmares and dreams.

I spun. Khimaer and Jackals and human soldiers still fought all around me. I spotted Aketo near the gate, locked in a fight between three women, all armed with dual-ended swords. Blood leaked down the side of his face.

I sent out the shards of magick, aiming for every unmasked body in soldier white. Not to deliver killing blows, but to injure them enough to surrender.

Two of Aketo's opponents fell to their knees as the shards struck them in the chest, blood spraying where the magick entered them, but the third, standing behind him, slapped the magick away with a hand suddenly cloaked in silvery-blue flames.

I screamed, calling Aketo's name, but the sound was swallowed in the discordant song of battle.

The woman raised her blade, preparing to cut him down, and every thought in my head went silent. Only one thing rose above the silence: I had to save him.

I refused to lose Aketo.

Between one breath and the next, I *moved*. Sword outstretched, heedless of who I might hurt in my haste, I harnessed the true speed he'd taught me—*cashina*.

Between one breath and the next, I sprinted for the gate. Blades spinning through the air seemed to slow, as graceful as dancers at Court, dipping and twirling to a grisly song.

It only seemed to take a few steps to cross the distance, but

I was still too slow to parry her strike. The sword gleamed, bright as the fire she'd conjured only seconds ago, mere inches from Aketo's back. At the last second, I shifted to instead shove him out of the way.

But as soon as I pushed Aketo, the soldier's blade bit into my left forearm. The pain was a distant fire I could ignore as I turned to face her. I bared my teeth, and she flinched back, viciously ripping her sword from my flesh. My vision wavered as hot blood spurting from the cut coated my palm.

I held up my bloodied hand. "This was a mistake."

It took little concentration to summon more magick. I lifted my sword in a two-handed grip, the edge of the blade dripping with blood magick. It didn't matter that this position left me wide open. She was too afraid to make the first move. The soldier's eyes darted behind her, showing the whites.

"Surrender," Aketo said behind me. "Look at your companions. Most have put down their weapons already. Will you die to keep someone else in a cage?"

I didn't take my eyes off the woman, who first shook her head when he spoke of surrendering, but Aketo had spoken truth. The last of the soldiers still fighting for their missing General were in the midst of surrendering.

It was over soon after that. Swords clattering to the ground. Dthazi began giving instructions on where they would round up the wounded soldiers and those loyal to them that required healing, but I didn't have time to listen.

I wrapped the cut on my arm with a piece of linen; it was deep enough to require healing, but I couldn't wait any longer. I took off running for the gate, Anali and Falun at my sides.

I skidded to a stop in front of the entrance to the tunnel, nearly sobbing at the sight of Daischa standing out front. For the look on her face was so gentle, so kind that I knew my earlier assumption was right.

"She's gone, isn't she?"

"Yes," she whispered, rocking Otho, who was wailing despite her best efforts. "She left in the night, Eva. When we realized, you were already gone."

❧ CHAPTER 28 ❧

Eva

I DREAMED OF death and hot blood soaking into my skin and soldier-white uniforms stained with worse things. I dreamed of bones snapping, the black wings of carrion crows, and my heart in Isa's hands, shredded until it was nothing more than meat.

I woke with the dawn, unable to sleep more than a few hours at a time these days. Aketo beside me didn't stir as I slipped from beneath his arm and out of the bed. It was good goose down, as comfortable as my bed in the palace.

Throllo spared himself little comfort despite his isolation in the North. It had been weeks since the night we'd faced Throllo's remaining soldiers, and I was still shocked at how much old fey art the man had repurposed to decorate the manor. Tapestries of ancient battles and marble busts and carved hunks of crystal.

It was a wonder he hadn't required a team of servants merely for dusting. I stepped into my boots, bundled myself in a fur-lined cloak, and left without waking Aketo. It was early enough that I only encountered one other person, my cousin Tavan, sitting in the manor's front courtyard. Frost blanketed the ground, grass crunching under my feet. I waved but didn't stop, mind too full of worries.

Had Throllo taken Isa straight to the capital? Had Mother already gotten news of the rebellion? The marching of soldiers filled my nightmares—thousands of men and women making their way north under her command. Somehow, I did not think we would have months to wait until my mother showed her hand.

Now that she had Isa back, they would be coming to deal with me. No matter how I spent my time, I couldn't forget every unspoken word between me and my sister. I'd never offered her forgiveness for lying about being fey, and I'd never said that, despite the lie, I still loved her. It seemed such a foolish emotion now, love for my sister. My sister who had betrayed me just hours after her promise to keep Otho and Daischa safe.

What good was that love?

I made my way through the streets of town until I reached the steps leading up to the Aerie. I was sweating by the time I climbed to their zenith, and warming my fingers with my breath.

Over the last week, the cold had become something you couldn't ignore. The air was thinner up in the Aerie, and more snow had fallen here than in the town. Not planning on staying long, I walked to the row of trees near the ledge. I removed my cloak and summoned my wings.

The shift came easier up here, inches from a terribly far drop. I conjured every detail of the wings and stepped off the edge.

✦

I returned to the manor a few hours later, sans wings, the muscles of my back aching at the strain of flying. I was surprised to find Osir waiting outside the bedchamber I shared with Aketo. I had spoken little to my older cousins since our arrival at Sher n'Cai. Tavan stayed busy as their most skilled healer and Lirra spent much of her time with Daischa, cooking and seeing to the needs of the elders in town.

Osir had joined Dthazi's scouting team and left yesterday morning to search for any sign of more soldiers in the surrounding mountains. They had anticipated being gone for several days.

"We found something, Eva. There's a camp a few miles from here, and it's filled with khimaer."

The words were barely out of his mouth before I took off, making for the front of the house. Dthazi and Aketo were waiting beyond the gate, at the place Throllo had doled out his punishments, but was now lots of overturned dirt and trees in the midst of being planted. Daischa was overseeing the project, moving many of the trees from the Aerie down here to create a grove of sorts as a tribute to the forty khimaer men and women who were killed in the fighting.

We were all finding ways to distract ourselves. Daischa had focused the lion's share of her attention on making the manor a home.

Once I'd saddled one of the horses in Throllo's stables, we

rode past the soldiers' barracks, now occupied with Dthazi's forces, and reached the gate of the Enclosure.

After we'd passed through the entrance, I sought the coalescence. Only half conscious of the pommel beneath my fingertips, I sought that cord of magick between me and Baccha.

The Hunter's prickly annoyance greeted me, the feeling more vivid than any I'd felt from him since leaving Ternain. I spurred my horse on, following the connection between us.

It didn't take very long to reach the clearing. After a while, we found tracks in the snow leading straight there. Since they weren't bothering to conceal their presence, we rode into the front of their camp.

Hundreds milled about the neat rows of tents.

Around us, a hush fell over the camp. I dismounted and scanned their faces, recognizing one from the times I'd seen through Baccha's eyes.

"Took you long enough, Princess," an all-too-familiar voice drawled from behind me.

A growl escaped me as I turned to face Baccha. He was unchanged, in his black leathers, loose braid down his back, kicking in the wind. He grinned broadly. "What? No warm greetings for me?"

I crashed into Baccha, shoving him into the dirt. He let me kick and punch at him, offering no resistance.

"This doesn't work if you don't fight back," I said, kneeling in the mud.

"You want to make me complicit in the beating you hoped to give me," Baccha said. "Cruel Princess, how I've missed you."

"I haven't missed you," I muttered.

"That's what comes with staying busy," Baccha replied, not bothering to call me on the lie. The emotions passing between us through the bond were too enmeshed for me to tell exactly what each of us felt. But Baccha had missed me, as much as I'd longed for his return.

"What are you doing here?" I frowned up at him. I hoped he didn't think all would be forgiven that easily.

"You might not have noticed, Princess, but I have kept an eye on you. When the Elderi learned you were heading to the Enclosure, I persuaded them to come here."

"Well, you missed the rebellion"—if one could call it that—"by a few weeks, Baccha."

He flicked my nose. "It's the thought that counts."

"Are you at least going to offer an explanation? Apologize?"

"I thought I'd save that for when we are alone." Baccha climbed to his feet and helped me up.

A silver-haired khimaer girl stood a few feet away, observing our exchange with a darkening gaze. Baccha turned toward her, an easy smile on his lips. "Ah, there you are, Mother Ysai. After all these months, it is my deepest pleasure to introduce you to Princess Eva. Ysai leads the Tribe."

I wiped the mud and melting snow from my palms and offered my hand. "Mother Ysai, thank you. Please join us in Sher n'Cai."

Did they really call this girl *Mother Ysai?* The title must've come with the role. I remembered Baccha saying that the woman who currently led the Tribe was an old friend of his, and that couldn't have been Ysai.

She shook my hand, but her expression was still frosty. "Thank you for the offer, but we will remain here."

I glanced at Baccha, but his expression offered nothing. "At night, the mountains are terribly cold. There is plenty of space inside."

"We are used to cold nights, but I thank you for your concern."

"I respect your decision, Mother Ysai," I said, raising my voice so it would carry, "but I must warn you all, I expect the Queen's Army is marching toward us at this very minute. I would not want to be caught outside when they arrive."

A striking older woman with crimson eyes and black wings tipped in white, like she'd dipped them in paint, appeared at Ysai's side. The look she gave Ysai was full of carefully restrained anger. "We thank you for your offer, Princess, and kindly accept."

"No," I repeated to Baccha for the third time. "Absolutely not."

"At least consider—"

"Why should I be tested by them?" I asked, pouring heated water into my tea. We sat across from each other in one of the manor's several sitting rooms. "And before you start on about history and traditions, I already know how it is supposed to work. The Elderi choose the Queen, right? Well, I'm their only choice, so what exactly is the point of this testing?"

I was on my third cup of tea. While I'd sipped the first, Baccha had told me about his journey north, about his "Aunt" in the Sister Citadel, and his capture and subsequent detainment by Ysai. During the second, I recounted our flight from Ternain, the journey across the Arym Plain, my first time shifting, Isa's betrayal, and that I didn't even know how many people I'd killed during the rebellion.

Baccha took my hand when my voice quavered, explaining the magick that had emerged from my skin. "I'm sorry, Princess."

Baccha was pleased to learn I hadn't considered killing my sister, which shocked me. I'd expected him to be as pragmatic as Anali when it came to the Rival Heir contest. When I asked him about it, he'd simply shrugged and said that hurting my sister would make me unhappy.

"Remind me again, Princess, how many soldiers are under your command?" Baccha asked.

When I did not answer, because I'd already told the bastard during my story of the rebellion, he answered himself: "Right. Not very many. Didn't you say the Queen is heading here?"

I was doing something about that, at least. I had written dozens of letters. I started with the Generals on Mateen's list, detailing the events of my nameday, why I'd fled Ternain, and why I'd helped liberate Sher n'Cai. I explained that I now believed the Queen had accused the Dracolan King of orchestrating my father's murder to distract from her own treachery, and that I did not expect the Queen would honor the time-honored Rival Heir tradition, in the event of my victory against my sister. I wrote to every noble House with lands near the mountains, calling for them to travel to Sher n'Cai and witness what would happen whenever the Queen arrived here.

It might have been futile, but it made me feel a bit better about the doom headed my way.

"I doubt any in the Tribe will fight with you against the Queen if you refuse the testing," Baccha went on. "They'll try to find another option for the throne. Ysai wanted to search the Enclosures for more blessed with Khimaerani's gift. The only reason we came here first was because I promised them you were a worthy candidate."

"Even if they do fight with us," I said, "we will still be outmatched a hundred times over. Mother could bring ten thousand men here."

"So I brought them all this way for nothing?" Baccha rose from his seat and began pacing. "Eva, they've waited over a hundred years for this. For a khimaer Queen, one blessed by Khimaerani. The only way I'll be free from my oaths is when they find a khimaer Queen to take the throne."

I blew out a sigh, massaging my temples as the beginnings of a headache pulsed at the base of my neck. "You should have led with that. What will it entail?"

"In the past, there were three trials. The only consistent rule they followed was that the last, and most important, trial was always used to address a problem in the Queendom."

"Will any of it be designed to kill me?" These trials were part of the inspiration for the Rival Heir tradition, so it was a fair consideration.

"I thought the Entwining still held," Baccha remarked. "Didn't you say you'd survived a fall that shattered a number of your bones? Don't tell me you're afraid of a few tests, Princess."

"Yes, well, I'd like to avoid the possibility, even so. I've had enough of people trying to kill me," I said, draining the last dregs of my tea. "Let's go. I suppose I should show you around."

~ CHAPTER 29 ~

Isadore

SINCE THE NIGHT she'd fled Sher n'Cai with General Sareen, Isa felt as though she were sleepwalking in the weeks that passed on horseback. She wouldn't speak to any of Throllo's men and had to keep her mental fingertips on the General during the day to keep him from accosting her.

She'd despised him immediately. When the soldier brought her to the General's manor, she'd eyed the walls crusted with ancient fey artifacts with distaste. She'd had to force the soldier to wake Throllo, and when the man had finally risen from his bed, it had taken quite a bit of persuasive magick to convince him of the wisdom of her plan.

He was to gather as many soldiers as he could and take her back to Ternain. But the moment Isa wormed her way into his head, she'd seen his true desire to collect her like one of his stolen artworks. She had to use her magick constantly, or she feared he would turn back and try to reclaim Sher n'Cai.

So much so that she was relieved when they entered the hill lands, called the Little A'Nir, and a group of patrolling soldiers intercepted them. They'd shocked her by revealing that her mother was not in Ternain, but at Fort Asrodei.

She couldn't have said exactly how many days passed between when she walked out of the caves, leaving her new brother behind, and when they arrived at Asrodei.

A sprawling tent camp rested at the base of the fort, with at least a thousand soldiers. Isa noted the flags dotting the camp with growing dread. Dozens of banners with her mother's sigil, a bolt of lightning wreathed in flowers, and their House Killeen sigil, a sinuous blade on a cobalt background, kicked in the wind.

After Isa mounted the lifts, she was hustled off by a team of maids, who scrubbed away the layers of grime on Isa's skin with fretful tuts. After they'd washed her hair and given her a dress to wear—one she recognized from her closet in Ternain—she was summoned to a meeting room.

Before she could knock, the door swung inward and her mother's voice drifted out. "I will hold you to those three weeks, General."

Isa stiffened as Throllo strolled through the doorway, smiling broadly. He was a knife of a man, slim, and with a rich, flawless complexion like oiled teakwood. He was handsome, long boned and elegant in his impeccably tailored uniform; a crest of untamed coils was the perfect contrast with the rest of him. "Ah, there you are, Princess Isadore. The Queen and I were just discussing your daring escape from your sister."

Isa sniffed and walked wide around the man. When she was Queen, she would deal with him.

When she was Queen . . .

The thought did not fit so neatly in her head now. She

recalled the words she'd spat at Eva, *You want to be Queen, don't you?*

Didn't she?

Mother was seated at a long table filled with maps. Ivory and obsidian figurines held down the corners. Other than a guard by the door, they were alone. She wore a cream riding dress, beaded with gold moons and stars.

"Isadore," Mother said, shock lining her face. She stared at Isa like she didn't recognize her.

Belatedly Isa realized she'd forgotten to don her glamour. No matter now, she glamoured her face into a facsimile of the Queen's and slid into the chair on her right side. "Mother. What are you doing here?"

"I've come to collect you, of course," Lilith said, twisting one of the sapphire rings on her finger. "It's time we dealt with your sister. A coronation in the spring will be nice, don't you think?"

Isa shook her head. "But you always said you planned to rule another five more years."

"Yes, I once thought so, but you're ready. You survived."

"There was nothing to survive, Mother, besides that man." Isa barely held on to her calm. "Eva never hurt me. Did you know Sareen hangs people for breaking curfew?"

"Oh, my Isadore," Lilith cooed. "Do you expect the man to use a gentle hand when dealing with those khimaer? You know how they are."

Her mother's syrupy-sweet tone drained the last of Isa's patience. "No, I don't know, Mother."

"You have been gone for months, Isa," her mother said, reaching out to pinch her cheek, her lacquered nails biting into Isa's skin. "Don't tell me your sister convinced you that you deserved to be kidnapped and dragged across the country. She stole you away."

"Only to give us a choice," Isa protested.

"I see. You've been letting her fool you into thinking she is vulnerable. Look what your sister does given freedom. Slaughtering soldiers who have sworn to protect her for people she hardly knows. You think she won't kill you? She will turn this Queendom into a charnel house if you let her, Isadore. We have to act first."

Memory dragged Isa back to the night before Eva's nameday.

You must strike first, Mother had said. She'd called Isa to her rooms, and was still wading through the papers on her desk when Isa arrived.

Isa had sat waiting until Lilith deigned to speak when she noticed the ring balanced on top of one of the stacks of paper. Her not-father's ring. *Is there any news from the border? Have the Dracolans made any new acts of aggression?*

They were all waiting for more news on the assassins who'd killed the King. Lilith had promised to get to the truth and find out who exactly had put a bounty on Lei's head.

Her mother looked up from her work, waving a dismissive hand. *I doubt the King of Dracol will do a thing, unless we send soldiers over the border.*

But how will we find out who wanted Papa dead? What if they're targeting you next, or me?

Lilith's face went still. *We are safe here.*

But—but, Isa sputtered.

Lilith's eyes were cold, and then, as if recounting something as dull as the weather, she said, *That is enough of you worrying about Lei. He was a liar and a fool I never should have welcomed into my bed.*

Isa had been disbelieving when her mother went on to explain that Lei was khimaer, and he'd been hiding it from them for decades.

They are a scheming, base race. That is why you must strike against Eva first.

With a mingling of dread and anticipation, Isa listened to her mother's simple plan to draw Eva away from the ball the next night. It would be over soon and the worst thing she would ever have to do would be behind her.

When she tried to imagine actually dealing the killing blow, she could never conjure it. But she knew how she would do it—ensnaring Eva's mind and taking her pain away before she ended it—and her mother's revelation made her all the more certain she was doing the right thing.

Eva *was* a liar. She'd pretended to love Isa and left her without ever looking back.

Or so Isa had believed. She couldn't deny that Eva had been as shocked as she was when she learned the truth about Lei.

Isa sat across from her mother now, watching as she plotted over maps of the A'Nir Mountains and Sher n'Cai. Small enamel figurines that reminded her of Lei were scattered across the table. It occurred to her that these maps, and everything else in Lilith's makeshift war room had belonged to her father.

"How long did you know Eva and Lei were khimaer before you told me?" Isa asked quietly.

The question must have shocked Lilith, by the muscle feathering in her jaw, though the rest of her face was placid. For a long moment, Isa thought Lilith was not going to answer, but finally she said, "A few months. Do you think I would have let a khimaer remain King for long if I knew?"

The words echoed in Isa's ears like a warning bell. She thought back to the question Eva had repeatedly asked her those first weeks of Isa's captivity.

Isa barely listened as her mother told her they would be marching north at dawn. "I hope to make it to the Enclosure in a few weeks. I brought all your winter clothes. Pack what you need and prepare yourself. It's time you finally faced your responsibilities and did away with your sister."

So much for keeping her promise to Eva. Leaving with Throllo was supposed to give them months. Months where Isa could decide, without her mother's or her sister's influence, whether she still wanted the throne. But she had never been able to stand up to her mother, so Isa stood and left the room.

～ CHAPTER 30 ～

Eva

A WHITE-CAPPED CROW winged through my window to deliver a message the same morning I was set to meet with the Elderi for my trials.

I was deciding whether I needed to arm myself, when the creature alighted on the vanity in front of me. I nearly jumped out of my skin as it peered up at me, unblinking and unafraid. Clearly the creature had been magicked.

I pulled the tube from around its leg and pulled out the roll of paper inside. The note was short.

Evalina,

We march on the Enclosure. If you turn yourself over to fight your sister, I will forgive the people of Sher n'Cai for their participation in your little rebellion. Fail to present yourself and they will die. It's time to be done with this once and for all. We arrive in a week.

There was no signature, but I knew my mother's florid hand. The crow gave a shake of its wings and took off.

Had Isa chosen this? I prayed Mother made this decision without her, but there was no way to know.

I finished dressing, even though my thundering pulse begged for me to sound every alarm there was, and considered canceling the trials. We could prepare for a siege. The glass atop the Enclosure wall would deter any hoping to climb it, and I doubted they could bring trebuchets through the mountains.

Or I could do as my mother requested. Face the battle between me and Isa that our every step had been leading to since I was born.

I crumpled the note in my hand and left my room.

I'd expected a private meeting with the Elderi, but it seemed word had gotten out. The entire receiving hall was full.

The room had been set up like its own Court, with the Elderi seated in high-backed chairs arranged in a semicircle on a raised dais, with Mother Ysai at the center. She looked different from the last time I'd seen her; Baccha had told me she also possessed Khimaerani's gift.

Daischa and her sons were given positions of prominence beside the dais. Dthazi winked at me and elbowed Aketo, who met my gaze, smiling slightly.

I reminded myself that even if I failed, making allies of the Tribe would be worth enduring this. I trusted the Elderi to ensure the people of Sher n'Cai weren't massacred in my absence.

I stood before the dais, hands behind my back, and recited

the words Baccha had told me: "I present myself, Evalina Grace Killeen, to the wisdom of the Elderi Council. I pray to be worthy of your approval, but if I am not, I pray you find another to sit on the Ivory Throne."

I don't know what I expected in reply, but the Elderi at Ysai's left side rose from his seat, leaning on a gnarled walking stick.

"The first of your trials is a feat of magick," intoned Eramin, the oldest among the Elderi, with a bull snout and twitching bovine ears that looked diminutive among his nest of gray coils.

"A feat?" I echoed. "What sort of feat?"

Arsa, the cranelike woman whom I'd met the day of their arrival, said, "The Hunter tells us you have been blessed by Khimaerani. We request a feat of magick to prove it, Your Highness."

Oh.

That.

I closed my eyes; sketches from Queen Assani's *On Mutable Flesh* floated through my thoughts. I had thought long on my chosen form, considering all the beauty I had encountered in Sher n'Cai these last weeks.

The sunlight on Daischa's scales; the ropes of her sable braids. Dthazi's large eyes that could see in the dark, and the fangs that poked out of Aketo's mouth when he pouted. Otho's chunky fists and kicking hooves. Baccha's fine-boned face peeking out from his curtain of hair as he bounced Otho on his knee. Tufted tails and deft wings. Springy antelope forelegs covered in soft fur.

An image began to coalesce in my mind. Winged and scaled and horned and clawed.

I opened my eyes, surprised to find a scaled tail wrapped

around my waist. Its ebon scales ended in a flare of golden feathers to match the ones on the tips of my wings. I spread them wide and bowed at the waist.

I straightened and was surprised to find Eramin and the rest of the Elderi beaming.

"Most well done," he thundered, stamping a cloven foot on the dais.

I heard the rustle of fabric behind me and froze at the sight of dozens of khimaer, and Baccha, kneeling on the floor. I gestured for them to rise, heat warming my face.

Arsa rose from her chair. "Your second trial is to settle a dispute between us." She inclined her head toward Ysai, the only one who did not seem impressed by my display. I didn't fault her; I, too, would not clap for something I had been doing for years. "You know that Lord Baccha has acted in service of the Tribe since the start of the Great War."

"I do," I agreed. I forced myself not to look behind me and see his reaction.

"Then you know that when he traveled to the South, he interfered with you despite our express commands. However, had he listened to us, we may not have learned of your magick. Should the Hunter have been . . . reprimanded for his inability to follow our directives, or should he be lauded?"

"If I recall correctly, you already have punished Baccha," I said, trying to smother the stirrings of real anger. What did they expect, for me to condemn him? Baccha was a cool wind in the back of my mind, offering peace.

"Previous imprisonment notwithstanding," Arsa said. "We would like to hear your assessment."

I embraced the tranquility my friend offered and drew in a

calming breath. "From what I've been told, Baccha swore to serve the Tribe because of his past sins. But he has been a great tool to you, because of his unique skill set. Is this true?"

"Yes," Arsa agreed. "He is the last of the famed magickians."

"So his obedience isn't truly the real benefit you gained by sending Baccha to Ternain. If so, how can you expect him to follow orders without consideration for the circumstances? I found Baccha; he didn't seek me out. And had he ignored our connection, that would've been in opposition to his purpose to discover knowledge about the crown." I glanced behind me, and found Baccha listening with a sober expression. "Baccha is by no means without flaw, but neither were the orders he was given. No, I don't believe he should be punished."

The Elderi began arguing among themselves. Ysai, apart from them, tipped her head in acknowledgment, though by the flat set of her lips, I could tell she did not agree with my conclusion.

Finally, Arsa broke apart from the others, palms pressed together as if in prayer. "We do not all agree, but I was given the task of assigning the trial, and it is up to my judgment whether you fail or pass this test." She dipped at the waist, carmine eyes crinkling as she smiled. "And I say you pass."

Arsa returned to her seat on Ysai's right side. Finally, the young woman stood.

"Princess Eva," Ysai began. "Since arriving, I have heard many stories about you. Of your magick and skill with a blade. Tales of deadliness. Nothing about this surprises me. Our ancestors fell to Raina's cursed magick, but I will not accept a Queen who believes all her problems can be solved with a sword. For your third trial, I assign to you this: Solve the problem of your Rival Heir sister without killing."

"What?" I gasped, then remembered myself. "Mother Ysai, how can I be expected to do that?"

"Killing is easy, clean, some would say." Ysai inclined her head, nose wrinkling. "It's much harder to seek a complex solution to your problems. I don't doubt you could kill your sister with one swing of that sword at your waist. But this task is not meant to be easily done, Princess."

⪼ CHAPTER 31 ⪻

Eva

A WEEK LATER, as Mother promised, they arrived.

Perched on the roof of what was once General Sareen's manor, I watched the rows of tents that hadn't been there last night. Thousands of soldiers blanketed the earth; from afar they looked like writhing ants.

When the scouts returned yesterday morning with news that two battalions of the Queen's Army were marching up the mountain, Dthazi and Aketo had gone to sweep the mountains around Sher n'Cai, making sure everyone was inside.

I faced my friends' grim expressions. Aketo, Anali, Falun, and Baccha had joined me on the roof and they at least deserved the truth. "A week ago my mother sent this."

I handed Aketo the note. His eyes scanned it, and the look of betrayal in his eyes was a knife in my side. "You knew?"

"I didn't tell you, because this problem is mine to solve," I said. "Before you ask, yes, I'm going to agree to it. Don't try to change my mind. I have to; this place would become a death-trap in a siege."

I'd already sent one of Mateen's Jackals with a note, accepting my mother's indicating I would meet them in the morning, and I hoped it would be enough to hold them off tonight. So far they seemed content to wait.

"What about the trial?" Aketo asked.

"What choice do I have? If I kill"—I swallowed back the bile rising in my throat—"Isa, I will be the True Heir, Elderi approval or not. But there's another problem to consider. I'm not certain my mother will be content to leave this fight to me and Isa."

I didn't want to believe she would interfere, but considering what the Queen allowed to go on in the Enclosure, my understanding of which lines Lilith would or wouldn't cross was no longer reliable.

"Baccha and Fal, I need your eyes on my mother. If it seems as though she is plotting to ensure only Isadore can walk away from our fight, it will be up to you to subdue her." I turned to Aketo and Anali. "If I fall, I need you two to promise you won't try to get revenge. Swear to me that you will help Dthazi get everyone into the caves."

The cave network in the A'Nir offered the only slim chance of escape if everything went to hell tomorrow.

Anali bit her lip, but nodded.

Aketo, eyes unreadable, pulled me aside. "What are you planning, Eva?"

I rose up on the tips of my toes and kissed him thoroughly. "To keep you safe."

✦

Around midnight, I stood before a tall standing mirror, holding a candlestick in one hand. I pictured Isadore's face in my mind's eye. Her small mouth always twisted into a pout, her eyes of freshly trimmed grass.

I hadn't ever attempted to shift my features, but it worked. I looked exactly like the guise Isa wore at Court, though I couldn't quite convey her disdain for everything and everyone she came across. I hoped no one would pay close attention to my threadbare cloak.

I snuck out of Sher n'Cai through the caves and walked right into the Queen's Army camp. A fair amount of soldiers were still awake, but no one stopped me as I searched for the tent that could possibly be Isa's.

It was as if I were being pulled through the camp, a puppet on a string, until I finally stopped before an emerald tent. A flag with a slim blade wrapped in ivy hung from a pike stuck in the ground outside.

Casting a furtive look at the nearby soldiers, I ducked inside.

Isa sat cross-legged on a cushion, a small lamp at her side. When she looked up to find me entering her tent, there was no shock on her face, because she'd been guiding me here all along.

"Good, you're here," Isa said. She sat cross-legged on a cushion, a small lamp at her side. "I think it's time we talked."

❧ Chapter 32 ❧

Eva

WHEN THE SUN was directly overhead, piercing the blue-gray storm clouds, Aketo signaled to raise the gate to the Enclosure. The crank required two sets of hands to wind.

Aketo was at my side. Baccha and the few who were left of my guard, just Falun and Kelis, walked behind us. The Elderi and the rest of the Tribe's forces followed at a short distance. It was a pitiable force when compared with a couple thousand soldiers Mother had brought to Sher n'Cai. After an hour of deliberation, Dthazi, Yaya, and their unit of fighters had decided to remain inside the Enclosure. They would be better used in an evacuation than in a battle.

I hoped it didn't come to that. When the gate was hoisted high enough and the dirt, stirred by its ascent, settled, I gazed out at the rolling waves of soldiers. Their white uniforms blended into the landscape, with mud up to their knees.

We had the high ground, but that was truly our only advantage.

Standing ten feet ahead of the first line of soldiers, Isadore and Mother were hand in hand. Mother wore her crown, a fan of rubies set in gold, and wore a pale blue dress, the voluminous skirts divided for riding horseback, its hem already muddied.

Isa was dressed for a fight in slate leggings, and boots laced up to her knees. A tunic, its sleeves pushed up to her elbows, and a glistening chain-mail cowl that covered her shoulders matched the rest.

Isa's hair was yet again silvery blond and she'd glamoured away her springy curls in favor of soft waves falling around her face. Even though it was another layer of our subterfuge, I couldn't help but mourn at the sight. And yet some small part of me was impressed.

Isa had made herself into this image of our mother for her safety. But she'd still broken out of Mother's thrall.

I felt overdressed in comparison. I'd borrowed it all from Daischa: the finely made chain-mail cowl was an old heirloom made from interlocking slivers of silver and gold, like a dragon's scales. My cloak was crimson silk lined with soft wool. The sturdy shearling tights and tunic were Osir's work.

We marched toward the army until we'd cleared the gate. My steps faltered as I noticed a contingent standing apart from the soldiers. The group of fifteen women were dressed in fine woolen dresses, designed to withstand the cold, and I could tell they were noblewomen by their bearing. Even the way they sniffed at my approach oozed Court disdain. It didn't matter that they weren't exactly on my side; they could still be witnesses for what I planned.

I waited to hear the crunch of stone on stone indicating the gate was closed.

I dropped Aketo's hand and stepped forward, boots crunching in the snow.

I drew in a deep breath—the smell of freshly turned earth, bitter draughts of kaffe, and sword oil filled the air—and called, "Before we begin, Mother, I have a request."

My mother took in the sight of me with barely suppressed rage. Immediately she began to twist one of the baubles on her finger, and her skin had gone nearly as pale as the snow on the ground. But she must have conquered her fury, because she laughed. The sound of it was like shattering glass. "A request? Very well, Eva. What is it you want?"

"Rescind control of the army and give the command over to whichever one of us survives today."

"While I'd have no trouble turning over command to Isadore, I cannot in good conscience give you the chance to tear through the Queendom, killing whoever you choose. I think not, Evalina."

Do not rise to the bait. "Fine," I said, crossing my arms. "Then simply swear not to interfere."

"The nerve of you, a rebel and a traitor, making demands of me. You are lucky I am still giving you a chance to gain the throne."

My hands curled into fists. "Did you think it luck when you were our age, being an only child? Not having a sister to kill?"

For once my words penetrated her icy calm. "I thought it unfortunate that I never had a chance to prove myself as you two do. I will grant your request. I swear no one will interfere."

"My thanks." I nodded and drew my sword. "Let's get this over with, then."

Mother whispered something in Isa's ear before my sister stepped forward. Two of the long-handled knives Isa favored were strapped to her back.

She pulled both free in a smooth, graceful movement, tossing her hair behind her.

Sword gripped in one hand, sturdy belt knife in the other, I ran for Isa. Eyes slit, I fought to avoid her gaze as we clashed.

Sword to knife, steel to steel. Neither of us reached for any magick just yet. I could sense that Isa was as curious as I to see how we matched up now. She met my every strike, parrying my attacks with blistering speed.

She was so quick, seeming to know where I intended to strike before even I did. But eventually Isa began to slow and I took my opportunity when she lifted both arms in a head-on attack.

I raised my sword, gritting my teeth as I fought to hold back all the strength in her. With my belt knife, I stabbed her in the side, not a deep wound, but blood welled, spilling down the handle and onto my hand.

Isa hissed, baring her teeth as she backed away.

I swiped the flat side of the blade across my forearm, leaving a smear of blood right over the tattoo of arrows. I dropped my belt knife as the quiver full of blood-magick arrows appeared in my hand. Lowering my sword to the ground, I smiled.

"Wait," Isa said, gasping to catch her breath. She hoisted both knives again, crossed in front of her like a shield.

But it was too late. I had already sent an arrow flying straight for her heart. It pierced her chest, disappearing into her skin in a spray of deep crimson. Heart's blood.

Isa's knives slid from her hands as she fell, face-first, into the snow.

Blood pooled around Isa's fallen body.

A roaring noise filled my ears as I stared at her splayed limbs, but as the sound of a high-pitched keen filled my ears, I remembered my true purpose.

Mother, skirts gathered in one fist, ran to Isa's side, kneeling in the spreading blood. She laid two fingers against Isa's neck, checking for a pulse. Finding none, she glared up at me.

It didn't occur to me until that moment that I had never seen my mother in a true fury. She kept such a tight leash on her emotions; I was familiar enough with her rage when stifled.

"You," she shouted, tears streaking her face. "You cursed nightmare. If only I hadn't failed to kill you when I had the chance."

As if her words were daggers, I stumbled back, struck. "No. *No.*"

"You never once suspected. Both of my daughters, too trusting for their own good. You aren't fool enough to think I will let you take the throne, are you?"

She sucked in a deep breath, reaching for the sky. The clouds swirled and thunder cracked, the mountain seeming to vibrate underfoot.

"You really did kill him," I whispered, shaking.

She climbed to her feet. "It's no more than he deserved. If only those Dracolans had struck when you two were together."

The howls of a dozen wolves reached my ears, and for a moment, relief coursed through me. I wasn't alone.

But as I looked behind me, the first bolt of Mother's lightning struck the ground where the wolves gathered around Baccha. Squeals and cries of pain filled the air.

I dove backward as another bolt struck the ground a mere hand's width from where I stood.

Hail began to fall and the squall surrounding Mother left her hovering inches above the ground. If this continued, she might bring an avalanche down on us all.

She held one of Isa's swords as she floated toward me, murder in her eyes. I was frozen, rooted to the spot by shock. Isa had warned me last night that Mother's reaction to her death would be terrible, but this? I couldn't believe it.

Too trusting. Not once had I considered my mother might be the one who sent killer after killer to end my life.

A bellow of rage sounded. I turned in time to see Baccha with his hand stretched toward the sky, in the same gesture as Mother's just moments ago. Baccha's hair, torn free of its usual braid, floated around him like a golden shroud. He looked like the Godling he was as power glowed beneath his skin.

The wind began to ebb away, calmed by Baccha.

My mother, feet firmly planted on the ground now, leveled the sword at me, eyes promising murder.

I stared down at the quiver still in my hand.

Killing is easy, Ysai had said.

It would have been so simple, sending one of these arrows to savage her heart. I was ashamed that I wanted to repay her for every pain. Every time she'd cut me down in front of the Court. For stealing my father from me and Otho and Isa. For her inability to love me.

For never once choosing me.

But simply because I could kill her didn't mean that I should. Even if I wouldn't mourn her death, Isa would. And I refused to do to my sister what Lilith had done to me. I wouldn't take my mother's life as she had stolen my father's.

I let my magick ebb away. I didn't need it anymore.

When she darted toward me, clumsy in her dress, I side-stepped her. I hooked an ankle round hers and she fell in the dirt.

When she tried to rise, I pointed my sword at her throat. "That's enough."

✦

Isa rolled over onto her back and growled, "Gods, Eva, that *hurt*."

"If you recall, it was your idea," I countered. It was Isa who suggested I use the arrows to make it seem as though I'd stabbed her through the heart. I'd aimed for an inch above her heart, not a shot I would've trusted on an actual bow. As it was, Isa's breathing had a labored, wet sound that worried me.

"Baccha," I called. "Can you heal my sister, please?"

My mother's eyes went so wide I could see the whites all around. Like she'd seen a ghost. "What is happening?"

I pointed to the soldiers who'd laid down their weapons. "You've confessed to ordering the killing of King Lei and repeated attempts to murder me in front of a sizable contingent of the army, Mother. I'm arresting you for treason and murder."

"You can't arrest the Queen for murder. And what treason? Lei was a liar and a fraud."

"An act against a future heir is treason, Mother, and so is using a murder you orchestrated to start a war with Dracol." I waved a hand at the crowd of soldiers, who had not taken my mother's confession kindly. Even the courtiers were aghast, trading troubled looks. "Do you think they will stand with you? I do not."

I walked to where Falun stood, carrying a small satchel. The shackles inside were the same ones Isa had worn months ago.

By the time I returned, it seemed something had broken in my mother. She didn't resist as I slid each shackle over her wrists. Of all the things, it was her compliance that cracked my heart in half.

It was over. It was finally done.

⪻ EPILOGUE ⪼

A Queen of Gilded Horns

"Ow!" I groaned, massaging the back of my scalp.

"If you'd like me to cut out the knots, I can get the shears now, Evalina," Mirabel scolded.

She'd woken me an hour before the sun was up. Apparently, the hairstyle she intended for today would require four hours of work. Lucky me.

Isa, seated in the corner of my bedchamber with her legs folded beneath her on a citrine velvet cushion, chuckled. She'd knocked on my door midmorning with a plate of buttery pastry, mazi fruit, and blood oranges.

Supposedly the kitchen staff had cleared the groves in Ternain and had more shipped in from the citrus groves south to account for the myriad of recipes for the coronation feast.

Mirabel had heard rumors that some of the cooks complained that I'd opened the feast to the public. We hired additional staff to make up for the new mouths to feed.

"Mirabel, will you braid my hair tomorrow?" Isa asked.

Despite the early hour, she was already made up. The kohl lining her vivid eyes seemed to make them glow. Or Isa could be playing with glamour. Hard to say.

She'd been suspiciously quiet when I asked about it.

"What will you do for me if I say yes?" Mira countered. She and Isa were like two cats who couldn't help but accept that they enjoyed each other's company.

A week after we returned to Ternain, Isa rescinded her claim for the throne before the Court. We had both Rival Heir diadems melted down and created a new crown for her.

And in a quiet ceremony at the Temple, Sarou and two Sorceryn supervised the removal of the Entwining. Though we'd both wondered what would be the harm in keeping the spell intact, the Sorceryn warned that magick left untended had a habit of growing strange. The connection between our souls was best severed.

Though I hadn't officially been crowned, I gave her a new title, Princess Advisor to the Throne, which so far meant she sat in the meetings between the Queen's Council and the half of the Elderi who'd remained in Ternain. The rest had gone to the Southern Enclosure on the edge of the Kremir. We'd sent notices that all detainment of any people on Myrean soil was now outlawed, but hadn't yet heard any news back.

Though every gathering of the Queen's Council and the Elderi was contentious, we were attempting to rewrite the Rival Heir laws. I was looking forward to seeing what they came up with. When I'd suggested a reversal back to the old system, of the Elderi choosing candidates, though perhaps with some qualifications more than a couple in a generation could meet, Ysai graciously told me their meetings were to be private from that moment on.

The other struggle with the Queen's Council had been deciding on the matter of my mother. The law was quite clear that Queens could not be executed, and thank the Gods because I would have refused, but jailing her in the dungeons of the palace indefinitely would not work either. The compromise we'd found was exile, though Isa and I had not yet determined a place where we were comfortable sending her. And I knew Isa still visited her once a day. I hadn't gone to the dungeons and had no plans to.

When Mirabel had finished with my hair, we all retreated to my closet, where three of the most ornate gowns I'd ever seen hung.

The first was pure white with a full skirt, seed pearls beading every bit of the low-cut bodice. I'd declined to wear this one immediately, as it reminded me of something Mother might wear.

The next was quite dramatic, its skirt made from long strips of crimson and black silk embroidered with the flowers tattooed on my arms, complete with blades hidden inside their petals. I'd been tempted by it, but when I saw my seamstress's final offering, I knew it was the one.

It was like liquid gold, falling in a clean sweep to the floor. Unadorned, simple, Queenly in its simplicity.

We finished off the fruit and pastries—priorities—and then Mira helped me into the dress, while Isa spectated and tried on my jewelry. She had already slipped into her own gown of vivid green silk embroidered all over with ivy leaves.

She gasped, finding a green enameled bangle in one of my drawers. "This is mine!"

"Absolutely not," I argued. "You gave that to me!"

We bickered back and forth until Mirabel began to hum loudly, drowning us out.

Around midday, an hour before the coronation was set to begin, three knocks sounded on the door. Baccha, Aketo, and Falun were waiting in the sitting room when I opened the door.

Baccha was in bloodred. The color set off his tan skin and flaxen hair perfectly. The only other color I'd ever seen him in was the gold of his jewelry. At the sight of my dress, he groaned, "I thought we agreed on red."

"I told you, Baccha. It's too reminiscent of blood."

"That is the point, Princess," he protested. Then he paused, face falling as if something terrible had occured to him. "Oh no. I've just realized this is the last morning I'll get to call you that."

I grinned. Somehow I suspected Baccha would still be calling me Princess long after I'd been crowned. If he did indeed stay in Myre. "I'll wear crimson tonight. Just for you." After the coronation and the party that entailed, Ysai, Baccha, and I would be meeting to do away with his oaths to the Tribe. Ysai, ever a purist when it came to rules, insisted we wait until after the coronation.

Like me, Aketo was in gold. "Shall we?" he asked, fingers lacing through mine.

He noticed Isa standing in the doorway behind me. "Uh, I think Dthazi went to your rooms."

Isa groaned. "I swore I told him I would be getting dressed *here*."

She left my rooms with the promise to meet us in the ballroom.

"One last thing," Mira called, a medium-size velvet box in her hands.

Just yesterday one of the palace's archivists had found it. The gilded crown of the past khimaer Queens.

I peeked inside, spying the pronged edges of the crown curling like horns.

"Captain." I handed it to Falun, a vision in soft dove gray that made his eyes a rich cerulean.

The only absence I regretted was Anali, who'd been reassigned as Lady Commander of the Queen's Army. The role had been filled by the husbands of Queens for the last nine generations, but if . . . when Aketo and I married, I wanted him by my side to aid in the difficult transition to freedom. Already the human nobility showed signs of revolt at the return of lands to their original owners.

Baccha looped his arm through Falun's, and dropped his head on Falun's shoulder. Even though he was a couple inches taller than Fal, it did not seem awkward. "Ready, Princess?"

"As I'll ever be," I said, smiling.

THE STORY BEGINS IN

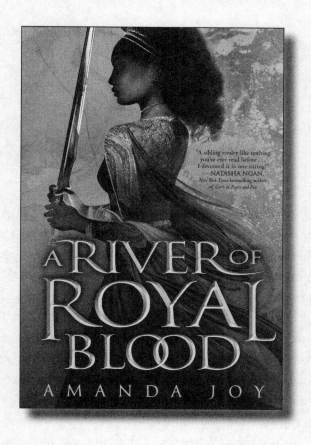

A RIVER OF ROYAL BLOOD

AMANDA JOY

"A sibling rivalry like nothing you've ever read before. I devoured it in one sitting."
—NATASHA NGAN,
New York Times bestselling author of Girls of Paper and Fire

TURN THE PAGE FOR A SNEAK PEEK

⇥ CHAPTER 1 ⇤

THE PASSAGE BENEATH my bedchamber was silent as a crypt, though as always, the Empress scorpions that nested in these forgotten tunnels started hissing disapproval the moment my feet touched the ground.

I crouched and checked the circle of cinnamon sticks and dried lavender I'd laid to deter the wicked beasts, and then knotted the hem of my skirt. If left hanging, the chime and rattle of its beading would echo through the passages, and although I'd never crossed paths with anyone here, I couldn't risk discovery.

I adjusted the belt knife in its soft leather holster at the small of my back. Whenever I shifted, nicks in the wooden handle scratched my skin, but it couldn't be helped. This knife was my only weapon plain enough to suit this disguise. In a floor-sweeping skirt and a top that bared my midriff but covered my arms and their tattoos, I could pass as a common human girl out for a night of revelry.

Flint struck stone inches from my face, sparks dancing through inky darkness. I jumped, a curse on my lips, but my hand fell from my knife. "I'd appreciate some warning next time."

"Just keeping you sharp," said the young man standing mere feet away.

Falun, second-in-command of my guard and my closest friend, towered over me in the cramped passage. He was long-limbed and graceful, though still not quite grown into his wide shoulders. Like many of the fey, who originally came from the North, Falun was fair-skinned and fine-haired. Even in the scant torchlight, his skin gleamed like mother-of-pearl. All the fey had a certain sameness—luminous skin, oversize eyes, pointed ears, and vibrant coloring—but Falun was among the most beautiful. His hair was streaked with apple red and dark gold, and the sharp line of his jaw emphasized his full-lipped smile.

Two nights ago, Falun had gone to my room at dawn to propose a journey to the kitchens and found me missing, my bed pushed aside, trapdoor hanging open. He knew I became restless at night, and instead of sounding the alarm, he'd waited until I returned. In exchange for such a kindness, I'd decided to bring him tonight, though I'd been very light on the details.

Falun held the torch to the passage wall, the dancing flames making his blue eyes flash silver as he inspected the words engraved on the stone. They were written in the khimaer language, the sinuous alphabet of the people who'd once ruled from this Palace. Nearly two hundred years ago, humans had wrested control of the Queendom from the khimaer, but signs of the previous rulers still lingered all over Myre.

Falun's eyebrows rose as he recognized the language. "How did you find this place?"

"When I was seven, Isadore and I found the trapdoor after her earring rolled under my bed." I didn't add that we'd found a similar hatch beneath hers and spent a year sleeping very little as we explored every inch of these passages at night.

I went to great lengths to avoid discussing my sister.

The tips of Falun's tapered ears went pink. "Isadore knows about this place? Don't you worry about seeing her?"

I snorted. "Why would my sister come here? There is nothing about the Palace that would make her want to leave."

"True enough." He swiped a hand across his face, but his grimace remained in place. "I'll regret this, won't I?"

"You won't, and you know it—why else would you have come?"

He leaned forward as if sharing a secret. "Actually I came to keep you out of trouble."

"And that works just as well." I grinned, even though I could protect myself. I snatched his torch and snuffed out the flames beneath my boot. "Follow me."

We ran through darkness so thick the only sign of Falun beside me was his hand in mine. After months of sneaking out through these passages, finding my escape route—and avoiding the scorpion nests—had become second nature. When Isadore and I were children, we'd stuck to the passages around our quarters, but when I returned to the capital ten months ago and began exploring again, I soon realized they tunneled through the grounds around the Queen's Palace, right up to its outer wall. The floors of the passages changed now from stone to tile to packed earth, a sure sign that we were close. After about a mile, we stopped at a steel ladder. Night air blew through an opening overhead.

I climbed to the top and emerged in an orchard with rows of flowering trees, though they didn't bloom during the scorching weeks of high summer, as it was now. Fresh air kissed my skin, heavy with damp heat. I breathed it in, my pulse a driving beat beneath my skin.

Almost, it hummed.

Falun joined me, following my gaze to a carved expanse of white stone.

The wall that marked my freedom.

I wasn't allowed outside it without a guard of at least twenty, per my mother's stipulations. Compared to my home for the previous three years—at Fort Asrodei, an army base in the highlands, where my father still lived—the Palace was cramped and held little of interest. Every room crawled with courtiers, the very last people I wanted encounter. Aside from training at the sparring grounds and attending Court every morning, I rarely left my rooms. These nightly excursions were my only escape.

We scaled the wall and dropped down into a vacant alley in the bloodkin sector.

Four races dwelled in Myre—human, fey, bloodkin, and khimaer. Of the four, only bloodkin, fey, and humans were allowed to live freely in the capital, and the city was divided evenly among them. Humans lived in the southern sector, fey in the east, and bloodkin in the north. The Red River was west of the city, where its red-brown waters were clogged with river ships and water markets.

Falun and I left the alley and emerged in a narrow avenue lined with abandoned flats and blood brothels. The men and women strolling beside us could've passed for human— the darkness hid the telling red tinge to their skin—but for the bloodletting knives at their belts, the scabbards marked with patterns to signify the wearer's trade. When bloodkin reached maturity at seventeen, they sustained themselves by drinking the blood of the living. The narrow blades weren't worn out of necessity—bloodkin largely used their fangs to feed—but were mandated by a law created so that humans who feared bloodkin could identify them at a distance.

The northern sector was a warren of streets so cramped you could barely tell them from the alleys. Most shops were shuttered and didn't look like they'd be reopening anytime soon. The Night Souk was buried within those tight streets. Because it was a smugglers' market, the peddlers set up their makeshift stalls at sunset and took them down by sunrise. When we arrived, business was still thriving, before fear of a visit from the City Guard sent many of the smugglers home early.

"Ya, ya," they cried. "Ho-chee-chee, ho-chee-chee! Best in Ternain!"

We passed towers of stoneware stacked haphazardly, vats filled with powder dyes, and burlap sacks of beans and spice pods. I stopped to exchange two coppers for a handful of spell-worked beads that wound through my curls with little effort and would fall out whenever I bade them. Clothiers hawked silks, stretching out their arms to measure the yardage and show off the vivid colors.

Gazes lingered on Falun as much as could be expected—he was, after all, lovely—and their eyes moved right over me, a plain human girl to all appearances. Exactly as I intended.

My minimal disguise worked for two reasons. No one expected a Princess in these streets, and so no one truly saw me. Knowing the young Princess was orange-eyed and wild-haired was different from connecting those features to a random girl in the market. My first nights outside the Queen's Palace, I thought if I let my cloak slip even once, someone would recognize me. But in the bloodkin sector, most had never seen any of the royal family up close. And even if they had, I'd been away for three years, and since my return, I'd rarely left the Palace. Few outside of it knew my face.

Still I was careful. I dropped my eyes to the ground whenever anyone met them, and kept my hands hidden unless haggling with a shop owner absolutely required it. If I had more ordinary magick, I wouldn't have bothered to hide my tattoos. Every human in Myre had magick inked onto their skin, but the white and red symbols—for marrow and blood—on my arms drew the eye.

Ahead of us, drums rolled like thunder. We'd finally reached the Patch, where bloodred tiles had been used to mend the broken paving stones of the sector's main thoroughfare. The tiles had taken on a different purpose soon after—a place to dance.

Gripping Falun's hand, I took off running toward the

sound, coming to an abrupt stop as we reached the press of bodies around the Patch.

Throngs of young fey glided through the street with flowers woven through lustrous hair and brass bells hanging from their wrists. *Glamour*, the fey ability to cast illusions over the world and themselves, made their glossy skin shine as bright as the moon. Beside them human girls in large groups held hands, swirls of silver paint on their tattooed arms glittering as they passed around tiny cups of *ouitʒa*, dark liquor made from the sugarcane that grew along the river.

Three-story *akelaes*—Myrean homes built around a central courtyard—painted in bright jewel tones filled the street, bougainvillea climbing terraces filled with candles as tall as my waist. Food carts were set up beneath the eaves, selling liquor and paper sheaths full of roasted nuts and boiled shellfish.

I collided with a bloodkin boy with flawless umber skin. He smiled, hands falling to my hips to steady me. He opened his mouth, but Falun's hand dropped onto my shoulder.

The boy frowned, but when he looked at Falun, his gaze warmed. "Are you new to the Patch?" .

Falun's cheeks reddened, mouth hanging open as he sought an answer.

"We aren't new," I said, removing both of their hands.

"See you on the tiles," the boy called as I pushed farther into the crowd. Falun followed, glancing over his shoulder as the boy disappeared behind a group of human girls.

One handed Falun two cups and ran her fingers through his hair. He smiled and the girl's eyes went soft with wonder.

She didn't even blink as he plucked her hand away. The ouitza burned a path down my throat. Falun sipped his, wrinkled his nose, and gave the rest to me.

The gathering opened up and I caught sight of the Copper Steps, the fountain, where coins were dropped in nightly; by morning about half had been retrieved by those who desperately needed them. I explained the custom to Falun, and we kissed our coins, wishing blessings for whoever would find them.

After we tossed the coins into the fountain, Falun leaned down to my ear, yelling over the sound of the drums. "You told me there would be dancing?"

We inched around the lip of the fountain to the back, where the patch of crimson tiles began. We'd made it just in time for the next dance. The drumming was the call to the dance, a prelude of sorts. Already boys and girls were lined up across the tiles, arms held aloft, sweat coating their faces.

Musicians sat across from them. There were five young men beating on makeshift drums, a willowy man with a fiddle, and the singer, a tall, imposing bloodkin woman with a hawkish nose and beaded braids hanging down her back.

I let go of Falun's hand and stepped onto the tiles. "Watch first, and then join me."

There was only one dance done on these tiles at night: *chatara*, the dance of new lovers.

It started in your feet and you started the dance alone.

The drummers began with a simple beat, building it gradually. Our hips rocked side to side, keeping pace with the rhythm. We twirled, hips winding in figure eights until the singer began to howl.

Gooseflesh prickled my arms as I swept them down and raised them back up to the night sky. I tossed my head, watching the moon as I moved through the steps—switching my hips and kicking my feet into the air.

The singer's magick swept through the crowd, carried by the sound of her voice. Bloodkin called it the *thrall*, because with it, they could ensnare the mind until they controlled every emotion and sensation a person felt. This was partly the cause for the laws mandating bloodletting knives, so that no one could be enthralled unaware, so that people could guard their minds against attack. Even among bloodkin, the singer's was a rare gift. Most believed bloodkin projected the thrall with their eyes, but some could also use their voices.

I felt the magick heightening my emotions as I danced. The singer's thrall turned all our emotions into a shared experience. As we danced, we became one in our wanting, and the awareness of our bodies sharpened until it was dizzying. I felt sweat slide down our spines and the scrape and glide of fabrics I wasn't wearing.

The smell of salty blood, orange blossoms, and incense filled the air—the scent of the singer's magick. It pulsed through the air, pushing every movement farther. Curls clung to sweat-dampened cheeks as I arched back, twining my arms above my head. Each movement carried echo and premonition, of the girl just a beat ahead of me, of the boy just behind.

And when the singer's voice broke, the sharp edge was

like nails dragged slowly across my skin. We all crowed with her as partners joined us on the tiles.

I didn't expect Falun yet, so I jumped when warm hands circled my waist, soft and dry and hot against my skin.

It was the bloodkin boy from earlier, smiling sweetly, springy coils of hair falling into dark brown eyes. "Your friend won't join us?" He looked to where Falun stood at the edge of the tiles. His eyes were wide but unreadable.

"Not yet." Our limbs twined together as we moved in sync. He caught my wrist and spun me around. I fell flush against him, warm from the ouitza and his touch. "Though I think he will join sooner with your convincing."

"You think so?" His warm breath touched my cheek.

"I know so." I smiled, beckoning Falun forward.

He didn't move. But there was naked wonder in his gaze—mine had been just as wide the first time I laid eyes on this place. The bloodkin boy, whose name I still hadn't gotten and hoped never to, waved him over. Still Falun didn't move.

I stopped dancing and held out my hand, wishing I had brought him here sooner. After a long moment Falun stepped onto the tile and gave my hand a squeeze.

I left him with the bloodkin boy and found another partner. One who didn't seem to see me at all, and only wanted to dance.

Even out here, there were things I couldn't allow myself. Princesses bound for death couldn't have romantic entanglements. It would be too cruel, for them and for me.

We reveled in the music, stopping only to drink, eat, and trade partners. An hour passed before Falun and I danced together; I coaxed his stiff limbs into rhythm and showed him how the deadly grace inside him was useful for more than swinging a sword. The bloodkin boy stuck fast to Falun and I tried to ignore the twinge of longing in my chest when they kissed.

They disappeared into the throng together and another's arms wound about my waist. I turned to find a young human man, his skin a soft, warm brown. He was tall, with muscle-bound arms tattooed in white. Something about him nagged at me. I had to crane my neck to get a good look at his face. His nose was at least twice broken, the end jutting to the left, and his eyes were hazel. A dark, inviting color, and yet when they caught mine, unease swept through me.

I stepped out of his embrace. He was wearing a City Guard's blue uniform and his eyes were warm with lust. He spoke in a ragged voice: "Pretty little thing, aren't you?"

I bared my teeth at him, spitting out a curse as I backed away.

His gaze, once leering, sharpened. "You . . ."

I could have my knife out and pressed against his throat in the time it would take for him to draw his next breath. I would have, if not for the crowd dancing blithely around us.

Keeping the City Guard within my sight, I searched for Falun but found no sign of him, no flash of red hair, no fine-boned face. I caught a glimpse of the Guard's cruel smile before the singer screamed out one word: "Raid!"

Bodies slammed into me on every side and I could still feel the Guard's eyes burning a hole in my back. My stomach knotted as more City Guardsmen in dark blue uniforms spilled onto the Patch, cudgels and short swords in hand. Cries of fear and the sound of weapons striking flesh filled the air.

I pushed toward the Copper Steps, mouth dry. At least once a week, raids on the smugglers in the Night Souk spilled into the Patch. Public gatherings were against the law in Ternain after midnight. Most of the time, the Guardsmen only arrested those who couldn't afford a bribe, and I always kept my sigil ring on me in case I was caught. It wasn't the raid that scared me. It was the Guard.

For a moment, it had seemed like he recognized me, but then why hadn't he told the other Guards? Either way, I had to lose him in the crowd. I would run until I found Falun or reached the Palace wall, whichever came first.

I slammed into a woman's back and she fell to the ground. As I helped her to her feet, a hand curled around my elbow.

Heart pounding, I reached for my belt knife and the Guardsman nearly wrenched my arm out of its socket.

"Eva, it's *me*," Falun said. "We have to get back to the Palace. *Now.*"

His skin had lost its sheen and his usually pointed ears were rounded like a human's. His hair shifted color as I watched, from fiery red to muddy brown—glamour. Our fingers laced together and his magick slipped over my skin like a wash of scalding water. We ran.

ACKNOWLEDGMENTS

Writing a second book demands so much more of an author than their first—or so I'd heard several times before beginning this journey. Even having seen friends struggle through that second-book slump, I remain shocked at just how difficult it was to write this book. There were many times—dozens, in fact—where I thought I couldn't do it. Luckily, blessedly, it wasn't all up to me. I can only begin to convey the vastness of my gratitude to everyone in my life, both professionally and personally, who made this book possible.

To Kiki Chatzopoulou: My first reader, writing partner, Sorceress of Plot, and best friend. Thank you for fielding my endless texts about plotlines and craft. Thank you for your faith in my writing. Most of all, thank you for your friendship and love.

To Laura Silverman and Anna Meriano: Thank you for the writing retreats, the Catan, and the group chat that keeps me going. You are the best of friends.

To my parents: Thank you for your endless support. I wrote this book between my home and yours, because there's a special magic in the place where I first began writing. Mom, thank you for dealing with Deadline Amanda and all the mess that entails. Dad, thank you for teaching me to use my voice, even when you disagree with what I have to say. I love you both.

To my brother Jordan: No one has listened to me go on and on (and on) about this book more than you. Thank you for that, and thanks for your limitless creativity, because it drives mine.

To my Luna: Thank you for the puppy snuggles and sweetness when I thought this book was trying to kill me. Your wildness and wolf howls will forever remind me of Baccha, little moon.

To my agents, Taylor Haggerty and Holly Root: Thank you for being the best agent team one could possibly hope for. Thank you for your wisdom, constant enthusiasm, and faith in me!

To my editor, Stacey Barney: I feel so privileged to work with you and to learn from you. Thank you always for your patience and your incisive editing genius. It's a joy to work together. Can't wait to celebrate this book in person one day hopefully soon.

To the team at Putnam and Penguin Teen: Thank you for your boundless enthusiasm and all the work you do championing books! Thank you to Anne Heausler for caring about moon cycles as much as I do and for your kind words. My deepest gratitude to Alexxander Dovelin and Samira Iravani. I am still in awe of these stunning covers. They are such a gift to me.

And last, but the greatest of these: Thank *you*, dear reader, for taking this journey with Eva and me. I hope you will join me on many more.

AMANDA JOY has an MFA from The New School,
and lives in Chicago with her dog, Luna.

You can find her on Twitter and Instagram at
@amandajoywrites